flyy girl

omar tyree

SCRIBNER PAPERBACK FICTION
Published by Simon & Schuster

SCRIBNER PAPERBACK FICTION
Simon & Schuster Inc.
Rockefeller Center
1230 Avenue of the Americas
New York, NY 10020

First Scribner Paperback Fiction edition 1997
SCRIBNER PAPERBACK FICTION and design are trademarks of Simon & Schuster Inc.
Designed by Deirdre C. Amthor
Manufactured in the United States of America

3 5 7 9 10 8 6 4

The Library of Congress has cataloged the Simon & Schuster edition as follows:
Tyree, Omar.
Flyy girl / Omar Tyree.
p.   cm.
1. Girls—United States—Fiction. 2. Afro-American girls—Fiction I. Title.
PS3570.Y59F58   1996
813'.54—dc20   96-24834
CIP

ISBN 0-684-82928-2
0-684-83566-5 (Pbk)

". . . don't give them *nothin'* unless they got something to give you.
. . . what you do is get a nice-looking nut dude with some money and
romance his ass. If you can get somethin' without doing anything,
then do it. But if you can't, then make sure you play with his mind
real good before you do. . . ."

It is best when some particular creations have no man-made laws.
Only then can we attack the harsh addictions of our deteriorated society.
It is not of an intelligent human being to ignore that which is real.
True answers come from what we can see, taste, hear, think and feel.

Omar Rashad Tyree

dedicated to
all sisters and brothers,
in memory of the
glamorous and exciting '80s

the early Years

drifting apart

"Happy birthday toooo you. Happy birthday toooo you. Happy bir-r-r-th-day dear Tra-a-a-a-cy . . . Happy birthday toooo you," the crowd of sixteen children sang, helped along by some of the parents who were present.

It was Sunday afternoon in Tracy's sixth year of life, nineteen-seventy-seven. She sat proudly on her father's lap at the table in front of her birthday cake. She cracked a broad smile in her cute red dress. Her newly tied ponytail dangled down her neck. Her hazel eyes enlarged as her daddy helped her to cut the two-layer cake while the other children watched excitedly, all wishing that it was their birthday.

Tracy's daddy, Dave Ellison, was deep cocoa-brown and hazel-eyed and had the lean figure of a trained athlete. He was a youthful twenty-nine-year-old, possessing the boyish face of a teen. Dave wore no mustache or beard, obeying his self-imposed hygiene regulation. He believed that his clean-shaven face presented a healthy and professional appearance at the hospital where he worked as a pharmacist.

Tracy's smooth, honey-brown skin was exactly half the richness of her father's tone. She had inherited his light-colored eyes along with the almond shape and long eyelashes of her mother, Patti. Tracy's eyes seemed to glimmer whenever the sun hit them, making them sparkle like a cat's eyes. She was average height for her age, not standing out among the other kids. But her daddy was tall, and her mother was no midget herself. Patti had inherited a considerable amount of height from her father, Jason Smith, who had died in a car crash a year ago. So Tracy, it seemed, was destined to be tall.

Tracy's cousins had always envied the attention she received. For her birthday, she received presents and money from all of her guests and relatives. Her aunts bought her new clothing and shoes that her cousins wished they could have. All but two of her six cousins were older than she was.

Patti, matching her daughter and wearing red herself, bought Tracy a pink Mickey Mouse watch. Dave gave her a small gold ring.

Most of the parents sat around eating ice cream and cake and watching the television set inside of the kitchen. Their kids played board games in the Ellison's large, finely decorated basement.

The kids began to scream and yell once Patti decided to put on a VCR movie. The 27-inch, floor-model, color television set was a brand-new RCA. Dave had bought it a week before the party. He had moved the old, 19-inch Sony, with stand, into Tracy's room. Her cousins envied that, too.

Out of four sisters, Tracy's mother Patti had captured the best man. And Patti had been considered the prettiest sister since their youth, with her light skin, curvaceous body and dark, almond-shaped eyes.

Dave was definitely a catch. His high income enabled them to move into a comfortable and scenic black neighborhood in Northwest Phila-delphia. In Germantown, they had the luxury of private lawns, patios, driveways and lots of trees, which surrounded their three-bedroom twin-house, things not affordable to the many Philadelphians who lived in crowded row-house areas. Patti worked at a nursing home as a dietitian, adding to their snug income.

So far, Tracy was their only child. Dave was an only child himself. Patti's three sisters each had two children.

Tracy fought with her cousins constantly. At most of their family gatherings, her mother and aunts tried unsuccessfully to keep them apart. Their unruly children could destroy an entire party with infighting. They had done it many times before.

The kids, ten girls and six boys, including Kamar, Tracy's only boy cousin, watched *Cinderella*. The girls were having more fun than the boys, who would have rather watched *Dumbo*. But it was Tracy's party, and she wanted to see *Cinderella* first.

The children spilled juice on the rug, left crumbs on the tables and got melted ice cream all over their bodies. Patti ran behind them, cleaning up to keep the house neat and pretty.

There were carpets in every room except for the kitchen, which had new blue and white tile floors. And when Patti finally gave up trying to salvage what was left of her clean house, she went and sat in her large kitchen with her sisters and the rest of the parents.

"Girl, this house is just beautiful," a parent said enthusiastically, as though the house had energized her.

"Yeah, girl, you just don't know how much we put into this house," Patti quickly responded, trying to be modest.

"Well, if my man had some money, I could've had a house like this, too," Patti's younger sister Tanya said. She stood inside the kitchen entrance leaning up against the wall. Tanya was well-curved herself, wearing a royal blue shirt and pants set with black shoes.

"Unh hunh, that's why I love to visit, just to be in this house," Patti's youngest sister Joy said with a giggle. "This feels better than being in the hospital." Joy was considered the silly sister. She was on the thin side, wearing an off-white dress and sitting in one of the kitchen chairs.

"See, I told you years ago, Joy, that that *boy* you was dating didn't have no sense. But you wouldn't listen," Marsha, the oldest sister, commented. Marsha was heavy-set and mean. She wore a wide, black, skimpy dress. She kept pulling it down over her hips under the kitchen table.

You need to stop trying to look cute in them tacky-ass outfits you wear, Patti thought to herself of her older sister.

"Look who's talkin'," Joy responded to Marsha while slicing a piece of cake. "You ain't got nothin' better than what I got."

"Well, that's only because the nigga left me. But I *gots* more, honey."

Patti began to feel uncomfortable, predicting where her sisters' conversation was headed. "Come on now, every time we get together we talk about the same-o-same-o. Now, this is supposed to be my daughter's party, so let's act like it," she told them.

"Aw, girl, listen to you," Marsha snapped. "You gon' get yourself a little college boy with some money, and then gon' tell us not to be jealous."

"Now hold on, one minute," Patti responded. "Don't start this dumb stuff tonight, Marsha, 'cause I'm sick of it. You can leave my house with all that."

Marsha shook angrily while trying to lift herself from the kitchen chair. "Fine! I ain't gotta stay here for this boring-ass party any-damn-way."

The parents, standing inside of the kitchen and the dining room, began to feel embarrassed. They all appeared as though they weren't listening to the argument, but they were.

"You know what, Marsha? This is it! If you can't show me any respect in *my* house, then you don't need to come here anymore. There's no reason for you to be acting like this toward me, or the rest of us."

"Fine, sista', you said it," Marsha huffed. She jumped on the phone and called a taxi. She then got her coat and rumbled to the basement door to call her two daughters.

"Trish and Marie, get your things, 'cause we goin' home!"

"No, I'll take them home," Joy interjected. "Ain't no sense in them being punished just because *you* can't get along."

Marsha looked offended. "Look, dammit, my girls *came* here with me and they gonna *leave* with me!"

Both of her daughters looked up from the basement stairway while listening to the confusion. Trish, the oldest, didn't care one way or the other, but Marie didn't want to leave.

Trish hiked up the steps and got her coat in a flash.

Marie whined while moving slowly up the stairs behind her. "No, mom-mee, I wanna stay," she whined.

"Get up them damn steps, girl! I'm sick of your whinin'," Marsha screamed at her, grabbing her arm.

"Come on, stop her," Tanya urged Patti. Tanya, the peacemaker, had the two youngest children.

"You know how she is, Tanya, so I ain't even gon' try," Patti told her.

Tracy came upstairs with the rest of the kids to watch the dispute. She felt good that her Aunt Marsha and cousins were leaving. She didn't want *them* at her party in the first place.

Dave had sneaked upstairs to his bedroom to watch a football game long ago. He decided to stay out of the sister battles. He knew it was coming. The Smith sisters had never gotten along since he had met his wife. They were all a larger image of their children.

"The man don't really love you. He only married you 'cause you messed around and got pregnant on him," Marsha said to Patti as she hastily headed for the door. "And I *should* tell him that you lied the first time."

Patti was shocked at Marsha's outburst. *I don't believe she said some shit like that in front of everybody!* she snapped to herself. A large vein in Patti's throat thumped erratically. She was embarrassed. She fought off a strong urge to go after her mean-spirited sister as she walked from the house. Patti felt like canceling the entire party to recuperate from Marsha's venom, but it was a celebration for her lovely daughter. She didn't want to let her inconsiderate older kin ruin Tracy's party. Nevertheless, a few of the parents could sense her embarrassment. They moved to gather their kids for home as well.

"Look, Patti, it's been nice, but I really have to be going. The kids have school tomorrow," one parent said.

"No, don't let this tear my daughter's party apart, Venice. I'm fine. Now come on, they can stay," Patti pleaded.

"Patti, I have some other stops to make," Venice argued.

Patti sighed and gave in. "Well, at least let me make you a few doggy bags," she offered.

Venice nodded as Patti hurried off toward the kitchen.

Patti quickly wrapped up leftover food and two large slices of cake in aluminum foil as she helplessly watched her daughter's party fall apart.

"See, that's why I hate them. They always mess stuff up," Tracy whined at the front door.

"I know. Every time they come over here they get mad at everybody for no reason," the little girl from next door agreed. The three boys from down the street, who were left, weren't concerned. With the diminishing number of girls, they went back inside of the basement to begin watching *Dumbo.*

DING DONG! . . . DING DONG!

"Mommy, somebody's at the door," Tracy called, running back to the kitchen.

"I heard it the first time," Patti responded to her. She marched out to answer it.

"Hey, Patti, how you doin'?"

She backed up to let him in. "I'm fine, Keith. How are you?"

"I'm okay. I just came to pick my daughter up," Keith said, eying his little girl who was sitting on the couch. She stared up at his slender, dark frame in alarm.

"Well, let me get you some cake," Patti told him.

"Okay," Keith said.

Patti took another trip to the kitchen.

Keith then approached his daughter on the couch.

"Hey, girl?" he asked her sternly.

"Yes, daddy," she whimpered.

"Didn't I tell you to leave at six-thirty? You got school tomorrow."

His little girl hunched her shoulders and drew a long face. "Yes."

"Aww, Mr. Keith, she was gonna come home soon," Tracy said in her friend's defense.

"Yeah, well, that ain't the point. Her daddy told her to come home on her own," Keith responded to Tracy. "It's ten after seven now, and she forgot all about what I had told her."

"Here you go, Keith," Patti said, returning with more cake wrapped in aluminum foil.

"Oh, thanks, Patti," Keith said with a smile.

Keith was not tall, nor as defined as Tracy's dad. His daughter, Raheema, favored him in the face, with her high cheekbones and aquiline nose. Her fair skin and long brown hair favored her mother.

Patti had always wondered why Keith was so mean to his wife and daughters. They were all beautiful. Yet he treated them with nothing but bitterness.

"Well, good-bye, Ra-Ra," she said, stooping down.

Raheema was as light as Patti and pretty cheerful. But Keith, in times of his evilness, could look like a blue-black, red-eyed wino.

"Say good-bye to 'Aunt Patti,' girl," he told her while Patti stood beside them.

Raheema was nerve-racked by then, and her voice showed it. "Good, good-bye Aunt, Aunt Pat-ti," she stuttered, with tears in her eyes.

Patti noticed her fear and made a point to see her to her house, next door. Keith had a snake's tongue, but he was no match for Patti.

"What's wrong, Ra-Ra?" she asked, as if she didn't know.

"Oh, she's just crying because she has to go home to get ready for school tomorrow," Keith answered for her.

"Well, you can come over tomorrow, honey. Okay?" Patti assured Raheema, pinching her cheeks.

"Yes," Raheema answered with a sniff. Then from out of nowhere, big tears began to fall from her eyes.

"Don't cry, Ra-Ra," Tracy perked, comforting her next-door neighbor with a hug.

"Matter of fact, I'm going over to your house to ask your mother right now," Patti responded.

She, Keith, Raheema and Tracy went next door, leaving the little boys inside the basement.

"Beth, Patti's down here!" Keith shouted up the stairs.

Patti could sense that he felt robbed of punishing his daughter.

Beth came down in her nightclothes. She looked tired. Her long brown hair was combed back, and her dark, ringed eyes stood out against her light-brown skin. She looked nothing like she did three years ago, when she and Keith first moved next door. Dave and Patti had moved to Germantown only a year before them. The seventies had been prosperous for blacks.

"How are you, girlfriend?" Beth asked, stepping up to hug Patti. Tracy smiled. And Raheema felt relieved with them in her house.

"I'm doin' all right. Yeah, umm, I just wanted to ask you if Raheema could spend the night on Friday," Patti said, changing her initial plan.

"Well, yeah, I guess so," Beth answered, sneaking a glance at Keith.

"Okay then, I'll be right over to get her after school. And then we'll go shopping together and get us some ice cream."

"Y-a-a-a-y!" Tracy squealed.

Keith took a seat on their long black couch and watched television in silence.

"Tracy looks so pretty today," Beth said, watching Tracy as she bounced in her bright red dress.

"Well, Ra-Ra is a little charmer, too," Patti told her.

Keith frowned. "Yeah, but she never listens. Mercedes listens, but I guess Ra-Ra thinks she's too cute."

"Raheema and Mercedes are two different people, Keith. You shouldn't even judge her like that," Patti contested.

Raheema became apprehensive hearing her father speak about her. She hoped "Aunt Patti" could win the fight. Beth always kept quiet. She never intervened when Patti and Keith would go at it about her own children. And since Beth wasn't up for the challenge, Patti stayed right in their business.

"Well, she better start doin' what she's told," Keith warned.

"She'll be all right. Come here, Ra-Ra," Patti said. She gently rubbed her fingers through Raheema's soft hair and rubbed her neck to calm her nerves. She knew she had won their argument. Raheema would be able to sleep in peace.

Patti left with Tracy and began to send the rest of the children in her basement home. She then readied Tracy for bed. It was nearly nine o'clock.

"Did Keith say anything to Ra-Ra when I went inside the kitchen?" Patti asked her daughter while tucking her in.

"Unh hunh. He said that she was 'sposed to go home at six-thirty."

Patti shook her head in disgust. "I knew it. That man ain't no good. He's just as evil as he wants to be."

Tracy chuckled and closed her eyes. Her mother then swept into her own bedroom. Dave was still watching television. He was leaned up against a pillow with his hands behind his head.

"You know what, Patti, I'm sick and tired of your sisters coming over here and terrorizing my damn house. I've worked *hard* for mine. Now if they got a problem with that, you best leave them out of our lives. Or at least out of *my* damn life."

"Look, Dave, now that's my family. Without me, they'll fall apart," Patti self-righteously assumed. "So even if they argue with me, they really do need me."

"Yeah, well, I'm gon' tell you what, soon you ain't gon' *need* me, because I'm a little worn out from this dumb stuff."

Patti started to undress. "Dave, it ain't all that bad."

"Yes the hell it is," Dave snapped. "Matter fact, they're not coming over here anymore. Period."

Patti stopped undressing and stared at him. "Why, Dave?"

"Because I said so. That's reason enough."

"Now you know that ain't even fair," Patti retorted. She caressed Dave's chest under the sheets. Dave pulled her hand away and rolled over. "Baby, come on," Patti pleaded.

"No, now, get off of me."

Patti sighed and turned the other way.

"Turn the TV off," Dave demanded.

"You're the one that turned it on."

"I don't care. You just got in bed. You're not all that comfortable yet."

Patti stayed in the bed, refusing to move.

Dave turned to face her. "What do you think, I'm playing? I told you to turn the shit off," he snapped, nearly pushing her out of bed.

Patti caught her balance to avoid falling onto the floor. She then went and turned the TV off. *I don't know who he think he is,* she thought to herself as she strolled back to her side of the bed.

"Are you satisfied now?"

Dave was playing his ugly tough-guy role. He had learned it years ago to keep Patti in check. And Patti enjoyed pissing him off. It was her childish entertainment.

Dave jumped up in an instant and grabbed her arm.

"What are you doing?" Patti whined.

"I'm tired of you playing that young-girl shit. You sleep on the damn couch tonight."

"Why?" Patti said, holding Dave gently by his waist. She gently squeezed him, hoping to turn him on.

"Get off me, Patti. You're a damn kid, girl, I swear," he told her as he knocked her hands away.

Patti shoved her breasts up against his chest. "Please, I'm sorry, baby," she pleaded. She tried to plant a kiss on her husband's lips. Dave turned away to avoid it.

"No, get off of me," he persisted, still trying to push her away.

Patti sighed and began walking toward her daughter's room.

Dave asked, "Where are you going?"

Patti teased him with a sly grin. "I'm going to sleep with my baby. She's the only one that *cares* about me," she told him.

"Look, I'm gonna give you about two seconds to go downstairs and sleep on that damn couch, like I told you," Dave warned her.

Patti really knew how to get to her husband. She smirked and said, "Okay already."

Dave mugged her in the back of her head. "You think this shit is a damn joke, don't you?" he asked her, pinning her to the hallway wall.

"Now wait a minute, Dave, you're hurting me."

"I'm hurting you? Shit, you're hurting me with these stupid-ass games you play all the time," Dave told her.

"How the hell am *I* hurting you? It looks like you're the one that has *me* pinned up against this damn wall," Patti retorted.

"Look, you're fucking with my peace of mind, Patti. Now we're damn near thirty years old. We're getting too old for this role-playing shit."

Patti looked at him seriously for a moment. "Dave, you're the one that started it. You could have turned that TV off yourself."

"Yeah, well I'm gonna end it, too." He released the hold on his wife and walked back into his bedroom, locking the door in her face.

Patti shook her head and grinned. She reminisced on the many other occasions where she had argued with her husband and ended up making sweaty love. Those were their best nights. She thought that maybe they would be having another one if she played along with him, but she was wrong.

Dave was seriously fed up. He longed for a more mature woman who would cooperate with him instead of aggravating him and forcing him to play Mr. Sweet and Mr. Sour. In fact, Dave had become so good at it that he couldn't tell the difference between his real self and his roles. He was beginning to feel like he was up for a living Academy Award.

Patti fell asleep on her living-room couch and spent the night there. She had anticipated her husband coming down to carry her back to their bedroom and make passionate love to her. But it never happened.

"Come on, Tracy, it's time to get up," Patti called.

"Okay, mom," Tracy answered, wiping out her eyes. She stepped out of her twin-sized bed and followed her mother to the hallway bathroom.

"Did I wake you up from a dream, baby?" Patti asked her.

"Yup. I was Cinderella, and the prince was just like dad."

"Just like dad? Well, didn't you have a beautiful dream."

Tracy smiled and said, "Yup, mom."

"Well, let's get you cleaned and dressed so you can eat your break-fast."

"Mommy?" Tracy asked, getting undressed for her bath.

"Yes, Tracy."

"Why does dad never eat breakfast with us?"

"Because he has to go to work early."

Patti helped her daughter into the tub.

"Why does he have to go to work early?"

"Because that's his job, honey?"

"Did you and dad fight last night, mommy?"

"No," Patti lied to her. "Why would you think that?"

"Because I heard you and dad in the hall last night."

"Well, we were out in the hallway, but we weren't really fighting."

Tracy looked in her mother's hand mirror while getting toweled off. "Why my eyes different from yours, mommy?" she asked.

"Because you got them from your father."

"Unt unh. Daddy's eyes aren't pointy like mine. And they shiny, too," Tracy argued, still looking inside of the hand mirror.

"Yes they are, Tracy. You just can't notice them on your father as much as you can on you, because you're lighter than your dad," Patti explained.

Tracy put her arm next to her mother's arm to compare complexions. "I'm tanner than you, mommy," she said.

"Yup, you came right in between me and your father."

"How that happen?" Tracy asked, as her mother put on her new birthday clothes.

"Ut oh, my daughter looks sharp to-day," Patti said.

Tracy smiled and spun around in her baby-blue dress. But she hadn't forgotten her question. "Hunh, mommy, how'd that happen?" she persisted.

"What?" Patti asked.

"How did I get like this?" Tracy asked again. She raised her arms up high to show Patti her color.

"You ask some complicated questions for a little girl, now don't you?"

They went down into the kitchen to eat.

"Tell me, mommy," Tracy pressed, as she took a seat in a kitchen chair.

"From genetics, sweetheart."

Tracy frowned. "Genetics? What's that? What's genetics, mom?"

Patti just couldn't believe how tenacious her daughter was. *She's going to be a very assertive girl,* she told herself. "I'll tell you what, you ask dad when he gets home."

"Awww, see, you don't tell me nothin'."

Patti looked at her daughter with piercing slit eyes. "You watch who you're talking to, girl! You hear me?"

Tracy nodded and began to eat her breakfast with a long face.

Tracy loved going to school. She had perfect attendance and was smart and popular. She drew attention like a magnet. She wanted as many friends as possible. School was where Tracy could show off. And the teachers praised her participation in class.

"Yup, and then my cousins messed it up. They *always* mess it up," Tracy was telling her group of girlfriends, Celena, Pam and Judy.

"I don't like my cousins either, 'cause they always wanna race and stuff," Judy said, standing short and chunky.

Celena, the tallest of the group, rose from their small bench at the far end of the schoolyard. "Aw, you just say that 'cause they always beat you," she said to Judy.

"Shet up, girl. That's why you gon' fail in school," Judy retorted, facing off with her.

"I got better grades than *you,*" Celena said.

"No *you* don't."

"Yes *I* do, 'cause on our first spelling quiz, I did *better* than you."

"Well, we just started, and that was the only one we had *anyway.*

Now! I busted *your* bubble," Judy responded, bumping flat chests with Celena.

"You can't beat me in nothin', *little* girl," Celena contested, staring down at her shorter friend.

"Who is you callin' *'little girl,' Stinky?"*

Tracy loved to hear the girls argue. It reminded her of her aunts and her mother.

Pam, the quieter friend, sat and watched the action herself.

"I'll kick you in your butt, *Big Mouth,"* Celena said as they bumped each other again.

"Do it then, *Stinky,"* Judy dared.

Both girls were pushing and shoving. Tracy got up to stop what could've turned into a real fight. "Stop y'all, we all friends," she said, moving in-between them.

"Well, that's why Celena ain't got no hair. At least I ain't *bald-headed* like *you,"* Judy said, starting up again.

"I ain't *bald-headed, girl.* I got more hair than *you,"* Celena snapped.

"GET OUT THE WAY, THE BALL IS COMING!" a boy shouted, running past.

The girls didn't move out of the way quickly enough. Judy got knocked down on her plump behind.

"Ay, boy? Why you do that?" Pam yelled at him. She was quiet, but a fighter.

"I'm sorry," the boy responded.

One of his friend's overheard him apologizing. "Ay, Tommy, don't say sorry to her, man," he said, staring and bumping into Pam. She swung immediately. The boy blocked it and punched her back in her neck.

"See, boy, I'm gon' tell on you," she whined.

"Go 'head then, girl. See if I care."

"See, Aaron, you always hittin' girls. My dad told me that boys who hit girls are sissies," Judy screamed at him.

"So what, girl? Who asked you?" Aaron retorted. "Come on, y'all, let's finish playing ball," he told his rowdy friends.

"Go ahead, you scared *sissy,*" Judy taunted him.

Tracy loved it. School was exciting.

Tracy's father picked her up from school, and she would tell him every-thing that had gone on while he listened to her constant chatter. Tracy went to work with her questions as soon as they entered the house.

"Daddy, how did I get like this?" Tracy asked, raising her arms.

Dave stretched out on the couch, failing to notice his daughter's raised arms. He stared up at the ceiling with his head plumped on a cushion.

"Daddy?"

"Yes, pretty," he answered her wearily.

Tracy raised her arms in front of him.

"How did I get tanner than mommy and lighter than you?"

"Because, God did it," Dave told her. He then closed his eyes.

"God did it?" Tracy mumbled to herself. Confused by her father's simple answer, she decided to crawl up on his chest and rest there on the couch with him.

"Hello, hello, sleepy-heads," Patti said, stepping through the front door an hour later. She hung up her jacket and immediately headed for the kitchen.

Tracy got up off her daddy's chest and followed her mother. "Can I help you, mommy?" she asked with wide eyes.

"Unh hunh, now get the little frying pan."

"Okay . . . Now what?"

"All right, now get the Kool-Aid mix."

"Okay, mommy . . . Here, mom, now what?"

"Go upstairs in my room and bring down the cups and bowls so mommy can wash them out."

"Okay, mom. I'll be right back." Tracy ran up the stairs and grabbed all the dishes she could find. "What now, mom?" she asked, running back inside the kitchen and breathing heavily.

"Aren't *you* full of energy," Patti commented. "Well, why don't you go and see if your father needs any help."

"Okay," Tracy said, running. She tugged on her father's arm at the living-room couch. "Daddy, wake up."

"Yes, pretty?" he answered, with his eyes still closed.

"Can I help you with something?"

"Yeah, sweetheart. Can you help your dad get up?"

Tracy looked at his long, lean body and remembered the last time she had tried, unsuccessfully, to lift him. She stepped back and shook her head. "No, I can't lift you, dad."

"Yup, well, I guess you can't help dad then," Dave responded to her.

Tracy, still filled with energy, hurried back to help her mother in the kitchen.

"Well, did you help your dad, sweety?" Patti asked her.

"No-o-o. Because he want me to help him to get up, and I don't have no muscles," Tracy whined.

Patti laughed at her. "You have muscles; they just aren't strong enough to lift your dad."

"Well, when I grow up, I'm gonna have bigger muscles. Right, mommy?" Tracy asked, tugging on her mother's apron.

"Yup, and you're gonna be as tall and as pretty as me."

Tracy smiled, pleased with herself. "I'm gonna marry me a man like dad, too."

Patti gave her a curious smile. "Do you like boys yet, Tracy?" she asked of her young daughter.

"NO! Boys get on my nerves!" Tracy shouted.

Patti chuckled. "Why do you say that?" she quizzed.

Tracy pressed her little hand on her hip and shook her head. "Because, 'dey rough and bad. And this boy named Aaron hit my friend Pam today," she huffed.

"Why did he do that?" Patti asked her.

"'Cause his friend Tommy knocked Judy down when 'ney was playing ball, and Pam was gon' hit him for it. So then Aaron came to get in it for Tommy, and he punched Pam in her neck."

"Well, did she try to hit him back?"

"Yeah, she tried to hit him first, but he blocked it with his arm."

"Did the boy get in trouble?"

"Mmm hmm, but he didn't even care though."

"Yeah, he sounds like a bad boy," Patti said, continuing with her cooking.

"My friend Judy said that boys who hit girls are sissies. Is that true, mom?"

"Who told her that?" Patti quizzed, turning to face her daughter.

"She said that her father told her."

Patti grinned. "Well, you go and ask *your father* if that's true."

Tracy ran back out and into the living room. "Hey, dad, are you a 'sissy' if you hit a girl?" she asked, tugging again on her father's arm.

Dave opened his eyes and stared at her. "Did your mother tell you to ask me that?"

"Mmm hmm," Tracy hummed. Then she smiled.

"Well, you tell her that I said she can't beat it."

Tracy ran back to her mother and stuttered, "He, he said you can't beat it, mom."

"Well, you tell him that I love him anyway."

"Mom said she loves you, dad," Tracy yelled out to him. Her father didn't respond. "Well, dad?" Tracy asked, expecting him to send another message.

"Well, pretty, I guess it's almost time to eat," he mentioned to her instead.

Dave still hadn't responded to Patti's message as they sat down to dinner.

Tracy was confused. Her daddy didn't say that he loved her mother. Why not?

"You don't love mommy, dad?" Tracy asked him at the table.

Dave looked frozen, as if he had lost his appetite.

Patti came to his rescue. "Of course your daddy loves me, Tracy. What kind of a question is that?"

Tracy backed off and hunched her shoulders. She was still a bit confused and apprehensive about the tension she had caused at their dinner table.

Dave quickly finished his food and headed out of the house after dinner.

Tracy was left alone to ask her mother plenty more of her questions.

"Mommy, where does daddy go at night?"

"To his friend's house," Patti answered while cleaning pots and pans inside the kitchen sink.

"Does daddy love you, mommy?"

Patti was getting agitated. "Yes, he does, Tracy. Now what is wrong with you?"

"How come he never says it then?"

"Look, now, stop bugging me. Okay?"

"But does he, mommy?" Tracy persisted.

Patti sighed, surrendering. Had she pushed Dave to his limit? Did he still love her? "I hope he still loves mommy, honey," she said to her persistent daughter. "I hope and pray he does."

Dave walked in at eleven on a Wednesday, early compared to some of his other nights out. He had begun to spend more of his free time away from home. He failed to touch Patti or talk to her for weeks at a time. He only chatted with her on occasion, kissing her every now and then.

He walked to the kitchen and got out a spoon with the cherry vanilla ice cream and started eating it from the box. Patti waited upstairs, listening to his footsteps. After a few minutes of debate, she decided to walk down the steps to join him. Carefully, she approached him as he sat inside of the kitchen. She calmly slid her hands over his shoulders from behind. Dave moved forward to release her hold. Patti then sat in front of him to look into his eyes.

Dave got up and went to the bedroom without a word, leaving the box of ice cream on the table and daring Patti to comment on it. Once upstairs, he walked inside of the bathroom to take a shower. Patti followed after him.

"Dave . . . where do you go at night?" she finally asked, trembling.

"I go the hell out. Where the hell do you think I go?" he answered while running warm water. He closed the door behind him and took a fifteen-minute shower.

When he had dried himself off and returned to the bedroom, Patti was waiting for him.

"Dave . . . are you seeing another woman?" she forced herself to ask him.

"What if I was? You wouldn't care. You're still my number one, right?"

Patti pressed the issue. "Are you, Dave?"

Dave pulled on his pajamas and slid underneath the covers. "Can I get some sleep, Patti? I'm tired. It's been a long day."

Patti snatched the covers from him in a frenzy. "Stop playing with me, Dave! DAMN IT, I'M SERIOUS!" she shouted at him.

Dave took a deep breath to calm himself as he sat up to speak. "Now look, Patti, you wanted to keep playing these little panty-games, and it ain't fun no more. I don't have any more energy for that. So look, give me back my sheets, and shut up before you wake up my daughter."

It was too late. Tracy heard them going at each other from her room. She sat up in her bed, wide awake, realizing that her mother was losing her daddy.

Several weeks more had passed, and Patti tried her hardest to avoid Tracy's daddy questions. Nevertheless, her mother's lack of answers didn't appear to stop Tracy from asking.

"Mommy, tell me how you met my dad?" she asked one morning.

Patti shook her head, exhausted by them. "You just won't quit, will you? Okay, girl, what do you want to know?" she said, sitting down to join her daughter eating breakfast.

"Where did you meet him at?"

"I met him at a college party."

"Daddy went there?"

"Yup, and he was one of the most handsome guys there."

"And did he like you?"

"Well, he came over and asked me to dance."

"And you said, 'yes'?"

"Of course I said, 'yes.' I wouldn't have said, 'no' to *him.*"

"And then you got married?"

Patti grinned and shook her head. "No, not that fast. First mommy had to get him away from all the other girls."

"How did you do that?"

Her mother reflected on "the good old days."

"By being more sexy than them," she answered. Patti then lost track of time as she thought back to the many weeks of seduction. She used to take Dave out to Fairmount Park at night and do wild and crazy things under the privacy of the trees. She used to sneak him into her house at night, while her parents and sisters slept.

Patti painted a facade of not appearing to be jealous whenever other women showed interest in Dave. She acted as if she was above them, which made Dave feel more comfortable with her. Patti was always two steps ahead of the game.

The long talk Tracy had with her mother about how her parents met made them run late. Tracy's girlfriends at school wanted to know why.

"Why was you late today, Tracy?" Judy asked at recess.

Tracy was usually one of the first students at school. "I wasn't late," she told her nosy friend.

"You was almost late," Celena interjected, siding with Judy.

"Well, *almost* ain't good enough," Tracy snapped.

Her friends caught on to her disdain and dropped the subject. They sat and quietly watched the boys play ball. They all watched Aaron, except for Tracy. Tracy was too wrapped into herself and her family to think of any boy.

"Aaron is the best one at keep-away. They can't catch him for nothin'," Celena commented.

Judy sat and stared.

"So?" Pam huffed. "What 'chew watchin' him for?"

"Because, he fun to watch," Celena answered.

Tracy said out of the blue, smiling, "Ay y'all, guess what my mother told me? She told me that she took my dad from a whole lot of other girls."

"She did?" Judy asked, stuffing her mouth with a cupcake.

"Yup, and then they got married and had me."

"WATCH OUT, GIRL!" Aaron shouted, zipping past them with other boys chasing behind him.

"HEY, AARON! WATCH WHERE YOU GOIN', BOY!" Celena yelled.

Tracy paid him no mind. She continued with her story.

"Well, anyway . . ."

"So are you saying that it's over?" Tanya asked her sister, Patti, that evening. They sat in Tanya's small living room. She lived in a small, three-bedroom house in Logan, Philadelphia.

"Girl, I don't know. I mean, he hardly talks to me," Patti responded.

"Yeah, that's how they get when they wanna call it quits. Either they ignore you or they get on your damn nerves until you can't take it anymore," Tanya told her.

Tracy was upstairs playing with her cousins Patrice and Kamar.

"I mean, what am I supposed to do?" Patti asked helplessly.

"Tell him that you love him and that you'll try your best to work things out," Tanya calmly suggested.

Patti snapped, "Are you serious? I'm not fuckin' beggin' him shit. He's the one cheating on *me.*"

"Well, okay, Miss Know-it-all. Why the hell are you asking *me* in the first place, since you got all the answers?"

They sat quietly for a few minutes before Patti apologized. "Look, I'm sorry. I'm just under a lot of stress right now."

Tanya was still annoyed. "You think I don't know that? Me and John have arguments, too. It ain't like I don't have to sit down and think things out myself sometimes.

"That's one of your damn problems, Patti. You always take other people for granted. Now you gettin' some of your own medicine."

"What, you think this is my fault?"

Tanya looked at her sister curiously. "I don't know, Patti. Is it your fault? You tell me."

Patti sat and thought about it. *Maybe I have overdone things a few times,* she told herself. *But it ain't all my damn fault! I mean, he's not even trying to talk it all out. He's just trying to punish some-fucking-body.*

"Dave, we need to talk. I mean, our marriage isn't over, is it?" Patti asked, settling into bed after putting Tracy to sleep.

Dave rolled away from her. He stared at the rain out of their bedroom window. "Ain't shit come out my mouth, did it?" he answered sourly.

"That's funny. I thought you said that *I* curse too much."

"Well, I've changed, and your shit is rubbing off on me."

Patti eyed his back. "Aren't you gonna take a shower?" she asked, attempting to provoke him.

"Why should I take a shower?"

"Didn't you make love to her?"

Dave paused. "No, I just went to dinner with her, and she kissed me," he lied. He wasn't dating any other woman, he simply wanted to give Patti something to think about. *Maybe she'll tell me to get out,* he thought to himself. He felt as if he was suffocating in their marriage. *Maybe I was too damned young to get married. I was just finishing school when she got pregnant.*

Patti wanted to kill him. *She fucking kissed you, hunh?* she felt like screaming at him while pounding her fists against his head and back. Then she thought about what Tanya had said earlier, and decided to use her head. "So . . . what are we going to do now?" she pleaded. "Are you ready to throw away your life with me and your daughter for this woman?"

"I think I need to take a little break for a while. I got this little apartment I've been looking at," Dave announced to her.

What? You need a damn break? Patti felt like yelling at him. She took a deep breath instead, leaning her head on his shoulder. "I don't want you to go, baby," she whispered into his ear. "We can work this thing out."

Dave shook his head, set on moving out. "It's too late for that now."

Patti rolled to the edge of the bed. She hoped maybe he would ask where she was going. She went down to the kitchen. She thought about grabbing a knife.

"Did you sleep well last night, sweetheart?" Patti asked Tracy at breakfast.

"Yup, I had a dream that I could fly."

"You did? And were you scared?"

"Unh hunh."

Patti gave her a medium-size box to open. "Your daddy bought this for you."

Tracy opened the box and pulled out a stuffed animal. "Wow, he got a suit on!" She held it up and hugged it to her chest. It was a tan lion wearing a black tuxedo with a white bow tie.

"When did daddy buy me this?" she asked.

"Last night, because he's not going to be around as much."

Tracy raised her brow in alarm. "He's not?"

"No, because he decided to move out," Patti told her.

Tracy's hazel eyes ballooned. "Why-e-e, mommy?"

Patti looked away, feeling both guilt and anger. "Because we don't get along anymore."

"Is he still gonna come see us?"

"Yes, but he won't be staying with us for a while."

"Well, when is he coming back?"

"I don't know."

"You don't like each other anymore?" Tracy squealed.

"I don't know, honey."

"Well, how can I go to play with him and ask him questions and stuff?"

"He never really played with you, honey. Do you remember any things that you and your father did together?"

Tracy thought about it. "No," she said, shaking her head. "But I like it when he's here, 'cause he makes me feel good."

Patti smiled at her and sat her daughter on her lap. "I know. Daddy made *me* feel good too."

Tracy smiled back and said, "Yeah, dad is fun."

"He sure is, baby, but now we're going to have our own fun."

"How?"

"Well, by going shopping and stuff, 'cause daddy said you're going to get an allowance."

Tracy was puzzled. "Allowance? What's that?" she asked.

"It's money after a certain period of time."

"He wants me to have money?"

"Yeah, he doesn't want his baby to be wearing rags. He wants you to wear nice things."

"Well, who's gonna pick me up from school?"

"I don't know yet, but let me tell you something, honey." Patti tossed her arms tightly around her daughter's growing body. "No matter what you do, my little princess, never let any little boy break your heart. It's a rough world out there for us girls, 'cause everything is geared for the boys to do. And they can just get up and walk away from you whenever they want to. Just like your father did."

Tracy nodded.

"They can do whatever they want, and we're supposed to sit back and be complacent," Patti went on.

"What's that mean, mommy?"

"That means you're supposed to sit on benches and talk to your little girlfriends until some boy wants to talk to you."

"Yuck, I don't like boys," Tracy told her.

Patti shook her head and smiled. "Yeah, I know. But you remember this, you hear? You always go after what you want in life, and never give anything away without a good reason."

"Yeah, 'cause I don't like to give candy, now."

Patti chuckled to herself. Her daughter was in another world. *She'll eventually understand what I'm talking about,* Patti told herself. *She'll learn.* "You're a beautiful little girl, and you stay strong, okay?" she said, shaking Tracy on her lap and kissing her cheek to cheer her up and get her off to school.

"Okay, mommy," Tracy responded with a smile. She then lifted up her arm in a bodybuilding pose. "I'm gon' be real strong."

Patti laughed at her. "Girl, you're just too much."

trouble next door

Two years had passed, and Tracy was hanging out with her mother regularly. They went to the malls, parks, museums and theaters. Tracy grew to love and respect her mother's points of view on everything. Mommy wore nice clothes, so Tracy wanted nice clothes, too. They watched TV together. They chose Patti's dates together. They did everything together, just like girlfriends. But nothing seemed to satisfy the void of Tracy's father. He still hadn't decided to come back home and stay with them.

Beth picked Tracy up from school, and Tracy would stay with them until her mother got in from work. But Raheema's home, although it was full, wasn't as warm and cheerful as hers. Their home seemed lifeless and dreary, even with all of its members.

Raheema's older sister, Mercedes, did nothing but homework. She and Raheema went to Catholic elementary school and wore uniforms. Raheema and Tracy would sneak around the house, getting into trouble and then drag Mercedes into it, making her life miserable. Their father, Keith, was strict and intimidating, so Mercedes stayed moody behind closed doors.

Mercedes was thirteen, and she had matured enough to communicate with boys. Keith would have more than he anticipated on his hands in due time. Young teenagers were starting to walk Mercedes home from school and hang out with friends who lived on her block.

"Ay, Mercedes, come here for a minute," a rather plain-looking boy said. He was nothing to get excited over. Mercedes' walnut-brown complexion, dark eyes and long silky hair aroused him, though. He thought she was gorgeous. She had the "Indian look."

Mercedes walked over to him. The boy stood with one foot in the street and one on the sidewalk. Beth was inside the house cooking, and Keith was not expected home for another three hours.

"Yes?" Mercedes asked the boy, keeping a good distance from him. She didn't like him or anything, she only wanted to see what he wanted.

"Come here. I ain't gon' bite 'chew girl, dag," the boy said with a smile.

Mercedes didn't want to be any closer to him. "What?" she asked.

"You got a thorough-ass name," he told her. "Ay Kev, ain't 'Mercedes' a decent name?"

"YEAH!" his friend shouted from across the street.

Mercedes smiled at that. She was flattered. She waited for the boy to ask her something else. She liked talking to boys but didn't want to get serious with them, *yet.*

The plain-looking boy studied Mercedes' white, blue and gray uniform. "So you go to Catholic school, hunh?"

"Yeah, but I don't like it," she said.

"You don't?" he asked, pointlessly.

Mercedes sucked her teeth and answered, "No."

"Why not?"

"Because I just don't."

"Uuuuww, Mercedes talkin' to a boy!" Tracy squealed, bolting from the house with Raheema.

"Yuuup, we gon' tell," Raheema warned.

"Hold up, I'll be right back," Mercedes told the boy. She ran to the patio steps. The two little ones ran inside the house and up the stairs to Raheema's room. Mercedes chased after them.

"Why you do that?" she hissed, yanking her sister's arm.

"Because daddy don't like you talking to boys."

"So, who cares what he likes? I hate him anyway. And you better not tell on me, either."

"Did you like 'dat boy, Mercedes?" Tracy asked excitedly.

"No. He was ugly," Mercedes answered.

"Does he like you?"

"I think he does. He wanted to talk to me."

"What did 'ju say to him?"

Mercedes looked down and frowned at Tracy. "Dag, girl, you writin' a book or something?"

"Well, what did 'ju say?" Tracy repeated.

"I didn't say that much. He just asked me about school and stuff."

Raheema remained silent, with her lips poked out.

"Mommy, Mercedes was talkin' to this boy today, and she said he was ugly."

"Mercedes is talking to boys now, hunh?" Patti asked while she searched through her closet for something to wear.

Tracy plopped on her mother's vanity chair inside of the bedroom. "Yup, and me and Ra-Ra saw her."

"You did?" Patti said, picking out a dark green dress.

"Yup, and then he chased us."

"*He* did what?" Patti responded, giving her full attention.

"I mean, *she* did."

"Oh, okay. I thought maybe you were out there playing or something."

"No, me and Ra-Ra was in the house."

"Well, *we're* going out to eat tonight, sweety," Patti said, changing the subject.

"Who we goin' wit'? Jus' me and you, mom? Hunh?"

Patti paused for a minute and gave her daughter a stern look. "What

I tell you about talking so fast? I can't even understand you sometimes. Everything that you do, you just have to be so *fast* about it. Slow down sometimes when you speak."

"Okay," Tracy perked.

"Now, mommy has a date, and I'm going to take you with me. So go wash your hands and face."

Patti scooted her daughter toward the bathroom.

"Okay," Tracy said, running.

Patti wanted to establish a family feeling with the new man she was getting close to. If Dave wasn't going to show any consistent responsibility, then Patti was ready to open up her options for a man who would.

Paul Greggory was tall, with smooth caramel skin and a mustache. He drove them to a romantic restaurant in his sporty Camaro. The service was impeccable. That was a plus for Paul. Tracy never liked waiting long.

The food was well prepared. Paul cut Tracy's steak and potatoes, buttered her bread and wrapped her napkin around her neck. Patti was impressed with his manners. Then he ordered ice cream for dessert, their favorite.

"Hey, mom, he got us ice cream," Tracy said cheerfully.

"Yup, he sure did. So do you like it, honey?"

Tracy hunched her shoulders in her tan dress. "It's okay, but I liked that place where dad used to take us better."

"And where was this?" Paul asked her.

"I don't know, but it was a long way though."

"And did they have cherry-vanilla ice cream there?" Paul asked her while winking at Patti.

Paul wore a navy-blue sports jacket and a cream-colored shirt with no tie.

"I'on know," Tracy answered him.

"We used to get sundaes," Patti said.

"Oh, okay. Well, we could've gotten a sundae. Would you like to still go get one?" Paul suggested to Tracy. He leaned over the table and smiled at her.

"I don't care," Tracy told him.

Patti watched to see if her daughter liked him.

They drove to the ice cream store where Dave used to take them. Tracy fell asleep in the car.

"Okay, Tracy, we're here," Patti said, grabbing on to a limp arm.

"Stop, mommy," Tracy whined.

"Don't you want the ice cream, baby?"

Tracy dropped her head back into the seat. "No, I wanna go to sleep." Patti got Paul to pick her up and walk her around, despite Tracy's protest.

Patti wasn't quite ready for her date to end. It was only eight o'clock.

They all sat with their sundaes at a small window-view table, where Tracy watched cars zip past on the highway.

"Mommy, I wish he had a car like that," she said, pointing at a red 911 Porsche, parked outside.

Paul chuckled. "Wow, she has expensive taste for a little girl, doesn't she?" he said to Patti.

"I'm not a *little girl*," Tracy responded to him. She started to kick her feet under the table while eating her sundae. She accidentally kicked Paul.

"What's wrong with you, girl? Stop that!" Patti yelled, grabbing her daughter's feet.

"That's okay, she didn't mean it," Paul interjected.

Tracy gave him an evil stare. "I gotta go pee," she said.

"You have to use the *ladies' room*," Patti sternly corrected her. She then rushed, hand in hand with her daughter, to the bathroom, leaving behind the half-finished sundaes.

Patti turned Tracy around by the shoulders once they had entered the bathroom. "What's wrong with you, girl?"

Tracy stared down at her patent leather shoes. "I don't like him. I wanna go home."

Patti looked startled. "He's a nice man, honey. Why don't you like him?"

"Because he gets on my nerves."

"He hasn't *done* anything to you, girl," Patti said, looking into Tracy's eyes. "Well, do you have to go or what?"

"N-o-o, I just wanna go h-o-o-me."

Patti sighed and led her daughter back to the melted sundaes at their table. "Look, Paul, she wants to go home. I'm sorry about this."

Paul nodded to her. "Don't worry about it. I know how kids can get," he said, setting a dollar tip on the table.

Tracy reached out to take the money.

"Put that back, girl!" Patti shouted at her.

Tracy cracked a mischievous smile. "I was just playin'."

Patti snatched her by the hand. "Now *you're* getting on *my* nerves. You're eight years old, and still acting like a spoiled baby."

Tracy giggled and climbed into the car for the long ride home. Patti knew that Paul had failed. Tracy didn't like him. It was unfair, but there was nothing that Patti could do about it. She would have to turn Paul down. Tracy didn't seem to like any of her mother's dates. And she definitely was not ready for anyone to take the place of her father.

"How 'bout we do this again sometime?" Paul asked when they arrived at Patti's front door. She had never invited a man inside of the house. Dave was still paying the bills, and Patti gave him that respect.

She answered Paul with knifing eyes, "I'm sorry, but I really don't think so."

"Well, we'll just leave the girl home next time," Paul suggested.

Patti unlocked the door. Paul tried to follow her in after Tracy. Patti glared back at him, stopping him before he strutted in. "And what are we gonna do, have a relationship without my daughter being involved?" she piped at him.

"No, I'm not saying that, but you and I need a little more time alone before we can work things out with her."

"No, that's all right," Patti said. She wished to end the date as quickly as possible, but Paul was making it difficult.

"Well, okay, I had a nice time. How 'bout you?" he asked, still appearing cheerful.

"Please, let's not get into this," Patti told him. "I have to think about things before I decide to go out with you again. And I'm sorry for the inconvenience."

Paul nodded and said, "Okay," as Patti slowly closed the door on him. He paced to his car, finally pissed off. "Damn kid!" he mumbled as he headed down the walkway.

Patti shook her sleepy daughter from the couch. "Wake up, girl, and go on upstairs to bed," she huffed.

"What, mommy?"

"You've just ruined my night, girl, that's *what.*"

"*You* wanted me to g-o-o."

"You still didn't have to act like you did, Tracy."

Tracy struggled to her feet and began a sullen walk up the stairs.

Patti calmed herself as she followed her. Tracy's comment surprised her, but she was right. Patti had wanted her daughter to test the man, and he had failed. Plain and simple.

"Ay Mercedes, come here for a second," the boy named Kevin called from behind. He always wore a baseball hat shoved down on his smooth, dark-brown face, right above his thin eyebrows. Kevin lived across the street. Mercedes had watched him playing football in the street with his friends for years.

"So you 'sposed to be talkin' to my boy Wallace?" he asked her.

"No, I don't like him," she answered with a frown. "Why?"

"Because, I wanted your phone number," Kevin told her nervously. He had watched her over the years as well.

"I can't give out mine. But I can take yours, though."

Kevin wrestled out a piece of paper and a pencil from his book-bag. "That's a bet," he said, writing his number down.

"Umm, Kevin, don't tell your friend that I don't like him, because I don't want him getting all mad at me. Okay?" Mercedes asked him. She was well aware of how boys acted when they were rejected. Her father had been a good example of that. Keith had fits all the time. Everything had to be *his* way.

"Oh, aw'ight. But when you gon' call me?" Kevin said to her.

"Tonight."

"Oh, bet. Like what time?"

"Like around eleven-thirty, when my father goes to sleep."

"What, you can stay up that late? I thought you had to go to sleep *early.*"

Mercedes smiled at him, bashfully. *"I do,* but that's the only time that I can talk to you without my parents *jumpin' down my back,* because they're real strict and all."

Kevin smiled. "So you gon' risk getting caught to call me? Oh, *I* must be *the man* then."

"Yup," Mercedes told him with a laugh. "So you're gonna be up?"

"Yeah, I'll be up."

Mercedes grinned. "All right then, I'll call you."

Kevin nodded and said, "Cool."

Mercedes walked into the house, smiling from ear to ear. She wanted to show her father that he could *not* rule her life. She had done everything that he had asked, and was still punished, getting beatings with her younger sister. Mercedes despised her father. And if Keith had anything to say about her boyfriends, she vowed to make *his* life as miserable as *he* had made *hers.*

Mercedes called Kevin that night and the other nights that followed. She began to smoke cigarettes in school with her girlfriends, buying Wrigley's chewing gum to hide the smell. She collected more phone numbers from neighborhood boys who were attracted to her. She turned down most of the "Catholic-school boys." Mercedes wasn't interested in *them.* And in a matter of weeks, she had met enough new boys to become an item.

"Hello . . . Kevin," she whispered on the phone.

"Yo, it's me. What's up, girl?" he answered, watching the late-night *Benny Hill Show.* "Ay, tomorrow there's no school. Can't talk to me regular?"

"Unt unh. I'm still supposed to be in bed, even if we do have off from school tomorrow," Mercedes told him.

"Dag, that's messed up."

"Ain't it though? That's why I hate my father."

"What 'chew gon' do tomorrow?" Kevin asked her.

"I don't know. Why?" Mercedes quizzed, having a good idea of what was coming next.

"You wanna come see me tomorrow?"

"I don't care," she whispered.

Kevin then fell silent as he thought of a fantastic idea. "Do you have any dogs in your driveway?" he asked her.

"No," Mercedes whispered.

"Are you still dressed?"

"Unt unh."

"How long would it take you to get dressed?"

Mercedes grimaced. "Why?"

"'Cause, you could sneak around to my basement through the driveway, *if* you're not scared to."

"I'm not scared," Mercedes told him. She felt sneaky excitement, like an actor in a spy movie. The enemy was her father.

"Well, are you down or what?" Kevin challenged her.

Mercedes thought about it. *Just do it, girl. Say, Yeah,* she told herself. "Yeah, I'm coming. Give me like twenty minutes."

"For real, you comin'?" Kevin asked her. He was surprised. He was just trying his luck. He didn't really think that she would sneak over to his house at night.

"Yeah, I'm serious," Mercedes assured him.

Kevin cracked a broad smile. "Aw'ight then. I'm gon' open the back door for you."

Mercedes hung up the phone. She tiptoed back to her room, put on some loose jogging pants with her white uniform blouse and a jacket. She walked into the bathroom and flushed the toilet to muffle her escape. She then snuck down into her basement and out of the door, making sure she kept it cracked so she could re-enter. She sprinted around back, filled with elation, and got to Kevin's. Kevin was at his door, grinning like a cartoon cat, awaiting her arrival.

"I thought you was jokin'," he whispered.

"Nope, I told you I was coming," Mercedes said.

Kevin's baseball cap was off, and for the first time Mercedes could glimpse his hair.

"You got a nice haircut," she commented. "Why you wear your hat all the time?"

"I take it off in school, but when I'm out on the street, I always wear a hat. I'on know why, it's just my thing. I like hats."

"Oh," Mercedes responded, forcing herself not to seem nervous. *Oh my God, I'm in his house!* she panicked. She noticed that Kevin looked even better with his hat off. He was a handsome teenager, wearing a high fade haircut with a long part on the left side.

Kevin walked over to her and unzipped her jacket. Mercedes didn't move to stop him like she wanted. "What, 'chew *scared* or something?" he asked, sensing her tension.

"No I ain't," she lied to him as he rubbed his hand up her lower back.

Mercedes was a well-developed thirteen. She got her pert body from her mother.

Kevin began to caress her breasts through her uniform blouse and leaned over to kiss her. But Mercedes didn't know *how* to kiss. She puckered her lips to his as she thought it was supposed to be done. Kevin then moved her toward the couch.

Mercedes rubbed up and down his back as Kevin ran his fingers through her smooth, long hair. He then unbuttoned her shirt, unclipped her bra and began to kiss her nipples.

Mercedes was quickly aroused. Kevin dropped to the floor on his knees and pulled down her clothes. Mercedes then went for his shirt, to undress him. Kevin, stripped naked, laid overtop of her in a push-up position. He struggled to guide himself *in*.

Mercedes whispered, "It hurts, Kevin." She moaned, quietly, as her nails began to scrape his back. And then it felt good to her, the friction and the increased energy. Her body loosened and folded in on Kevin as she squeezed him.

"Do it feel good?" he asked her, breathlessly. He made note to be as gentle as he could with her. He knew that Mercedes was a virgin. She had never had a boy even kiss her before him.

"Yeeeahh," she moaned.

Kevin increased his speed, beginning to lose control. He flexed and sucked in air as his body jerked uncontrollably. Then suddenly he pulled himself from her and grabbed the towel that he had set on the floor alongside the couch.

Mercedes watched him as he strained and breathed, crazily. And she was upset that he had stopped.

"Why you do that?" she asked him.

Kevin looked at her, confused. "You don't wanna get pregnant, do you?" he asked her with a frown.

Mercedes shook her head as he climbed back on the couch with her. "No," she told him.

"Well, I had to pull out. I ain't got no rubbers."

"Oh," Mercedes responded, realizing she had a lot to learn about sex.

"That was good as shit though," Kevin told her. Mercedes began to smile as he cuddled her. She leaned up and kissed his pretty brown face, sparkling inside and planning on *"doing it"* with Kevin again, and as much as possible.

"Mommy, why do I have to go over Mr. Keith's house?" Tracy pouted.

"Because I'm going out."

"Aw, you don't want me to go?"

"No, because it's Friday, and I'm *not* coming home *no time soon.* All you're gonna do is mess up my date and fall asleep," Patti said, grabbing her purse.

"No I'm not, mom. I promise. Ple-e-ease," Tracy pleaded.

"No! Get your jacket and bag. I am *not* taking you with me," her mother persisted.

"Aw, see, I was gonna be good, too," Tracy said with a long face.

Patti chuckled. "You're a trip, girl."

They walked next door, hand in hand.

"Beth, I'm gonna let her spend the night, because I don't know how long I'm going to be out, and she's only gonna mess up my date. Is it okay?" Patti asked.

"Sure," Beth told her. "We're not going anywhere. I haven't been out, except for the movies, in a long time," Beth said with a grin.

"Well, girl, you better do *something* before you start to rust in here."

Tracy ran up the steps to play in Raheema's room.

"What are you doing here?" Raheema asked her.

"My mom said I could spend the night."

"She did? Y-a-a-a-y! We can play all night then," Raheema cheered.

"No we can't, 'cause Mr. Keith gon' make us go to bed," Tracy argued.

Raheema piped down. "I know. But we can play when he thinks we're sleeping," she plotted.

"Where your sister at?" Tracy asked her.

"In her room, sleeping."

They went into Mercedes' room. Mercedes was stretched out. She reminded Tracy of Snow White. Tracy decided that maybe Mercedes had been dreaming about boys and needed a kiss to wake her.

Tracy looked into Mercedes' face. It was expressionless. Mercedes did not toss and turn, make noises or anything. Her hands were firmly grasped around her pillow, as if she had fallen asleep thinking of holding someone.

The two little ones left and went back to Raheema's room.

"She pro'bly dreamin' 'bout a boy," Tracy said.

"Yeah, that ugly boy who was out there talking to her," Raheema responded.

"No, it's not *him,* Ra-Ra. Mercedes don't like *him.*"

"Well, that's the only boy she talks to."

"*You* don't know, Ra-Ra, 'cause you don't see who she knows in school."

"So, she probably don't talk to nobody in school."

"Shet up, 'cause you don't know nothin'. *You* still a baby," Tracy snapped.

"I'm older than *you.* My birthday is before yours. *Now!*" Raheema retorted.

"So, Ra-Ra, you still *act* like a baby."

The two faced off, and neither would back down.

"You can't *beat* this baby," Raheema challenged.

"You wanna bet?"

Tracy slapped Raheema in the face. Raheema tripped on her toys and bumped her head on her low-leveled bedpost. She immediately screamed out in pain.

Keith, just in from work, ran into her room, followed by his wife.

Beth catered to her daughter. Keith looked to Tracy for an explanation.

"What the hell is goin' on in here?" Keith asked, sternly.

Tracy cringed, but she hinted a smile. "We was fighting."

Beth noticed Tracy's gleeful expression and said, "You could have hurt her real bad, Tracy. That's not funny."

"I'm sorry, Ms. Beth. I just got mad, that's all."

"Well, where the hell is Mercedes? She should have been in here watching them anyway," Keith shouted.

"She, she in her room, sleeping," Raheema stuttered, wiping tears from her eyes.

"She's *sleeping?*" Keith asked, baffled. "Is she sick or something?" he asked his wife.

"No, but she's been sleeping all day," Beth answered.

Everyone followed Mr. Keith into Mercedes' room to see what was wrong with her. Keith clicked on the light and woke her up. Beth, Raheema and Tracy looked in from the door.

"Wake up, girl! Are you sick or somethin'?"

Mercedes wiped out her eyes with closed fists. "No, I'm just tired," she muttered.

"You're *tired?* Girl, you didn't even have school today. What 'chew do to be so *tired?*"

Mercedes squinted her eyes from the glaring light. "I'on know."

"Well, get up. It's time to eat," her father told her. "And you make sure these kids don't get in any more fights."

Mercedes felt overjoyed about her secret. Keith didn't seem as smart as he used to be. He wasn't as scary either. He thought he had everything uptight, but Mercedes had proved him wrong.

She ate dinner silently. She washed the dishes, pondering over her passive mother. Beth had allowed her father to be God in their house. *He's not God,* Mercedes thought to herself.

She cleaned the floor, the kitchen table and the refrigerator without a complaint. She then watched television, ignoring Raheema and Tracy. They contributed to her torture. Mercedes was beginning to hate them as well.

She wondered how Keith became her dad in the first place. He was too damned mean to have a woman like her mother. *What did she see in him?* she asked herself. *He doesn't even act like he likes us.* All Keith seemed to do was pay the bills and control their lives.

Patti stayed out late. She picked her daughter up early Saturday morning. Tracy didn't bother to ask her mother how her date went. She daydreamed about her daddy coming over to see them. Dave hadn't been to see them in a few months. He mailed Tracy's allowance checks to the house religiously, but Tracy wanted badly to see him. Dave added the needed spice to her young life.

"So did you have fun last night?" Patti asked her.

Tracy was watching *Space Ghost* in her room. She was sitting on her bed with crossed legs and her face in her hands.

"No, 'cause we didn't do nothin'," she pouted.

Patti frowned. *I know she can speak better than that,* she told herself. But she decided to ignore it. She sat down and joined her daughter on her bed. "You didn't?"

"No. We started fighting."

"Fighting? Why?"

"Because, *Ra-Ra* don't know nothin'."

Patti was confused. "Well, what were you two talking about?"

"We was talkin' 'bout: don't girls sleep in the daytime when 'ney thinkin' 'bout boys?"

"What I tell you about trying to talk so fast?" Patti snapped.

"Okay," Tracy said with a nod.

"What does sleeping in the daytime have to do with anything?" Patti asked her.

"Because, Mercedes is talking to boys, and she was sleeping all yesterday."

"That doesn't mean that she was necessarily dreaming about a boy. She could've just been tired."

"No she wasn't. She never sleeps in the daytime."

Patti pondered the subject. "I don't know, girl," she said to Tracy. Mercedes was old enough to mess around. Tracy could have been right. But if Mercedes was seeing boys, it would serve Keith right. He had tortured her enough. And whatever it was that she was doing, it seemed to be making Mercedes' personality a lot stronger. Patti had noticed the recent glow on her face. *Hmm. Maybe Tracy's onto something.*

DING DONG!

"Mommy, somebody's at the door!" Tracy yelled.

Patti walked out from the kitchen wondering who it could be. She looked through the peephole and was shocked.

"Who is it, mommy? . . . Who is it?" Tracy repeated.

Patti finally answered her. "Guess who, honey?"

"DAD-DY!"

Tracy jumped into his arms, and Dave kissed her on the lips, spinning her around the living room.

Patti watched with a smile. She was still happy to see him. And she still loved him. *Nevertheless, he should have called first,* she thought.

Dave just thought he'd drop by. It was *still* his house.

"So how's my little girl?" he asked, sitting on the couch with Tracy on his lap.

"I'm okay, daddy."

"You're still talking a lot in school?"

"Not like before."

"You cooled off a bit, hunh?"

"Yup, because 'dey stupid in school, anyway. They don't know nothin'."

Again, Patti frowned at Tracy's speech. "I've been trying to get her to slow down and *pronounce* her words when she speaks to people, Dave."

Dave nodded his head. "I see. She wants to talk so much she can't get all of her words out," he commented with a laugh.

"It's not funny," Patti told him.

"But you're still a little brainiac, right?" he asked his daughter.

"Yup," Tracy answered him with a glow.

Patti watched them enviously. She was begging for Dave to say something to *her*. He hadn't even looked her way. She felt an urge to sit down beside him, but her pride wouldn't let her "kiss up." Her nerves pushed and pulled, torn between love and dignity. Then Dave intensified her struggle.

"So what has your mother been up to?" he asked Tracy.

"She been goin' out to dinners and stuff."

Patti was pissed as well as embarrassed. *Now how is he gonna sit up in here and ask Tracy that when I'm right in his damn face?* she thought to herself. "Why not ask me?" she said to her separated husband.

Dave turned to face her with a seductive smile that made Patti nervous. "Well, what have you been up to?" he asked.

Patti took a deep breath to maintain her composure. She was about to explode on the inside. "I got a new job at this abortion clinic. I had enrolled in a night-school training program, and—"

"Where was Tracy while you were doing this?" Dave asked, cutting her off.

"She was next door."

"Yeah, dad, I was at Mr. Keith's house."

"Okay. But you know what, my little girl? Daddy bought a surprise for you."

Patti left the living room for the kitchen, annoyed that he had led her on. "Damn, he gets on my nerves!" she mumbled. "I don't even know why I tried to talk to him."

Dave pulled out a small box and opened it, displaying a gold chain to his daughter.

"Wow, daddy, that's for me?" Tracy asked.

He put it around her neck. "Yup, sweetheart, it's for you all right. Now go show your mother."

Tracy ran into the kitchen to show it off. "Look what daddy bought me, mom."

Patti looked down at Tracy's neck and felt a spark of jealousy. She couldn't help it. Dave didn't bring *her* any presents. He didn't even want to talk to *her.* Hell, she felt like throwing his ass out. But it was still his house.

This motherfucker got me trapped, he knows it, and he's toying with me! Patti snapped to herself. "That's nice," she told her daughter while hiding her rage.

Tracy ran back into the living room and jumped on her father's lap.

"What did your mother say?" he asked her.

"She said it was nice."

Dave smiled and shook his head. "Go tell your mother I got a surprise for her, too."

"Okay, daddy," Tracy responded, running back to the kitchen.

"Daddy said he got one for you, too, mom."

Patti tried to hold back a colossal smile. *See that! He's fucking with me!* she fumed. Her smile exploded through anyway. "Ask him what it is."

"What is it? dad, mommy said."

"You tell her I said to come here."

Tracy loved the message game. She ran back to the kitchen again. "He said come and get it, mommy," she fibbed.

Patti slowly walked out into the living room and sat on the couch. She then took Tracy into her arms and held her daughter on her lap.

Dave laid back against the couch and waited for Patti to say something.

"Well, what do you have for me?"

"Nothin'. I just wanted to look at you."

Patti felt bubbly with joy. "Why do you want to look at me?" she asked him with a slight blush.

Dave sat up and ran his fingers from the back of her neck and through her hair. "Because you're so pretty."

Patti rocked her daughter, letting off some of her swelling anxiety. She was about to ask her husband why he left her when Dave leaned over and kissed her on her neck. Patti responded, lifting her head. He was touching her, passionately, for the first time in years.

Dave stopped and chuckled to himself as he got up to leave.

Patti was frantic. "Where are you going?" she asked him hastily. She stood up so quickly that she unintentionally dropped Tracy to the floor.

"Hey, mom," Tracy yelped.

Dave responded with a grin, "Calm down, girl. I'm coming back. I'm just gonna run out to the bank and get some money so we can go out today. Okay? Is that all right with you?"

Patti mellowed out with a smile. "All right," she said, feeling a bit foolish. Dave still knew how to push her buttons.

The Ellisons went out to the suburban Willow Grove Mall. Dave bought his daughter a few new dolls and dresses and a new book-bag with bright neon colors. He bought Patti a pair of shoes to match a gold dress she had purchased. They hadn't shopped as a family since Tracy was four years old.

They sat inside of the mall's restaurant area and ate lunch. Dave looked around curiously while Patti sneaked peeks at his hazel eyes in blissful silence.

"Daddy, why do people sleep in the daytime?" Tracy asked him with a French fry in hand.

"Well, some people sleep in the daytime when they have nighttime jobs. Or you might have a hard day, or exhaust yourself doing something physical, like playing sports or something."

"But what if you a girl and you don't have no job yet?"

Her father grinned. "Oh, well, in that case, I'd say she's running around with boys at night and tired herself out. Boys can take up a lot of your energy," Dave said, creating a big story to amuse his wife with their memories.

Patti beamed across the table.

"See, mom, I told you. Dad knows I'm right," Tracy said.

Dave raised his brow. "What is she talking about?" he asked Patti.

"She thinks that Mercedes is running around with boys, because she slept late yesterday."

Dave responded, smiling, "Yup, that'll do it."

Patti grinned. "Not necessarily, Dave."

"Well, as long as we've been living next door to them, that girl ain't did nothin' to be tired. How old is she now?"

"Thirteen," Tracy answered, butting in.

Dave shook his head and laughed.

"What's so funny?" Patti asked, smiling herself. She was overjoyed to be with him again. Marriage and a child with Dave had created a comfort zone between them that none of Patti's dates seemed to be able to reach. Dave felt the same way about her. After two years, he thought he was ready to come home.

"I was just thinking about this girl who everybody was after when I was young," he said. "Her name was Rita. Her father was mean, too, and that girl did everything she could to get into something."

Patti nodded. "Unh hunh. I knew this girl like that, too. She was just as quiet as she could be. And she was nasty as can be."

Tracy got a kick out of hearing her parents talk about their youth. She was learning about "the birds and the bees" much faster that way. If her parents only knew how much and how fast Tracy picked up on things, they would not have spoken so loosely around her.

"I know one thing," Dave said, "Keith damn sure ain't the most charming man. I think he must have scared Beth into marrying him."

In the passing weeks, Mercedes collected more phone numbers from only cute guys. She had increased her popularity around the neighborhood. She was still seeing Kevin whenever she got a chance. But Kevin was bored with her and started to avoid her calls. Mercedes was learning her first big lesson about boys: never become a submissive sidekick.

"Ay Mercedes, come here for a minute," said a light-skinned boy named Hakeem. He had spoken to her before, and he was known as a fighter and a troublemaker. He lived on the rougher side of Germantown in a row-house, across Chelten Avenue.

Hakeem had wavy light-brown hair and sleepy eyes. Those eyes attracted Mercedes. She liked his boldness as well. And he had a voice that demanded attention, so Mercedes remained apprehensive as she walked over to him on her way home from school.

"Are you still talkin' to Kevin?" he asked her. His rowdy friends hung close by.

"Yeah," she answered.

"Well, you know what? I wanna talk to you anyway," Hakeem told her. He looked over her body, imagining what it looked like through the Catholic school uniform. "So what's up with that, Mercedes?"

Mercedes was afraid to alarm him. She immediately changed the subject. "Where are you coming from?" she asked pleasantly. She wanted to avoid his question. Her heart was still full with Kevin.

"Look, can I get your number or what?" Hakeem pressed.

"I can't give out my phone number."

"Why not?"

"Because my father doesn't allow me to."

Hakeem shook his head, defiantly. "Naw, I'm not tryin' to hear that, slim. Ay Lou, write my number down, man, 'cause she gon' call *me*," he said to one of his friends. "Now you better call me up, 'cause I'm *not* playin' wit' 'chew."

Just like that, Hakeem had won Mercedes over. He knew what he wanted and how to get it. She started to imagine what he would be like in bed.

"What time do you want me to call you?" she asked, peeking at his six-pack of friends, who were patiently waiting for him.

"I mean, whenever you get a chance. I ain't in no hurry. As long as you call me this week."

"All right then, I'll call you," she told him.

She memorized his phone number, repeating it over and over again before she tore up the piece of paper that his friend had written it on and threw it away. The word on the street was that Hakeem could box anybody his age. He was her new champion, and he was well respected.

Mercedes dreamed up fantasies while doing her math problems. But although Hakeem was a new kid who had jumped into her heart, she still felt for her first love. She refused to let Kevin go. She still preferred him over any other boy. Kevin wasn't as decisive or as respected as Hakeem; she just couldn't break his love spell.

She crept down to the kitchen phone that night and dialed.

"Hello . . . Kevin."

"Ay Mercedes, why don't you stop callin' me for a while?"

"Why? What I do?" she whispered.

"Look, I'm just tired of you. Okay? Damn!"

"Why you gotta treat me like this, Kevin?"

"'Cause we had a little somethin', and now I wanna move on."

There was a moment of silence while Mercedes thought it over. "I hate 'chew then, boy," she said, hanging up on him. "I'on need him," she mumbled to herself.

She then dialed Hakeem's number.

"Hello. Can I speak to Hakeem?"

"Who is this?" a deep voice boomed.

"Mercedes," she answered.

"Hold on. YO, PUNCH! The phone is for you, man!"

Mercedes was amazed that there was so much noise in Hakeem's house after eleven o'clock at night. He would probably have a lot of stories to tell of staying out all night. She could imagine him taking her to adventurous places on the weekends. His crew probably did wild and crazy things every day, just for the hell of it. Mercedes could not *wait* to be with him!

"Hello," Hakeem answered.

"Hi, it's me."

"Me? Me who?"

"The girl you gave your phone number to."

"Oh, what's up, girl?"

"What's up wit' 'chew?" Mercedes asked, attempting to sound "cool."

"I thought you was gon' call later on this week."

"Well, I surprised you, didn't I?"

"No, 'cause I knew you was gon' call me eventually, and if you *didn't*, I was gon' punch you in your mouth for lyin' to me."

Mercedes heard laughter in the background. She suspected that Hakeem had company over, or a lot of brothers. "That's why they call you 'Punch'?" she quizzed him.

"You don't wanna find out why they call me Punch," he told her.

Mercedes grinned. Hakeem was tough as nails, and rambunctious. "You got a lot of company over or something?" she asked.

"Naw, my cousin, Lou, lives wit' me. Him and my brothers are drunk."

Mercedes thought they probably got drunk every night and acted like fools, like her father would do whenever his friends came over. That was the only time Mercedes could stand her father. Keith was entertaining when he was drunk.

"How many brothers you got?" she asked.

"Three. What about you?"

"I got a little sister."

"So you're the oldest, hunh?"

"Yeah, but I know you're not," she guessed.

"Nope, I'm the baby. But I'm still the man, though."

"What do you do to have fun, Hakeem?"

"Talk to pretty girls like you."

Mercedes turned giddy as a baby. "I'm serious, Hakeem," she said with a huge smile.

"I told 'ju already," he responded. "Sike, girl. You wanna know what I *really* do to have fun?"

"Yeah, Hakeem, tell me."

"Well, as soon as you come over, you gon' find out," he joked.

Mercedes could see that Hakeem wasn't for *beating around the bush*. He was into *cutting down trees*.

"How we gon' do anything when your brothers gon' be there?" she asked, starting to play it his way.

"Oh, they not gon' be in here. Plus, I got my own room. Two of my brothers stay in the basement."

"What about your parents?"

"Most likely, they gon' be at work when you come over."

Mercedes heard footsteps. "Hakeem, I gotta go. Okay?" she said quickly. She turned the light on and got a tall glass from the cabinet. By the time her father walked into the kitchen, Mercedes had a glass of water in her hand as she squinted her eyes to act as if she had just woken up.

"Hey girl, you had to get some water too, hunh?"

"Yeah, my throat was dry," she said in a husky voice, faking sleepiness.

Hakeem was *it!* Mercedes would give him his chance and he would give her excitement. She figured it was a fair trade for a relationship. And her body would be her ammunition.

Hakeem was on the prowl, looking for Mercedes after school that next day.

"Yo, Mercedes, come here!" he yelled after waiting on the corner for her. He was standing with his crew again.

"I know what you gon' say, and I only hung up because my father was comin'."

Hakeem walked over to her, smiling with slit eyes. "Well, what's up? When you gon' come over to see me?" he asked.

"Whenever you want me to," Mercedes answered seductively.

"Oh, shit! I like that attitude," Hakeem told her. "I think me and you gon' do lots of things." He reached out to hold her hand.

"I hope we will," Mercedes responded to him with a smile.

"Aw'ight then. Call me tonight," he told her.

Mercedes headed up her block.

Hakeem turned to go with his friends.

"Yo, Punch, she sounds like she on you, like a *champ,*" his cousin Lou said.

"Yeah, I know. I like her too though, now. At first, I just wanted some ass. But now, I think she's aw'ight. She's thorough as shit, Lou."

"Yeah, cuz', she's real pretty," one of his friends commented with a nod.

"Yeah, I *know* she is," Hakeem told him, grinning with confidence. "I'ma make her my girl, cuz'. Straight up."

boyſ -N- girlſ

Aaron was the most popular boy in fifth grade. He continued to make noises in class, play ball outside of class, and get into mischief after school. He was still the fastest, and all the teachers knew him by first and last name—Aaron Barnes. The girls grew from hating him to adoring him.

Aaron stood up to the older guys and protected his ground inside the schoolyard. He was silly, yet he had a maturity about him that no other boy in his grade possessed. And whenever he was calm and laid back, it caused confusion for the girls, who would swear they knew his every move.

Aaron didn't show any interest in girls, though. Girls were "stupid." They were too talkative and petty, complaining all the time. They preferred to sit on benches and get in his way, which always pissed him off.

The girls still liked him no matter *what* Aaron did. If one of them had Aaron's heart, they could brag about it and quickly become the envy of all the other girls in the fifth grade. No one could fill a classroom with laughter like he did. He was their hero, with big bright eyes, chestnut-colored skin and wild, curly hair.

Tracy shoved her girlfriend, Celena, during recess. "Go ahead and talk to him," she said.

Celena resisted. "No, girl. I'm scared."

They were all getting bigger, but they had maintained their same bench inside the schoolyard since first grade.

"If you like him so much, what are you scared for?" Tracy asked her tall and lanky girlfriend.

"Because. What if he don't like me?" Celena responded.

"Then he just doesn't like you then."

"Well, you go talk to him."

"I don't like *him*. Y'all the ones all after him."

"How come you don't like him, Tracy?" Judy asked her.

"I don't know. I just don't," Tracy said.

"You don't think he's cute?" Celena asked.

"Yeah, he's cute," Tracy answered. "But so what?"

"So you should want to make him your boyfriend. That's what," Judy said.

"Why? *Celena's* the one that likes *him,* not me."

"But you're prettier than me, Tracy. He might like you," Celena argued.

Tracy sucked her teeth. "Aw, you're just scared of him. I *should* go tell him that you like him."

"No, don't do that, Tracy," Celena said, nervously.

They watched Aaron running around at recess, avoiding all the other boys. They all seemed too slow to tag Aaron. He moved quickly and accurately, like Tony Dorsett of the Dallas Cowboys.

"See, he's better than *all* of them," Celena bragged.

Tracy nudged her toward the field.

"Go talk to him, then."

"No, because he'll think that I like him."

"But *you do* like him."

"Yeah, but you can't let *boys* know," Celena said, matter-of-factly.

"Why not?" Tracy demanded.

"Because, if they know you like them, then they gon' try to talk to you," Pam spoke up.

Tracy threw her hands on her hips. "Well, ain't that what you *want* them to do?" she asked.

"Yeah, but you don't want them to chase after you," Celena told her.

"Why not?"

"Because, girl, then they stop bein' fun if they're spendin' all their time chasin' you," Judy said.

"Oh. You mean like Tommy?" Tracy alluded.

Celena smiled. "Yeah, like him."

They all laughed. Tommy was a pushover. He would do anything a girl told him.

"Well, don't you want the boys to talk to you?" Tracy asked Celena.

"Sorta," Celena answered.

"What? What do you mean, *sorta?"*

Pam stood up and explained it to her. "See, you want them to talk to you, but you don't want them to act like they like you."

Tracy frowned at her. It all sounded ridiculous to her. *"Who* told you this stuff?"

"My older sister. *She* got a boyfriend," Pam said.

"Well, who told *her?"*

Pam sucked her teeth. "I don't know, Tracy. Dag."

"Well, that stuff is stupid. Why wouldn't you want to know that a boy likes you?"

"Because, that takes away the fun of it. That's like knowing what you're getting for Christmas," Judy put in.

Tracy laughed at that one. "Well, I wanna *get* whatever I *want* for Christmas. And if I want me a boy wrapped up in big box, then that's what I wanna get. And I could probably get it, too. But I don't *want* no stupid boy."

Celena mumbled, "That's because you're spoiled."

"Yeah, your dad buys you anything you want," Judy commented to Tracy.

Tracy was proud of it. "That's right," she told them.

• • •

Tracy had her own house key. She was ten years old, and since they lived next door to Beth and Keith, Patti decided to give her that responsibility. Dave still hadn't moved back in with them. He kept making excuses about his apartment being closer to his new job and whatnot. But he stayed over on most weekends.

Tracy walked home with her girlfriends, still confused about the boy-versus-girl games. She figured if she liked a boy, she would go after him. If the boy didn't respond to her, then he wasn't worth her time anyway. Any boy would be dumb to turn her down, or at least so Tracy thought.

She started wearing even nicer clothes. She had dressers and a closet full of different styles and colors. She could wear different things for almost a month. Being the only child was heaven.

Although Tracy seemed to have everything she wanted, there remained a hollowness to be filled. Something was missing. She was running out of things to do to entertain herself. She was tired of sitting around the house asking her mother unanswered questions and watching television. She was bored. The only time she was happy was when her father came over. But Dave seemed to be spending more of his time with Patti. Tracy was a bit jealous of her mother since her daddy wasn't home every day. There simply wasn't enough of him to go around.

Tracy thought she understood her father better since she was older. Her father didn't want to be tied down. Even though he loved his wife and daughter, he needed his space. And Tracy figured if she couldn't have her dad, then she'd find a substitute.

"Hey, honey, I'm home," Patti announced, peeking into Tracy's room.

Tracy sat on her bed, watching *Woody Woodpecker.*

"Hi, mom," she answered, glumly.

"What's wrong, honey? Why you look all down? Did something happen in school today?"

"No, I'm just bored. It's nothin' to do."

"Well, guess what?" Patti perked. "Mommy has some good news."

"What?" Tracy asked her, curious.

"I'm going to have a baby boy in about four months. That's why mommy's stomach is getting so big."

Tracy looked at her mother's stomach. She had watched enough television shows to know that babies came from parent's loving. "From being with dad, mom?" she asked with a grin.

"Yeah, honey. Your father wanted to have a son."

Tracy gave her mother her undivided attention. "Does that mean he's coming back?"

Patti hesitated. She didn't want to give her daughter any false expectations. "Well, we're still working on that," she answered carefully. "See, your daddy and I had to work out a plan where we can *all* be happy."

Tracy failed to see how that *plan* was working. She wasn't all that happy. Nevertheless, she smiled and rubbed her mother's stomach. "Is he gon' look like daddy?" she asked.

"He might, but I don't know. He could come out light, dark, or like you."

"Dad said that God does it."

"Yeah, that's just because you wouldn't be able to understand it."

"Well, tell me then."

First Patti frowned. "Look now, I don't feel like it," she said. Then she piped down and smiled. "But isn't it great that you're going to have a little brother?"

Patti went to the kitchen to begin fixing dinner. Tracy thought over the news. A little brother *could* bring some entertainment to her life. He'd be cute and cuddly like the babies on TV. But he couldn't be like her dad, if he was only a baby. It wouldn't work. It would take too long for him to grow up, and he would always be younger than her. How could he answer any of her questions? She would always know more than he would. Tracy began not to like the idea. Babies always cried on TV. What if he turned out to be a big cry-baby.

· · ·

The next day at school, Tracy wanted to know if Aaron really hated girls as much as they all thought he did. No girls really tried to talk to him. They just smiled and giggled whenever he walked by. No wonder Aaron didn't like *them*. They *were* "stupid." But not Tracy.

She decided to break the norm and talk to a boy *first*. She didn't like Aaron or any other boy. Tracy could care less if he liked her or not, as long as he responded to her.

The bell rang to end class, and Tracy watched Aaron get his football from his locker. She followed him and his friends through the hallway and into the schoolyard. Her girlfriends watched her, all wondering what Tracy was up to.

The boys began to play keep-away. When the ball finally landed near her, Tracy picked it up and tried to throw it back to Aaron.

Aaron frowned at her. "What 'chew do that for, girl?" he asked her sternly.

"'Cause, I just wanted to help."

"Aw, you can't even throw, girl. How you gon' *help* somebody?"

"Teach me how to throw then," she challenged him.

"No," Aaron said, walking away from her with his football in hand. Tracy followed him. "Why not?"

"'Cause you a girl," he told her.

"So? I can learn to play if you teach me." Tracy was optimistic about it. *How hard could it be to catch and throw a ball?* she figured.

"You can't catch. *Girls* don't play football," Aaron hissed at her.

Tommy took the ball from him. "I'll show you how to play," he said, giving Tracy the ball. Tommy was light-skinned with reddish-brown hair and freckles.

Tracy's girlfriends moved in closer. They all wanted to join in, but the fear of embarrassment prevented them.

"NO! I want *Aaron* to show me!" Tracy demanded. She was going to *get* what she wanted.

The boys began to giggle, recognizing Tracy's challenge to Aaron.

"No, girl. Dag," he said, taking his ball back.

Tracy hated him. She vowed that he would teach her to play catch if it was the last thing he did. Aaron had survived that round, but he would give in eventually, Tracy was sure of it. But at that moment, as she walked back toward her girlfriends, all she felt was hatred for him.

"What did 'ju say to them?" Celena asked excitedly.

"Nothin'! I *hate* that boy!" Tracy fumed.

"But what did you say?" Celena persisted.

"I asked him to teach me to play football."

"Why you ask him that?" Judy butted in.

"I don't know, girl."

"See, *I told you* not to let them know that you like them," Celena reminded her.

Tracy was quickly getting annoyed. "Shet up, Celena, because I don't even like him."

Celena backed down.

Then Pam asked, "So why you go to talk to him then?"

"'CAUSE I FELT LIKE IT!" Tracy snapped, squaring off in Pam's face.

They all teamed up on Tracy.

"You don't have to get all mad at us, just because he don't like you," Judy said.

"I don't like him *either!*" Tracy shouted, balling up her fists in frustration. A gathering crowd pushed Pam into her. Tracy lashed out with a barrage of punches. She was a *girl,* but she played boxing with her dad, so she was good at using her fists.

Tracy was suspended three days for fighting. Patti was furious that evening. She had received a call at work about her daughter beating up a girl at recess. Patti had just been telling her companions at work how much of an angel her daughter was. She lied and said that Tracy had fallen ill at school when she received the call. "It was probably an upset stomach or something," Patti told them. She couldn't stand being embarrassed. Her sisters had embarrassed Patti throughout her life.

"What the hell is your problem, girl?" she huffed at her daughter once she had gotten home with her.

"It wasn't my fault, mom, she was picking with me," Tracy whined.

"About what?"

"I don't know. She just doesn't like me," Tracy answered, lying herself. She held her hands in her lap, twitching nervously and refusing to look at her mother.

"You look at me when I'm talking to you!" Patti told her. Tracy looked up for an instant, hunching her shoulders in fear. "Now you're telling me that this girl picked on you for no reason? Is that what you're telling me?"

"Y-e-e-e-s."

Patti threw her hands to her hips. "Go on upstairs, girl, and do your homework. And you get no TV for the rest of this week."

Tracy was disappointed with all the trouble she had gotten into, just to find out why some "dumb boy" didn't like girls. She hated boys even more, with reason. She wished she had never been curious about it. Aaron was immature after all. He was no better than the rest of the boys. Yet he did tell her "no." No one had *ever* turned *Tracy* down.

During one of her days home from school, Tracy played with her cousin Marcus while staying over at her Aunt Joy's house. Marcus was two years old and fun to play with. After being with him, Tracy felt delighted that she would soon be having a little brother of her own.

Tracy hadn't seen some of her cousins for years. Their number had increased to ten. Tracy had only been with two of her four new cousins. They were all boys, except a baby girl that Marsha had had.

"Can I help you, Aunt Joy? My mom lets me help her," she asked her aunt inside of the kitchen. Joy's older children were off at school.

"No, I'm almost finished," Joy told her, stirring dark brown beef gravy. "So why were you fighting yesterday, princess?" her aunt asked her.

"Because, this girl was teasing me."

"She was *teasing* you? What was she teasing you about?"

"Because," Tracy said with a helpless grin. Her aunt was trying to get the truth out of her.

"Oh, I'm beginning to see now," Joy responded.

"See what?" Tracy quizzed her.

Joy smiled at her with shiny white teeth. "You were fighting over a little boy," she said.

"No I wasn't," Tracy quickly responded, startled by it.

"Come on now, Tracy, you can tell me. I won't tell your mother," Joy promised her.

Tracy giggled, covering her mouth to hide it. "I wasn't trying to talk to that *boy.*"

"Mmm hmm, I know you were. I was trying to do the same thing when I was young," her aunt said.

Tracy gave in. "Well, I didn't like him *anyway.*"

Joy chuckled. "Yup, those little boys can tear your heart out, but no girl can live without them."

"I can," Tracy proudly announced. "I'm not *ever* gonna talk to another boy again."

Tracy was not allowed to return to school until Monday. She felt like a new student when she had returned. Everyone was ahead of her in class assignments as if she had been left behind. Even the smell in the hall seemed different. And everyone was staring at her.

Curious students whispered about her as she walked through the halls. Her mother had told her to ignore them, but it was aggravating. Tracy wanted to lash out and finish off the entire hallway. But then she would end up suspended again.

Tracy was unusually quiet in class. She was silent at recess as well. Her friends were scared to talk to her. They all figured she was still mad about Aaron not teaching her to play football, so they sat and watched without speaking. Pam made sure she went nowhere near Tracy.

Tommy stopped playing football to talk. He smiled at Tracy and said, "I heard you beat up Pamela."

"Yup, that's why I got suspended last week," Tracy told him, pleased that someone was willing to talk to her.

"Well, if you still wanna play football, I'll teach you."

"Okay," Tracy said, forgetting that she hated boys.

Tommy had a red-headed temper, but he was sweet when he wanted to be. The other boys dared not to say anything about him taking the ball to play with her. They all mumbled under their breaths.

Tommy and Tracy played catch all through recess. Tracy's friends watched, hesitantly. Anything could trigger Tracy's wrath. None of them were willing to take that chance.

Tommy even walked Tracy home after school. He was as nice as any *boy* could be. Tracy started to like him. He was wonderful. She had no idea that a boy could be so friendly and understanding toward *girls*. He then sat outside of her house with her. Tracy felt like she was grown. Talking to Tommy was relaxing.

After going in the house, Tracy went up to her room and dozed off as she watched *Tom & Jerry*. Then suddenly she was shocked to attention, sitting up wide awake in her bed.

I forgot about something, she thought to herself, frantically. *Or did I forget to do something? No! I forgot to see somebody.*

Tracy stared at her television trying to remember what it was. Something was missing from their normal school day and she couldn't figure it out.

"AARON!" she yelled at her television. "Aaron Barnes wasn't in school today," she reminded herself. Her little heart began to patter. No wonder school had been so dull. Aaron made school exciting. Without him, there was little to talk about and nothing to remember.

Tracy grew restless. She knew she had to face him. She couldn't get Aaron Barnes off of her mind. In her daydream, she imagined *him* teaching her to play football. It was the strongest feeling that Tracy had felt for anyone besides her father. And it was the first dream she had had of any *boy*. Aaron Barnes was *it!* Tracy Ellison had been bitten by the love bug.

Tracy wore one of her prettiest skirts to school on Tuesday. It was royal blue with white and gold hemlines. And she wore the rubber-soled blue shoes that her father had bought her, anticipating playing catch.

Tracy walked through the halls with a new attitude, expecting to be happy. Aaron hadn't arrived in class, but Tommy was there, and he was in her way. Tracy decided to ignore him while she waited patiently for her young Romeo to enter the classroom.

Tommy asked a few questions, trying to get Tracy's attention. She answered him snobbishly, still trying to ignore him. But Tommy stayed right in her face. Tracy then asked to be excused to the bathroom. While walking through the hallway, she spotted Aaron turning the corner. Tracy slipped inside of the bathroom and went to the mirror to see how she looked. She was impressed and confident. But no confidence could match Aaron's. Tracy knew it. She was as scared and as nervous as Celena was.

Walking back into class was like performing on stage for the first time. Tracy felt like everyone was waiting for her to do something. From the corner of her eye, she noticed Aaron looking at her. She quickly turned away from him, acting as though she was still angry. Nevertheless, Aaron's cute brown face and big energetic eyes were glued to hers. As he started to smile in her direction, Tracy held back a bomb of excitement. She was ready to nab Aaron, despite what anyone said.

Tracy walked slowly to where the boys played football during recess. She took Celena with her for security. Aaron played with all of his concentration while Tommy ran near them every chance he got. But Tracy's eyes were for Aaron only.

Every time Aaron did something, Tracy clapped her hands and shouted. Aaron shook his head and frowned at her. She didn't care what he did, as long as he noticed her.

Tommy was getting jealous. Even though they were on the same team, he began to purposefully bump into Aaron. After a while, Aaron realized what was going on. He ignored it a few times because Tommy was his best friend. Yet it was getting on his last nerve. He felt he could easily beat Tommy, but he didn't want to fight over *a girl*.

Tommy bumped into Aaron one time too many, and that was it. Aaron had to straighten it out, once and for all.

"Look, I don't like that girl, man, so stop trying to start a fight with me," he said, loud enough for Tracy to hear.

Tracy's nerves were shot. She had gone through all kinds of troubles for him, and yet he could just throw her efforts away in front of all of his friends. He hadn't even spoken to her. He was simply not interested.

Tracy felt like running away to cry, but her mother had told her to be strong, so she concealed her pain. And she felt dedicated to a new project: to get Aaron Barnes to like her before they graduated from elementary school.

"You want me to walk you home, Tracy?" Tommy asked after school.

"No," Tracy told him. She then crossed the street just to get away from him.

Tommy responded by following her. "Why not?"

"Because I don't *want* you to," Tracy snapped. She wasn't interested in Tommy anymore.

"We can go to the store, and I'll buy you some candy," he told her.

"I don't want no candy, boy."

"Aw, come on, Tracy, you let me walk you home yesterday."

"Well, that was *yesterday.*"

"I bet if I was *Aaron,* you'd let me walk you home. And he'll *never* do it," Tommy snapped back at her with gleaming red hair.

Tracy gave Tommy the evil eye. "How *you* know, boy?"

"'Cause he just won't. He don't like girls."

"Well, I don't like you either."

"I didn't say that I didn't like you," Tommy said, confused that she had heard him wrong.

"So. I don't like *you* anyway, so leave me alone."

"Stupid," Tommy mumbled, turning away from her.

"Who you callin' *stupid,* boy?" Tracy said, facing him.

"I wasn't talking about you."

"Yes you was. I heard 'ju."

"Okay, I'm sorry," Tommy said, hopping back over to her. "Please, I just got mad. So can I walk you, Tracy, please?"

"NO! Leave me alone, boy!"

• • •

Tracy felt better after turning Tommy down. She walked into her house and stared out of the window. It was too cold to stand outside. She thought about what she would do the next day at school to get Aaron's attention while watching cars drive up and down her block.

Mercedes walked up with a boy who handed her a gold chain. She snuck him a kiss on the lips and headed toward her house. Tracy looked at the boy to see if he was cute. After confirming that he was, she ran to the door to invite Mercedes in.

Tracy smiled at her. "Who was that boy, Mercedes?"

"My boyfriend."

"Why he give you that chain?"

Mercedes tried it on. "Because he wanted to. Look," she said, pulling out a football jersey from her book-bag. "He let me hold this, too. He's a senior on the football team."

"Uuuuw, he's too old for you," Tracy squealed.

Mercedes cracked a devilish grin. "Girl, he's only two years older than me. When you get older, you can go wit' older guys."

"Where you gonna wear that without your father knowing?"

Mercedes responded with a frown. "Fuck him. I hate him."

Tracy cringed, shying away from the foul language Mercedes was using.

"He's always trying to tell somebody what to do. That's why he don't know what I be doin' now."

"What 'chew be doin'?" Tracy asked her.

"Girl, you too young to know."

"No I'm not, Mercedes. Tell me."

"Do you have a boyfriend yet?"

"No, but I like this boy named Aaron, though."

Mercedes took off the chain and put it inside of her small leather pocketbook. "Does he like you?"

"No, because he's into playing football and stuff."

Mercedes stared at Tracy curiously. "Did you try to kiss him yet?"

Tracy was horrified. "NO, GIRL!"

Mercedes was getting "nasty."

"Some boys respond better when you kiss them first," she said, grinning at Tracy's uproar.

"But I don't wanna kiss him," Tracy whined.

"Well, I guess you can't get him then, 'cause once you give a boy something, he'll give you things, too. I got a lot of stuff, now."

"Why, you was kissing boys a lot?" Tracy asked her.

Mercedes burst out with wicked laughter. "I've been doin' *way* more than that," she said.

Mercedes is *nasty,* Tracy thought. "Well, *I'm* not gon' kiss no boy, just for him to like me."

"You won't ever get the ones you want then," Mercedes told her as she left.

Tracy thought it over. She would never go as far as *a kiss* to get a *boy*. Aaron probably wouldn't let her get close enough to kiss him, anyway. He'd probably get mad at her.

"Mercedes! Come in here and sit down!" her mother shouted at her as soon as she walked into the house. "Now I know you've been running around here with these boys lately. And I saw that one give you the chain. I want you to give it back to him."

Mercedes waited to hear all that her mother had to say. She knew Beth was permissive. Mercedes had little respect for her mother. Beth had never lent a hand to help her in disputes involving her mean-spirited father. She didn't deserve any respect in Mercedes' eyes.

"Now look, your father has given you a lot of time to go out and all, since you're fifteen now, but that doesn't mean you can run around with all these different boys."

"Aw, mom, ain't nobody runnin' around with a bunch of boys. I know him from school."

"Oh, you think you're grown now, don't you? Well, I know about them late-night phone calls you make, too. You're not slick."

"So what, mom? I'm tired of him. I'm ready to move out and go live at Aunt Mary's house and go to public school anyway. I hate going to Catholic school."

"Mercedes, you don't want to live in that neighborhood with all that shooting and stuff going on," Beth said, disturbed by her daughter's plans.

"It ain't like I'm gon' walk outside and get hit by a bullet. It ain't that bad!"

Beth pleaded. "They got drugs and stuff down South Philly, you know, and you don't need to be down there."

"Well, I ain't stayin' here much longer," Mercedes revealed. She began to take off her uniform.

Her mother continued pleading, "What's so wrong with living here? This is a beautiful neighborhood."

"I mean, I got no problem with the *neighborhood*. I just hate living with *him.*"

"He only acts like that because he doesn't know how to show his love."

"Mom, I'm tired of you telling me how you understand him and all, 'cause I don't. I'm sorry!"

"Well, if you'd listen—"

"No, mom, I'm tired of listening to you. I don't know why you married him anyway!"

Mercedes stomped upstairs to her room. Beth followed after her. Raheema listened in from her door.

"I don't know who you think you're talking to, girl. That's your father," Beth said.

Mercedes faced her mother and yelled, "Look, mom, could you leave me alone, please?"

"Stop being hard-headed, girl."

"Ain't nobody being hard-headed. Just leave me the hell alone!" Mercedes shouted.

Raheema stood at her door, watching from the hallway.

Beth reached out to smack Mercedes, but she was too slow. Mercedes grabbed her hand.

"Okay, mom, you tough now after *he* beat you up all these years, *right?*" she said harshly. Mercedes looked her mother straight in the eyes.

Beth left the room in shock. Raheema pledged right then and there that she would never be as devious as her older sister. Mercedes was no longer afraid of Keith, and she showed outright disrespect toward her mother. She might have even hit her mother back if Beth had succeeded in slapping her. It was more than Raheema could take. Mercedes' actions scared her more than her father's did.

Raheema began to think that her sister was possessed. Mercedes had transformed into a cursing, sneaky monster who seemed to fear noth-ing. She no longer did her homework like she used to, and she began to receive bad grades on her report card. She would leave for the movies on Saturday mornings and not come home until late at night. She even refused to go out with the rest of the family on occasion. And Keith never forced her to go.

Mercedes was getting away with everything. She could openly argue with her father and not be hit or punished for it. Mercedes began to say what she wanted to his face. And she had been sneaking around with boys for two years.

Raheema quietly went to her sister's room and observed her while she listened to her earphones, blocking everyone out.

Raheema walked over and tapped Mercedes on the shoulder.

"What do you want, girl?" Mercedes asked her, snappishly.

"I'm scared for you, Mercedes."

"Girl, get out of my damn room. You stupid, and he gon' ruin your life, too."

"Yeah, but I won't turn out like you, 'cause I hate you!"

"So what, Ra-Ra? I always hated you, so get out!"

Raheema left Mercedes' room in tears. She loved her sister, but she feared what she had become. Mercedes cared less about the family. She cared only about herself. She was no longer the quiet sister Ra-heema used to know, so she decided to stay away from her.

• • •

Aaron repeatedly dodged Tracy's attempts to get his attention at school. Tracy brought him candy from home, and Aaron refused to take it. She offered him some of her lunch, and Aaron took it and walked away. She even spread rumors around the school that he liked her. Aaron simply ignored it, while still playing football.

One time at recess, Tracy took Aaron's ball after convincing Tommy to give it to her. When Aaron said that she could have it and that he didn't care, she turned to walk away, only to have him swoop by and snatch it back from her. Tracy even tried to take his jacket, embarrassingly taking the wrong one.

Finally Tracy asked Aaron to go with her. He walked right by her, putting his hands over his ears, telling her "no." Tracy hung around the lunch table where he sat to eat. Aaron didn't seem to notice. But she knew that he knew. All the girls commended Tracy for trying so hard, but they would never adopt her methods. Tracy was obsessed with the boy.

She began to let older sixth-graders walk her home to make Aaron jealous, but he would only laugh and call her "stupid." The older boys respected him for keeping her hooked, but Aaron didn't care. The sixth-graders began advising him to talk to her. Aaron acted as though he didn't have any ears. And finally Tracy was willing to kiss him. Patti kissed her father when she wanted him to stay. So why couldn't Tracy kiss Aaron?

Tracy walked into school with a plan to kiss Aaron on the lips. She only needed him to listen to her to pull it off. She didn't really think it would work, but it was worth a try.

"Ay Aaron, that girl, Tracy, likes you, man. Why you be ignoring her?" a sixth-grader said before walking into school.

"Why don't you go with her?" Aaron retorted.

"I tried to. But she don't like me. She likes you, man."

Aaron frowned at him. "What she like me for?"

"I'on know, man. Some girls never make no sense."

"I know, so why should I talk to her?" Aaron asked as they entered the building.

"'Cause she's pretty, man."

"So what? I got a sister that's pretty, too."

"What that got to do with anything?"

"So I'm not interested," Aaron answered. "My sister makes me sick, like all girls."

"Well, Tracy ain't your sister, man."

"So, she a girl, and she acts like my sister."

The sixth-grader grimaced his long, brown face. "Man, stop acting stupid and just talk to her."

Aaron sighed, finally giving in to suggestion. "Yeah, aw'ight, man. I'll talk to her. But I still don't like her."

Aaron walked into his advisory class and immediately noticed Tracy staring at him. She was out to wear him down.

Tracy called him over to her as soon as they got a break from class. She didn't think he would come to her, but she called him anyway.

"Yeah, yeah, what do you want?" he asked her nonchalantly.

Tracy looked up the hallway, watching her girlfriends watching her. "I got something for you," she whispered. Everyone liked surprises, Tracy had figured, just like her and her mother. Her father was full of surprises. Maybe Aaron would like a surprise, too.

"What?"

"I'll tell you at recess. Okay?"

"Yeah, aw'ight," Aaron told her. He didn't think much of it.

Tracy went out and watched him playing football at recess as usual. She waited patiently for him to notice her without bothering him. Aaron looked over at her after scoring a touchdown and remembered that she had something for him. He told his team to hold the ball for a minute.

"Well, what do you have for me?" he asked her.

Tracy told him, "You have to go inside with me to get it."

Aaron started to walk away. "Oh well, never mind then."

Tracy snapped, "Okay, forget you if you don't want it."

"What, girl? What do you want?" Aaron shouted, walking back.

Tracy said, "Come on," as she grabbed his hand.

"Where y'all goin'? Tommy shouted at them.

Aaron followed Tracy into the building, feeling silly. His friends decided to play on without him. Luckily for Tracy, Tommy didn't follow them to mess things up.

Her girlfriends watched them excitedly as they entered the building. But Tracy hadn't told any of them what she was doing.

Aaron asked, "Now what do you want, girl?" as soon as they stepped inside of the building. They stood inside the stairway.

"This," Tracy said, kissing Aaron on the lips.

Aaron looked into her slanted hazel eyes with his big browns, and was shocked. Tracy thought he'd get mad, so she backed away from him, staring curiously.

Aaron said, smiling, "Kiss me again."

Tracy smiled, filled with sneaky energy. "Okay."

Aaron closed his eyes and puckered his lips, kissing Tracy again.

Despite their begging, Tracy didn't tell any of her friends. She just smiled and said nothing. She found more excitement in not telling them. It was her little secret. Tracy felt on top of the world.

She got Aaron to walk her home, and even Tommy saw them. Tracy felt good about that. *I told him Aaron would walk me home,* she thought to herself. *Now, boy!*

She kissed Aaron again in front of her door, and went inside the house. She jumped and danced around the living room, pleased with her accomplishment. Tracy had been as cunning as her mother had said she had been when she was younger. Tracy felt proud and smarter than boys. Aaron wasn't such a hot shot after all. All she had to do was get his attention.

DING DONG!

"I got it, mom," Tracy called, running to the door.

"Hey, girl," her father said, picking her up for a hug and a kiss. He liked the idea of ringing the doorbell instead of using his key. It was an announcement that he was home, and he knew that it would please his daughter to be surprised.

"Mom, daddy's here!" Tracy screamed excitedly.

Dave followed his daughter to the kitchen, while Patti worked on dinner. She wasn't all that happy to see him, though. Patti wanted to press the issue about him moving back in. He had stalled long enough. And they were having another child soon.

Dave said, "Come here, woman," and opened his arms wide.

Patti approached him reluctantly, thinking about arguing her point. Yet arguing with him would only give her selfish husband another excuse to keep his getaway apartment.

Dave ducked under her arms to feel her stomach.

"Oh, so you came over to check up on your future son, hunh?" she asked as he rubbed her rounded belly.

"That's right. I came to see if you're eating right and taking care of my boy."

"Well, you would know if you stayed for a while," Patti hinted.

Dave ignored it. He figured he was spending a lot of time with her as it was. He still had to work five days a week. *You see that?* he thought to himself. *I can't satisfy her. As soon as I move back in, she's gon' want me to do something else.*

"Yeah, dad, and he gon' look just like you," Tracy commented about the baby.

"Nope, he gon' look like your mother," Dave refuted, taking a seat at the kitchen table.

"Why? Ain't he gon' be a boy?" Tracy asked him.

"Yeah, but mommy does more, so he's gonna look more like her."

Tracy didn't understand his logic, so she changed the subject. "Daddy, why do boys hate girls?"

"Boys don't hate girls, they just don't like hangin' around them too long," Dave told her. As soon as the words left his lips, he regretted saying it.

Patti gave him an evil eye from the stove and remained silent. *He's gonna say some more shit like that and I'm gonna kick his ass right out of this house. I don't give a damn if he is paying the bills,* she told herself.

"Well, why do you have to give boys stuff for them to like you?" Tracy asked her father.

Dave eyed her sternly. "Give them what?"

"Candy and stuff," Tracy answered. She surely wasn't going to tell her father about a kiss.

"Oh, well, that's because some boys are greedy."

Every comment Dave said added fuel to Patti's fire.

"Tell me about it," she mumbled. "They just expect to get everything that *they* want."

"Well, some *women* can be greedy, too," Dave responded. "And a lot of times they don't know what the hell they want until it's gone."

Patti dropped what she was doing. "Don't try that shit with me, Dave. You know damn well I didn't want you to leave."

Dave stood up and began heading for the front door. "I guess this is that pregnancy thing."

"No, it's *not* a *pregnancy* thing. It's a *common sense* thing, Dave," Patti snapped, following her husband into the living room. Tracy could hear her mother's voice cracking as she spoke.

"Don't leave, dad," Tracy pleaded to her father.

Dave exhaled and took a seat on the couch. He then opened his arms wide so Tracy could climb onto his lap.

Patti decided to calm herself. Even though she was angry at him, she still wanted Dave to stay for dinner. She headed back to the kitchen without another word.

Dave stayed and ate dinner with them and decided to spend the night.

Tracy felt like she owned the place on her next school day. The school had her name on it, and she had *personally* hired all of the teachers *and* the principal. She had gone after the most desirable boy in the fifth grade and "got him."

Tracy's friends followed her around still, begging for her to tell them something. Aaron ate lunch with Tracy at her table and even stopped playing football when she called him. Everyone knew that Tracy had won him over after that. But no one knew how, unless Aaron had told them. Tracy didn't want people to think that she was nasty, so she decided to keep the kiss to herself. And she definitely wasn't kissing Aaron again. He just didn't know it yet. Tracy had decided that kisses were too much. *I don't want to get pregnant,* she thought to herself.

Aaron approached her after school, wearing a tight, dirty baseball cap. His wild hair fluffed outside of the edges. And his clothes were ragged from playing football. Even his jacket was ripped.

Tracy wore a pink jogging suit, white running shoes and a colorful coat. She felt embarrassed by Aaron's appearance. She didn't feel like having him walk her home, looking so "bummy." She also noticed a rip on the side of his pants. *Yuck.*

"Do you want me to walk you home?" he asked her.

"I don't care," she said. Tracy didn't have the courage to treat Aaron like she did Tommy. But she wished that she did.

"Okay then," Aaron told her.

Tracy hoped that they could start some kind of an argument so she could get rid of him. Arguments always seemed to get rid of someone. But it was no use. Aaron was becoming a Tommy, and Tracy no longer wanted him around.

Before dumping him, Tracy got Aaron to teach her to play catch, and Tommy was angry. She then got Aaron to tell her girlfriends that he always liked her, and Tommy was furious. Aaron and Tommy had patched their friendship up the last time she came between them, but it was different once Aaron admitted to liking her. Tommy felt betrayed.

Tommy waited for Aaron after school and attacked him, but Aaron managed to duck his punches. They squared off, standing face to face, fists to fists on the sidewalk, as the other students watched with Tracy. Aaron still proved to be faster and got the most punches in. Tommy's nose was bloody and his lip was cut before someone broke it up.

Tracy walked home alone, because Aaron decided to parade with his friends about his victory. She felt better off without him. She liked to brag about him more than she liked being with him.

"MERCEDES! I GOT SOMETHING TO TELL YOU!" Tracy shouted, running to catch her next-door neighbor, who was heading up the block ahead of her. Mercedes waited for her and decided to go into Tracy's house to hear her little story.

"My boyfriend beat this boy up for me today," Tracy bragged.

"He did? Why?" Mercedes asked, intrigued.

"Because Tommy was jealous."

Mercedes frowned at her news. "Well, you better watch out, because after boys do that, they start acting like they own you."

Tracy looked confused. "They do?"

"Yup. I had a lot of boys fight over me," Mercedes told her, "and then they always get a big head."

Mercedes left big impressions on Tracy's mind. She gave Tracy things to think about. What if Aaron did change? He had already decided to go home with his friends instead of with her. Tracy decided to watch out for him. If Aaron did or said anything that she didn't like, that would just as well confirm it. He had a big head.

Tracy didn't see him as she walked through the halls at school. She didn't look at Aaron when he did arrive. He didn't say anything when he saw her either.

The bell rang for recess, and Tracy headed to her bench with her friends. Aaron played football with his. Tracy didn't bother to call him anymore. But after school, Aaron was waiting for her.

"You want me to walk you home?"

Tracy had an attitude. "Do you want to?" she responded sourly.

Aaron said, "It's up to you, 'cause I don't really care."

Tracy tossed her head. "Well, if you don't care, then go your own way then."

"What?"

"I said, no, since you don't *care* no more."

"Well, I ain't wanna walk you home no way, girl," Aaron huffed at her.

"Fine. Leave me alone then," Tracy shot back.

"Aw, you stupid anyway."

"I'm *not* stupid, boy."

Aaron bit his bottom lip and balled his fists. "Say somethin' else, girl, and I'll punch you in your mouth!"

Tracy shut her mouth. She knew that Aaron would do it. He had hit lots of girls.

"I ain't like you anyway," he told her before walking off in the opposite direction.

"Yup, you was right, Mercedes. Aaron didn't say nothin' to me all day. And then he gon' try to walk me home," Tracy explained.

"So what did you say to him?" Mercedes asked her.

"I told him no."

"Well, don't worry about him. There's other fish in the sea."

"I'm *not*. This boy named Patrick likes me *anyway,*" Tracy said.

"Yup, Tracy, I'm gon' be moving soon," Mercedes announced to her.

"Why-e-e?" Tracy squealed with large eyes.

"'Cause I'm tired of living with them," Mercedes answered sharply. Tracy listened as Mercedes went on: "All my life my father made me kiss up to him. I couldn't even go to parties and movies and stuff." Mercedes paused and said, "Yup, girl, I wish I had a father like yours."

"But my father don't live with us no more."

"Well, at least you can do what you want then."

◊

Mercedes had everything planned. She knew she would be leaving. She had already packed up most of her things. Her mother and sister didn't bother her anymore, since she was so anti-social. Mercedes told them months ago that she was leaving. And she meant it.

Beth tried to convince her daughter to stay, but it was a waste of time. Mercedes wanted to be on her own. And as long as she found a job and helped to pay the rent at her aunt's apartment, Mary was willing to let her stay. "I never liked your evil-ass father either," her Aunt Mary had told her.

Mercedes had plenty of boyfriends, but she never stayed with anyone for more than four months. One guy she dated for two weeks. She dumped him after she found that he was boring. Mercedes had no time for boring guys. She was only attracted to the free-spirited type, the kind of guys who did whatever they wanted to do.

Going to Catholic school had restricted Mercedes from wearing the glamorous clothing that public school girls wore. She never was into Catholicism anyway. Most of the black students that she knew only went to Catholic school because their parents liked the discipline. It had nothing to do with religion. Mercedes figured that with a job and enrollment in public school, she would be on her way to becoming a well-dressed star while obeying her *own* rules.

"Hey, dad, I'm goin' to that Prince concert Saturday," she told her father, anticipating rejection.

Keith sat in his La-Z-Boy chair, watching television. "You don't know how to ask no better than that?"

Mercedes stood near the television, opposite him. "Well, can I go to the concert Saturday night?"

"No. You've been to enough places this month."

"Oh, so it's a limit on what I can do, hunh?"

"Girl, I'm about tired of your damn mouth."

Beth walked in from the kitchen and listened.

"Well, I'm tired of you always telling me what I can't do."

Beth said, "He's only trying to protect you, honey."

Raheema listened from the top of the stairs.

"I know one thing. She got about one more time to talk back to me," Keith said to Beth.

"Yeah, right, you always sayin' that," Mercedes retorted.

Keith jumped up from the chair to grab her.

Mercedes backed away from him. "This is it, dad. I'm leaving. And if you try to stop me, *I'll kill you!*" she warned venomously.

Keith stopped and looked at her as if she had lost her mind. "Girl, you ain't gon' kill a damn thing," he said, stalking her.

Mercedes screamed as she backed around the dining-room table, "Mom, I'm telling you! Get him away from me!"

"All right then, girl. If you wanna leave so bad, then get the HELL OUT!" Keith shouted at her.

Mercedes ran through the living room, rushed up the steps and flew past her little sister.

Raheema watched in shocked silence.

Mercedes ran into her room and grabbed her suitcases.

Keith asked, "What the hell is wrong with that girl?"

"She's just hard-headed, that's all," Beth answered.

"She been runnin' 'round wit' them damn boys, puttin' that shit in her head," Keith responded. "Well, she can take her ass outta here. See if I give a damn."

"She don't mean what she says, baby," Beth said, rubbing Keith's back.

"Aw, Beth, you probably been lettin' her get away with shit while I been working."

Beth went back to the kitchen, realizing that arguing with Keith was useless. *Like father, like daughter,* she thought to herself.

Keith hollered at Raheema, "Get your ass in your room and do your homework! I break my ass every day for that damn girl and she gon' act like a fool," he ranted, sitting back down in his chair and facing the television. "Matter of fact, she ain't going no-damn-where," he decided.

Keith headed up the stairs to Mercedes' room. Raheema heard him coming and jumped back to her homework.

Keith beat on Mercedes' locked door.

"Leave me alone! I HATE YOU!" she yelled.

"Open this damn door. I know what you need. You *need* a good ASS-KICKIN'! That's what you need."

Mercedes broke down into wild tears. "Just let me live my life! LEAVE ME ALONE! I hate you, I hate you, I hate you!"

Keith stared at her locked door, perturbed, and walked away. He went downstairs and back to the kitchen with Beth. "What did I do to that girl to deserve all this?" he asked his wife, who busied herself cooking dinner.

Beth said, "I guess she needs some time to herself. She just need to be free."

"Free? What 'chew mean, *free?* She ain't no damn slave around here!"

Beth didn't answer him. *It sure seems like it sometimes,* she told herself.

Keith said, "I've been letting that girl get away with murder lately. I should have kept the strap on her hot ass."

"Well, maybe that's why she acts like that now," Beth responded nervously.

Keith stared at her for a second. "Okay, now *I'm* the bad guy, hunh?" He walked back upstairs to his bedroom and slammed the door.

Mercedes ran out with her luggage. Raheema listened to her make several trips, deciding to come out of her room. Mercedes' things were piled at the front door in no time.

Raheema came down to talk to her. "Please, Mercedes, don't leave me here," she squealed with tears in her eyes.

Mercedes hugged her and backed away. "I'm sorry, girl, but I gotta get out of here . . . You wanna come with me?" Mercedes asked her sister.

Raheema shook her head. "No. You're just gonna get in trouble."

Mercedes looked down at her little sister and felt sorry for her. She felt sorry for herself. She felt sorry for her mother. They could have had a beautiful home. But Keith had to ruin it for all of them. "It's not gonna get any better around here, girl. I wish you luck," Mercedes told Raheema. She then paced to the kitchen to see her mother.

Beth said, "I've called a cab and your aunt, to tell her that you're on your way."

Beth hugged her older daughter with no hard feelings. She was happy Mercedes had the courage to step away.

Mercedes hugged her mother and began to cry. "I'm sorry, mom," she choked, "but I gotta get out of here."

Beth had nothing to say. All she could think of was, "Be careful."

Mercedes nodded and began to lug her things outside. A yellow cab arrived at the sidewalk as Beth and Raheema watched from the door. Mercedes was off to live a life on her own.

Raheema wiped her tears and hugged her mother. She didn't want her sister to leave. She wished they could all remain a big happy family. Mercedes only cared about herself. What did she know about anything? She was only fifteen. But Mercedes thought she knew it all.

chasing boyfriends

Having a little brother was supposed to bring diversity to her life, but unfortunately a newborn baby in the house brought Tracy nothing but agony.

Jason cried all night during his first year with them, and Tracy was forced to assist her mother in changing him, feeding him, watching him and keeping him busy, which had severely reduced her free time.

Twelve and going on thirteen, Tracy was about to enter her last year of junior high school. She had been watching Jason on weekends during the school year because her father's work shift had changed. He had been working nights and on weekends with plenty of overtime.

Patti pissed a bitch about her husband's new work schedule, but Dave still had to pay the bills. "If his ass would move back in, he could save four hundred dollars from that damn apartment of his," she hissed to her daughter. Dave seemed to love working, but Patti thought of it as another convenient excuse for him to remain absent from the family.

It was aggravating for Tracy to have to keep an eye on Jason while her friends went out to the mall and to the movies. She started to argue with her mother as if *they* were married. And once summertime rolled around, Tracy was sick of watching Jason. *He shouldn't be my responsibility anyway! I'm not his mother!* she snapped to herself.

"Mom, he can just sit here and watch TV by himself."

"I told you to watch him while I clean up this house."

"But I gotta get ready to go with my girlfriends."

"I don't care, girl!"

"God! I'm tired of this!" Tracy huffed, as she sat and watched Saturday morning cartoons with her brother.

Patti had gotten Dave to lug the television set from the basement into the living room, so she could have something to keep Jason busy. She was not in the basement much, and neither was Tracy, so there was no sense in leaving the television set there.

Jason, named after Patti's late father, was two and a half years old and talking. He had Dave's dark brown skin and his mother's dark, almond-shaped eyes, a precious sight to see. But once he had gotten restless from watching cartoons, he jumped off of the living-room couch and ran back into the kitchen.

"TRA-CY! Get in here and get him!"

Tracy, Raheema and three other friends caught the H bus on Greene Street and went to the Cheltenham Mall. They were all anticipating going to high school in a year, and most of them were interested in boys.

Raheema, the only Catholic school student, didn't know as many people as Tracy and the other girls. Catholic schools were smaller than most public schools.

Once they had arrived at the mall, the five girls ran in and out of the arcade looking for cute boys to talk to them. Many of the boys knew Tracy from school, so she was no big deal to them, but Raheema was a new pretty face. She got more attention than the other girls. All of the boys wanted to talk to her.

After a while, Tracy started to intervene, filled with jealousy. Yet she grew tired rather quickly of getting in Raheema's way. *Dag, Raheema's lucky!* she thought to herself as she began to watch, spiteful of all the attention her next-door neighbor was receiving.

"Ay, what's your name?" a dimple-faced boy asked Raheema. He was standing next to a pinball machine inside of the arcade.

"Ra-Ra," she said, smiling and backing away.

The dimple-faced boy seized her hand to keep her near. "Where you live at?"

Raheema yanked her hand away. "Diamond Lane."

"Do you have a boyfriend?"

"No. I don't want a boyfriend," she told him.

"Why not?"

"Because I don't."

"Well, can I talk to you as a friend?" he asked her nicely.

The other girls watched enviously.

Raheema then turned to them to rescue her from the jam she felt she was in. She asked no one in particular, "Aren't we ready to go?"

"Answer his question," Tracy said. She was purposefully trying to keep Raheema crammed.

"Well, if *she* won't talk to you, *I* will," Tracy's girlfriend, Jantel, interjected while walking toward him. Jantel was a deep brown and skinny. She was very forward and athletic. She was one of the fastest girls on the track team at school. In fact, Jantel was faster than many boys her age.

The dimple-faced boy stood there in a daze, waiting for Raheema to respond to him.

Raheema shied away from him and slid behind the rest of the girls.

Tracy whispered, "He's cute, Ra-Ra. Why don't you want to talk to him?"

Raheema said aloud, "Because I don't want to."

"Dag, you stupid," Tracy told her.

Raheema did the same to every boy who approached her at the mall that day. The other girls had no idea why Ra-Ra acted like she did. They all wished that they could take her place somehow.

"Uuw, look y'all, it's try-outs for cheerleading," Jantel said, noticing several fliers stapled to the telephone poles. As usual, Jantel led the pack on their way home.

The other girls ran over to join her as she read it aloud. Cheerleading was a sure method of meeting some top-quality boys. And football clubs in the Police Athletic League traveled around the city to play other teams. It was a great idea. They would become an important part of a new social organization.

Tracy hurried home to tell her mother about the cheerleading. Patti told her that she could join. She had not seen her daughter that excited in a while. The first day for try-outs was coming up in a week.

It was the beginning of August. Tracy turned thirteen in September. Raheema was a teen already, but she didn't even bother to ask her parents about joining a cheerleading team. She thought it was out of the question. Keith would never let her join something so sexually suggestive, with little girls shaking their little hips and wearing little skirts while chanting sing-songs.

Tracy and her friends went to try-outs on that first Saturday in August. Thirty other girls were out for the same thing, but only fifteen of them could make the squad.

Tracy worked hard on her cheers at try-outs and stayed to watch the football players while they practiced. She was sure she was going to make the team. And she was right. Jantel had survived the cut with her.

The football players were immediately attracted to Tracy, but she had her eyes on the star running back. Steve had the admiration of all the boys on the team, and the coaches seemed to brag about him every day. Steve was going to be her next boyfriend. Tracy was sure of it.

She began to picture being with him even before the season started. After every touchdown he scored, she would wait on the sidelines and he would wink his eye at her. Then he would buy her a hot dog and soda and let her wear his jersey after the game.

Tracy expected to be the most popular girl on the team. She wanted to be the captain of the cheerleading squad, too. During the halftime shows, all of the parents and spectators would have their eyes glued to her.

Once the team started having scrimmages, Tracy asked enough about Steve to find out his age, address and the school he went to. She was not chosen to be the cheering captain, but that wasn't that important. Steve being her boyfriend was Tracy's priority.

Tracy then found out that Treasure, the captain of the cheering team, had already asked Steve for "a chance" to "go with her," or in other words, to be her boyfriend. Steve liked her too, so he told her that he would. Yet Tracy didn't believe that Steve *really* liked Treasure. *He doesn't like her more than he likes me. She just asked him first,* Tracy assured herself.

Steve scored three touchdowns in their first game, and all of the fans were yelling out his name. Tracy was really pressed for him then. Part of her fantasy was coming true. Steve was the star of the team.

Tracy waited for him after the game and asked Steve how much he liked Treasure. Steve was pleased that Tracy was interested in him, but he was still loyal to his new girlfriend. He told Tracy that he liked Treasure a lot. Treasure even wore his jersey.

Tracy was on regular speaking terms with Steve after the second game. He began to notice Tracy a lot, but he still "went with" Treasure, or in other words, was still her boyfriend.

Tracy began to hint to Steve that she liked his number. Steve would always smile and fall silent instead of responding to her. He realized what Tracy was hinting at. She liked him, and she wanted to wear his jersey instead of Treasure. Tracy was slowly but surely wearing Steve down.

After their third game, which was played at their home field, Tracy noticed him walking home by himself. Steve's friends had remained behind to watch the older boys play.

Tracy debated whether she would talk to him or not. It was still early that Saturday afternoon, and his girlfriend, Treasure, was nowhere to be found. Once Tracy decided that she would, she left Jantel and ran off to catch up to him.

"Hi, 'Stevie.' Are you going home already?" she asked him from behind.

Steve was as brown as Tracy's brother Jason, and his low haircut made his perfectly rounded head look like a well-roasted peanut. He held his Wilson helmet in his hand.

"Yeah," he told Tracy with a smile. Tracy's assertiveness made him seem bashful.

"Why?" she asked him.

"Because, I have a homework assignment to do. I have a science project that I have to turn in on Monday."

"Oh," Tracy perked, remembering that Steve attended an advanced private school. Yet she failed to believe that he was that dedicated to doing homework on a Saturday. "Walk me home, Steve. Please," she responded to him.

Steve resisted her. "Well, I wanna finish my project today, so I can watch football tomorrow. The Eagles are playing Dallas," he told her.

Tracy grabbed onto his arm. "Aw, come on, Stevie. Please. I don't live that far."

Steve let out another bashful smile. "Okay."

Dag, that was easy, Tracy thought to herself. She had expected to do more begging.

"So you still go with Treasure?" she asked him as they began to walk.

"I don't know," Steve answered. Treasure had not been paying him much attention after the second game. She didn't even wear his jersey anymore.

"Well, do you still like her?"

"Yeah, I guess so." He sounded like he had said it out of obligation.

Tracy pressed him, smiling in her blue and gold uniform. "Do you like me?"

Steve grinned and said, "Yeah."

I got him! Tracy told herself. She giggled, filled with self-assurance. He had given her the confidence she needed, and Tracy was set to go for the kill.

"Let me see your helmet," she said, reaching out for it.

Steve gave it right to her. Tracy took it and smiled. She then accidentally dropped it on the ground while trying to hold it erect. Steve picked it up and made sure it wasn't broken.

Tracy felt embarrassed by her clumsiness. "I'm sorry," she told him.

"Don't worry about that. This is a good helmet," Steve responded. He beat on it with his right hand and said, "See?"

Tracy looked at him with sparkling hazel eyes as the sunlight hit them dead on. Steve shied away to avoid their magnetism.

Tracy could tell that he was nervous. "So are you gonna quit Treasure and go with me, Stevie?" she asked him bluntly. She could tell that Steve was a pushover.

He hunched his shoulders, still not looking Tracy in those scary eyes of hers. "I don't care."

"Well, can I hold your jersey? I'll wash it for you and everything," Tracy told him excitedly.

Steve *wanted* to say "no," but he couldn't overcome Tracy's persistence. "Yeah, you can hold it," he said, reluctantly, "but don't mess it up. And don't lose it, either."

He took his blue jersey, with gold numbers trimmed in white, right off of his back.

"Thank you, Stevie. You so nice," Tracy cheered, pinching his brown cheeks.

Steve cracked another smile.

Tracy then jumped onto his back, turning him into a horse. "Give me a piggy-back ride."

"Okay," he agreed, straining to carry her weight. "Let me put my helmet back on first."

"Okay. I live right up the street," she lied to him. She actually lived *two* blocks up.

Tracy smacked Steve on his helmet as he walked with her on his shoulders about halfway to the corner before putting her back down.

"Why you stop?"

"Because my back is hurting."

"Aw, boy, I thought you was a strong running back," Tracy huffed at him, disappointed.

"You can't tackle me," Steve said, teasing her.

Tracy retorted, "I don't wanna tackle you." She expected for Steve to get angry and stand his ground after a while, but he was already under her spell.

"Tracy, I have to go home now. Okay?" he told her, once they had reached her house.

Tracy rolled her eyes at him. "NO! I didn't say you could go home yet."

Steve pleaded, "I have to though. I have something to do."

"Well, go ahead then. See if I care, boy," Tracy warned him, childishly.

Tracy was dying for Steve to reject her so she could at least have a challenge. But he simply couldn't. Tracy was too much for him.

"All right, I'll stay," he whined.

Tracy made Steve sit out on her steps while they played with her little brother until the sun started to go down. After realizing that her daughter was holding the boy hostage, Patti finally sent Steve home. Tracy then walked him to the corner and punched him in the arm. Steve told her he could take it and walked away giggling.

Tracy skipped back up the block, pleased with how easy it was to twist Steve around her pinky-finger. "I can make him do whatever I want," she said to herself with a devilish grin.

A black Mustang convertible pulled up to the curb as Tracy walked back to her steps. Out jumped Mercedes. Tracy had not seen Mercedes since she had left home, more than two years ago.

"Look, I'm just going in to see my mother for a few minutes," she said to the young man sitting behind the wheel in sunglasses.

"Aw'ight, I'll be back," he said. He pumped up the volume on his car's radio and speeded up the street.

Mercedes walked to the steps and spotted Tracy smiling at her. "Hey, girlfriend, how you been doin'?" she asked. She hugged Tracy and backed away to see how tall she was getting. "Damn, you're getting big, girl. You gon' be able to hang out with the old-heads soon."

Tracy blushed as she looked Mercedes over. Mercedes wore black designer shoes with a matching pocketbook and a blue leather skirt with a multi-colored sweater. Her neck was dripping with gold, and she wore huge gold earrings that shone in the dark. Her hair was fabulous and asymmetric. Mercedes looked gorgeous, like a teenage movie star who had returned for a visit home.

"Where you get those earrings?" Tracy asked her.

"My boyfriend bought them for me. But how you been, Tracy?"

Tracy was stunned. She practically forgot everything that she wanted to tell Mercedes. She was too wrapped up in Mercedes' outfit, the car, the boyfriend and the glamour. "That was a decent car he had," she commented, impressed.

Mercedes responded with a smile, "I know. Ain't that car smooth, girl? Well, look, my old man ain't in the house, is he?"

"No. Mr. Keith works overtime now, just like my father."

"Good, 'cause I came to see my mother right quick."

Tracy was astounded as she continued to observe. Mercedes entered her house with her old key. Her mother was watching television when she walked in.

"Hey, mom, how's life been treating you?" Mercedes perked.

Beth was shocked. "Girl, it's about time you came up here to see your mother! It's so dag-gone far, going all the way down South Philly."

They hugged each other and took a seat. Mercedes immediately pulled out a pack of Newports from the Gucci purse inside of her pocketbook. She lit one up and started to smoke without even asking her mother if she would mind.

Raheema came down from her room, saw Mercedes and frowned. She didn't see what Tracy saw. Raheema's idea of success was totally different. Mercedes was still just a teenager to Raheema, a teenager trying to be a grown-up.

Mercedes ignored her sister's glare.

"When you start smoking?" Beth asked her.

Mercedes lied, "Like last year, sometime."

"That stuff leads to cancer," her mother told her as she fanned the smoke from in front of her.

Mercedes took another puff. "Look, mom, I ain't come over here to be lectured."

"Well, leave then. Nobody wants you back here anyway!" Raheema shouted at her. She headed back up the steps and went to her room. "She got some nerve!" she mumbled to herself as she slammed her bedroom door. "She just thinks she can come back here and do what she wants. I hate her! She ain't nobody."

Mercedes felt slightly annoyed by this. She decided that she would leave sooner than she had expected. *Raheema's still acting like a big-ass kid!* she snapped to herself. *She needs to grow the hell up! This is my God-damned life, and I'll live the way I wanna fuckin' live!*

"Where you goin'?" Beth asked, as her oldest daughter stood up in haste.

"I'm gettin' up out of here, mom. I see I'm not welcome anymore."

Beth said, "Let me tell you a few things before you leave. Now you may think you got them streets and all, but that's a life for losers. So please screw your head back on and do the right thing."

"And what's the right thing, mom, to move back in here with y'all?" Mercedes asked, sourly.

Her mother was speechless. *That's what you need to do,* Beth thought to herself. But it was no use in trying to advise Mercedes. It would have been a waste of breath.

Mercedes walked out the door. The young man wearing sunglasses was parked and drinking a soda. "Come on, let's get out of here," she told him.

Mercedes threw her head back against the black leather interior. Her friend then revved up his sporty black Mustang. They left listening to Kurtis Blow as her mother shut the door.

Two teenaged girls went to sleep that night with different thoughts on Mercedes. To Raheema, her older sister was still a monster, but to Tracy, Mercedes had become a star. Raheema vowed that she would never be anything like her, while Tracy planned to try her best to emulate Mercedes' glamorous style.

"Did you quit her yet?" Tracy asked Steve before practice.

"Yeah, I told her last night."

"Well, how come you didn't call me?"

"Because, you didn't give me your phone number yet."

"Oh, well, I'll give it to you one day," Tracy said, walking away from him.

"Did you wash my jersey?" Steve asked her, following close behind.

"Yup. I'm gonna wear it to school tomorrow," she told him.

Tracy walked over to where a few of the cheerleaders had gathered and heard Steve's ex-girlfriend, Treasure, talking about her.

"Tracy thinks she's *it,* and I didn't want Steve *anyway.*"

"If you got somethin' to say, then say it to my face, girl," Tracy challenged her.

"I didn't say nothin' to you," Treasure responded, backing down.

"Yes you did. I heard you. I'm not *deaf.* How you gon' sit up here and lie to me?"

The girls gathered around, expecting a fight.

Treasure said, "Well, you can have Steve if you want him, because I don't."

Steve hunched his shoulders. *What did I do?* he thought to himself in a panic.

"Yeah, you just mad because I took him," Tracy commented.

Treasured stepped away, still mouthing, "Like I said, you can have him. He ain't nobody."

The heat cooled off when the cheering coach started them off practicing their drills. Tracy thought about what Treasure had said during practice, and felt cheated, like she had bought a loaf of stale bread. She debated Treasure's comments. Was Treasure simply jealous, or was Steve just a flunky?

Tracy began to mess up her cheers as the other girls snickered at her. They didn't seem to care much that she "went with" the most popular player on the team. Then again, Steve was not popular on the streets like other boys were; he was only a running back. No one paid any attention to him after the game was over. Everyone would shake Steve's hand and talk about him during the game, but after that, Steve was pretty much a loner.

With the confusion over Steve on her mind, practice became much longer and harder for Tracy. After a team meeting, the boys were excused from practice earlier than the cheerleading team, so they all walked over to watch the girls. For the first time that season, Tracy could see who the best-looking players were while their helmets were off.

Steve was not all that cute compared to some other boys. It was up in the air as to whether or not Tracy should drop him. *A lot of players look better than him,* she told herself. Nevertheless, Tracy decided to hold on to him for a while. Steve still scored the most touchdowns.

"Ay, Carmen, that's not the right way to do it!" a boy wearing a blocked haircut yelled.

"Shet up, Amir!" Carmen hollered back, smiling at him.

"I know, he always got something smart to say," Jantel commented.

"He need to leave people alone," Carmen added.

The block-haired boy sucked his teeth and spun around to show them his backside. "Y'all can all kiss my—"

"You get out of here before I tell the coach," the tall cheerleading instructor interjected.

Amir curved his mouth after spotting her.

Tracy was excited for a second, wondering who he was. Amir looked as if he could be her twin. His skin tone matched hers perfectly, and only the coolest boys wore blocked haircuts.

Amir was the middle linebacker on defense, and he made most of the tackles. He had an obvious muscular build, Tracy could tell by his broad shoulders. *He could tackle Steve,* she thought. She couldn't wait until after practice to ask more about him.

"Ay Jantel, give me the juicy fruit on Amir. You know, who does he go with, how old is he, where does he live? Girl, tell me everything," Tracy piped.

Jantel broke into laughter. "Unt unh, girl, you don't wanna talk to him."

"Why not?"

"Because, he's fresh. He be squeezing on girls' butts and feeling all on them and stuff. That boy is freaky. I wouldn't talk to him. But he talks to Carmen anyway."

"Does Carmen know that he's nasty?" Tracy asked.

"Yeah, but she don't care."

"She *don't?*"

"Nope," Jantel responded. Then she whispered to Tracy. "I think she be '*doin' it*' to him. I heard she fresh, too."

"Oh my God. For real?" Tracy asked with a grin.

Jantel nodded. "Yeah. That's what I heard."

Tracy went home thinking about Amir. She didn't want to be nasty with him, but she thought about him anyway. Steve had not been Tracy's boyfriend for a week, and already she was planning on dumping him. Steve wasn't any fun. Tracy needed to chase just as much as boys did. It was a game of choosing and chasing and dumping.

Tracy walked into her house and noticed her little brother smiling at her. Jason stared at her with his dark almond eyes as though Tracy was a ghost. Then he began to laugh. Tracy walked over to him, wondering what was going on.

Dave jumped out of the closet on her. "I GOTCHA!"

Tracy screamed as her father grabbed her from behind, "OOOWWW!"

He let her go and started to laugh himself. "I didn't know I could scare a big old girl like you all that bad."

"Yeah, dad, you surprised me," Tracy told him while she caught her breath.

Jason dashed and jumped on his father's legs.

"Dad-dy," he yelped.

"Yeah, what's up, little man?"

"He talks a lot, now," Tracy said.

"I know. I talked to him while you were at practice. How's the team turning out?"

"We 3–0, dad."

"Yeah, that's pretty good. Your mother told me you had one of them sitting on the step for three hours," he said to her.

Tracy started to giggle, embarrassingly. "Aw, dad, why mom telling you my business?"

"Because you don't have no business yet. And if you *think* you got some business, then I plan to *stay* in your business," Dave told his daughter with a grin.

Tracy smiled back at him and decided to tell him her business. "Well, that was this running back named Steve. He makes most of the touchdowns."

Her father nodded and started to reminisce. "Yeah, I remember when I played little league. I was the middle linebacker, crushin' kids."

"You played on defense, hunh, dad?" Tracy asked him, curious. Amir was middle linebacker, too.

"That's right. I liked to hit. Them cats on offense were the soft guys."

"Did you have a girlfriend?"

Dave smiled with boyish charm. "Well, I don't think I wanna tell you about that."

Tracy laughed, assuming that her father had had plenty. "Did the running backs have a lot of girls?" she asked him.

Dave answered, "Yeah. They had the most. All the girls were into the touchdown thing. They weren't really into the hitting. They all liked the quarterback, too."

"So what type of girls did you get?" Tracy pressed him.

Dave smiled again, knowing that he was planting some bad seeds in his daughter's head. "I ended up with the girls who ran around chasin' boys. I always got them rough tomboy girls. We had a bunch of fun though," he answered her. "Your mother was a tomboy."

Dave left back out that night, as usual, after filling Tracy's head with his memories. Tracy was no tomboy, but she was more aggressive than most girls her age. She never planned on sitting around being prissy, and waiting for boys to talk to her. Tracy was a boy-chaser indeed.

Tracy observed Amir for the rest of that week. It became clear to her that he was known around the neighborhood as a bad kid. He had been run off of many neighborhood streets by angry parents. Amir was always into something.

Tracy watched Amir making tackles more than she watched Steve run hand-offs during their fourth game. It became exciting to hear those hard, cracking hits. Every time Amir would get someone good, the crowd would moan, "WHEW! Damn, that boy can hit!"

Amir knocked two opposing players out of the game. He had done it before, yet Tracy had paid the defense little attention before her father's comments.

The fans talked about Amir's brutal hits more than the touchdowns that fourth game. What a coincidence it was for Steve to be over-shadowed right when Tracy was thinking about dropping him for Amir.

After the game, Tracy and Steve went to the movies along with Jantel and a few of Tracy's other girlfriends. She wanted to leave Steve at home, but when Carmen hugged Amir after the game, Tracy decided that it was better to have something than nothing.

The movie line at the Cheltenham Twin Theater was long, filled with teens and a few adults. They all had to wait in line a half hour to see a new Chuck Norris film. Several boys from other teams were there. They all walked up and shook Steve's hand as they talked about the upcoming games. That cheered Tracy up a bit, but it was not enough to keep her satisfied with him.

Steve bought her popcorn and found good seats. They sat quietly as Tracy's girlfriends ran their mouths about who was who and who was cute and who was not while watching boys walking up, down and through the aisles. Tracy was bored. All she could think about was Amir and Carmen. She then asked for some candy. Steve gave her a dollar out of his allowance money for her to go and get what she wanted from the refreshment stand. Tracy then faked going to the bathroom several times before the movie started to look at other young couples, noticing how happy they seemed.

Life seemed dull with Steve. He never gave Tracy any tingles, except for when he scored touchdowns. She was beginning to see that she didn't really like him as a person. She only wanted the star of the football team.

A pack of wild, yelling boys stomped into the theater after the previews had started. Tracy noticed a few of them from school. The boys jumped from seat to seat, joking around with each other. Tracy and her girlfriends began to pay them more attention than they did the big screen. They continued to wrestle each other right up until a few angry parents cussed them out.

"AY, AMIR, get me some popcorn while you up there!" one of the boys yelled.

Tracy couldn't believe her ears. She watched the shadowy figure walk up the aisle. He was the right size and height, wearing a baseball cap. *Oh my God, he's here!* Tracy thought, excitedly.

"I'm going to get a hot dog," she told Steve.

"Yeah, I bet," Jantel commented with a laugh.

Crowds of people packed the refreshment lines all hurrying to be served before the films started. Tracy eyed Amir's broad back, with three people separating them. She slowly walked nearby and showed herself off like a young model, hoping that Amir would notice her tight yellow sweater and Sergio blue-jeans.

"Dag, this line is all long," she said to no one in particular. She was begging for Amir to respond to her.

Amir smiled at her. "You gon' have to go to the end of the line, like everybody else," he said. Then he began to laugh.

"Shet up, boy," Tracy snapped at him, holding his name at the tip of her tongue.

Amir let her get up in front of him as the line moved. When it stopped, he leaned against her butt. Tracy felt him and wondered if he did it on purpose.

The line moved again. Tracy was reluctant to move with it, not wanting to move away from him. Amir then pushed her ahead.

"What's your name?" he finally asked her.

"Tracy," she said without turning to face him.

"Where you live?"

"Right around the corner from you," she lied. Tracy thought that he would be shocked by this.

"How you know where I live?" he asked her instead.

"Because I've seen you around," she responded, still moving forward.

"Well, how come you never said nothin' to me?"

"I don't know."

"So you gon' be out tonight?" he asked her.

"If it ain't too cold," Tracy answered. "I'm on your cheerleading team," she finally revealed to him. It was eating her up inside that he didn't know who she was.

"Wow, tell me something I didn't know," he said to her with a grin.

Tracy laughed softly, relieved. Amir had noticed her. "How you know?" she quizzed him.

"You hang out with Jantel and that girl Raheema."

Tracy sucked her teeth at hearing her next-door neighbor's name. "How you know *her?*" she asked with a grimace.

"Who?" Amir said, making Tracy have to say it.

She sighed and said, "Raheema."

"Oh. My friend was trying to talk to her. I saw y'all hangin' out in the mall before."

"Oh . . . Do you think she's pretty?" Tracy just had to ask.

"Yeah, she's all right," Amir told her.

They both seemed to forget about the movie. They stood inside the lobby and talked even after they had been served.

Amir asked, "Why, are you jealous of her?"

"NO! I ain't jealous of *her!*" Tracy responded radically.

"Yes, you are," Amir rebutted. "But I like you more than her." He ran his hands over Tracy's neck and shoulder and then through her hair. It gave her a chill. Tracy wanted more, but then Amir left her abruptly. Chuck Norris was in action.

Tracy followed him back inside the theater and returned to her seat with a bag of candy.

"That sure was a long trip to get a *hot dog,* Tracy," Jantel joked. Her friends broke into laughter.

"Yeah, what took you so long?" Steve asked Tracy.

"The line was long," she said with an attitude.

"Oh," Steve said. He quickly dismissed it. Tracy was angry at how gullible he was for believing her. It was a waste of time to go to the movies with *him. He is so boring!* she thought to herself.

Tracy was glad to get back home from the movies with Steve. When she had arrived home, she found Raheema sitting out on her front steps.

"What are you doing here?" she asked, hoping that Raheema was leaving soon. Raheema had definitely become a rival to Tracy.

"I have to spend the night over your house because my parents are going out all night," she answered, blandly. Raheema was not pleased with the idea of having to be baby-sat any more than Tracy wanted her over there.

Tracy saw it as an opportunity to settle their differences. She wanted to get to the bottom of things with her neighbor. Raheema was rejecting some top-quality boys for no good reason.

Tracy asked, "Do you know some boys named Amir and Todd?"

"Yeah, that boy named Todd wanted to talk to me," Raheema told her, not at all excited about it. "He used to try and wait for me when-ever I came home from school. I don't know why. I kept telling him that I didn't want any boyfriends."

"What does he look like?"

Raheema gave Tracy a good looking over. "He's a little lighter than you and shorter than you," she said.

Tracy was taller than Raheema by *at least* three inches.

"You didn't like him?" she asked.

"He's all right."

"So didn't you want to talk to him?"

"I did talk to him. I told him that I didn't want a boyfriend."

Tracy sucked her teeth. "Girl, what is wrong with you? How come you get all of the boys?"

Raheema smiled. Tracy was really pissed off about the attraction that boys seemed to have toward her.

"I don't know," Raheema responded to her. "I don't even pay them no mind."

They walked inside the house.

"You don't like boys at all, do you?" Tracy asked.

"I like your little brother. Jason doesn't want anything from me like the other ones do."

Tracy sat down on the couch. "What are you talkin' about?"

"Boys only want one thing," Raheema said, still standing.

"And what's that?"

"You know what I'm talking about," she answered, feeling embar-rassed that she was asked to say it.

"Well, you probably never gon' have a boyfriend then."

"Tracy, like I said, I don't *want* any boyfriends. I don't want to be *used.*"

"Why you thinking that? I'm not *used.* I don't give them *nothin',"* Tracy bragged. They quieted down a bit once they heard Patti walking around upstairs and approaching the steps.

"Well, how are you two doing?" Patti asked them.

"Okay," they mumbled in unison.

Patti looked at them suspiciously and mumbled, "Mmm hmm, you two are down here gossiping. Well, when you want some *real* answers about the dating thing, you just let me know. I can tell you two a lot of things about what *not* to do. But other than that, you're on your own, because these damn men are definitely trifling," she told them before heading inside of the kitchen to get herself some ice cream. "Damn selfish fool gon' tell me that things are fine the way they are," she continued to mumble to herself from the kitchen.

Raheema and Tracy began to smile at each other. But Tracy was a little embarrassed. She knew who her mother was talking about, and she was sure that Raheema was smart enough to figure things out.

They continued to sit, silently, until Tracy's mother had passed them again. Patti then reached the top of the steps and told them, "You can go on back to your boy-talk now."

Tracy and Raheema smiled at each other again.

"Are you ever gonna get married?" Tracy asked Raheema.

Raheema looked at her incredulously. "What? How you go from boyfriends to getting married?"

"Just answer the question," Tracy snapped.

Raheema took a deep breath and shrugged her shoulders. "I don't know."

Tracy looked over Raheema's light skin and long, dark brown hair. She had given up on trying to figure her out.

"What did you do today?" she asked, changing the subject.

"I did my homework and watched TV."

Tracy frowned. "That's all you did today?"

"Yeah. Why?"

"Ain't you bored with your life or something? God!"

Raheema hunched her shoulders. "No, not really. I mean, sometimes I get bored, but everybody gets bored once in a while."

"Yeah, but at least we do more than you," Tracy told her, standing up.

Tracy went up the steps pondering how dull Raheema's life seemed. They ended up playing board games while discussing their futures until three-thirty in the morning. They both slept hard that night with the future on their minds.

Raheema wanted to become a successful doctor or a lawyer, and live in a big white house. She still didn't know if she would marry or not, but if she did, she would not hesitate to divorce any man who would use or abuse her. She would wait her entire life for a loving, respectable husband if she had to do so.

Tracy wanted a house filled with kids and a fun-loving husband who would fulfill all of her dreams. Her husband had to be exciting, generous and full of surprises. Tracy didn't care what her occupation would be. As long as she had a handsome husband who met all of her criteria with money to boot, she would be happy. "As long as we're not poor," she had told Raheema.

They awoke late Sunday morning and watched the Eagles play the Giants. Raheema didn't show any interest in football. She ate sandwiches and talked about her teachers.

Ever since her sister, Mercedes, had left the house, Raheema had received nothing but A's in all of her classes. Mercedes' leaving seemed to be an inspiration point for Raheema to do the best that she could in school. Keith praised her and put her older sister down in the same sentence. "Raheema's studying the way a smart girl is supposed to study, not like that crazy sister of hers. I can't even remember her name," he would comment with a laugh. But he really did miss his first daughter. He couldn't get Mercedes off of his mind. Whenever his friends came over, he would tell them the same story of how Mercedes was his "darling girl" who had turned rotten on him, and how Raheema had turned out to be the good girl. "The Jekyll & Hyde Sisters," he called them.

Tracy, on the other hand, had gotten A's and B's and had never missed a day in school, except for when she was suspended for fighting. Neither Patti nor Dave worried about Tracy's schoolwork. They continued to treat her like a little woman. Patti let Tracy do almost anything she wanted. *Tracy's not a bad girl,* she thought. *She knows what to do and what not to do. I trust her.* And her father trusted her as well. Tracy had had a good behavior record.

• • •

Steve heard about Tracy talking to Amir in the lobby at the movies during practice that week. Amir hung out with a rough crowd. Steve was intimidated by him, so he didn't want any hearsay going around. He decided to keep the fact that he knew to himself, but he surely didn't trust Tracy anymore.

It was an unusually hot day for October. Everyone seemed to be at the playground where they practiced. Tracy watched out of the corner of her eye to notice if Amir's friend Todd was there. Tracy was curious to see what he looked like.

After practice, Tracy talked Jantel into following Amir home with her. She was scared to say anything to him with his buddies still around. Amir spotted them and refused to speak.

Tracy sneered at him. "Oh, you don't know me now?"

"Nope," he told her, laughing with his friends.

Tracy smiled at his sarcasm. "Come here for a minute, Amir."

"Hold up, y'all, let me see what she wants."

"Yo, we'll get back with you then," his friends told him.

Amir walked over to Tracy. Close up, and with his hat off, Tracy noticed that his block-shaped hair had dents in it from wearing his helmet. And unlike Steve, Amir didn't shy away from her hazel eyes.

Tracy asked him carefully, "Why don't you walk me home?"

Amir shook his dented head. "Naw, 'cause I'm 'bout to do something."

"Come on, Amir. Please," she begged him.

Amir began to laugh at her, unmoved by her pleading. His friends then yelled from down the street, "YO AMIR, WE 'BOUT TO HAVE WATER BALLOON FIGHTS!"

"OH, BET!" he hollered back, immediately taking off to go and join them.

Dag, I had him, Tracy thought.

"Let's go around there," she said to Jantel.

"All right."

They ran two blocks up and watched as the boys chased each other like buffoons, screaming and hurling water balloons. Amir then threw one at Tracy. She got hit before she had a chance to duck. Water splashed all over her clothes and hair. One of his friends followed his lead and bombed away at Jantel. The girls quickly became target practice. After getting splashed a few more times, Jantel started to cry, but Tracy was still having fun.

An angry parent roared from his patio, "AMIR, LEAVE THEM DAMN GIRLS ALONE!"

Tracy and Jantel headed on their way back home.

Tracy asked, "What 'chew start cryin' for?"

Jantel whined, "They hit me in my eye."

"YO TRACY, HOLD UP!" Amir shouted down the block to them. Tracy turned and waited for him at the corner. Jantel marched home while rubbing her left eye. Once he had caught up, Amir walked home with Tracy.

"Why she start crying?"

"Because one of y'all hit her in her eye."

"Well, you 'bout to go in the house?" Amir asked.

Tracy smiled, anticipating something "juicy." "I don't know. Why?" she quizzed him.

Once they had reached Tracy's house, Amir sat on her steps and looked up at the moon. " 'Cause," he told her, hinting at companionship.

Tracy grinned and sat down beside him. "You got me all wet," she complained, feeling a cool draft.

Amir said, "Come here. Let me see how wet you are." He sat Tracy right down on his thigh pad. "Dig it, you are wet."

"Shet up, boy," she teased.

Amir looked at her lips. Tracy could sense what he was thinking. He then wrapped his hands around her waist before she had a chance to respond and kissed her. Tracy couldn't resist him. Amir's arms were pretty strong, and Tracy began to like how tightly he held her.

Amir suddenly backed away.

"What 'chew stop for?" Tracy asked him, curiously. She looked up at her house and then next door to make sure no one saw them. She then hopped off of Amir's lap in a panic. *Oh my God! What am I doing?* she asked herself. *I could have gotten busted, right in front of my house.*

" 'Cause," Amir said again.

Tracy hopped down a few steps to distance herself from him. "'Cause what?"

Amir paused. "You wanna come over my house Monday?"

"I'on care," Tracy said without thinking. She simply went with the feeling, and the feeling from Amir was good.

Amir grinned, surprised that she had agreed. "How old are you?"

"Thirteen. Why?"

"Oh, I was just asking. So you coming to my house, Monday, after school, right?" he asked again, just to make sure.

"Aw'ight," Tracy chirped, still filled with sneaky excitement. She then got up to go inside the house as Amir took off running, carrying a big smile on his face.

Tracy thought about the next thing that comes after kissing that night. It tickled her stomach to think about the possibility of "doin' it." *I don't know,* she told herself. *I don't know if I want to.*

Tracy bragged about her football team's record at school. They were still undefeated and on their way to a sure championship. Students wore jerseys from other teams and argued with her up and down the halls in between their classes. Tracy had forgotten all about going over to Amir's house. She wasn't ready to go past kissing yet. She had hardly done that. Amir had been the first and only boy Tracy had kissed since Aaron Barnes, at least five boyfriends ago. Having a boyfriend was like watching television to Tracy. She didn't have to get too involved, she would just change the channel and watch something new.

Tracy came across three girls inside of the lunchroom. They had some interesting gossip to nose in on.

"I know, he is nasty. He only want you for one thing," a slim brown girl was saying.

"Yup, and that's why I don't talk to him no more," a darker brown girl responded.

"But Todd is cute though, ain't he?" a lemon-skinned girl interjected.

"Yeah, but forget Amir. Bunk him, y'all, 'cause he's just a user."

The shock was enough to ruin Tracy's day. Raheema was right. It came back to Tracy that she was supposed to go over Amir's house after school. *I'm not going to that boy's house,* she thought. *He ain't gettin' none from me. That boy thinks I'm stupid. He's out here trying to get everybody.*

"Ay, girl, what's up?" Amir called, as soon as Tracy stepped out of her building. Several football players from her school shook his hand. Tracy wasn't impressed. She kept pacing by, ignoring him.

"Where you goin'?" he asked her.

"I'm going home."

"I thought you said you was gon' come over today."

"Did you get out of school early?" Tracy asked, avoiding his question.

"Yeah, we get out earlier than y'all every day. I'm in high school."

Tracy frowned at him. "You don't trust me or something? I said I was gonna come."

"Oh, I'm supposed to *trust you* so you can sell me out?" Amir retorted.

"You can't take my word for it?" Tracy asked him.

Amir shook his blocked-shaped head. "Nope."

"Well, you go find yourself somebody else then," Tracy responded to him, walking away.

Amir went back to his friends.

"Yo, what happened, man?"

"Fuck that girl, cuz'," he answered, sourly. "She ain't nothin'. Bet, here comes Carmen."

Carmen walked out from the building, switching her firm young hips and wearing a bright red jacket. She stood out from everyone, and her soft brown skin smelled of cocoa-butter cream.

Amir waited for her to walk near him. Carmen tried not to notice. Amir stepped in her way.

"Where you goin'?"

"I'm goin' home," Carmen responded nervously.

"No you ain't. You goin' wit' me," he told her, snatching her by the hand.

Carmen asked, "Where we goin'?"

"We goin' to my boy's crib. Why, you don't wanna go wit' me?" he snapped, letting go of her hand momentarily.

"I didn't say that."

"Well, shet up and come on then."

ALMOST TIME

Tracy shot up in height during the football season to tower over most of the boys. She lost her babyface look, and she began to wear her hair shoulder length and curled. Although she was just thirteen, her size made her appear seventeen or eighteen. Tracy had developed into a vivaciously curved young lady, with a new hobby, observing herself inside of the mirror.

Raheema grew a bit herself, but neither she nor her older sister, Mercedes, had grown anywhere as tall or as well-defined as Tracy had. Tracy outgrew most of the girls her age, beginning to look more like a high-schooler than an eighth-grader. She was beginning to attract the attention of much older guys as well. High-schoolers had always gathered after school to entice younger girls who were willing to step up in competition. And at least physically, Tracy had crossed over into the bigger, faster league of the dating game.

On a Friday afternoon in the frost of winter, Tracy headed home from school, sensing plenty of the lustful teenaged eyes glued to her backside. Expecting them to approach her, Tracy was *more* than willing to test her tempting skills of persuasion with the older guys. By the time she reached the corner, one high-school boy had decided to try his luck.

"Ay, sexy, come here for a minute," he said, smiling with assurance. He knew he was older than Tracy, and young-girls were easy to talk to.

Tracy cracked a grin and walked over to him, swaying her newly developed hips as she pouted her medium-full lips and licked them wet as she stood.

The boy anxiously thought about what to say to her. *What's the coolest line?* he mused. "Yeah, umm, what's your name?" he asked, warming up his game.

"It's Tracy," she answered him, huskily and slow. "Why?"

"'Cause you look good, and I wanna get to know you."

Tracy used her stabbing hazels to dazzle him. "You looking for a girlfriend, or just somebody to mess wit'?" she quizzed him.

The older boy was stunned. "What? Oh, I mean, I'on know," he said, stumbling.

"What's your name?" Tracy asked him.

"Jeff."

"Where your girlfriend at, Jeff? *I know* you got one. Don't you?"

Jeff backed off, trying desperately to get himself together. "I ain't got no girlfriend," he mumbled. His self-assurance was gone in the wind. Tracy had turned out to be more than what he had expected.

"Why not? You look cute to me," she told him, while moving in closer to him. Tracy always knew when she had a boy on his heels.

Jeff laughed nervously. "Come on now," he responded, losing eye contact with her. She was invading his comfort zone.

Tracy knew she would reject him. Jeff was not cool enough to gain her consideration. She just wanted to practice *her* game, and she was doing extremely well.

Jeff asked, "Where's your boyfriend?"

Tracy fixed the new gold ring that she wore on her right hand. "I don't have one."

"Oh yeah," Jeff responded meaninglessly. He was hesitant to continue. The young girl was more than he had bargained for.

Tracy locked in on his eyes with hers. She knew the effect that this would have. Only the most confident boys could survive her intent stare. "Are you finished?" she asked him seductively, loving every minute of it.

"Yeah, but umm, I'll see you around, aw'ight," he stammered.

The high-schooler backed completely away, embarrassed with himself. Tracy turned to walk home, beaming from ear to ear.

"Yo, you didn't answer me," he pouted. His friends were approaching.

Tracy turned with a smile and said, "Bye," breathlessly. She figured that Jeff *had* to show off for his friends. *All* the guys did it.

When Tracy arrived at home, her neighbor, Raheema, was at the door. Tracy was tempted to gossip with her like she had done with Mercedes, yet she quickly realized that their interests in life were different. All Raheema talked about was what the teachers did in school. She was not interested in any of Tracy's boy stories. Nevertheless, they decided to chat. Tracy went into Raheema's house, getting out of the cold.

Raheema said, "All you talk about is boys, and I remember when you didn't even like them."

"Well, all I know is that Todd was cute. And you should have talked to him."

"Don't play dumb with me, Tracy. I heard about you kissing him in the driveway."

Tracy twisted her lips. *"You* didn't want him." She had moved on from Amir and on to his friend Todd.

Raheema huffed, "I know I didn't. I don't *want* any boys, thank you."

"Oh, you think you so smart, don't 'chew?"

"No, but I'm not getting *used* by any boy, that's for sure."

"How you know?"

"Because I won't talk to them," Raheema answered frankly. "That's why I'm going into dance class, to do something that doesn't involve boys."

"What dance class?" Tracy asked, feeling left out. Football season and cheerleading were over.

"None of your business," Raheema snapped. She had outdone Tracy again.

Tracy went home and waited impatiently for her mother to arrive with her brother. She wanted the 4-1-1 on Raheema's dance class, and she had a fool-proof plan of how to get it.

"Hey mom, I think it would be good for me to be in a dance class. You know how bored I get after doing my homework."

"Yeah, okay then," Patti responded, while taking off her son's coat and hat. "Where is it at and all?"

Tracy grinned. "I don't know all that, but Ra-Ra's in it, so Ms. Beth probably knows."

Patti called Beth about the dance class. It was held near Patti's sister Tanya's house in Logan. Patti called Tanya to see if she wanted Patrice, or "Reese," as they called her, to take dance lessons, too. Tracy didn't expect that. But Reese was not that bad when she was not around her other cousins, Trish and Marie. Reese took sides with them rather than with Tracy because she was afraid of them.

On the first day of dance, their instructor went over the calendar schedule for the four-month dance session. During their first exercises, Tracy snickered at her cousin Reese's form, while Raheema did the same to her. For all three of them, it was more hard work than expected. Tracy found out rather quickly that dance was definitely more complicated than cheerleading.

A flock of rough boys played basketball inside of the recreation center where the girls held their dance lessons. The boys watched the girls with excitement. Every year the boys anticipated the pretty new girls that dance classes attracted to their rec center. It had become a ritual, and it was only a matter of time before they would start to mingle with the girls. On Tracy's third night of class, a boy finally approached her.

"Ay girl, you cute as shit," he told her. "Why don't you come over here and talk to me when you finish?" he said.

"Thank you," Tracy responded to him. She began to smile in his direction before she took a good look at him. Once she got a better look at him, Tracy thought that he was ugly. "That's okay. My mom is coming to get me," she told him.

The forward boy persisted. "So what? She ain't here yet."

Tracy lied and said, "Well, I have a boyfriend."

The boy then got an attitude and grimaced at her. "Dude ain't here either," he said, walking closer to her.

Tracy scrambled to her feet from her stretching position. "Naw, that's all right," she said. The boy then moved as if he was about to grab her. Tracy quickly dashed toward the dance instructor. "Ms. Hamilton, that boy is after me," she squealed.

"Leave her alone, Ricky!" Ms. Hamilton screamed at the boy.

The boy smiled. "Aw, I was just playin' with her, Ms. Hamilton, that's all."

Tracy was excited about the close call when her mother arrived. She told Patti what happened, and her mother laughed good and hard. Raheema rode home with them after Patti had dropped her niece, Reese, off.

"Hey, dad. What's up?" Tracy perked when she had arrived home with her mother.

Dave sat watching television with his son. He looked at Tracy as if he was in shock. *"Damn!* Who are you?" he responded, jokingly.

They smiled at each other and shared a laugh.

"She just blossomed like that overnight," Patti told him with a grin. It was Dave's first time seeing his daughter in a leotard.

Dave said, "Come here and turn around." Tracy felt embarrassed as she turned around in her baby-blue tights. "Gir-r-r-l, you got a big butt back *there,"* Dave said with a laugh.

Tracy gushed, "Yup, dad, I grew. Didn't I?"

"You damn sure did. Your mother's gonna have to put a curfew on you now."

Patti said nothing.

Tracy smirked as she sat down beside him. "Yup, dad, this ugly boy tried to talk to me today," she told him.

"Did you give him your phone number?"

Tracy looked disgusted. "No, that boy looked like a monster."

Dave grinned. "Those are the best ones. They'll do anything for you."

Patti had had enough. She marched to her usual spot in the kitchen. She was no longer crazy about seeing Dave as long as he insisted on playing presto man, popping in and out of their lives.

"Naw, dad, you can have that. My man has to look *good*," Tracy was telling him.

Patti came back out from the kitchen wearing her apron. "How was your dance class, other than the boy?"

Tracy shrugged. "I mean, it was okay. It's a lot of work though."

Little Jason jumped up on Tracy's lap to get some attention.

"Get off of me, boy," she huffed, pushing him away.

"Stop, Tracy. He's just being friendly," Patti reasoned.

"I'm tired of him jumping all over me, mom."

Dave grimaced. "Oh, you're *that* mature now, hunh?" he asked. "I remember when you were running around here with a snotty nose and doo-doo stains in your drawers."

Tracy threw her hands over her ears in embarrassment. Dave and Patti laughed as she tried to block them out.

Patti asked, "How are you getting along with Reese?"

Tracy smiled, still feeling stunned. "She's all right. She doesn't say much to me."

"She's your cousin, Tracy," Patti fumed at her.

"Yeah, but they start stuff all the time."

"Well, how is Raheema doing?" Dave asked.

"She's all right, too. We just have differences in opinion."

"What about Mercedes? What she been into?"

"She's been all over the place by now," Patti answered him. She had recently talked to Beth about it. "Mercedes is out there in them streets, chasing after the money."

Tracy added, "Yup, she got some real nice clothes, too."

"Didn't you need some new jeans?" Dave asked Tracy as he pulled out his wallet.

"Yeah. I'm starting to outgrow everything now," Tracy answered him. She watched her father peel off five twenties.

Dave handed it out to her. "This is all I got for you right now."

Tracy took the money with a nod and cracked a grin. "Thanks, dad. Me and mom can go shopping this weekend."

Again, Patti decided to hold her tongue to keep the peace. *A couple pairs of jeans does not excuse you from acting like an asshole,* she thought to herself.

Saturday came quickly, and Tracy went out shopping at the mall with her mother. Tracy tried on clothes in every store they entered. She just *had* to have brand-name fashions. Patti urged her to buy bargains, but bargains ruin teenaged reputations. Tracy wanted to dress stylishly.

She bought Coca-Cola, Guess and Gloria Vanderbilt jeans along with an Adidas sweat suit and three pairs of shoes. She then went with her mother to a jewelry store for a gold bracelet.

Dave's hundred dollars was spent after the first two pair of jeans. Patti ended up paying for her daughter's other things. And since Tracy wanted to keep up with the trends, she worked it out with her father to receive seventy dollars for shopping every other week. Soon her closets were filled with gear.

Tracy began to out-dress everyone at school, and every boy wanted her phone number. When Christmas time came, she had clothing under the tree. Tracy could not get enough. She spent hours matching and ironing clothing for each school day. She would then change her outfits several times each morning until she was satisfied with what she planned on wearing.

Tracy became a hot topic with the boys in her neighborhood. With the increase in her already large ego, she decided that *no one* was good enough for her. She had far surpassed Mercedes' popularity at thirteen. And Tracy had not given up *any.* She was a proud virgin.

"Ay, what's up, Tracy? Who's your boyfriend?" an eighth-grader asked inside the school hallway.

Tracy closed her locker. "Don't worry about it," she told him.

"Dag, I'm just askin'."

"Well don't, and get away from my locker."

As the bell rang, the eighth-grader asked, "Can *I* talk to you?"

"Excuse me, I'm late for class," Tracy said, walking by.

"Well, I'll walk you there."

"I don't *need you* to walk me to class, boy. I got legs."

The boy smiled admiringly, as Tracy stepped away from him. She walked through the hall with her head high, strutting around as if she was a teenaged queen and was late for her class.

"Tracy, you have two more times to walk into my class late, and then you'll have a detention," the teacher warned her. Ms. Patterson was a white woman in her early thirties, shorter than Tracy and with jet black hair and glasses.

Tracy smiled nonchalantly. She was unfazed by the teacher's warning.

Ms. Patterson asked, "Tracy Ellison, what did I just say?"

"Hunh? I don't know."

There was a pause. Tracy was becoming a distraction to the class. "I am sick and tired of you daydreaming in my class," Ms. Patterson yelled at her.

Tracy rolled her eyes. "Well, don't ask me no questions then."

"Do you think that you're too *good* to answer questions, Tracy?"

Tracy sighed and ignored her.

"That's it! GO to the principal's office, because I'm SICK OF YOU!"

"I was *paying* attention," Tracy snapped.

"Well, turn around, sit up, and listen."

A boy snickered at Tracy from the back of the class.

"What 'chew laughin' at, boy?" Tracy said to him.

"Aw, shet up, girl. You think you *it* now, just because you got your Christmas presents on."

The students roared with laughter.

"I ain't get this for Christmas," Tracy ranted.

"Yes, you did. You even got Christmas glitter on your jeans."

"GET OUT! Both of you! NOW!" Ms. Patterson hollered.

"Aw, Ms. Patterson, I didn't even do nothin'," the boy whined, throwing his hands in the air as he pleaded.

Tracy frowned. "Yes he did."

They left for the principal's office with a note for detentions. The boy's long arms swung loosely from his tall, walnut-colored frame as he strolled in front of Tracy.

"See, boy, you got me in trouble," Tracy said to him.

"Yeah, I know. But Santa Claus *was* good to you this year. Wasn't he?" the boy joked.

"Shet up," Tracy snapped with a smile.

Long-arms was a regular comedian.

They sat inside of the main office lobby with five other students, all waiting to be seen by the principal. There were two girls and three boys. Tracy was the most glamorous thing in the room. She wore black leather boots with a long gray skirt and a matching gray sweater. She wore lip gloss and two gold chains that were neatly draped over her sweater, and a black leather purse dangling from her shoulder. She felt embarrassed to have to sit inside of the lobby with six low-ifes.

Tracy sucked her teeth. "I'm tired of waiting in here."

"Shet up, girl. Do you think I like bein' out here?" the long-armed boy snapped at her, demanding respect and attention. He smiled at her once Tracy had piped down. "Sike, I'm just jokin' with you," he said.

Tracy lied. "I *know* you was."

Long-arms grinned at her. "But for real though, you look cute. I don't want you to think that I don't know it."

"Thank you."

"Yup, I feel like taking you into the bathroom and just *giving it* to you," he said with a smile. Tracy couldn't believe what he said, and he kept a straight face when he said it.

"I mean, you think I'm jokin', but I'm serious," he added.

Tracy smirked with nervous energy. She was scared to say anything. Long-arms seemed to turned everything into an embarrassing joke.

"You know we gon' be here all day after school," he commented.

"For real?" Tracy asked, unaware. She had never had a detention before.

"Yup, so you might as well come over to my house and have dinner."

Tracy smiled. "You a trip."

"So, Tracy, who's your boyfriend?" he asked her. "Because I'm ready to give dude a handshake."

"I don't have one."

"For real?"

"Yup."

Long-arms cracked a broad smile. "You might as well give me your number then," he said, taking out a pen and notebook to write it down. The other students eyed Tracy to see if she would oblige.

Tracy didn't think the boy was good-looking, but he *was* funny. She could not refuse him. The boy was simply amusing, and his offbeat comments kept her on her toes.

He smiled at her, half-expecting that she would give it to him. "So what is it?"

Tracy ran her number off to him. "Eight-four-two, five-four-three-seven."

He sloppily jotted it down. "Aw'ight, bet. When can I call you up?"

"I got dance class tonight, so I won't be home until nine."

"Aw, you into that stupid shit?" he snapped, for another laugh.

Tracy giggled at it herself. "It ain't stupid," she argued.

"Yes that shit is. Y'all be in there doin' all that jumpin' around and stuff for like a year, to do *one* show."

Tracy began to laugh with the other students. Long-arms was the life of the party. "So what?" she told him. "It builds your body though."

"Yeah, 'cause I'ma tear *your* body up."

The boy's rash humor was intriguing to Tracy. He was even taller than her, for a change.

"You know my name, right?" he quizzed her.

"Umm, it's Travis, ain't it?" she said, acting as if she was not sure about it.

"Yeah, that's it," Travis said. He chuckled, knowing that she knew.

The principal roared, "You two! Get inside of my office!"

Tracy didn't have a love-at-first-sight feeling about Travis, but there were definitely sparks between them. He had plain looks, but a lot of character. Travis was unafraid to speak his mind, and Tracy could not wait to talk to him after her dance class.

"One, two, three, four, and one, two, three, four," Ms. Hamilton chanted, coordinating the class. "Raheema, what's wrong with you today? You're not in the rhythm at all, honey."

"I'm not feeling too well," Raheema whimpered.

"Come here." Ms. Hamilton pulled Raheema over to the side of the room. *Lord, I hope and pray that this girl isn't pregnant or something,* she thought to herself. *She has her whole life ahead of her.* Ms. Hamilton had come in contact with all kinds of problem children over the years. "What's wrong?" she asked Raheema, privately.

"I got a D on one of my tests. I'm scared that I'm gonna get in trouble," Raheema answered, with tears in her eyes.

Ms. Hamilton was relieved. "Baby, you're not gonna get in trouble for *one* D," she contested. "Don't you have straight A's on your report card?"

Tears rolled down Raheema's cheeks. "Yeah, but that doesn't mean anything."

"What do you think is going to happen to you?"

Raheema wiped her eyes. "My father's gonna say that I can't dance anymore."

"Honey, he's not going to do that. The show is coming up soon."

"Yes he is. I know it."

"Well, what if I talk to your parents?"

"You can only talk to my mother. My father won't listen to you."

"Okay then. I'll give your mother a call tonight."

Ms. Hamilton spoke to Beth about her daughter's situation. Beth told her that her husband was not upset, but that Raheema would have to study more on the weekends to compensate for time lost to her dance lessons.

"Hey mom, did I get any phone calls earlier?" Tracy asked, just to make sure. It was after nine o'clock. Travis was supposed to have called her by then. *Maybe he forgot about my dance class and called me earlier,* she thought.

"No. Were you expecting one?"

"Yeah," Tracy said, disappointed.

BRRRRIIIINNNNNGG!

"That's for me, mom. I'll get it," Tracy said while scrambling for the phone. "Hello, this is Tracy," she answered.

Patti sneered at her. "Now you know better than to answer the phone like that," she huffed.

"Yo, what's up?" Travis responded.

"Nothin'. I thought you were gonna call me at nine o'clock."

"I would have, but my mom was on the phone."

Patti decided to head up the steps and put Jason to bed. He had fallen asleep during the car ride from Tracy's dance class.

Tracy immediately got more comfortable, plopping her feet up on the coffee table. "Well, I got home late from dance class anyway," she said to Travis.

"So why you ask me if I called, then?" he snapped.

Tracy smiled. "Because you said you would."

They talked all night and about everything. Travis made Tracy laugh for hours. When it had reached midnight though, Patti decided that enough was enough and abruptly ended their conversation.

"Tracy, get off of this damn phone."

"Okay, mom. We're almost finished."

"I mean, now, girl."

"All right," Tracy snapped. "I'll see you tomorrow," she said to Travis, glumly. *She could of at least came and told me instead jumping all on the phone like that,* she fumed to herself. *That was embarrassing.*

"Aw'ight then," Travis told her as they hung up.

Travis began to laugh once they had hung up the phone.

That next school day, Tracy wore her Coca-Cola jeans, white sneakers and blue Adidas sweat-suit jacket over a white tennis shirt.

"Ay, what's up, Tracy?" a clean-cut boy asked her inside of the hallway.

"Hi, Martin," she responded.

"Oh, you're speaking to me today, hunh?"

"Yeah, but don't get excited about it."

Jantel came to talk to her. "Tracy, you hear about those girls wanting to beat you up?" she whispered.

"What girls?" Tracy asked, quizzically.

"I heard that it was Jackie and Sharon."

Martin butted in. "They're not gon' do nothin' to you. If they do, I'm jumping in it."

"What they wanna fight me for?" Tracy asked Jantel.

"I'on know," Jantel answered.

"Well, *who* told you this, Jantel?" Martin quizzed.

"I heard Crystal telling some girl in the bathroom."

"Well, what she got to do with anything?" Tracy asked.

Jantel hunched her shoulders. "I'on know that either."

Tracy grabbed her things. "Come on."

They marched down the hall after Tracy. Crystal was shutting her locker as they arrived.

"Ay Crystal, Jackie and Sharon said they was gon' jump me?" Tracy asked her.

Crystal backed away as if she was in on it. "I didn't say that," she responded, frantically.

"Jantel said she heard you in the bathroom."

Crystal took a quick look at Jantel, who was embarrassed that Tracy put her name in it. "Well, I didn't say that, and *she* need to mind her own business."

"Yes you did. I heard you talking about it in the bathroom," Jantel spoke up.

"Won't you get the facts straight if you gon' start spreadin' gossip on somebody?" Crystal snapped at her. They squared off with each other. Jantel stood about three inches taller, but Crystal was ten pounds heavier.

Tracy butted in. "Look, I'm gon' let you know right now, Crystal, they *better not* jump me, 'cause I'm gon' get all of y'all if they do."

"And I got her back," Martin interjected.

Crystal stared at him. *That boy better go ahead somewhere. My boyfriend'll kick his ass,* she thought to herself.

Other students began to watch. They were shocked by Tracy's bravery. Then again, Tracy was taller than Crystal, Jackie *and* Sharon. Only Sharon was near Tracy's size.

Crystal backed off, with a message to tell her friends.

When Tracy was late again for the same class, Ms. Patterson had a mouthful to say. "Tracy, get out of my room. I've decided to write a pink slip on you. You've been late to this class *several* times now, and you never pay any attention while in class. I'm surprised that you're even passing."

"No, Ms. Patterson, these girls were trying to get me after school, so I had to straighten that out, 'cause I don't play that."

"Come here," Ms. Patterson responded to her. She walked out of the class and shut the door behind them. "Now who's after you?" she asked, peering through her thin-rimmed glasses.

"Jantel told me that it was Jackie and Sharon, but I think that Crystal Johnson has something to do with it, too."

"Well, why are they after you?"

"I don't know, but I don't appreciate it."

"You and Travis have detentions today, right?" Ms. Patterson asked, changing the subject.

"Yeah," Tracy answered. *What does that have to do with anything?* she mused. *I'm about to get jumped after school, and she's sittin' up here asking me about some damn detentions!*

"Well, where is he?" she asked of Travis. "I've been noticing that he's been absent from school a lot."

Tracy hunched her shoulders and frowned. "Well, I don't know where he is," she said, still annoyed about Ms. Patterson giving her the third degree. She had more pressing concerns. Tracy had anticipated seeing Travis in school and had even dressed for him, yet he was not there. To top it off, she had a fight on her hands.

"Well, look, you go to your detention, and I'll see about these girls," Ms. Patterson informed her.

Tracy felt relieved. "Okay."

After her detention, she rushed home to see what had happened to Travis. Travis was not home when she called. Tracy let the phone ring six times before she hung up. She then sat in the house, bored, with no dance class scheduled. She watched television in the living room before falling asleep on the couch.

"I got some Chinese food here, Tracy," her mother walked in announcing, waking Tracy from her unexpected nap. Jason followed close behind as Patti took the food inside the kitchen.

Tracy climbed to her feet and followed them. She got a plate and tasted the food with a grimace. "Did you get this from the same place we usually go, mom?" she asked.

Patti frowned after tasting it herself. "No. I know it probably doesn't taste as good."

"Nope. It tastes overcooked."

"What happened in school today?" Patti asked, ignoring the plate that Tracy pushed away.

"Oh, these girls were gon' try and jump me after school, mom."

Patti raised her brow. "For what?"

"I don't know, but I got it straightened out."

Patti nodded and suddenly snapped her fingers. She then stood up from her chair and got her pocketbook. "I need you to do me a favor. Go down on the avenue and get me some cake dressing. It comes in a little tube in the bakery," she said, describing the size of the tube with her hands.

Tracy hurried out of the house with the unfinished Chinese food setting on the table. She walked through the whipping cold, wondering where Travis could have been and what he was doing. As usual, the neighborhood boys hung out on the corners of Wayne and Chelten Avenues in their long down coats and colorful ski jackets. Tracy ignored their suggestions. She bought the cake dressing and headed home a different route to avoid them.

A crowd of teens was gathered at a small street intersection. A bloody-nosed boy came shuffling through the pack with a bruised and battered face. Tracy tried her best to back away and was helplessly surrounded by the flowing crowds.

"What's up, girl?" Travis said to her out of the crowd.

Tracy grabbed on to him for protection. "Travis, what's going on?"

"Oh, Victor just beat some dude up."

"Who is Victor?"

"You never heard of Victor? He's thorough as shit. He just whipped dude ass," he responded, excitedly.

"Who does he hang out with?"

"He hangs out with the High-Low crew: Mark Bates, Tyrone, Peppy, and all them other hoodlum dudes."

"He hangs out with *Peppy?* I *hate* that boy," Tracy commented. "What does he look like?"

"He's a dark-skinned, pretty muthafucka with a lot of flyy gear," Travis answered. "But it wasn't like I be lookin'," he joked with a grin. "Naw, dude is pretty decent. Straight up."

Tracy could tell that Travis had a lot of respect for him. That only made her more interested.

"What's his last name?"

Travis stopped himself. "Wait a minute now, we gon' stop talkin' 'bout dude. What's up with me and you?"

Tracy laughed it off as they began walking toward her house.

"Where we goin'?" Travis asked her.

"I'm goin' home," Tracy told him with a smile.

Travis had found himself halfway down the block with her. He then shrugged his shoulders and threw up his hands. "I might as well walk you home then."

"Where were you at during school today?" she asked, changing the subject. She had looked forward to seeing him.

"I ain't go to school."

"So where were you? I called your house, twice."

Travis grinned. "Oh, you really wanted to talk to me, hunh?" he responded, pleased with her concern.

"Shet up," Tracy said, grinning back at him.

"I was at my boy's crib. I'm goin' over there after school tomorrow, too."

"What do y'all do over there?" Tracy asked as they crossed the street.

"Nothing, really. We just watch television and videotapes and shit. My boy got one of them chill cribs. His mom works like twenty-four-seven. She ain't never home."

They reached Tracy's house and chatted a bit more before she went in. Tracy promised to go to his friend's house with him after school the next day. Travis promised her that other girls would be there, and Tracy trusted him. She was curious to see what they all did to entertain themselves.

After getting out of school, Tracy followed Travis and three other girls behind his loud friends. She had a funny feeling about following a group of mischievous teens to a boy's unsupervised home. Jantel had turned down her offer to tag along, and Tracy had become apprehensive about what they all planned to get into. Travis responded sourly at her suggestion. He didn't want Jantel tagging along. "All she gon' do is get in the way," he said.

Get in the way of what? Tracy thought. *I hope Travis don't think he's gonna get anything from me.* Travis was not attractive enough for Tracy to jeopardize her virginity, but it sure looked like a party of couples.

Once they arrived at the boy's house, all of the girls watched television while the boys ran around collecting money for something. Tracy was baffled and curious. She felt uncomfortable. The boys were not even talking to them. *What the hell are they doing?* she panicked. Tracy wanted to leave after the first ten minutes. It was a big mistake.

Once their money was gathered, one boy left the house. The others then decided to converse with the girls. A shockingly attractive boy sat in a chair opposite from Tracy. He was tanned-skinned with small dark eyes and dark curly hair. His thick dark hair was tapered on the sides and long on top.

Tracy could not take her eyes from him. She looked over his new Nike sneakers and his red and blue Fila sweat suit. *Dag! I wish I was here with him instead of with Travis,* she thought to herself.

"Ay Bob, did he go to get it?" the girl wearing a green Champion sweatshirt asked him.

Bob said, "Yeah, he'll be back in twenty minutes."

"What are we waiting for?" Tracy asked.

Bob laughed. "We waitin' for some weed. You ever smoked weed before?"

"Unt unh. I don't do that."

Bob smiled at her through dark slit eyes. "Why not? It gets you in the mood. It makes you feel nice as hell."

"Yup, girl. It makes everything in the world seem funny," the green-sweatshirt girl responded.

Bob said, "Dig. Remember that time we got *on* over Mark Bates' house?"

Green-sweatshirt girl nodded her head and smiled.

Bob stared back at Tracy. "Do you go with Travis?" he asked her.

"No," Tracy said, overjoyed that she didn't.

"Y'all just friends, or do you like each other?"

Tracy hunched her shoulders and smiled. "I don't know."

"You don't know?" Bob asked with a frown of confusion.

Travis called from the kitchen in the nick of time, "Ay Tracy, come here."

Tracy got up in her long, black boots and blue Gloria Vanderbilt jeans. The tight-fitting jeans hugged her firm behind quite snugly.

Bob could not take his eyes off of her either. "DAMN!" he howled, shaking his dark, curly-haired head.

"Ay Bob, you better cut that shit out, cuz'," Travis warned with a chuckle. "So what's up? You gon' get *on* with us?" he asked Tracy inside of the kitchen.

Tracy made up her mind. "Naw. I ain't really down with that."

"So what we gon' do then?"

"I'on know," she said. She felt unsure with Travis. She was more interested in Bob.

"Have you ever had sex before?" Travis asked her bluntly.

"Yeah," Tracy lied, embarrassed.

"Aw'ight then. We gon' go to my boy's room when dude gets back with the nickel bag."

Tracy wanted to tell him "No," but she knew she'd seem young if she caused a scene, so she kept quiet.

"Aw'ight," she said, nonchalantly. *I ain't doing nothin' though,* she told herself as she turned and walked back to her seat inside of the living room.

Tracy sensed Bob's eyes glued to her behind again. All he did was smile at her, and Tracy was immediately tantalized. She wanted to lose her virginity to him, and she didn't even know him. Bob gave her that sexual feeling.

The errand boy had finally gotten back with the small yellow bag of marijuana. He brought two more boys with him. Tracy really felt uncomfortable then. They spread the crushed dried leaves right out on the table in front of her and started rolling joints. Tracy was praying that they didn't ask her to smoke any. And they didn't.

The two quiet girls were dragged up the stairs. Bob sat there giggling at Tracy. He didn't seem interested in anything after he had gotten high.

Tracy grinned at him. "Why you laughin'?"

"'Cause you funny." His dark eyes got smaller, making him look even cuter to Tracy.

"Tracy! Come here!" Travis yelled. He led her up the steps and into the back room. He then patted his lap for Tracy to have a seat on it. She sat on his lap hesitantly, feeling nervous about it.

Travis began to rub his hands over her breasts. Tracy began to breathe slower, deeper. Through the thin walls, she could clearly hear moans and a squeaky bed from the next room. It added to Tracy's sensuality, but not for Travis. He tried to kiss her. Tracy turned her head to avoid him.

"What's wrong?" he asked, holding her tighter.

"Nothin'," Tracy said. She didn't want to say it, but she hoped that he would get the message. Travis put his hands on her pants zipper. Tracy grabbed his hand to stop him.

"Come on, now," Travis whined.

Tracy took a deep breath to force out her suppressed comments. "I don't wanna do this."

"What? See now, why you playin' wit' me?" he fumed at her.

Tracy got off of his lap. "I'm goin' downstairs," she said.

She hurried down the steps and saw the same sociable girl sharing a joint with Bob.

Travis came down after her. "Ay Tammy, come here for a minute," he said. Tammy wasn't attractive. Tracy thought *she'd* "do it" with anyone. Travis and Tammy went up the steps.

Tracy was left alone with Bob, who immediately began to giggle.

"Why you keep laughin' at me?"

"Come here," he said. He stood up and looked her straight in the eyes. "You ain't down wit' Travis, hunh?"

Tracy shook her head. "Unt unh."

"Get your coat and stuff," Bob told her, caressing her hand.

Tracy wanted to be with *him*. They left, holding hands and heading for Bob's house.

"Come downstairs," he said. Tracy took her coat and bag. "My mom might be comin' home soon," he warned her.

Tracy stood inside of his red-carpeted basement. Bob walked over to her and pulled her body to his, kissing her. She then felt his hands, running down her back as he squeezed her behind. His pants tightened as she felt his masculinity throbbing against her leg.

It was all happening too fast, and Tracy wanted more. She could feel Bob's vibrations through her jeans. It took him a while to get her zipper down. He then peeled her clothes to her ankles. Tracy felt the basement draft whip around her bare lower body, while Bob began to peel his own clothing to his ankles. That was when Tracy saw *it* approaching her legs.

It was difficult for Bob to position himself on top of her because her pants were not completely off, making it hard for him to spread her legs. Bob then tried to force it with Tracy resisting and pulling back.

"Bob, take my pants off," she whispered.

He sat up and thought about it. "I'on know, 'cause my mom is comin' home soon."

Tracy sighed, disappointed. She leaned up with him. "Well, try again like this."

Bob tried, but it was no use. He then saw shadows through the basement window.

"Oh shit! It's my mom and my sister!"

Tracy pulled her pants up in a hurry. Bob snatched her coat and bag and led her to the back door. She ran out of his house and down the driveway, excited about the suspense. Bob ran back into his basement and turned on *Inspector Gadget*. His long-haired mother walked down into the basement and looked around. Bob sat and smiled at her, nervously.

"What's up, mom?"

"Boy, you think you so slick. I know you had a girl in here," his mother said, glancing at the back door.

She looked at Bob with an evil eye. "I keep tellin' you, boy, them damn girls gon' get pregnant. Now you keep runnin' around here like they won't trap you. Because it's a whole lot of confused little girls out here who are just dying to have some pretty babies. You hear me?"

DING DONG! DING DONG!

"Jantel, I got something to tell you!" Tracy screamed.

Jantel opened her door. "What?"

"You know some boy named Bob?" Tracy asked, throwing her book-bag to the floor.

"He got real curly hair?"

"Yeah, and he hangs out with Travis and them?"

Jantel got excited. "Yup, that boy is cute as I don't know what. *All* the girls like him."

"*I* was just over his house," Tracy bragged.

"Uuuuw, for real?" Jantel squealed, happy for Tracy.

"Yup, and he *did it* to me," Tracy fibbed.

Jantel whispered, "How it feel?"

"It felt gooood."

"Dag, I would love to *do it* with *him*. You go with him now?"

"Yup," Tracy lied again. She wanted to go with Bob though.

Jantel sighed. "Dag, you lucky, girl. How did you meet him?"

"I was with Travis, but I didn't want to *do it* with him, 'cause he ugly, so I left with Bob."

"Uuuuw, you nasty, girl."

"Shet up, you would want some from him, too, so don't even try that goody-two-shoes role," Tracy retorted.

"Yup, if he asked me," Jantel admitted to her.

Tracy went home and daydreamed about having kids with and marrying Bob. She hardly knew the boy, but he was s-o-o-o-o cute that it didn't matter. He was the best-looking boy she had had yet. He even dressed nice. Tracy planned to get his phone number and go finish what they started. She forgot about Travis. She told herself that she only liked him because he was funny. But Bob was someone she could *really* be with. As far as her virginity . . . oh well. *Everybody has to lose their virginity one day,* she figured. And Bob was an excellent choice to lose it to.

Tracy wore her best outfit, hoping Bob would come to see her after school. She wore a blue leather skirt suit that everyone talked about. It was one of the expensive outfits that she had received for Christmas. Tracy caught all eyes and nothing but compliments.

"You look like a knock-out today, girl," Jantel told her.

Tracy cracked a wide smile. "Yeah, I know. I hope he comes up here today."

"Well, if he don't, he doesn't know what he's missin'."

"Maybe we could go to the movies tonight," Tracy suggested. It *was* Friday.

Jantel nodded. "Yup, you should ask him, Tracy. And I can go with y'all."

Tracy shook her head with a grin. "Not this time."

Jantel sucked her teeth. "Oh, you're going solo on me now, Tracy?"

"That's right," Tracy piped.

A few boys whistled up the hall at her. Tracy ignored them.

Jantel said, "See, *everybody* is on you."

"I know, but when you look like *me* they can't help it," Tracy responded with a laugh. Her head was definitely getting big.

They went to their classes like any other day, but Tracy got real nervous when the final bell rang. She chewed gum violently to calm her nerves. She then slowly walked to her locker to get the books that she needed for homework. Other girls stared at her jealously.

Tracy didn't look around for Bob after school. Her nerves were too shot. In fact, she began to hope that he wouldn't show. Jantel walked alongside her.

"Hey girl, what's up?" a voice called from behind.

Tracy turned around and smiled, no longer nervous. "I didn't get your phone number yesterday," she said to him.

Bob acted as if he didn't hear her. "Check you out," he commented.

"They said you was flyy, but *damn!*" He looked inside of Tracy's coat to peep her leather suit. His breath smelled of marijuana, and his clothing was not as classy as it had been the day before.

Tracy looked him over. "So what 'chew want?" she asked snappishly.

"Oh, I just came to see you."

"Well."

Bob laughed at nothing. Tracy frowned at him.

"When you gon' come see me again?" he asked.

Jantel began to walk away, fanning herself. "This is too much heat for me," she joked.

"Hold up, Jantel, I'm coming with you. What did you say, Bob?" Tracy asked him, making him repeat himself. It was happening again; Tracy was quickly losing her interest.

"When you gon' come over again?" Bob repeated.

Tracy waved her hand in front of her mouth. "Dag, you been smokin' weed." It didn't seem to bother her before.

Bob grinned and said, "Yeah, we got *on* again."

"Was Travis with y'all?"

"Yeah, he was there." Bob was laughing at everything. "But umm, I'ma get back wit' 'chew. Aw'ight? I got something to do. I just wanted to see you right quick."

"All right then," Tracy told him, glad that he was leaving. She watched Bob walk away like a lunatic, bumping all into people with the sun making his dark curly hair shine. He was cute all right, but he was also damaging his looks by taking drugs.

Tracy turned to head home with Jantel. She asked, "Did you see how *on* he was?"

"Yeah. I thought you didn't notice," Jantel commented.

Tracy thought things over. "Dag, I don't know about him now. He was lookin' like a bum."

"He's still pretty though, Tracy."

"No, he ain't all that. His hair was all crazy-looking."

They laughed as they crossed Wayne Avenue.

Jantel asked, "Are you gonna get with him this weekend?"

"I don't know. I got this dance show tonight. I almost forgot about it, and I'm going to that party tomorrow."

"Carmen's party?" Jantel asked.

"Yeah. You goin', too?"

"Yeah, girl," Jantel answered excitedly. "Everybody's gonna be there. But I hate when them older guys come to the parties, like Mark and Peppy and them. All they do is cause trouble."

"How old are they?" Tracy wanted to know.

"Like sixteen or seventeen. Why, you like one of them?"

"No. But do you know Victor?"

Jantel looked at her and shook her head with a scowl. "Oh, no, girl, he's the main one," she said.

"Why you say that?"

"Because, he's *always* fightin' somebody."

Tracy nodded. "Yup, he beat this boy up just Wednesday night. Is he cute?" Tracy had heard that he was good-looking from several sources, but it didn't hurt to ask again.

"Yeah, he's cute," Jantel answered. She said it as if she hated to admit it.

Jantel's demeanor alarmed Tracy. "Why you say it like that?" she quizzed.

"Because, he uses girls to get what he wants. He ain't no damn good. He got *a lot* of girls. And they be all fallin' for his ruthless behind."

Tracy could never seem to keep one particular guy on her mind for any long stretch of time. Victor was good-looking, older *and* popular. He had a way with women and could fight. Tracy wanted to meet him so badly it was killing her. Her attraction to boys was impulsive. Tracy just had to have whomever she wanted right away. *Maybe he'll be at Carmen's party tomorrow night,* she pondered. And if he did show, Tracy planned on being ready for him.

. . .

The dance performance was a huge success. All of the parents and plenty of guests watched the sixteen girls display what they had learned over ten weeks of dance lessons on a large theater stage on Broad Street. Raheema was happy for the first time in a long time. She was receiving an opportunity to be rewarded for something other than report cards. She danced her heart away, especially for her father. She wanted him to be proud of her. Even Tracy's father, Dave, had made it out for the evening.

"Are you doing anything tomorrow night?" Tracy asked Raheema while gathering their things inside of the dressing room. She figured she would try and turn a new leaf with her neighbor.

"No. I have a lot of work to do," Raheema answered her, still overjoyed about the event.

"Do you think you can go to a party with me tomorrow?" Tracy pressed her.

Raheema shook her head, still smiling. "I'm not interested in parties."

"Why not?"

Raheema sighed, tired of having to explain things to Tracy. "Tracy, I'm just different from you. I mean, I don't get all excited about boys and parties and stuff."

"Well, you were excited about this show," Tracy reminded her.

"Yeah, because I was interested in this."

Well, I tried, Tracy thought. "Okay then."

Tracy got ready to go to the first big-time party of her life. It was "a dollar a holler" to get in. Everyone from the neighborhood would be there.

Tracy took a shower, washed and blow-dried her hair, put on some new underwear and snuck some of Patti's perfume. She decided to wear a blue silk shirt with an off-white vest and pants set with her blue suede boots. She clipped on all three of her gold chains and was ready to head to the party, smelling good and looking good. She called Jantel over so she wouldn't have to walk to the party by herself.

Plenty of teenagers were out that night, all heading to Carmen's house-party. Tracy eyed all of the young hoodlums, trying to spot the one that fit Victor's description. Only a few people were dancing when Tracy and Jantel had made it inside of the packed basement. It was still early, so most of the teens stood around bobbing to the DJ's beats.

Tracy recognized several of the boys whom she had had a crush on over the years. Aaron Barnes was there with his friends, Amir with his, and even Steve was there. They all gazed at her, remembering when she was theirs, wishing that they could have another chance.

Tracy had *never* looked as good as she did at Carmen's party. The high school girls were staring at her as well, as if Tracy was too much for her own good.

While waiting for Victor and the older guys to strut in, Tracy was shocked to see Travis and Bob walk through the door with their crew.

Bob noticed Tracy immediately. He then pulled her by her hand for a dance. Tracy refused him, but Bob wouldn't take "no" for an answer. He grabbed her hand and pushed her into a corner. "Come on, now, dance with me."

"Stop. I don't feel like it," Tracy told him, pulling away.

"Naw, you gon' dance with me," he persisted, smelling of marijuana again.

He dragged Tracy to the dance floor. She gave in, but she no longer cared how cute Bob was. He was a drug addict. She continued to watch the stairs for Victor over Bob's shoulder.

Peppy shouted down the steps as he crashed the party with eight other guys, "YO-O-O, THE BOYS ARE IN THE HOUSE!"

Tracy said, "Hold up, Bob, I'll be right back." She hastily jerked Jantel's hand through the packs of teenagers. "Which one is Victor?" she asked in Jantel's ear.

Jantel looked through the crowd to spot Victor. "He's not over there," she said, still squinting in the direction of the rowdy party-crashers.

Tracy was pressed. "Are you sure?"

"Yeah. I could spot him easily. Victor always stands out. He's not over there with them."

Across the room, a sleepy-eyed boy asked Peppy, "Yo, where Vic at, man?"

Peppy smiled. "He's wit' that flyy-ass girl we met downtown in The Gallery."

"Oh, for real? He's always with some girl, ain't he?"

"Ay, man, some of us got it like that."

the fast Lanes

A Loss of Virginity

"Come on, mom!"

"Look, girl, I said I was comin'!" Patti shouted.

Tracy was impatiently waiting with Jason, ready to go to the mall. "Dag, you always takin' all day."

"You know what, Tracy, if I hear you say another word, I'm gon' smack your mouth off!"

"Sit down, boy, dag. I'm tired of you," Tracy said, forcing Jason to sit on the couch. Patti stormed down the stairs and grabbed her. Tracy broke her hold, dashing quickly away to avoid her.

"Girl, come here, because I told you about that," Patti said, dressed in a purple jogging suit with white tennis shoes. Her daughter had thrown on some raggedy jeans and an old blue Guess shirt.

Tracy laughed. "What I do, mom?"

"See, you think I'm playing with you. Don't you? You keep acting up, Tracy, and you won't get any summer clothes."

"Come on, mom, it ain't even worth all that."

They went to the Cheltenham Mall to shop for summer outfits. Since

Carmen's party, nearly three months ago, Tracy still had not been able to see this guy named Victor. She had been to four more parties since then, and he was never there. Nevertheless, she continued to think about him.

Tracy and her mother shopped for bargains from one store to the next as Jason tagged along, pouting. Everyone was interested in Hawaiian shorts, so Tracy gathered several pair with matching colored socks. She bought two pair of sunglasses, a Hawaiian cloth pocketbook and a pair of white leather sandals.

Jason, tired of being cooped up inside of department stores, dashed away from his sister's hand after coming out of Gimbels. Tracy ran after him. Jason ran through and around people before she finally caught him. She then marched him back to Patti, who stood smiling. Jason twisted and pulled, trying to get away, but Tracy had a tight grip on his kid-sized jumper.

"He's fast, mom," she said, surprised.

"I know. Maybe he can run track or something."

"Yup. Maybe," Tracy agreed, maintaining a grip on her brother as he continued to try and twist free.

"N-o-o-o," he wailed.

Patti said, "Look, I'm going over to sit on this bench. Why don't you take him to get some ice cream?" She pointed to the store and gave Tracy five dollars.

Jason squealed, jumping up and down, "Y-a-a-a-y."

"Hold up, boy," Tracy told him.

She ordered eggnog for her brother and butter pecan for herself. She then noticed a couple walking toward her as she and Jason headed back to their mother. The boy was slightly taller than Tracy, wearing a white Adidas sweat suit and Nike sneakers. His dark, chocolate-brown skin vividly stood out from the bright white clothing he wore. His face was smoothly handsome, and he had a sharp blocked haircut with an attractive pair of connecting eyebrows. His confident smile soothed Tracy's soul.

The girl he was with was the same bright, honey-brown tone as

Tracy, with short-cut asymmetric hair. She was wearing sunglasses, a pair of Hawaiian-colored pants, a red shirt, and matching red socks, and she was carrying a light-brown leather pocketbook.

Tracy felt embarrassed that she had left the house wearing a pair of wrinkled pants and a shirt. She was envious because *she* did not have a boyfriend to walk hand-in-hand inside of the mall with. Her butter pecan ice cream cone had lost its flavor. Tracy walked back to her mother, long-faced.

"What's wrong with you?" Patti asked her.

"Nothin'," Tracy responded, sitting on the bench next to her mother.

"Shucks, girl, you look like you just lost your best friend."

Tracy chuckled, continuing to stare at the couple. The forgotten ice cream began to drip down her hands.

"Look what you're doing. It's getting all over you," her mother warned her.

"I got it, mom!" Tracy licked her hand, watching as the couple ordered their own ice cream, and the girl paid for it. They began to walk through the mall again as a crew of boys hurried from behind to catch up to them.

One boy shouted, "YO VIC! HOLD UP, MAN!"

Tracy immediately sat alert, appearing to be energized. It was *him!*

The boys shook Victor's hand as his girlfriend waited at his side. Tracy was pressed to get another look at him. She waited for his friends to leave, and then watched as Victor and his Hawaiian-dressed companion went inside of a record store.

"Mom, I'll be right back," she told her mother.

"Boy, your sister thinks she's grown," Patti said to her son as she watched her daughter switching through the mall.

Tracy strolled into the record store plotting on getting close to Victor, but Hawaiian-girl was too close to him. She held three cassette tapes in her hand: New Edition, Rick James and DeBarge. Tracy took peeks at Victor's handsome dark face as she skimmed through the Pop section. He had perfect features. *He does look pretty,* she thought as she watched him.

When Tracy decided to circle them, Victor caught her eye. For an instant, she was breathless as her heart jumped with excitement. Victor quickly turned away, and Tracy felt broken-hearted, yearning for his attention.

She walked out, slowly, misled by her attraction to him and thinking, *He'll never talk to me.* Victor, like a train, zoomed by her with money in his hands. Tracy quickened her pace behind him to see where he was headed. Victor stopped in the middle of her path, like a car at a red light. Tracy slowed down, feeling silly while she wondered if he knew that she was following him. She thought then about her sloppy clothes and wished she had never gotten close. But Victor smiled at her.

"Ay, come here. Ain't your name Tracy?" he asked.

She obediently came to him. "Yeah. How you know?" she asked, gasping.

"Because, I heard you was one of the flyyest young-girls around the way. And I've seen you before," he told her. "You live on Diamond Lane, right?" he asked, looking over her tall curved frame.

Tracy's rep had surprisingly grown. *Even* Victor *has heard about me,* she told herself with a grin. "How you know that?" she wanted to know.

"Oh, I've been watchin' you," he said, backing away with a smile that was worth taking a picture of.

Patti noticed their brief chat as her daughter headed back to the bench. "Are you ready to go?" she asked.

Tracy nodded as her mother got up from her rest with her son in hand and walked toward the exit.

"Do you know that boy you were talking to?" Patti asked her daughter, curiously.

"Yeah," Tracy lied, keeping her cool. She didn't really know him; she had only heard things about him while longing to meet him one day.

"Well, that boy is somethin' else," Patti responded.

Tracy lost her poise. "Why you say that?" she asked, excitedly.

Patti shook her head. "He was at the hoagie shop with a whole heap

of guys and beat some boy up. I felt sorry for the boy, but to hell if I
was gonna get involved in it with the way these kids act today. They
don't have respect for anyone."

"Why, what he do?" Tracy asked.

"The boy apparently said he was gonna get him for messing with
his girlfriend. Yup, girl, this was three nights ago, when I was coming
home from work."

"Well, how come you didn't tell me about that?"

Patti frowned. "What, I have to *report* to my thirteen-year-old
daughter everything I see or do? I didn't figure that you knew the boy.
How old is he anyway?"

"Sixteen."

"Sixteen! God, that boy looks young," Patti responded, shocked.
"He got one of those baby faces. He looks your age, to me."

Tracy chuckled as they climbed inside of the car in the parking
lot.

Patti began to think about her husband, Dave, and his baby face. She
missed not being able to share everything with him. A half of a man
didn't seem like much of a man at all. Yet no one else interested her.
She had tried the dating game before, only to come up empty, especially with Dave popping up around them the way he did.

"Tracy, would you like to go to the movies with us?" Patti suddenly
asked her daughter.

Tracy looked puzzled. "I didn't know y'all were going to the movies," she said, looking back at Jason, who sat fastened inside of the
backseat without a clue.

"Well, I figured since we're already up here and it's still early, then
why not?"

Tracy thought about getting home to tell Jantel the news. She then
noticed the empty look on her mother's face and made an easy decision.
Her mother was lonely. "Okay, mom. I'll go."

Patti looked as if a huge burden had been lifted from her shoulders.
She had not been spending much time with her children while sweating
over her situation with Dave, and even though it was only a movie, it
was better than going back to an empty house.

Tracy then convinced her mother to walk back through the mall instead of driving around to the theater.

"You just want to see that boy again," Patti told her with a smile.

Tracy giggled. *That's right,* she thought. Yet Victor was nowhere in sight.

Once they had arrived back at home, Tracy put her new clothes away and went outside to sit on her steps before the sun went down. It was a beautiful Saturday in April. She felt wonderful after meeting Victor. He had the self-assurance of a king and was charming like a prince. He even seemed thoughtful and informed. *He probably knows more about me than I know about him,* Tracy mused. *And his eyes; they just go right through you!* If he ever touched her, Tracy thought she would lose control. No wonder Victor had so many girls. He made her feel special, filling her day with just a minute of his time, and he said that he was watching her.

Raheema and her mother pulled up in Beth's new Toyota Tercel after they had gone shopping.

"Hi, Tracy," Beth perked before going in.

Raheema stopped to chat with her neighbor.

"How are you doing, Tracy?" she asked, as if she felt good about something. Raheema appearing to be excited was a rarity. She took her bags in and returned to sit on Tracy's lower step. Tracy was speechless as she observed her, envying Raheema's long brown ponytail. *She just gotta show that hair off!* Tracy thought.

"So what's been up, Tracy?" Raheema asked, sounding more hip than her usual Catholic-school self.

"Nothin'. What about you?" Tracy answered, tight-lipped. She was still wondering what her neighbor was so happy about.

"I'm going to a play tonight," Raheema informed her without being asked.

Tracy smirked. *So that's what it is.* "A play? For what?" she queried, frowning as if it was corny.

Raheema frowned back at her. She felt that Tracy was acting child-ish, afraid to try new things. "Because it's cultural."

Tracy could imagine it, a bunch of white people talking at the top of their lungs about Shakespeare and music and art and about the torture of love. Yet Patti had taken her to a few African-American plays at the Freedom's Theater when she was younger. Maybe a play wouldn't be as bad as she thought.

"Is it a black play?" she asked with new interest.

Raheema shook her head. "No."

Tracy grunted, "Hmm." *So she's going to see some white people like I thought,* she reflected. "Jantel is having her party tonight," she informed her neighbor. She knew Raheema wouldn't care, but she decided to tell her about it anyway.

"Skinny Jantel? I'm not going to her party."

"Jantel ain't all that skinny no more," Tracy commented, defending her friend. Over the years, Jantel had become her *best* friend. They had spent the most time together.

"Well, you know how I feel about parties," Raheema said noncha-lantly. She was sick of telling Tracy.

Tracy shook her head. "I don't know how you're ever gonna grow up, if you all worried about boys using you and stuff," she alluded. Raheema's fear of boys was her real reason for her not liking parties. *She probably can't even dance,* Tracy figured.

"Whatever," Raheema retorted.

"Yeah, okay, girl, but you can't run from boys your whole life, so you better get used to them now," Tracy piped.

Raheema stood up to go in. "Well, most likely, when I'm older, I doubt if it will be *boys* that I'm interested in," she remarked.

"Smart-ass," Tracy mumbled as her neighbor excused herself.

Tracy got ready for Jantel's party after eating. She was certain Victor would be there.

"What time can I expect you back in?" her mother asked her.

Tracy was apprehensive. Patti had never asked her what time, she had always told her to be home before the midnight curfew. "Ah, I don't know," Tracy stammered, confused.

"Well, since it's Jantel, you can stay later if you like," Patti told her.

Tracy was visibly pleased. "For real, mom?"

Her mother nodded to her. "Yeah, as long as you don't leave the party and go off some-damn-where with some boy, getting into something you don't have no business getting in," she warned with a raised index finger.

Tracy sucked her teeth. "I'm not gonna do that, mom."

"All right then, you can stay out later. And I want you to call me before you decide to head home."

"All right," Tracy perked. *Dag, I need to hang out with my mother more often. That movie put her in a good mood,* she told herself. She sat around watching TV until it got late. The latecomers always attracted the crowds. The party started at nine, but it was after ten before Tracy finally decided to go.

"What are you doing?" Patti asked her.

Tracy grinned as she stood up from the living-room couch and walked over to turn the television off. "I'm leaving right now, mom. I just wanted to walk in a little late."

Patti grimaced, reflecting to when she was a teen. "Mmm hmm," she grumbled, "you just make sure you remember what I told you."

Tracy shook her head, heading for the front door. "I'm not gonna run off with no boy, mom. I promise."

"Okay," Patti told her teenaged daughter.

Tracy walked through the empty streets toward her best girlfriend's house, hoping that everyone would already be there, particularly Victor.

"Ay, what's up, Tracy? Why you stop callin' me?" Travis asked, catching her on the street.

"Because," she responded, still walking.

As usual, Travis was high on drugs. He jumped at her and yanked her by the arm. "Hold up, girl. I don't appreciate that shit. You don't just brush me off."

Tracy shouted, "Get off of me!"

Travis let her go after seeing how serious she was. He stood back and admired her beautiful body and fashionable dress.

Tracy arrived at the party and greeted Jantel, who was collecting dollars at the door.

"What took you so long, Ms. Thang?"

"I had to do somethin' for my mother," Tracy lied. She then cracked an enormous smile. "Is Victor here yet?"

"Unt unh," Jantel told her. "I haven't seen him."

"Are you sure?" Tracy asked, still pressed.

Jantel looked at her as if her girlfriend was crazy. "I'm at the door ain't I?" she huffed.

Tracy smirked and walked in.

Victor was sneaking out of a girl's back door on a nearby street. He stopped to have a few last-minute words with her. "Was it good?" He wore a yellow Izod jacket and blue Calvin Klein jeans. The girl wore a pink terry-cloth bathrobe, and nothing else.

"Yeah," she said, smiling.

Victor asked her as he gently held her hand, "So are you in love with me now?"

"Yeah," she responded in a daze. She was a pretty brown-skin, but Victor had messed up her hairdo with his passion, running his hands wildly through her hair during their teenaged lovemaking.

Victor asked, "When you want me to come over again?"

"Whenever you want to," she answered him.

Victor's grin was sinister. "It's up to you."

The pretty brown-skinned girl nodded her head with a long, passionate stare. "All right then. You can come over after school, Monday."

Victor asked, "Are you sure you want me to?" It was part of his game, to make her surrender to his young and powerful ego.

"Yeah, I want you to," she answered, nearly hypnotized.

Mission accomplished, Victor smiled and gave her a kiss. Then he ran off for home.

· · ·

Victor was sure he could charm his way inside Jantel's party. He showered up, redressed, patted on some Grey Flannel cologne and sprinted from his house. He didn't even carry a dollar with him to pay.

"Come on, Jantel. If I had a party, I would let you in free," he argued at Jantel's front door.

Jantel was far from believing him. "The only reason I'ma let you in is because my girlfriend wanted to see you," she said, running her big mouth.

"What girlfriend?"

"My girl, Tracy."

"Oh, she was looking for me, hunh?" Victor said, smiling. He grinned, planning on seducing Tracy.

Victor walked down into the basement and gave Tracy a wink. Tracy thought he would stop and talk, but Victor strolled over to chat with his slim-brown friend, Mark Bates.

Mark asked, "Yo, what up, lover? Did 'ju hit it?"

Victor said with a smile, "What, you don't know? You better ask somebody," he bragged of his sexual conquest. "Man, she in love with me now. I tore that ass up like a god. Ask her about it, she'll tell you."

Victor knew that Tracy was watching him. Jantel gave up her info, and told him everything. Victor could do that to a girl, make her give up her soul for a hint of his young love. He decided to have a little fun with Tracy, doing what he did best, playing head games. He floated over to a light-brown-skinned girl, who was already waiting for him.

"I thought you said you was gonna call me, Victor?"

Victor gamed her; in other words, he made up a clever response to keep her interested. "I would have called you, but I just got back from shopping with my brother. He wouldn't let me use his car phone," he outright lied.

"Your brother has a car phone?"

Victor shrugged. "Yeah. It's no big deal, especially if he won't let me use it." He moved closer to her, feeling over her body, compelling

her to try and kiss him. Victor then moved away, successfully teasing
her as she began to whine to him:

"Why you playin' with me?"

The guys envied Victor and admired him, especially when he was at
work with the girls. He was their hero.

Tracy watched, jealously, from a distance.

"I just don't feel like kissin' right now."

"Why, you got new girlfriend in here?" the girl assumed. "See,
Victor, you get on my damn nerves," she responded, pretending to
push him away. She loved the attention that he was giving her.

Victor said, "Look, 'Sam,' are your parents asleep yet?" He was up
against the wall with her.

"I'on know," she responded.

"Well, if you want, I could come over tonight," he suggested, nonchalantly. He couldn't let her think that he was actually excited about
it.

Samantha answered him quickly, "I don't care."

Victor stared into her soft brown eyes. "But do you want me to?"

Samantha snapped, weary of his teasing, "I said, yeah."

"No you didn't. You said you don't care," he corrected her.

She smiled, bashfully, at his quick wit.

Tracy was fed up! She romped back up the stairs.

"So what time should I come over?" Victor asked the girl.

"I'on know."

"What time will your parents go to sleep tonight?"

"I'on know. They'll probably be waiting up for me."

Victor leaned over to whisper. "Aw'ight, look 'Sam,' why don't you
go home and act like you sleepin' so they won't wait up for you. Then,
around one o'clock, I'll come around and sneak in your basement."

Samantha was tickled by the idea. "Aw'ight then," she agreed,
impressed at how sneaky he was.

Victor looked to see that Tracy had left. He then turned and kissed
her. "You feel better now?"

"Yeah," Samantha said, licking her lips.

Victor sent her home and halted at the steps. He didn't want Tracy to see him until Samantha had left.

"He a trip. I hate that boy," Tracy was telling Jantel. She hushed herself when she noticed the light-brown-skinned girl whom Victor had been attending inside of the basement.

Jantel asked, "You're going home already, Samantha?"

Samantha lied, minding her own business, "Yeah, because I gotta go to church early tomorrow."

Jantel nodded and led her to the door, returning to Tracy. "See, that girl used to go with Victor," she said.

"Yeah, he was just talkin' to her in the basement."

Victor popped his head up from the basement door.

"Ay Tracy, come here. I wanna dance with you," he said, as if it was a closed case.

Tracy declined. "Naw, that's all right."

"Well excuuuse me," he said, smiling.

Victor left, returning to a crowded basement. Jantel smiled at Tracy in the kitchen while she fixed hot dogs.

"Are those the last of the hot dogs?" Jantel's mother asked, walking into the kitchen with them. She was tall, but not half as slender as Jantel was.

"Yeah, that's the last of them," Jantel answered her.

"Well, that's it," her mother commented. "Them greedy niggas don't get no more. They'll eat you out of a house and home."

The girls giggled as Jantel's mother began to straighten up the kitchen. They then decided to finish their discussion inside of the living room.

Tracy whispered to her friend excitedly, "Should I go dance with him?" She hoped that Jantel would say "Yes," so she could blame her if anything went wrong.

"It's up to you," Jantel said, knowing Tracy too well.

"But do you *think* I should?"

Jantel smirked. "If you want to," she said, keeping it Tracy's decision.

Tracy headed down the steps to search for him. Victor was already with another girl, but he promptly stopped dancing when he saw Tracy.

He walked over and asked her sternly, "So do you wanna dance with me or what?"

Tracy answered him, feeling privileged, "I don't care."

Victor led her through the crowds and to the DJ. "Ay yo, Spin, put 'Computer Love' on for me and this sweetheart."

DJ Spin said, "Man, she a sweet little chumpee, cuz', wit' pretty-ass eyes. Aw'ight then, I'll play it after this."

Tracy wanted to thank the T-shirt-wearing DJ for commenting on her eyes, but she didn't receive a chance to. Victor whisked her back to the dance floor, with his friends making room for them on demand. Tracy was impressed by the amount of respect they gave him. Victor had the party in check.

"So you changed your mind about dancin' wit' me, hunh?" he whispered.

Tracy responded harshly, "I'm dancing with you, ain't I?" She wanted to establish respect, but Victor just smiled. He slow-dragged with her, rubbing her firm behind and starting to lick behind her ear. Tracy's nipples hardened.

Victor whispered as he ran his fingers down the back of her thighs, "Do you like me?" He licked her neck as everyone watched in amazement. "I know you like me. Don't you?"

"Yeah," Tracy admitted, no longer caring.

Victor ran his hands to her lips and kissed her, only to pull away when she got into it. He then led her to the wall and leaned up against her as Tracy tossed her hands around his back. Victor started to kiss her again, rowing her body side to side, back and forth with his. He was possessing her, doing what he did best.

"Computer Love," by Zapp, went off. DJ Spin followed up with "Do Me Baby," by Mel'isa Morgan.

Victor whispered through the song, positioning Tracy's mouth, "Stop kissing so hard. Do it slowly." He then stopped and looked into her twinkling hazels. "Do you want my phone number? 'Cause I'm 'bout t' roll out of here."

"Yeah," Tracy answered.

Victor wrote his number on a piece of paper for her and left the party.

For the rest of the night, Tracy did nothing but think about how romantic he was. She already suspected that she would lose her virginity to him, only wondering when their moment of love would be.

Victor walked up to Samantha's door with a cocky stroll as he wet his lips with his tongue. He walked right into her basement and sat on a couch to take his shoes off. Samantha wore a gray bathrobe, with only her panties and bra on under it.

"You feel nervous?" he asked.

"No."

"Are your parents sleepin' yet?"

Samantha watched him take off his clothes, "Yeah, they sleep. They went to bed an hour ago."

"Did you bring a blanket down here?"

"Yeah, Victor, but why do we have to *do it* on the floor?"

"Because it gives you more leverage and it feels better," he told her, opening her robe.

Samantha was fifteen, with a tender body that was without scars. "Don't do it so fast, 'cause I like it slow," she told him.

Victor said, "Look, once it starts feelin' good, it's hard for me to slow down." He slid off her underwear and unclipped her bra, bringing her to the floor with him to lie over a soft blanket.

Sam wrapped her legs around his as Victor kissed her naked body and guided himself inside of her, gripping her by the waist and slowly thrusting. He then increased his speed, beginning to pound into her.

Samantha ran her hands to his hips and attempted to slow down his pace. She could feel herself shaking under his weight. She then pulled his body down to hers, wildly caressing his back and neck.

Victor pulled away when she had finished and started up again as if life itself depended on his speed. He flexed overtop of her, losing his poise and crashing back to her chest as he began to suck in air. And they laid there in fresh sweat, completed and not wanting to move, remaining for an hour, until Victor snuck back home.

"Was you at Jantel's party Saturday?" Carmen asked Tracy that Monday at school.

"Yeah. Why you ask me that?" Tracy wanted to know. She wondered if something was wrong.

"Was Mark Bates there?" Carmen asked her.

"Yeah," Tracy responded, shutting her locker.

"That boy is a liar then," Carmen snapped. "He told me he was gonna be at his grandmother's house."

"Do you talk to him or somethin'?" Tracy quizzed.

Carmen smiled and said, "Yeah, sorta."

"You know Victor, that hangs with him?"

Carmen got excited. "Yeah, that boy is *the shit*. He got everything uptight."

"He does?" Tracy responded with a smile. She already knew how well-respected Victor was, but she didn't mind hearing it again and again; it all increased her liking of him.

They dodged junior high school students walking the hallway.

Carmen said, "Yeah, and his brother plays basketball for college. He be on TV and everything."

"How old is his brother?"

"Like, twenty."

"And everybody knows Victor?"

Carmen grinned, curiously. "Why, you talkin' to him?"

"No, I just met him," Tracy answered, minding her own business.

"Well, everybody knows Victor Hinson."

"That's his last name?"

"Yup, because I remember when he played for the Raiders."

"He played for the Raiders?"

"Yeah," Carmen said. "He was number twenty-four on defense. He was on the older pound team."

They hurried to their classes with Tracy thinking about how popular *she* could become from hanging out with Victor. More people talked about him after class. He was in high school, yet all of the students in junior high knew of his rep, and he was known all throughout the neighborhood of Germantown. He even borrowed his brother's white Jetta, driving around on missions to entice unsuspecting girls. *And he wanted* me *to have his phone number,* Tracy mused happily.

The final bell for school rang, and Tracy hurried out of the building. To her surprise, she then was surrounded by interrogating younger girls.

"Ay, Tracy, I heard you was kissing Victor at the party?"

"Yeah," she answered, not caring if they knew.

"You gon' go with him?"

"I don't know," she said, heading home and feeling proud.

"Well, you should, because I would."

Tracy got home and found a boy talking to her next-door neighbor, Raheema. She decided to eavesdrop while sitting out on her steps.

The boy asked, "Can I have your phone number?" His sharp brown face shone under a yellow Kangol hat.

"I told you 'no,' four times already. God!" Raheema snapped at him.

"Why not?"

"Because I said 'no.' " Raheema darted in the house and left the boy outside with Tracy. Tracy smiled at him, hunching her shoulders.

He asked her, "Why she act like that?"

"Because her father is mean as hell and she always be trying to please him. I'd say, 'Bunk him,' if I was her."

"Is he a big dude?"

"NO!" Tracy exclaimed with a laugh. "You'd probably kick *his* ass. He ain't nothin'."

The Kangol-hat-wearing boy laughed himself before heading off. "Tell Raheema that I like her anyway," he said.

Tracy knocked on Raheema's door. Raheema let her in.

"Why was you so mean to him?" Tracy asked her. "That boy was nice."

"So what, Tracy? I just wish that they would leave me alone," Raheema told her. "You can have them, all of them."

Tracy smirked and shook her head, vehemently. "Girl, you're just stupid!" she said, leaving back out. Raheema didn't pay her any mind.

Tracy had been told to begin picking up her brother at four o'clock each afternoon from a new nearby day-care center he would be attending. She had completely forgotten about it even after Patti had reminded her several times. Patti came home with Jason in hand and was pissed.

"Tracy, I thought I told you to pick him up?"

Tracy cringed and threw her hands to her face. "Oh my God, mom, I forgot all about it."

"Mmm hmm," Patti mumbled. "I ask you to do something as small as that, and you can't remember."

"Dag, mom, it was only the first day."

Patti frowned at her. "I had been reminding you for weeks, Tracy. I mean, what the hell is on your mind, girl? I told you to pick him up this morning."

"I know, mom, but I forgot. Dag! You act like he's gonna die or something."

Patti looked at her daughter sternly. "This is about responsibility, Tracy. Now if I can't count on you to help me out around here, then don't count on me to do you any favors."

Tracy immediately reflected on being able to stay late at Jantel's party. "Well, I didn't ask to stay later at Jantel's party. You said that I could." Her mother was being petty.

"This ain't about a damn party, Tracy. This is about you acting more responsible around here," Patti fumed. "Now don't forget to pick him up tomorrow." She angrily took off her jacket and set her bags down before walking into the kitchen. "And what did I tell you about these damn dishes?" she screamed at her daughter from the kitchen.

Tracy walked into the kitchen and washed the dishes without a word. Patti left her alone and went up the stairs to her room, feeling a touch of guilt. She was losing control of her emotions, but to hell if she was going to apologize. No one apologized to her. *I guess I'm just supposed to do every-damn-thing around here,* she huffed to herself. She closed her door and stretched out on her bed to take herself a nap. *I don't feel like cooking shit tonight. I'll just order them some pizza,* she decided. *I need a damn vacation. Calgon, take me away.*

"I don't believe she's all mad at me just because I forgot to pick him up *one* day," Tracy was saying to herself inside of the kitchen. "Everybody makes mistakes."

She finished washing the dishes and decided to give Victor a call to take her mind off of her unstable mother. Jason was watching the late cartoons inside the living room.

Victor answered Tracy's call on the first ring. "Hello."

Tracy greeted him without volunteering her name. "What's up?"

"It's about time you called," he told her.

Tracy was confused. "Who you think this is?" she quizzed, praying that he wouldn't call her by another girl's name. He had only given her his number two nights ago. But Victor knew his girls. No one else would play on his phone, so it had to be Tracy. Tracy was not trained, yet.

"It's Tracy, right?" he guessed.

"Yeah," she answered, surprised.

"I thought you was gon' call me earlier," he told her.

"I was, but I ain't get a chance to," she lied to him. Tracy laid out across the couch, wishing that he was there with her instead of her brother, Jason.

Victor responded nonchalantly, "Oh, aw'ight."

Tracy asked, "What are you doing tomorrow?"

"I'on know. Why?" Victor quizzed, thinking she may ask him to come over. *This girl might be faster than I thought,* he mused.

"Won't you come see me tomorrow, at my school?" Tracy asked him, sounding as innocent as her tender age.

Victor smiled. Tracy wanted to show him off. "Aw'ight. What time do you get out?"

"Three o'clock," she responded, as if he should have known.

Victor snapped, "Don't get smart, girl, 'cause I don't have to come."

Tracy played it off. "Sike, I was only playin'. But I gotta go now because my mom has to use the phone."

Victor grinned, knowing that she was lying. He shook his head. *Yup, she needs a little discipline,* he thought. *She thinks that she's playing me for a sucker, but I got something for her.* "Aw'ight then. I'll check you out tomorrow."

Tracy happily hung up the phone. She was pleased with herself for standing her ground with Victor, and for getting him to agree to come see her after school.

Mark Bates asked, "Who was that?" He sat wide-eyed and slim-brown in the chair across from Victor.

Victor said, "That was that young-girl named Tracy."

"Oh, the chumpee that lives on Diamond Lane?" Mark said with a grin. "She a tough little junh, cuz'. She looks *damn* good."

Victor smiled and said, "Yeah, I know." He kicked his Fila's up on the old, brown coffee table in front of him.

Mark said, "Yeah, she dimed on me, too. She told my young-girl, Carmen, that she saw me at the party and shit."

Victor chuckled, looking at himself inside of a hand mirror. "That's why you don't give no alibis to no young-girls, cuz'. You just tell 'em that you got somethin' to do. If they press you about where you gon' be, just tell 'em that it's business. Girls like shit like that. As long as they think you out making money, it's cool."

Mark laughed. "You be knowin' these young-girls, hunh, cuz'?"

"Damn right," Victor said. "I done had too many not to. Plus, my brother used to school girls constantly, so I kinda picked the game up from him."

Tracy wore another classy outfit to school the next morning. She wore a pair of sunshades around her neck for a fashion statement. She planned on bragging about Victor all day long.

Tracy said, while strutting up the hall, "Yup, Jantel, and then I told him I had to get off the phone before I messed it up. I was kind of nervous."

Jantel smirked. "For real? I would have been nervous talking to him, too. I'm nowhere near his league," she admitted. *You ain't either, Tracy,* she thought of saying. Then again, Tracy had gotten all of the other boys she had gone after, so maybe she could get Victor.

"Well, he's gonna be up here for me today," Tracy continued to brag. She opened her locker to get out her books for the next class, and Travis' long arms grabbed her swinging door.

"So, I heard you talkin' to Vic," he said to her.

"Could you *get* off my locker, please?"

Travis was getting on Tracy's last nerve.

"Aw, bitch, don't get loud with me. He's only gon' *fuck you* and leave, anyway!" he lashed out at her disrespectfully.

"Yeah, aw'ight," Tracy responded in a low tone. She was afraid that Travis might haul off and punch her if she provoked him. But Travis laughed and walked off, swinging his long, reckless arms.

"He ain't shit," Tracy told Jantel as soon as he had left. "He's just mad because I didn't give him nothin'. The old drugged-up dog."

Tracy went to all of her classes on time, for a change, waiting anxiously for the final bell to ring. She walked out of the building with much anticipation and found that Victor was nowhere in sight. Travis laughed in her face and called her some more names. Tracy was embarrassed with a capital "E." She had practically told the entire school that "Victor's coming to walk me home today."

When Victor didn't show, Tracy appeared to be either a fool or a liar to all of her peers. Either way, she was obviously not pleased with it. She rushed right home to give Victor a piece of her mind.

Tracy howled over the phone, "Ay Victor, why you stand me up?"

"Oh, I was tryin' to get up there, but I had to get this book from the library to do this report. I'm just walking in the door now," he quickly lied to her. "And another thing, don't you *ever* get an attitude with me. I'm not one of your young-boys," he snapped.

Tracy was startled. "Oh, my fault. I didn't know that. I'm sorry."

Victor then filled her head with his game. "Yup, I was just about to come around there to see you. But you know what? To hell with that now."

"I said I was sorry," Tracy pleaded.

"Naw, fuck 'dat. That 'sorry' shit don't change nothin'. You think I'm one of those suckers you be dealin' with."

Tracy whined, "No I don't. Please come see me, Victor."

Victor said, "Aw'ight, I'll be around there, just as soon as you're ready for me to come."

"I'm ready," Tracy said thoughtlessly.

"No you're not, and don't call me back until you've thought about it."

Victor hung up on her ear. Tracy looked at her receiver, realizing what he was referring to. And he was right, she wasn't ready.

Tracy then went to pick up Jason from the new day-care center. Peppy, a mean-spirited, light-skinned boy whom Tracy never liked approached them on the sidewalk as they headed back home. To Tracy, Peppy was mad at the world and set on destroying it.

"Ay, dummy," he said to her, unprovoked. He was walking toward her and Jason from the middle of the street.

"Who you talkin' to?" Tracy asked, frowning at him.

Peppy let out a sinister laugh as he came closer.

Tracy quickened her step, pulling Jason along to get them away from him.

Peppy said acidly, "What you runnin' for, you little stupid bitch?"

Tracy was stunned. "Now why you gon' say that to me, Peppy? I didn't say shit to you." Little Jason stared at him. "God, I can't stand you, boy!" Tracy shouted.

"Girl, you ain't all that."

"Ay yo, Peppy, leave her alone, man!" Victor shouted from up the street. He wore a red, white and blue baseball hat, a navy blue Members Only jacket and blue-jeans.

Peppy said nervously, "My fault, man, I didn't know you was talkin' to her."

"I don't care if I was talkin' to her or not, cuz', you gots to stop fuckin' wit' people," Victor snapped at him. He stopped right in front of Tracy and her brother. Peppy shut his mouth and headed on his way. Tracy stood with Jason, impressed.

Victor asked Jason, "What's up, cool?" He extended his hand for a shake. Jason smiled shyly and shook Victor's gold-ringed hand. Tracy got bubbly inside.

"I used to have a jacket like this when I was young," Victor told Jason as he pointed to the miniature baseball logo on Jason's jacket. Jason wore a matching red hat. "He a cute little dude. He gon' be like me when he grow up. Ain't 'chew?" Victor asked him.

Jason cracked a smile and imitated Victor as he nodded his head.

"So what's your name, cool?"

"Tell him, 'Jay-son,' " Tracy said, sounding it out with him.

Her brother bashfully raised his hands to his mouth.

Victor chuckled, grabbing the brim of his hat, and giving his full attention to Tracy. She was admiring his every move. "You remember what I said, right?" he asked her, licking his brown lips. His smooth and pretty dark face glimmered whenever the sunlight slipped under his hat.

"Yeah," Tracy answered, like clay in Victor's hands.

"Aw'ight then. I'll be *waitin'* for that call," Victor told her as he headed off on his way.

Jason squeaked, "Who is that?"

"Victor Hinson," Tracy answered him, loving even the sound of his name. Victor Hinson was *the shit*.

Tracy stretched out in her bed that night, feeling herself and wishing that it was Victor. She wanted to know what it would *feel* like to make love. She imagined how it would happen, envisioning Victor on top of her, kissing down her neck and to her breasts, and then sucking and caressing them with his dark fingers running down to her stomach. She imagined herself, cupping his pretty face inside of her hands and begging for more as he moved with her, like two human snakes as they passionately kissed again and again, like they did in the movies.

Tracy wanted to know what it would *feel* like to have someone *do it* to her. She took her morning shower and felt all over her body, making herself excited as the warm water tingled her. She kissed the shower walls and ran her hands between her legs, thinking that she had gone absolutely crazy. And then she knew that it was time to lose her virginity.

Tracy could not wait for Victor to take her. Her newly developed body was ready for exploration, and she was tired of waiting. She couldn't concentrate on anything, while continuously day-dreaming about Victor *doing it* to her.

At lunchtime in school, Tracy inadvertently listened to more girl talk going on at the far end of her table:

"Yup, and she said he got her like ten times," a short and chubby girl was saying. She reminded Tracy of her elementary school girl-friend Judy.

"Well, I told him I wasn't into that, 'cause he a nut anyway," a taller girl responded.

"For real, Paula? You said that?"

"Yeah, 'cause you just don't *give it* to boys if they don't know how to *get it,*" Paula said. She was as light as Raheema, but her hair was snap short.

"He must be stupid then, 'cause you nasty as hell," her short-and-chubby friend responded.

Tracy giggled to herself.

Paula laughed. "I know, some boys believe anything you tell 'em. Like this guy named Bruce, I told him that I was pregnant, so I couldn't do nothin' with him."

The girls howled with laughter.

Short-and-chubby said, "You crazy, girl. Well, who did you give some to?"

Paula told her, "Light-skinned Jeff, and umm, curly-headed Aaron. That's all."

Tracy snickered at her end of the table. She got up to leave for class, feeling that she was above *their* level. They were only talking about small-time guys. Tracy considered herself in the major leagues.

She rushed home, hoping to catch Victor in his house when she called. At first she was reluctant to dial his number, quick to change her mind about her decision to lose her virginity to him. But after beating out her fear, she forced herself.

"Hello. Can I speak to Victor?" she asked, recognizing an older voice.

"Victor's not home." He rudely hung up the line before Tracy was able to leave a message.

Tracy felt deprived. *Rude bastard!* she snapped.

Patti told her that she would be going out Friday night, and that Tracy would have to watch Jason. "I'm not gonna let my life rot away while your father acts like an asshole," she grumbled.

Tracy immediately started to plot. Later on that night, she called Victor again, but no one answered his line. It tortured her that she couldn't get in contact with him. For the first time, Tracy felt satisfied with a guy without losing her interest.

The next day, Tracy called Victor once again to no avail. After Patti had arrived at home that evening, Tracy ran out to the store on Chelten Avenue, seven blocks away from her house, supposedly because she needed some school supplies. While out on the street, Tracy made sure to walk down Wayne Avenue, where Victor was known to hang out. The avenue seemed packed with everyone but him. She spotted Peppy and wanted to leave Victor a message, but never through *him.* She then bumped into Mark Bates before heading back to Chelten.

"Hey, Mark, I heard you talkin' to my girl Carmen," she said to him, grinning away.

Mark nodded lightheartedly. "Yeah, she told me that you dimed on me," he responded.

Tracy smiled, filled with guilt.

"Unh hunh, keep on smiling," Mark joked with her.

Tracy wasted no time. "Have you seen Victor?" she asked.

"Why?"

"Because I had something to tell him."

Without explanation, Mark abruptly pulled Tracy's arm and led her around the corner.

"Where are you takin' me?" Tracy asked him, puzzled by his sudden actions.

"Don't you live up this way?"

"Yeah, but I didn't want you to walk me."

Mark pushed Tracy toward her house anyway. "So what you want me to tell Victor?" he finally asked her.

"Just tell him that my mom is goin' out Friday night."

Mark smiled, proud of his boy's successful job of turning Tracy out. *Damn! I wish I had it like Vic,* he thought to himself. "Aw'ight then," he told Tracy. "I'll tell him."

Tracy, still wondering why he had run her around the corner, dismissed it and walked home. She was pleased that she had dropped her message off.

Mark headed back toward Wayne Avenue and approached his buddy. "Ay Vic, come here for a minute." Victor was with yet another attractive teenaged girl, waiting for the bus to take her home. "Tracy was just down here," Mark told his admirable friend. "I saw you coming and I ran her around the corner."

Victor looked back at the slender, tanned-skinned beauty and smiled, making sure she would not get suspicious of their conversation.

"Yo, she's flyy as shit, cuz'," Mark commented about the girl, who was wearing a shiny red Adidas sweat suit with large gold earrings.

Victor said, "Yeah, I met her up at Cheltenham Mall. And yo, she got a good *shot* downstairs. You know what I mean?"

Mark nodded. "It was good, hunh?"

"Man, was it ever," Victor emphasized.

"Well, Tracy told me to tell you that her mother is going out Friday night," Mark told him with a grin.

Victor cracked a wide, confident smile. "See that, Mark? I told you I would pop that young-girl. It ain't even been a week yet."

Friday came quickly. Tracy cleaned up her room and got everything set for what she thought would be one of the most memorable nights of her life. She packed all of her clothing away in her dressers, and all her shoes inside the closet, and she then straightened up her bed. She changed the sheets and displayed her best-looking pictures and stuffed animals on her dressers to make everything neat and pretty for her most important visitor.

Tracy walked out on the avenue to buy some ice cream before her mother was ready to leave. Patti told her to come right back, limiting the amount of time her daughter had to search the streets for Victor. In desperation, Tracy went as far as to ask a few girls if they had seen him, only to receive their jealous snarls in response. By the time she had gotten back to her house, Tracy had given up on her chase. She sat in her neat room and stared up at the ceiling in despair. *All he has to do is call,* she told herself.

Patti spotted her long face. "What's wrong with you, girl? You go out every Friday, so don't even try pouting in here tonight. I have a life, too, Tracy."

"I'm not thinking about that, mom," her daughter told her.

"Well, what are you thinking about?" Patti asked. She was decked out in a beige skirt suit with a white blouse and black stockings and shoes, set on reclaiming her life from Dave.

Tracy knew she had to throw her mother off track so she wouldn't get suspicious. "Well, my stomach was hurting today, and I had the runs," she lied. Tracy smiled, knowing it was a good one.

Patti laughed. "Well, you'll be all right; just stay close to the bathroom. You didn't embarrass yourself at school today, did you?"

"No," Tracy answered her.

Patti wrote down a phone number where she could be reached and placed it on Tracy's dresser. "Look, now, I gotta go, so here's the number to the place, if you need to call me."

"Okay."

Patti left out, and Tracy took Jason downstairs with her to watch television. She made a relaxing spot on the couch to get her brother to fall asleep, and after an hour Jason was out like a light. Tracy then carried him up to his bed and headed back downstairs, praying for her late-night romance to come true. She sat and ate her ice cream, and before she knew it, it was ten-forty-five and she had dozed off herself. Victor should have been there by ten.

Tracy struggled to her feet and headed toward the stairs. She was disappointed and ready for bed, but right as she reached the first step, she could see, through the front window, a figure approaching her door. She ran to the door excitedly. Victor stood on her top step, waiting for her to let him in.

Tracy said happily, "Hi. I thought you wasn't comin'."

Victor looked around as he walked in. "You gotta nice crib," he said, half ignoring her excitement. He knew she would be pleased to see him.

"Thank you."

Tracy followed Victor into the living room as he wandered around. He wore a red Polo jacket, a plain white T-shirt and black jeans. A gold rope chain shone around his neck.

"So, what time is your mom coming home?" he asked her.

"I don't know," Tracy answered.

Victor turned to look at her. "You got carpeting in your basement?"

"Yeah," Tracy answered. She led him to the basement door as if she was giving him a tour of the house.

Victor said, "Let's go down here, just in case your mom comes home, 'cause I wouldn't want to be caught inside your room." He walked down inside of the basement as Tracy followed him. "Go open the back door so we won't have to do it if she comes," Victor instructed her while he took off his jacket.

Tracy did as she was told. Victor then gestured with his right hand for her to have a seat on his lap.

"What 'chew want?" Tracy asked him, playfully.

Victor pulled her onto his lap. "So what we gon' do, Tracy?"

Tracy looked at his hair, noticing how thick and dark it was, with little shiny waves and curls all tangled inside of the perfectly blocked shape. *Damn he looks good,* she thought to herself.

"I'on know," she moaned. Tracy was feeling nervous and unsure of herself.

Victor pulled her down to his lips and gently kissed her neck. He then licked around to her ear, like he had done at the party.

"Do you want me to make love to you?" he asked her.

"I'on care," Tracy moaned as he kissed her lips. Victor stood her up to take off her clothes. Tracy then felt an impulse to stop him. "I don't know about this, Victor," she said, gripping her pants, as he tugged at them.

Victor pushed her away and said, "Look, I told you to call me when you're *ready.*"

Tracy whined, "Well, I thought I was. But why I gotta give you some just to be with you?" She wanted Victor to stay and argue with her like most boys would, but Victor had had too many girls for that.

"Call me when you're *ready!* Okay?" He snatched up his red Polo jacket and headed toward the basement door.

Tracy's heart pounded. She watched him walking away and couldn't help herself. "Okay, Victor! Don't go!"

Victor stopped at the door. "Well, what 'chew gon' do then? Because I got places to go and people to see if you're planning on wasting my time down here." He held his jacket across his left arm, holding the doorknob with his right hand. Tracy knew that he meant another girl. She decided that she would rather give him *some* than to be left alone, thinking about him.

"Well, what do you wanna do?"

Tracy nodded like a child with her hazels twinkling inside of the dark. She started to slowly take off her clothes. Victor came back in, and he watched her. Tracy undressed, piece by piece, as her heart raced, feeling trapped by young lust, confused for love. Soon she sat naked on her basement couch, not yet fourteen, and about to lose her virginity.

Victor yanked out a quilt from her mother's laundry basket and spread it out on the floor. Tracy looked up at him in submission as he began to take off his clothes.

"Is it gonna hurt?" she asked him, innocently.

Victor held in his laugh as he spread her thighs. "Only a little bit," he said, again kissing her neck. He played with her to arouse her young body for easy access. Tracy could feel him, bumping up against her leg as they passionately wrestled with tongues, fingers, arms, legs, elbows and knees. Victor was erect and throbbing against her, and Tracy quickly exhausted herself from the foreplay.

"Victor, put it in," she said, afraid to touch him.

"Are you sure you want me to?" he whispered.

Tracy pleaded, whispering back to him, "Yeah. Do it."

Victor tried, and Tracy resisted with a squeal. Her legs began to shake with anxiety as he barely entered her. She then tried to pull back from his grasp to avoid the pain, like she had done with Bob. Victor clutched her by her shoulders, pushing himself through.

"UNNNHH, VICTOR!" Tracy howled desperately.

Victor began pushing her legs back with his arms. Tracy attempted to grab the rug. Failing at that, she began to claw away at his back as she moaned, "UNNNHH! VICTOR, I LOVE YOU! I LOVE YOU!"

Oh my God! I can't believe I'm actually doing this, she thought to herself.

When he had finally finished, they lay there intertwined until Victor had regained his energy. Tracy watched him as if she was a wide-eyed toddler at an amusement park while he redressed, astonished by his dark and beautiful muscular physique. Victor had a perfect black body. And after being with him intimately, Tracy understood firsthand why all the girls loved him.

Victor asked, "What's wrong?"

"Nothin'," Tracy answered shyly.

"Well, I got to go, all right?"

"Okay," she responded breathlessly.

Tracy got up to walk him to the door, remaining butt-naked inside of her dark basement. She locked the door behind him and carried her clothing upstairs to her room. She then fell out across her bed, feeling relaxed and robbed of all her energy as she slipped into a deep and peaceful sleep.

Jason tapped on his sister's shoulder Saturday morning.

"What?" Tracy strained, making sure that her sheets covered her naked body.

"I want some cereal," her brother squealed. "Tray-cee." Tracy didn't respond, so Jason shook her. "Tray-cee!"

"Stop," she snapped at him.

Frustrated, Jason ran into his mother's bathroom hollering, "M-O-O-O-M! She won't get up!"

"Well, you tell her *I* said so," Patti mumbled while brushing her teeth.

Jason pleaded for action. "But she won't get it."

Patti finished brushing her teeth and marched into Tracy's room. "Look, girl, if you want to go out tonight, then you better get up and get him something to eat."

Tracy couldn't believe her ears. It seemed like only yesterday when her mother was pleasantly buddy-buddy with her, and in one week she had turned completely sour. *Now I know what people go through when their parents get divorced,* Tracy thought, *because she's starting to act crazy. I don't have anything to do with what dad does.* She took a few seconds to gather her energy and then slid some clothes on to do as she was told. And again, Tracy was given the responsibility of baby-sitting Jason while her mother ran errands.

"Hello. Is Jantel home?" she asked from the phone inside of the living room. She just *had* to call her best girlfriend and update her on the news.

Jantel answered, "Hello."

"It's Tracy, and guess what happened last night."

"What?"

"Victor came over here."

"For real? What did y'all do?"

Tracy smiled. *"You know."*

"Uuuuw, y'all got nas-sty."

"Yup, and it was gooooood. But girl, that shit hurt like hell at first."

Jantel cracked up. "It did?" she asked, with tears of laughter flooding her eyes. Jantel had always assumed that having sex would hurt. She had heard horror stories from several different sources to confirm it, and unlike Tracy, she was in no hurry to lose her virginity.

"Shit, yeah, it hurt, girl!" Tracy told her. She quickly looked over to Jason, hoping that he paid no mind while he watched Saturday morning cartoons. Tracy then decided that it would be wise for her to watch what she said around him, because Jason was at an impressionable age.

"Are you going to that party tonight?" Tracy asked Jantel on another note.

"On Haines Street?"

"Yeah."

Jantel grimaced and shook her head against the receiver. "No way. All they do is fight around there. Don't go to that party, Tracy. You don't even want to get mixed in with them people," she warned.

Tracy thought about her warning, but her mind was already made up: she was going to the party. Victor would probably be there, and it would give her another chance to be near him. She called Carmen, who went to all the parties, and set a time for them to go together.

Haines Street was packed with nothing but guys, outside and inside, and Carmen seemed to know all of them. There was limited elbow room inside of the smoky basement where the party was being held, and Tracy began to see why so many fights broke off. She searched the room with her eyes, feeling sure that Victor would be there. But she could not spot him, although most of his loud friends were there. Tracy immediately figured that he was off with another girl, doing what he did best.

"What's up, pretty?" an older guy with a fresh haircut said to her. His greased wavy hair glimmered under the dim green party light.

"Nothin'," Tracy said, and since Victor was not around, she was more than ready to leave.

"What's your name?" he asked.

"Tracy."

"Yeah, well, you got a boyfriend?"

"No, but I'm talkin' to somebody."

"Well, you don't go with him, so I figure that me and you can talk."

Mr. Waves looked all right, but Tracy had already been satisfied, so he was beginning to get on her nerves. He was too pressed.

"Do you know Victor Hinson?" she asked him.

"Oh, damn, you talkin' to him?"

Tracy nodded, and Mr. Waves backed off.

"My fault then."

Tracy smiled to herself, proud of Victor's rep. She then moved into a corner and spotted Carmen French-kissing some tall guy. And she was lonely.

"Ay, what's up, slim? You flyy as you wanna be. You got the fresh-ass gear on and everything. What's your name?" another boy asked. He was not as attractive as Mr. Waves, and his breath smelled like a ton of cigarettes, so Tracy ignored him. "Hunh, what's your name?" the boy repeated as she moved away. "Oh, aw'ight then! It's like that?" he said to her back. "Bitch!"

"You ain't like dude right there, hunh?" yet another guy said to her. Tracy looked to see a cute brown face under a red Kangol cap.

"Naw," she answered, uninterested in conversing. She was still satisfied with and longing for Victor.

Cute-brown asked, "Well, who are you in here with?"

"Nobody you know."

The boy was caught off guard by Tracy's blunt response. He figured that he was being respectable with his conversation. "You don't have to get like that on me," he told her. Tracy pictured him as a "Tommy-type," who would want to spend every hour of the day with her, so she simply wanted to get him off of her back, and fast.

"I'm talkin' to somebody, okay. Damn!"

Cute-brown moved away from Tracy and joined some of his friends.

Tracy sat there on the wall, deserted and staring at Carmen, who seemed to be having the time of her life.

Before she knew it, two hours had passed, and Tracy had danced with several dull boys.

Carmen finally joined her. "Ay Tracy, you wanna go with these guys I know?"

Tracy frowned. "Who?"

"Come on, I'll introduce you to them." Carmen dragged Tracy away to a couple of tall basketball players. "This is my girl, Tracy," she said.

"You live on Diamond Lane, don't you, right next to some girls named Mercedes and Raheema?" one of the boys asked Tracy.

"Yeah, how you know?" Tracy perked. *Damn, everybody knows me!* she thought to herself excitedly.

"Because, my cousin lived up there. And I seen you before."

"Yeah, Mercedes don't live there no more. But who is your cousin?" Tracy wanted to know.

"Well, he's an old-head now, but do you remember some guy named Kevin?"

Tracy nodded with a grin. "Yeah, I remember him." *Kevin was Mercedes' first man, like Victor is mine,* she reflected with a smile.

"Well, y'all down to go with us?" the other tall boy asked Carmen.

Tracy felt that they were harmless and friendly. She had no objections. The party had turned out to be a dud anyway.

They left the party and walked a few blocks to Carmen's friend's house. She was still hugging and kissing him while on their way. Tracy had completely forgotten about her mother's warning concerning leaving parties with guys. It had happened too fast for her to think about it, and once it did cross her mind, she had already done it.

The boy's parents had gone out for the night, and Carmen slipped right up the stairs to be with him. Tracy had just met the other guy, and she didn't like him sexually. They sat downstairs and watched Eddie Murphy's *Delirious* on tape. Tracy laughed, while wondering where the guy's parents were. She felt nervous knowing that the boy sitting next to her probably expected to do something. She dared not to mislead him, so she decided not to even look his way. She kept her eyes glued to Eddie and his blunt style of humor.

The tall boy asked, "What time you gotta be home?"

"Twelve o'clock," Tracy answered. It was already a quarter after eleven, and it would take Tracy twenty minutes to walk.

"You want me to walk you?" he offered.

Tracy planned on being short and sweet with all of her answers. "I don't care," she told him. She was relieved he was not going to try anything.

He then stood up with her and said, "Come here for a minute," as he leaned against the front door.

Tracy stopped with arms-distance between them.

"Come here," the tall boy repeated, tugging her arm toward him. He was trying to pull her closer, and Tracy correctly assumed that he wanted a kiss, so she promptly backed away.

"No, that's all right. I just met you," she told him.

They both stood there inside of the vestibule area, confused about the next move. The tall boy then gave in and opened the door for her. Tracy didn't feel comfortable about him walking her home anymore, and he didn't *really* want to. It was an embarrassing situation, so Tracy decided to walk home alone, despite the danger.

While on her way up a dark street, she noticed a young drunkard on a patio. Spotting her, he walked out toward the pavement. Tracy frantically crossed the street.

"Hey, good-lookin', come here, baby. I'm not gon' hurt you, I just want your phone number."

"No, that's all right," Tracy responded, running. She ran all the way to Wayne Avenue where she spotted the usual people from her neighborhood before she stopped, bumping into Jantel, who was walking out from the ice-cream store.

"Girl, you missed it!" Jantel exclaimed.

"I missed what?" Tracy asked, while catching her breath. She was still more concerned about her own story.

"Victor beat up this guy, and the cops came looking for him. Because this guy hopped out of a car with like four of his boys, and Victor had all his boys, right. So then Victor fought him with these rings on his hands and messed cuz' face up. And now the cops are after him."

"For real?" Tracy asked, forgetting about her own story. She *had* survived it.

"Yup, because the guy was jealous that Victor was seein' this girl."

It didn't much matter to Tracy how many girls Victor had. He had loved her for one night, and she was satisfied, yet she longed to have his personal and intimate attention again. And soon.

Tracy approached Carmen at her locker at school that Monday. "Ay, Carmen, you a trip, girl."

"Why, what I do?" Carmen responded to her, while gathering her things for class.

"Some drunken guy chased after me Saturday night."

Carmen laughed. "How is that my fault? I didn't tell you to leave."

"You *knew* I didn't know that guy."

"But you still could have waited for me, Tracy."

"Girl, I had to get home. Everybody's parents don't let them run the damn streets like yours do."

"Well, that ain't my problem," Carmen huffed. She rudely began to walk off toward her class.

"Yeah, all right, just see if I ever go to a party with you again," Tracy told her.

Carmen stopped for a second. "You the one that wanted to go, Tracy. I didn't call you for that party."

Tracy was speechless as Carmen stood her ground. The girls parted in a truce.

Classes were winding down before finals in June. The summer vacation was right around the corner. Tracy hadn't seen Victor much at all in the weeks that followed, and he didn't return any of her phone calls. *It's funny how I could catch him in his house when he first gave me his number,* she pondered, *but now he's never home.*

Meanwhile, more and more boys learned Tracy's name, but none were interesting enough to sway her preoccupation with Victor. *Now I know how my mother feels, dealing with my father,* she mused.

Tracy felt she could handle seeing and befriending Victor without having to give him *any*. She wanted to present herself like a lady. All she wanted was some of his time, and begging was useless, so she planned to make herself visible at all of his hang-outs until he would decide to be with her again.

Tracy ventured to the playground, displaying her summer Hawaiian look with sky-blue sunglasses that matched the blue in her outfit, and she dragged her best girlfriend, Jantel, along with her for backup. They sat down on the benches with the older girls, watching the guys play basketball. The older girls were not such a big deal to Tracy, or so she told herself. It was important for her to lessen the stature of the competition to keep her own self-image high. To get a number-one guy like Victor, Tracy figured she had to be a number-one girl. Every young lady at the playground was familiar with the rules of the dating game, and each of them were out to attract the best guys with their glamourous looks, attitudes and fashions.

Victor showed up with his friends at mid-afternoon and did not attempt to speak to Tracy. Nevertheless, Tracy continued to long for his attention as she watched his every move out of the corner of her eye, while pretending not to. Every few minutes, a girl or two would flock to Victor, and he would say a few words and go on about his business, which at the time was playing basketball with his friends. No girl seemed able to keep his attention for any length of time, and arguing would only make him ignore them, just like with Tracy's father.

Tracy smiled, reflecting on their similarities.

When Victor finally approached their bench, Tracy was ready to explode. He then looked and smiled at her. She stared back at him and returned his favor. It was obvious that she had been watching. Tracy realized that Victor was more than likely three times more experienced at playing mind games than she was.

"Ay Victor, there go that young-girl, man," one of his friends said, referring to Tracy.

Victor grinned. "I see her, but I'm just gon' make her sweat for a while."

"Shit, cuz', I don't see how you do it. You got all these little young-girls in love."

Victor said, "It's all in the mind, boy. You tease 'em and let them make their choice. If you're *the man,* like *me,* they'll be on you." Victor took a shot at the hoop and missed. "Shit! Let me get that one back."

His friend responded, "Well, every time I give a girl her freedom of choice, the bitch ends up dumpin' me."

Victor chuckled, and looked over at Tracy with another smile. Tracy turned away in embarrassment.

"Shawn, cuz', you have to know how girls think, and then you'll know how to deal with them. All girls are ruled by curiosity, so the less they know about you, the more they wanna know, and the more they wanna find out. So you just keep 'em guessin'. Watch this."

Victor swiftly walked over to Tracy and sat without speaking.

Jantel had had enough. "Hi, Victor," she said. Tracy was acting like an airhead to her. *Just tell him how you feel about him,* she wanted to advise her friend.

Stupid! Tracy thought. *Why she have ta' open her dumb mouth? Damn, she stupid!* The last thing Tracy wanted to do was seem obvious, even though it was a given to Victor. She was only there to see him.

"Oh, you not gon' speak to me?" Victor asked Tracy after waving to Jantel. Tracy couldn't help but to smile.

Victor chuckled at her and got up to leave.

Tracy asked Jantel, "Why you do that, girl?"

"Well, you didn't say that I couldn't say nothin' to him. We've just been sittin' out here for hours, doing nothin'. God!"

Victor came back and whispered in Tracy's ear, "I got something to ask you. Okay?" Tracy turned to eye his beautiful dark face, shining in the sunlight. Being that close to Victor again gave her goose bumps.

"What?" Tracy asked him.

"I'll tell you, just make sure you don't leave the playground," he answered her before he walked away. He returned to his friends as

Tracy wondered. He then walked off with them, heading toward the stores on Chelten Avenue.

Tracy obediently remained at the playground, watching the older boys playing basketball while she waited patiently for Victor to return. After a while, Jantel was ready to leave. *She* wasn't in love with Victor, and *she* thought that Tracy was acting ridiculous.

"You're actually gonna stay here and wait for him?" Jantel asked her friend.

Tracy sucked her teeth. "Jantel, if you don't wanna stay with me, then you can go home," she responded.

"Hmm," Jantel mumbled, standing up from the benches. "Well, I'll see you tomorrow then," she announced. "Happy waiting," she added.

"Whatever," Tracy said with a smirk as she continued to wait. She was afraid to leave, loving Victor without betrayal. And when the sun started to go down, she grew restless, still waiting, foolishly.

"Are you waiting for somebody?" one of the glamorous older girls asked her. They were all beginning to fade away.

Why don't you mind your business? Tracy wanted to snap. "No, not really. I just like watching basketball," she said instead.

The girl's friends snickered at Tracy as they began to walk off. "Don't get no splinters in your ass, waiting for no nigga, girl. 'Cause ain't none of 'em worth it," she said to Tracy as she walked off behind her friends.

Shawn said, "Ay Victor, man, that's ugly how you doin' her." They were heading back from the store.

Victor sucked his teeth. "Man, shet up. I know what I'm doin'. You gotta discipline these young-girls," he responded tartly. "She goin' through my little trainin' session." He munched on his barbecue chips and took a drink from his soda. "Plus, I'm waitin' for my pop to roll out, so I can take her to the crib and hit that ass again. I'm gon' hit it from the back this time."

When they got back to the playground, Victor looked over at Tracy, who was sitting by herself, and decided that he had trained her enough. It was nearly eight o'clock and his father would be gone from the house by then.

"Come here, girl," he said. His stare was serious as his connecting eyebrows rose. Tracy walked over to him slowly, feeling ashamed but important. If Victor wanted her, then she was surely a somebody. "When you want me to come over again?" he asked her sternly.

"I'on know. It depends on when my mother goes out," she answered, neglecting what she had told herself about not giving him *any*.

Victor said cheerfully, "Well, guess what? We can go to my house right now. But you probably don't want to though." He started to walk away from her, toward a hole inside of the playground gate.

Tracy lost her cool. "I didn't say that!" she gushed. There was no way for her to refuse without losing him. "I'll go with you," she said bashfully, as she followed after him.

Victor responded, "Come on, then." He led her through the hole in the gate. "YO, I'LL CATCH Y'ALL NIGGAS LATER!" he shouted, smiling at his friends and taking Tracy's hand.

"Damn, cuz'. Just let me be that nigga for *one* day," Shawn said to no one in particular.

"Dig it, man. Victor got all the flyy bitches."

Victor and Tracy walked around the corner, hand and hand. He wore a white Adidas shorts and shirt set, clean as usual. Tracy felt like a queen, ready to make love again to King Victor.

Victor looked into her hazels. "You know, I never realized how sexy your eyes were until I seen them in the light today," he told her.

"Thank you," Tracy responded, tickled brown. *God, I love him!* she thought to herself.

Victor told her to wait outside on his patio for a moment while he went in. Tracy waited, happy to be with him. He then came back and gestured for her to come with a flick of his wrist. His house was beautiful. Tracy looked at his brother's basketball pictures, noticing the family attractiveness.

"Your brother is my complexion," she commented, standing in front of the imitation fireplace.

"Yeah, my mother is your complexion," Victor told her. "Us niggas come in all colors." He approached her from behind, putting his hands around her waist and kissing the nape of her neck. Tracy rubbed his hands and leaned her head forward, loving it.

"Tracy, I want you to do me a favor. All right?"

"Yes," Tracy responded, dizzily.

Victor turned her around and looked her in her eyes. "Go upstairs to the last room in the hallway and take off your clothes. I'll be up in a few. And get under the covers while you're at it."

Tracy didn't even hesitate. She did exactly what he had told her, waiting for him under the covers, naked and unashamed.

Victor walked into the room and turned off his light. Tracy felt his smooth dark body as it joined hers under the sheets. He turned her over on her stomach and pushed her knees forward as he entered her from the back.

Tracy whined, "Ooww, Victor. I don't wanna do it this way."

He gripped her by her waist and began to pull her into him. Tracy dropped her head into the pillow, fighting the pain until it no longer hurt her.

"Did you miss me?" he asked her.

"Yesss," she moaned, breathlessly.

"Do you like it?"

"Mmm, hmm."

"Do you want me to stop?"

"No."

"Good," he told her, kissing the nape of her neck again.

Tracy rolled over and rubbed his chest when he had finished. He was her *man* and she loved him. Victor allowed her to lay with him on his bed, butt-naked and under his sheets, as Tracy peacefully fell asleep in his arms.

Victor leaned away from her and looked into her face as she dozed off. *She's just so young and pretty,* he told himself. He ran his dark fingers through her hair. "I like you," he whispered in her ear, *but I just can't let my guard down,* he thought to himself. His older brother had told him that young-girls were the worst ones to fall for, "because they don't know enough about relationships, and they're not mature enough to handle all of their emotions," he had said. Nevertheless, Victor liked Tracy's loyalty to him, so he considered her trustworthy.

Victor continued to have sex with Tracy throughout the summer, whenever he wanted. He never seemed to spend any quality time with her though. Tracy was pleased when she did have him. She saw no need to complain. He would come to her block and simply look at her a certain way, and she knew exactly what it meant.

Tracy had a problem with not being able to tell Victor "no." On restless summer nights, she even went looking for him. Time spent with him was never boring, and Tracy enjoyed her small part in his fast world.

"Ay, girl. Is your name Tracy?" a short, well-curved girl asked from the bottom of Tracy's walkway.

"Yeah," Tracy answered. She had been sitting out on her steps with Raheema.

The short girl said angrily, "Well, I got somethin' to talk to you about. Was you lookin' for my boyfriend?" she asked.

Tracy looked at the two girlfriends the short girl had brought with her, knowing they were all in high school.

"I don't even know your boyfriend," she said.

"Yes, you do. You know Victor Hinson, girl. Don't fuckin' try to lie to me," the girl snapped.

Tracy was glad that she was in front of her house. If anything jumped off, she was ready to make a dash for her door.

"I'ma tell you now, if I ever hear about you bein' with him again, I'ma kick a bone out your young ass." The three girls walked away after soundly ranking Tracy.

Raheema grinned. "See what trouble boys get you in?" she said.

Tracy sat speechless for a second. She then sucked her teeth and sighed. "Aw, that bitch know he be runnin' around *doin' it* to everybody. She stupid to even go with him," she said.

Raheema asked with a smile, "Well, what about you?"

Tracy smiled back. "So what, Ra-Ra?"

Raheema giggled helplessly. "Well, if I talked to a boy, first I would make sure that he didn't live around here."

Tracy grinned, curiously. "Oh, so you like boys now, hunh?"

Raheema defiantly shook her head. "No. I'm just saying if I *did.*"

oN the flip side

"See them girls right there, Bruce?" said a short, round-bellied, brown-skinned boy inside of the Cheltenham Mall lobby.

"Going into the arcade?" his taller, lighter-toned friend responded. Shiny waves mopped his head, flowing to the right with a part on the left.

Round-belly said, "Yeah, cuz'. We can get some ass from them, Bruce. They live up Wayne Avenue. I'll talk to the dark-skinned one."

His friend was hesitant. "Naw, cuz', I'm not talkin' to that other girl."

"Why not, man? Bruce, she looks good as shit, and you a pretty boy, too. Man, you can get with her," Round-belly assured him.

Wavy-head contested, "Naw, cuz', I can't really deal with them type of girls." He could tell that the girl was flyy; she had clues of high maintenance written all over her face, hair and body.

"Man, all you got to do is talk, and she'll be on you."

"I don't know, cuz'. She looks like one of those material girls to me, and I ain't really thorough enough to talk to them."

Round-belly said, "Man, shet up, as pretty as you are."

Wavy-head smiled as they went inside the arcade.

Round-belly said, "Ay Carmen, what's up, baby?"

"Oh my God! What's up, Bucky?"

"You tell me."

Bruce stared nervously at Tracy, who was looking at him.

"Yeah, this is my boy, Bruce," Bucky introduced him.

Carmen said, "Hi, this is Tracy."

"Hi you doin'?" Tracy said.

Bruce was too afraid to talk. He silently nodded his head.

Carmen asked him, "Don't you go to Northeast High School?"

"Yeah," Bruce answered, nervously.

"Do you know Victor Hinson? He goes there."

"Yup, he live up y'all way, right?" Bruce said, opening up. He leaned up against Mario Brothers' Donkey Kong.

Carmen responded, "Yeah, he do." She then looked at Tracy and smiled.

Bucky told them, "Yeah, well, we might be around there to see y'all. Aw'ight? So I just want y'all to know that we're comin'."

"Aw'ight," Carmen said.

The two boys walked out from the arcade.

Carmen asked Tracy, "What 'chew think about Bruce?"

"He was pretty as shit," Tracy told her.

"I know. Wasn't he? You see all them waves in his head?"

Two days had passed before Bruce and Bucky pursued their plans. They found Tracy's house on Diamond Lane, and ended up meeting Raheema and Jantel.

"Yo, what's up, Jantel?" Bucky said with a grin. He seemed to know everyone. "Don't that girl Tracy live here?" he asked, pointing to the house next door.

Jantel responded blandly, "Yeah, why?"

Bucky frowned. "Boy, you got an attitude," he commented to her.

Jantel did not particularly care for him. Bucky was known to be disrespectful to girls. "Yeah, whatever," she huffed.

Bruce interjected, "Well, she probably ain't home anyway." He then smiled at his friend. "Man, you always arguin' wit' girls, cuz'."

Raheema had been staring at wavy-headed Bruce from the time he walked to her steps. He didn't notice it at first, but once he did, he was drawn to her like a magnet. She had the most innocent pair of eyes, and he was not afraid of *her* attractiveness. Raheema seemed soothing and down to earth as compared to Tracy.

Bruce asked Jantel, "What's your friend's name?"

Jantel smiled, expecting Raheema to brush them off as usual. "Why don't you ask her?"

Bruce looked at Raheema and they smiled at each other, to Jantel's surprise.

"My name is Raheema," she answered.

Oh my God, she likes him! Jantel assumed from Raheema's dreamy look. *Wait until I tell Tracy!*

"That's a different kind of name. I like that," Bruce said to her.

"What's your name?" she asked.

"Bruce."

"Are you in high school?"

"Yeah."

"I'm going to high school in September."

He grinned at her. "Oh, you gon' be a freshman, hunh?"

Raheema nodded. "Yup."

Bucky smirked and began strolling down the street. "Yo, man, I'll be back," he told his friend. He didn't want to get in Bruce's way, and he was obviously taken by the girl.

Bruce said, "Aw'ight," and sat on the steps to continue talking to Raheema.

Jantel then decided to leave the two love birds alone herself. "Well, when you see Tracy, just tell her that I'll call her up tonight," she said with a smile. *Dag, everybody's talking to somebody but me. Maybe I should give that boy Damon that runs for the Philadelphia Express a chance. He likes me, and he's kind of cute,* she told herself as she walked off.

Bruce asked Raheema, "So you got a boyfriend, pretty?" He felt much more confident with her than he did with Tracy. Raheema was definitely more his speed.

"No," Raheema said, staring into his eyes.

Bruce leveled with her from "jump-street," or in other words, from the beginning of things. "Well, to tell the truth, I'm at the point now where I would like to settle down and find a girlfriend myself. And you're such a nice girl and all that I wouldn't mind you being the one."

Raheema blushed. "Well, I don't know if I'm ready for a boyfriend yet."

"Yeah, well, I can understand that. We just met each other, so we'll just be friends for a while until we find out how much we like each other."

Bruce left once his friend Bucky came back. Talking to Raheema had been relaxing to him.

Bucky said, "Ay Bruce, don't talk to that girl, cuz'." They headed down Chelten Avenue, back home toward Chew.

"Why not?" Bruce asked.

"That babe ain't fuckin', man."

"Oh, I know that."

"How you know?"

"'Cause, I can look in her eyes and tell. That's gon' be my girl, man," Bruce announced.

Bucky laughed. "I'm tellin' you, cuz', leave that nut bitch alone."

"You crazy. I ain't hardly tryin' to let *her* go," Bruce snapped. "See man, that's all I want is a pretty girl, who I like. I don't need them flyy, hip-hop girls."

Bucky responded, shaking his head, "Aw'ight then."

They walked home to the East Germantown area, across Chew Avenue.

• • •

"Ay Bucky, the party gon' be live tonight, right?" Bruce was asking.

"Yeah, cuz', it's gon' be many hoes up in there," his friend responded as he groomed himself, getting ready to leave out.

Bruce wore leather-trimmed jeans, a Members Only jacket, a gold pinky ring and a pair of seventy-five-dollar Fila sneakers. Bucky slid on his blue silk shirt with black, snake-skinned shoes and a matching belt. He wore dark blue Louis Rafael slacks and a gray Sergio jacket. Silk shirts were *in* in Philly at the time. The year was nineteen-eighty-five; the day was Saturday.

"Bucky looks like a million dollars," Bruce said with a laugh. He wrapped a twenty-dollar bill around his finger for status; all of the guys who had money to spare were doing it.

"I'm tellin' you, Bruce, you should get classy, man. The bitches love it."

"My gear is aw'ight," Bruce retorted. "But yo, 'Buck,' I'm gon' go up to Raheema's house to see if she wants to go."

Bucky frowned. "Man, that girl can't go to no parties. You wastin' your time."

"Well, I'm gon' go see anyway."

Bruce left immediately, taking the long walk by himself. When he got there, it was eight-thirty, and Raheema and Tracy were outside talking. Bruce hesitated after seeing Tracy there, but then he walked up as if everything was cool.

Raheema greeted him excitedly, "Hi, Bruce." Bruce was apprehensive, wondering what Tracy was thinking, and what she planned to do about her thoughts.

"Wasn't you at the mall, earlier this week?" she asked, as if she was not quite sure.

Bruce answered, "Yeah," nonchalantly.

Tracy wore a pair of tight black jeans and a red Sixers jacket. Bruce was more interested in Raheema, wearing a long royal-blue skirt and a colorful blouse.

"So, Raheema, you wanna go to this party with me tonight?" he asked her.

Tracy was immediately jealous. "Some boys just asked us about that," she interjected.

Raheema said, "I gotta go ask," to Tracy's surprise.

Oh my God! Jantel was right; she do like him, she thought to herself with a smile. Her neighbor then ran into the house and left Bruce alone with Tracy.

Tracy asked him with a devilish grin, "You came up here with Bucky, looking for me yesterday?"

Bruce lied and said, "Bucky was lookin' for you."

Tracy stood up and walked closer to him on the steps. Bruce turned away to avoid her hazel-eyed glare.

"You like Raheema?" she quizzed.

"Yeah, and I wanna go with her," Bruce answered bluntly.

Tracy felt like cursing him out. *Why does everybody want to go with* her? she fumed. Bruce continued to avoid her, giving Tracy a challenge.

Raheema came back out with a jacket, and Tracy was shocked.

"They said that you can go?" she asked, confused by it.

"Yeah," Raheema told her. "I told them that I was going with you and your friends, and they said to be back before curfew. That's all."

Tracy grinned, excited as ever to see how Raheema would act at her first house-party. Her neighbor was finally ready to start experiencing life.

Tracy dashed into the house to tell her mother where she was going, and then the three of them headed to the party, which was eight blocks away. Tracy and Raheema giggled behind Bruce's back at how pretty he was while on their way. Tracy then slid her hand near his butt. Raheema grabbed her hand and playfully hissed at her.

"Stop that, Tracy," she whispered with a grin.

Tracy whispered back to her, "I would *do it good* to *him.*" But she realized that Bruce would rather *do it* with Raheema.

By the time they had arrived at the party, it was nine-thirty. A gang of teenaged boys were crowded outside. Bruce recognized none of them, as they jealously began to stare at him. He had *two* pretty girls. *Who the hell is he?* they thought.

Although she didn't feel like associating with them, Tracy was familiar with several of the boys. One of them even called out to Raheema, but she refused to respond. They entered through the front door and paid their dollars. A girl then led them into the basement and down the crowded stairs.

Bruce walked down the steps and into the packed dance floor accompanied by two *fine* young women. And no sooner than he had reached a comfortable spot inside the room with them a boy rudely stepped in front of him, addressing Raheema.

"What's up, Raheema? Come here for a minute. I got somebody for you," he said as he tugged at her hand.

Bruce cut him off as Raheema pulled her hand away. "Naw, cuz'. She wit' me."

"If she really with you, then let her say it," the boy contested.

Bruce responded, ready for a fight, "Yeah, well, you see that she ain't goin' nowhere."

Tracy was impressed, but it made Raheema afraid of him. She hoped that Bruce was not a control freak like her father. Yet Bruce was simply standing his ground. *Dude had no business grabbing her from me like that,* he thought. *Who the hell he think he is?*

The boy walked away to join a group of his friends, and Bruce began to fear for his safety. He wondered where Bucky was.

After his nerves calmed, Bruce helped Raheema from the wall to dance with him. The DJ played "Angel," by Anita Baker. Bruce and Raheema caressed each other as Tracy watched them enviously. She was then appalled, noticing Victor kissing another girl. Tracy was horrendously jealous. Her heart burned inside of her chest with rage. Victor had not given her *a treat* in three weeks. Tracy counted the days.

"I wanna go home," she snapped to Bruce and Raheema. They were dancing as if they were married.

Bruce said, "Aw'ight, just wait until after this song." It didn't take much for Bruce to grow a hard-on, and he wanted to stay close to Raheema to get his thrills.

"I wanna go home," Tracy repeated.

Bruce looked at her with an evil eye. "Come on, now. We gon' roll, but just as soon as this dance is over." He regained his stance with Raheema.

Tracy glared at him. "NO, BOY! I want to go home! NOW!" she roared like a baby. Teenagers glanced at her as she hastily began moving through the crowd and toward the stairs. Bruce followed with Raheema, hating Tracy. She acted like a big kid. The thug types tried to entice her with conversation as soon as they walked outside. They were the guys no one wanted *inside* the party.

"Ay, come here for a minute, Tracy," one of them called.

Tracy already had an attitude. "NO!" she screamed at him.

He looked to his friends and frowned as they laughed at him. "What the hell is her problem?" he asked.

Bruce and Raheema held hands, pacing behind her.

Tracy looked back to Bruce and decided to pick with him. She had nothing better to do, and she knew that he was pissed. Tracy had ruined his hard-on. "You mad at me, 'Brucie'?" she said, giggling.

Bruce smiled at her humor with no comment. *This girl is a damn kid,* he told himself. *But she sure is attractive,* he could not help thinking. Tracy carried herself with a lot of passion.

"Are you gonna walk us back home?" Raheema asked him.

"Naw, 'cause that's outta my way."

"Well, what's your phone number, so I can call you?"

Bruce gave it to Raheema aloud. Tracy overheard it as they headed on their way back up a well-lighted Chelten Avenue. It was only ten-thirty.

Bruce then stepped to Bucky's house and waited out on the steps.

"BRUCE!" a girl yelled from her patio across the street. She ran over to the steps with him, looked into his scar-free, chestnut-colored face, and began to shake her head.

Bruce asked, "What 'chew do that for?"

"I was looking for you all night, 'cause my mom had left."

"Aw, for real?" he asked, disappointed that he had missed out on an opportunity.

"Yup, but nobody knew where you was," she told him.

His friend Bucky knew, but he couldn't tell her. "Damn!" Bruce exclaimed. "Well, when is she goin' out again?"

"I'on know. But you blew it tonight."

The girl scrambled back to the house as her mother called her. Bruce continued to sit and wait on Bucky's steps, feeling idiotic.

"Hey, dummy," Bucky said. His words seemed to drop out of the sky, as Bruce was caught daydreaming. "I just came from gettin' some ass. But what did you do, lover-boy?" his friend asked him with a laugh.

Bruce answered glumly, "Nothin', man. I went to that party with Raheema, and Tracy messed everything up. Stupid-ass girl!"

Bucky joined him on the steps. "Jackie was lookin' for you," he said.

"Yeah, I know. She just told me."

Bucky shook his head. "You hard-headed, man, and that's why you never gon' get no ass. Now Bruce, if you would've stayed with me, you would've gotten with Jackie t'night. And we could have gotten with them other babes next week."

Bucky shook his head and smiled. "So did you get her number, Bruce?"

Bruce shook his own head. "Naw. She can't have phone calls, so I gave her mine."

"She can't have phone calls?" Bucky asked, not believing what he was hearing. "Get the fuck outta here! See man, you going out like *a nut* again, Bruce, just like you always do."

That Sunday morning, Bruce watched baseball while thinking about the chances he had missed out on with girls. He could not seem to catch any lucky bounces. He shook his head and refused to answer the phone when it rang. He didn't care if it was for him. He felt miserable and wanted to be left alone. Everyone else seemed to be having sex but him.

"Bruce, the telephone!" His mother called from upstairs.

"Who is it?"

"Some weird name like Ra-ha, or *something.*"

Bruce jumped up on the phone. "Hello."

"Hi, Bruce. What 'chew doin'?" she quickly asked him. She seemed to be in a hurry.

"Nothin'. I didn't think you was gon' call this early." Bruce looked at the time on the VCR clock under the television stand. It was a quarter after one.

"I know, but I had something to tell you."

"What?" he asked.

"My parents went to church, and I wanted to know if you'd come over."

Bruce got excited. His pants tightened below the zipper. He asked her hysterically, "Like what time?"

"Right now."

"Right now?" he repeated, to make sure he was not hearing things.

"Yeah," she confirmed.

"Aw'ight then. I'll be up in like twenty minutes."

Bruce tossed some clothing on and ran all the way up Chelten Avenue. It was a twelve-block jog. He got to her corner and slowed down to gather his breath with his pants wet from expectations. He knocked on Raheema's door, and no one answered, so he tried again.

Tracy walked out of her house, laughing.

"What are you doing up here?" she asked.

"None of your business," he snapped at her.

"Well, Raheema ain't home."

"Where did she go?"

"To church, with her parents."

Bruce felt like a numbskull. He was confused about the phone call. "Umm, do you have my phone number?" he asked Tracy quizzically.

Tracy said, "No. You didn't give it to *me.*"

Bruce shrugged and started to walk away, still bewildered. "Well, tell her I was up here."

"Oh, you can't sit and talk to me?" Tracy responded. She was wearing a pair of tight blue-jeans and a red tennis shirt while standing inside of her screen door.

Bruce looked at her cracked open door and wondered. He had already had another hard-on. He felt desperate to get *some*.

He grinned, walked back and asked, "Who's home at your house?"

"Nobody." Tracy lied, grinning back at him. Patti and Jason were both home. Tracy just wanted to see what Bruce would say to her.

Bruce thought about it, no longer caring about the consequences. "Can I come in?"

"I can't have company when nobody's home."

"Aw'ight then. Fuck it," Bruce huffed, heading back on his way home. He sprinted back down the street, disappointed again.

Tracy laughed and walked inside. *He's funny,* she thought to herself. *I'm gonna have some good fun with him. He should have never tried to talk to Raheema instead of me.*

Patti took her son and daughter shopping Monday evening after work. She bought Tracy some of the new fads in fashion. Tracy had been saving up for a pair of Guess glasses and a gold herringbone chain, and with the combined money that her father had given her and with Patti pitching in for the balance, Tracy got what she wanted, plus some. The school season was rolling back around soon, so sales were plentiful. Patti bought her children new coats for the winter, and a few new pairs of winter shoes.

Tracy walked into Germantown High School on the first day of classes with her head up high, and noticed that it was a fashion show in itself. All the teens had new gear.

The older boys at "G-Town" came off to her with conceited attitudes. They knew that she was a freshman. Nevertheless, Tracy was confident that she would quickly rise to the cream of the crop at her new school. She considered herself too *flyy* not to.

She arrived home that first afternoon and stumbled across Bruce and Bucky, who were out talking to Raheema. Tracy looked at Bruce and smiled. Bruce then frowned at her as his friend Bucky took a peek at her attention-getting behind. He shook his head, enjoying the view and realizing that his partner was making his usual mistakes. *I would have never chosen Raheema over Tracy,* he reflected.

Tracy said, "Hi, Ra-Ra."

"Hi, Tracy," her neighbor perked. Raheema seemed to be in a good mood again. She had been much more pleasant since meeting Bruce.

Tracy greeted her and proceeded to stare at her neighbor's new *friend.* Bruce turned his head. Bucky smirked at him, wishing that his friend would take his advice, for a change. Tracy decided to go inside the house and get ready to pick up her brother from the day-care. Bucky then took another walk.

Bruce asked Raheema, "So what are we gonna do?"

"I have to think about it, Bruce."

"Look, I'm not leaving here without a girlfriend," he pressed her.

Raheema had been avoiding giving him an answer for weeks. Bruce could tell that she still was not ready to have a boyfriend. But he liked her too much to let it go.

A group of three boys approached them from up the street and started to misdirect Raheema's attention, which was aggravating to Bruce. He had important business to take care of.

"Who is this right here, Ra-Ra? Is this your boyfriend?" one of the boys asked.

Another guy commented to her boldly, "Ay Raheema, when you gon' come and see me?" The three of them were relatively all the same size and age as Bruce, trying to scare him off. *Why should we let this new guy come around here and get with Raheema when she wouldn't talk to any of us?* they pondered to themselves. One boy looked away, realizing that Bruce was not intimidated by them.

One asked Bruce, "Is this your girl, cuz'?"

Bruce lied, as he smiled to lighten up the tension between them, "Yeah, man."

Raheema snapped, "I didn't tell you, 'yes.' "

"Aw'ight then, forget it," Bruce said angrily.

Raheema continued to reprimand him. "I don't know why you even said that."

"Because I wanted to!" he flared up at her. "Look, just forget it. Okay?"

Tracy listened in from her doorway and giggled.

The boys saw that Bruce was not to be played with and headed back on their merry way into the streets.

Raheema was still upset about it after they had left. "You didn't have to tell them that." She felt mistreated. The last thing in the world that she was going to stand for was some *boy* trying to make her decisions for her.

Bruce told her what his intentions were. "Look, if you think I'm gonna come to see you and have some punk dudes try to scare me off, then you got another think comin'. I *want* to go with you, so I'll let them *punks* know right away where I'm comin' from. Now, if you can't deal with that, then fine, 'cause I'm not goin' for no dumb shit."

Raheema was speechless.

Tracy hid behind her door, impressed. She then walked out of the house to get her brother from the day-care center as if she had not heard a thing. She spotted Bucky heading back up the block to return to his friend.

"Your friend is a trip," she said to him.

"Why you say that?" Bucky asked.

Tracy answered with giggle, "He just got mad as hell at her, and told her off." Tracy had never witnessed a boy talk to Raheema the way Bruce had.

Bucky grinned. "For what?"

"'Cause, these guys came around here tryin' to punk him. And then Ra-Ra said he shouldn't have said what he did."

"What did he say?"

"He said that they went with each other."

Bucky frowned and headed back to Raheema's steps, gesturing for them to leave. Bruce had said all that he could. He then asked Raheema to walk him to the corner. Bucky followed them, shaking his head in disappointment. *He's doing it to himself again,* he thought.

Bruce pressed her. "So are you gonna go with me, or what?"

Raheema remained unsure about it. "Yeah, okay," she said, just to get him off of her back.

"I'm serious though," Bruce told her. She had answered too quickly for him to believe her.

"I said, 'okay.' "

Bruce smiled and happily tried to kiss her lips. Raheema refused. He then headed off with his friend, grinning from ear to ear.

"I told you I was gon' get her," he said on their way back.

"We'll see what happens," Bucky mumbled. He still felt Bruce was crazy for not wanting Tracy.

Raheema didn't call, but Bruce came to see her during the weeks that followed anyway, and Tracy was always there, bothering him. She decided not to tell Raheema that Bruce had tried to come on to her. She would use it instead as a last-resort weapon against him.

Bruce had a one-track mind when it came to Raheema. Nothing turned him away from her, kiss or no kiss. Bucky called him stupid though. His friend Bruce seemed to be the only one in the relationship. He could only see Raheema on Fridays and Saturdays, with no phone calls in between. And after a while, Bruce slowly began to lose interest.

It was late October on a Friday night, and a party was happening around the corner from Diamond Lane. Bruce went to see if Raheema wanted to go, and she refused. Bucky then called him another dummy.

"Ay Bruce, come here for a minute, man," he called, while out in front of Raheema's steps. Bruce walked over to him reluctantly. Bucky whispered, "Man, for the last time, leave, that, nut, bitch, a-lone. You wastin' your time with her, man."

Tracy and Carmen walked out of Tracy's house, getting ready to head to the party themselves. She and Carmen had become better friends, since Jantel was reluctant to do some of the things and go to some of the places that Tracy was becoming interested in. Tracy and

Raheema, on the other hand, were no longer friends. They were beginning to despise each other, and Tracy was still jealous of her neighbor.

"Bruce, come here for a minute," Raheema said, as soon as she noticed Tracy leaving out. Bruce left Bucky and walked back over to her. Raheema then whispered, "Put your arms around me and make her jealous." Bruce did everything she said. Tracy hated them both for it, and Bucky could not stop shaking his head. His buddy was a damned fool!

"Thanks, Bruce," Raheema told him, after Tracy and Carmen had passed by.

"Oh, so I can't get a *real* hug and a kiss, hunh?" Bruce asked, feeling cheated.

"Yeah, but I don't feel like it right now," Raheema said with a smile. Her relationship with Bruce was becoming one based more on entertainment than on feelings. She walked back to her steps and patted a spot for him to sit down next to her. And when Bruce followed her, his friend Bucky was fed up.

"Ay Bruce, I'm goin' to the party," he announced.

Bruce responded gleefully, "Aw'ight, I'll be around."

Bucky frowned at him, wanting to tell them *both* off. He held his tongue instead. *Well, I guess this dick-head will learn one day,* he thought to himself of his friend.

Bruce arrived at the party late and snuck inside the back door to find Bucky observing the crowds.

"Ay yo, man, I snuck in," he told his friend.

Bucky responded, chuckling, "Yeah, I didn't pay either, because I know the bitch." He obviously had little respect for women.

Moving through the crowds inside of the packed basement, Tracy bumped into Bruce on purpose.

Bruce turned and noticed her. "I'm 'bout to punch that girl in her head, man," he said in a low tone. Bucky laughed. His rough demeanor was slowly but surely beginning to rub off on Bruce. They had only been close friends for a little more than a year.

"You wanna dance?" Bruce turned to ask a cute, brown-skinned girl with long hair and long eyelashes. She was a beauty, with a face fit for the cover of a youth magazine.

"I don't care," she answered him, smiling like she liked him. "What's your name?" she asked, as their bodies met.

"Bruce."

"You live around here?"

"Naw, I live down the hill."

"Oh. Well, what are you doin' after the party?"

"I'on know. Why?" Bruce asked, hoping for sex.

"I'm going to my girlfriend's house afterward, and her mom's in Atlantic City. So we lookin' for something to do."

Bruce smiled, not believing his ears. It must have been his lucky night. He was already glad he had decided to come to the party instead of sitting out with Raheema on her steps all night.

"Oh, so you want me to come with you?" he asked the girl.

"Yeah, if you want to," she said, still staring. "Oh, my name is Stacy."

Bruce took her to the wall. He was getting rock hard under his jeans. *I might have a chance to finally get some ass,* he told himself.

A voice slipped into his ear from behind, "Yo, what's up, Bruce?" Bruce turned and spotted Victor Hinson, who was attempting to press a girl up against the wall himself. It was a sign of the times for teenagers to get what they called "exotic" at parties.

Bruce shook Victor's gold-ringed black hand, and smiled.

Stacy then spoke to his attractive dance partner. "Marsha? What time are we leaving?"

Marsha responded, referring to Stacy *and* Bruce, "Whenever *y'all* ready."

Stacy's girlfriend was as good-looking as she was. *Birds of a feather flock together,* Bruce told himself with a grin.

Smiling with shiny white teeth, Victor said, "Bruce, *we're* goin' to their crib." Bruce was well informed about Victor's reputation. He definitely felt he would score if Victor was with him. Victor Hinson was *the man!*

Interjecting, Tracy's girlfriend Carmen howled, "Ay Stacy, don't talk to him. He got a girlfriend."

Bruce turned to his left, nervously, thinking that he had been busted. Tracy was laughing in the background.

Victor pushed Carmen away and said, "Don't believe that shit, Stacy. Bruce is my cousin. She just mad 'cause he didn't wanna talk to her."

Bruce was impressed with Victor's quick tongue. He was like lightning with his game. And his reputation was well deserved.

"Oh, I wasn't worried about that," Stacy responded.

"Ay Bruce, come here," Jantel said, tapping him on his shoulder. She whispered, "Raheema wants to see you," while giving Stacy an evil eye. She and Raheema had become good friends, since Tracy was hanging out more with Carmen.

Bruce frowned. "For what?"

"Because she wants to see you," Jantel said, as though it was obvious.

"But I was just with her," Bruce whined, not willing to leave the party.

"All right then. I'll just tell her that you were *busy*," Jantel warned.

Bruce sighed and looked back to Stacy. "Ay, I'll be right back. All right?" he told her.

"Okay," Stacy said loyally.

Bruce moved through the crowds as Tracy kept an eye on his every move.

"What did you say to him?" she asked her estranged girlfriend, Jantel.

"I told him that Raheema wanted to see him," Jantel told her.

"She does?"

"Yeah."

Tracy then thought about their friendship. "Do you still like her?" she asked of Raheema with a grimace.

"Yes, I do, Tracy," Jantel huffed. "Do you still like Carmen?" she asked back.

Tracy sucked her teeth and was speechless. Jantel then walked off to do her own thing, since Tracy had new interests.

From out of nowhere, Bucky grabbed Bruce's arm before he had made it to the back door. "Where you goin', man?"

"I'll be right back, cuz'."

Bucky scowled at him. "Man, don't—" He then stopped himself in mid-sentence, realizing that he would be wasting his breath. "Fuck it," he said to his friend scornfully. "You're gonna do what you want to do anyway."

Bruce left the party and walked back around to Diamond Lane, where he found Raheema waiting for him on her steps. He sat down next to her, began to talk and quickly forgot all about the party. And when Raheema was ready to go back inside, he tried to kiss her once more before they said their good-byes, only to have her turn him down again. By that time it was after eleven o'clock. Bruce darted back to the party.

Tracy smirked at Bruce's arrival. "That's why they left you," she said, teasing.

Bruce ignored her. "Where did Vic and them girls go?" he asked Bucky.

"Oh, they were lookin' for you, but you had left."

"Well, how come you didn't tell them where I was?"

Bucky grimaced. "Man, you ain't tell me where you was goin'."

Bruce ran from the party to find out where Victor and the girls had gone. Block after block, he desperately gave people their descriptions, and no one seemed to know where they were.

Bruce was pressed for sex. He walked home, brokenhearted again and pissed at his brainless decisions. If he would have listened to Bucky and left Raheema alone, he could have *scored.*

Bruce ventured to Raheema's house early that Saturday morning. Raheema was out on her steps at first, but once she spotted Bruce approaching in a pair of tan Timberland shoes, black jeans, a brown leather jacket and brown Gucci glasses, she ran back into the house, considering herself not dressed well enough to be with him.

Tracy sat out on her own steps and laughed at Raheema's silliness. She smiled at Bruce, but he turned away.

"Uuw, Bruce, can I see your glasses?" Tracy squealed, reaching out her hands as if he had told her that she could.

"Naw," Bruce responded, slapping Tracy's hands away.

Tracy dropped her eyes, pretending to be hurt by it. "You so mean to me," she whined.

Raheema exploded out of her house, screaming, "Why don't you leave him alone, Tracy!"

Tracy laughed it off. She figured she would wear Bruce down eventually. The challenge made it more fun, and Raheema surely would not be able to keep him long. Every boy had his needs, and Raheema was not willing to meet any of them.

Tracy went in and got her brother. She then took Jason for a walk to the corner to get away from her neighbor and her handsome but pitiful boyfriend.

Bruce got bold and walked up to Raheema's door, suspecting that no one was home. He knew what kind of cars her parents drove, and neither of them were parked out in front of the house.

"Who's home, Raheema?"

"Nobody," she told him, happy to be home alone.

Bruce opened the door to walk in, and Raheema slammed his hand to stop him.

"You can't come in my house, boy! I don't know what *your* problem is!" she yelled at him.

Bruce embarrassingly laughed it off. "Your pop must really got you uptight, hunh?"

"*No,* I just don't *want* you in my house. That's all."

Bruce felt like a nitwit. Raheema had pulled his last straw, and he had no energy left to deal with her. He needed an excuse to get away. "Well, I gotta go shopping with my mom today," he lied to her, while backing down the steps. "I'll see you."

"*Leave* if you want to, boy. I don't care," Raheema hissed at him.

"Now why you gon' get like that, Raheema?" Bruce pleaded to her.

"We've been goin' with each other for over a month now, and you won't even kiss me."

Raheema refused to let her defenses down. She gave Bruce an evil stare and slammed her door in his face. She wanted badly for him to stay, but she did not know how to control her emotions. How was she supposed to feel toward a boy? And how could she keep him interested without kissing him, letting him tell her what to do, and then ultimately being *used* by him?

That's it! Bruce snapped to himself. He was tired of playing Mr. Niceguy with Raheema and getting no results. He planned on going after the primary prize: sex with Tracy. Bucky was right; *later for love.*

Bruce was too angry to feel nervous about approaching Tracy. She was still *flyy,* but he had gotten used to her, and he was no longer timid around her. He quickly met up with Tracy at the corner and stopped to talk.

"Tracy, I know I've been mean with you, but me and Raheema are finished, and she's the only reason I was acting like that," he said.

Tracy wanted to smile, but she kept a straight face. "Well, I don't really want to talk to no boys right now. I mean, I just wanted to be *friends* with you," she lied with a straight face.

Bruce looked bewildered. He was too mentally drained and psychologically frustrated to even respond. Tracy only wanted him when he was connected to Raheema, like some kind of a silly competition. He frowned, realizing it, and walked away in a state of depression.

Tracy felt sorry for the boy. *He's just gonna have to get smarter with girls,* she told herself. *Nobody likes a pushover.*

Bruce mumbled as he walked down the street with his head hanging low, "I'm a damn fool."

Bruce asked Victor about Tracy when they saw each other in school. Victor said, "Man, I was runnin' up in her all summer long. That young-buck was addicted to *my* shit. I got them panties whenever I wanted to."

Bruce was weak with jealousy. He thought that he would never be a lady's man. He turned them off with his niceness. He only dreamed that he could be like Victor one day.

Tracy continued to haunt Bruce's thoughts, with her glamour, her self-assurance and her sensuality. Bruce longed through November and into December, fantasizing that he would get another chance.

"Hey, dad! You bring my Christmas money with you?" Tracy asked, running down the stairs.

"Damn, girl, let me settle down first," her father responded to her. Dave had grown a smooth mustache and a beard, looking closer to his age than what he did previously with his hairless babyface.

"Aw'ight, just as long as you know what time it is," Tracy told him with a grin.

Dave strolled over toward the couch as Tracy's brother ran and jumped on his legs. He then dragged his son along with him as Jason clung tightly to his thigh, giggling with glee. Their father then sat on the couch with him as Tracy joined them.

"So how you doin' in school?" her father asked her.

"I'm doin' all right. High school ain't even as hard as I thought it would be."

"Well, why would you think that *that* high school was hard?" Dave asked, referring to their neighborhood Germantown High School.

"Because, everybody talked about high school, *in general,* like it was supposed to be a big change or somethin'."

"Well, it's more of a social change than an academic change, unless you would've gone to Central or Girl's High, like *we* wanted," Dave alluded.

Tracy sighed, tired of hearing about "those nerd schools."

Her father warned her sternly, "Now you make sure you stay away from them drugs, stay in school, and don't get pregnant."

Tracy brushed his comments off with a laugh.

"I'm serious, girl," her father told her.

"I'm not taking no drugs, dad. And I like to dress too much to miss school. Then I can show off my clothes and stuff."

Dave smiled. "Yeah, I know."

"Shet up, dad," Tracy said, playfully slapping his shoulder.

"What about these young guys your mother told me been calling you? You got a boyfriend yet?"

Tracy giggled, embarrassed. "Mom ain't tell you that. 'Cause I don't have any *boyfriends*."

Dave grinned. "Why not?"

"All the good ones are taken."

"Aw, here we go with that stuff," her father commented with a smirk.

Tracy smiled. "What?"

"You girls always talkin' 'bout *the good ones get away*. And most of the time, what you consider a 'good guy' is really a bad guy. And you probably got a *real* 'good guy' out there that's dying to be your little boyfriend."

"No it ain't. They be goof-balls. I want a *decent* guy."

"See, that's exactly what I'm talkin' about."

Tracy looked at herself in the diamond-shaped mirrors on their living-room wall. "I mean, dad, I am too *fine* to get some regular guy. I feel that I deserve the best guy I can get."

Dave smiled, proud of his handsome genes. "I see. You're thinking just like your mother used to think," he commented while wrestling with his son.

Tracy paused for a second. She looked toward the top of the stairs, wondering what her mother was doing. She had to know that Dave was home, with all of the commotion that they had made. *Mom's probably refusing to see him,* she thought to herself.

"Did you tell mom that you were coming?" she asked her father.

Dave didn't respond to her, as he was too busy playing with Jason. "What did you say?"

Tracy was not sure if it was her place to comment on their relationship. *But he's asking about mine,* she told herself. "I said, 'Did you tell mom that you were coming?' " she forced herself to ask again.

Dave thought to himself for a second. "Yeah, she knows," he said solemnly.

Patti never did come down to see him during his short visit. Dave would have stayed longer had she come down to see him, but he understood how she felt, and he wasn't ready to give up his freedom yet. He realized that he was being selfish. *But I'm still taking care of the bills around here,* he told himself. Patti still would not allow another man inside of the house, and Dave's paying of the major bills seemed to serve as his psychological leash on her. As long as Patti continued to live there in his house, Dave figured he could keep tabs on her actions.

Tracy's father left after giving her four hundred dollars for Christmas and promising her brother that Santa Claus would put some big toys under the tree for him.

Tracy thought about her father's comments on good guys versus bad guys, but her mind was made up. She looked in the mirror again and decided that weak-minded niceguys were meant for girls of a slower caliber. She was not attracted to guys who didn't have anything going. It wasn't her fault that they were "slow." *They should go after the girls who are more their speed,* Tracy thought. Because she was in the big leagues.

Tracy came home from school and noticed Mercedes climbing out of the driver's seat of a blue Honda Prelude. She was driving, nineteen years old and still looking sharp. She wore a long black leather coat against the winter chill.

"Hey, girlfriend," she called.

"Hi," Tracy responded, hugging her.

"Damn! You got tall as shit!" Mercedes exclaimed, looking Tracy over. "And look at that *ass* on you, girl. Give me some of that."

Tracy cringed. "Ill, you sound fruity," she joked.

Mercedes frowned at her. "Oh, girl, shet up. I don't go that way. Let's go in your house and have some girl talk. It's freezing out here."

They went inside, and Mercedes took a seat on the couch. She then opened up her coat, revealing a royal blue súede dress laced with gold chains. Tracy counted six of them, which doubled her collection of chains. Mercedes had a new pair of gigantic gold earrings as well, and her hair was fabulously styled as usual.

"So what's been up, girl?" she asked Tracy.

"Your sister had a boyfriend," Tracy told her.

"Get out of here," Mercedes piped. "She did? What dummy would go with her?"

Tracy chuckled. "Some boy named Bruce."

"How he look?"

"Oh, he's cute, but he was slow."

"Yeah, he *gots* to be slow to deal with her," Mercedes commented, taking out a pack of Newports.

"Yup, I liked him at first, but after I seen how stupid he was, that was it," Tracy added, not saying anything about Mercedes smoking in her house.

Mercedes took her first drag and puff. Then she asked, "So who you been seeing, girlfriend, 'cause I know you gave up them panties by now?"

Tracy answered bashfully but proud, "The only one who got some was this boy named Victor."

Mercedes' eyes lit up. "Victor Hinson?" she asked excitedly.

"Yeah, how you know?"

Mercedes chuckled through the smoke. "I used to mess wit' his older brother," she answered. "So little Victor was takin' it to you, hunh?"

Tracy admitted through a smile, "Yeah."

"Well, did you get anything from him?"

"What 'chew mean by that?"

"I mean, did he give you some gear, some money or *something*. I know you didn't just *give him the pussy* for free, did you?"

Tracy answered, feeling ashamed, as if she should have *known* better, "Oh, well, he just got what he wanted and left."

"Girl, what did I tell you before?" Mercedes said, seriously. "Do you smoke?" she quizzed.

"No," Tracy snapped, not caring what Mercedes felt about it. Tracy didn't like cigarettes, and neither of her parents smoked.

Mercedes puffed her cigarette with dark slit eyes, dressed to kill and sparkling with gold. She tossed out her gold-ringed, cigarette-holding hand and ran down the game from the girl side of things. "I told you, don't give them *nothin'* unless they got something to give you. Now I know Victor is a suave young-boy and all, but you won't get nothin' out of it, 'cause I had his older brother, and I know. They some stingy motherfuckers. Half the time, girls end up buying them shit.

"Now what you do is get a nice-looking nut dude with some money and romance his ass. If you can get somethin' without doing anything with him, then do it. But if you can't, then make sure you play with his mind real good before you do. 'Cause see, a lot of guys are stingy until you give them some pussy. But once you do, they start actin' dumb, all in love and shit."

Mercedes straightened out a few of the gold rings on her fingers. "But watch out for the hustlers though, 'cause they'll try to hurt you."

"What about getting pregnant and stuff?" Tracy asked, thinking about what her father had warned.

Mercedes dug into her bag and pulled out a plastic case. "These are birth control pills. You just take one of these every day." She then wrote a number down on a piece of paper. "You go into this clinic and they'll give you the right dosage for your body and stuff. And it's all confidential," she added. Mercedes gave Tracy the number. Tracy immediately thought about Bruce, plotting to seduce him.

"Hi, mom," Mercedes said, as her mother opened the door.

Beth's eyes ballooned. "Where have you been?" she queried, hugging her daughter excitedly. Mercedes had chosen to live on the wrong side of the tracks, but she was still her Mother's first child.

"I've been around, but I've been busy."

Raheema came out from the kitchen and listened in from the dining room.

"Well, what have you been up to?" Beth asked, stepping back to take a look at Mercedes, whom she had not seen in six months.

"I got a job at Mellon Bank. And right now I'm living with this guy who's in law school."

"Law school? Well, that's great! Do you plan to get married to him?"

"I mean, we'll have to see what happens. He may not want me after he finishes school. You know how these sorry niggas out here get. But how've you been doing, mom?" Mercedes asked, changing the subject.

"I've been hangin' in there, you know."

"How's Ms. Patti doin'? I forgot to ask Tracy while I was over there?"

"She's just fine. Everybody's fine," Beth said. She looked over at her younger daughter and wished the two of them could settle their differences. "Raheema, get on over here and say 'hi' to your sister, girl."

Raheema got up, hesitantly, and walked over to them. She had been feeling lonely since Bruce had stopped coming around, and she had been thinking about Mercedes. *She's still my sister,* she told herself.

Mercedes squealed, "Whaaat? My little sister wants to hug me and shit. This *must* be Christmastime!"

Beth was glad the fighting was over.

Mercedes said, "Well, since *we've* made up, then I guess it's okay if I ask about the old man. So how is he doin'?"

"Well, you should wait and see him. I know he's just dying to lay his eyes on you," Beth suggested.

"I'll tell you what, mom, I'll come back tomorrow and see him. 'Cause tomorrow is Friday, and I still have some things to do," Mercedes responded, ready to leave back out. She never did stay long. Spending too much time in that house seemed to bring back depressing memories.

Raheema and Beth watched her car as she pulled off.

Raheema asked, "What do you think, mom?"

"She's doing all right, honey."

"Do you think she's telling the truth about that lawyer guy?"

"Well, it doesn't really matter, honey, as long as she's alive and well."

Beth closed the door as they walked back inside.

• • •

Bruce and Bucky got ready for another party. The local YMCA on
Greene Street, off of Chelten Avenue, was being rented out. Bucky
took all day, while Bruce was dressed in an hour. They expected to
"rack-up," or in other words, to collect many phone numbers that
night.

Bruce wore new, gold-framed Neostyle glasses that cost over a hundred and fifty dollars. He spent money recklessly, but usually it was
only on himself. Bucky called him "a stingy muthafucka."

They were on their way, both wearing expensive black leather bomb-
ers. When they had arrived, crowds were packed outside, as they
greeted and shook the hands of all the people they knew, while setting
up to romance pretty girls.

Girls stared at Bruce, and he felt lucky as they paid their three dollars
and walked inside. He moved over to a sexy, big-butted girl and asked
her to dance. She looked at him as if she was in love and agreed to it.
She then moved in closer to him as the DJ mixed The Boogie Boys'
hit rap song, "Fly Girl."

Bruce smiled. "I guess this means you like me, hunh?"

"I guess it does."

"What's your name?" he asked.

"Joseline," the sexy, big-butted girl told him.

"That's a pretty one."

"I know. But what's yours?"

"Bruce."

Joseline squeezed his behind as they danced. "You got a girlfriend,
Bruce?"

"Not at the moment, but I do want your phone number." Bruce's
private was getting harder and harder.

Joseline whispered, squeezing his behind again, "I'll give it to you,
if you promise to give me some."

She was too aggressive and downright nasty for Bruce's taste. They
continued to dance until the DJ mixed in "The Show," by Slick Rick

and Doug E. Fresh. The place rocked with one of the most popular rap tunes, but they then decided to take a break as Joseline wrote her number down. Bruce left her and went to the other side of the room to get another number, thinking that he was *the shit*.

Bruce asked a sharply dressed, dark-skinned girl, "Ay pretty, you wanna dance?" She gave her Gucci bag to her girlfriend and started to dance with him without a word. She kept her distance and did "The Wop." She then turned around and moved closer to him, as he leaned up against her. Bruce soon turned to avoid it though, tired of having a hard-on.

After a while, Bruce grew weary of dancing. "Ay look, let's go over here so I can talk to you right quick," he said suddenly. He pointed to some chairs, off to the corner of the large gym. The girl retrieved her Gucci bag from her girlfriends and decided to oblige.

Bruce moved their chairs so that they faced each other. "So, what's your name?"

"Tasha."

"That's a nice one."

"Thank you," she said, smiling.

Bruce asked, "What would you say if I told you I would like to be your boyfriend in the future?"

Tasha hunched her shoulders. "I'on know."

"Well, my name is Bruce."

She grinned and extended her hand to his. "Okay."

Bruce then slowly placed his hand on her knee, while looking around the gym to make sure that Joseline didn't catch him.

He asked Tasha calmly, "Have you ever made love before?"

She lied and said, "Yeah."

"How old are you?"

Tasha lied again. "Fifteen." She really was fourteen.

"You got a boyfriend?"

Tasha finally told him the truth. "No."

Bruce smiled through his gold Neostyle frames. "Well, you gon' think about *me*, right?"

"Yeah," Tasha said, bashfully, believing that he was cool.

Bruce asked sternly, like he had witnessed Victor do, "So what's your number?"

"Five-four-two—"

"Wait, write it down," he told her, cutting her off.

Tasha took out a piece of paper from her bag. Bruce supplied her with a pen. She then wrote her number down, and Bruce got up to look for Bucky.

"Look, I'll call you up when I get a chance. Aw'ight?" he told Tasha, strolling away as if he was *the shit*.

"You better," Tasha retorted playfully. She was planning on telling her girlfriends all about him.

While on his search for his friend Bucky, Bruce spotted Carmen. *Oh, shit!* he panicked. His heart began to race. If Carmen was there, then Tracy might be as well. He was not prepared to see her, especially while he was on a roll. Bruce felt inferior when he was around Tracy. Then again, he figured, *This might be the best time to talk to her. She'll see how many other girls like me.*

Before he could even look, a familiar voice husked in his ear, "Hi, Bruce."

Tracy stepped out in front of him with a straight face, twinkling eyes and shiny gold chains, wearing an orange sweater that hugged her pert breasts. Her legs were slightly opened, suggestively, and Bruce was thinking about *doing it* to her on site. There was no way to get around her. He was shocked, stunned, dazzled and immediately afraid of her. He knew he wasn't *the shit* when up against Tracy. And she was *only* fourteen!

Bruce said, "What's up?" and moved past her nervously. He hastily entered the bathroom like a scattering alley cat and looked into the mirror, stalling for time. He wanted to talk to her, but he could not help feeling goofy and corny around her. Tracy had already told all of her girlfriends that Bruce liked her. The word was out, and he was scared to even look at her.

Walking back out into the party, he spotted Tracy's huddle of friends waiting for him. Tracy was in the middle, like a football quarterback. Cool and confident boys moved in, asking her to dance, but Tracy turned them all down.

Bruce went over and asked someone else to dance, but he could see Tracy staring at him from his left side. He had a feeling she was waiting for him. He felt like a winner, deciding to keep her guessing; that way he would be in command.

Yet Tracy destroyed his plans, deciding to approach him while he danced instead of waiting for him. "Ay, Bruce, you don't wanna dance with me or somethin'?" she asked seductively. She made it sound as if she was desperate and begging for him. And Bruce liked it.

"No," he responded to her.

The girl he was dancing with became apprehensive. "Is she your girlfriend or something?" she asked, reading Tracy's tone.

"Naw, she just likes me," he told her.

Tracy moved over to a nearby wall to continue staring at him. She was worried. Her plan to seduce him would never work if Bruce was no longer interested. And she was still standing there, several songs later, turning boys down as Bruce watched her watching him.

Bucky walked up beside him, grinning. "Tracy's here."

"Yeah, I know."

Bucky chuckled. "Well, you gon' game her up or what, man?" he asked, right in front of the other girl, not caring if she heard him. Tracy was more important in his eyes. She was one of the *flyyest* girls there.

"Yeah, but I'm gon' make her wait some more," Bruce told him.

Bucky looked at his watch. "Yo, man, it's almost twelve o'clock, and she might have to go home soon."

"Umm, excuse me, but it seems you have *other* things on your mind," Bruce's dance partner commented as she walked off from him. *Who does he think he is?* she fumed to herself. She felt slighted.

Bucky looked at Bruce and hunched his shoulders. "Fuck her, man. Go talk to Tracy."

Bucky was right, Tracy did have to leave soon, but she refused to. She told Carmen that she would stay until Bruce decided to talk to her.

Bruce finally called her over to him.

Tracy walked over to Bruce real slow, as if he was controlling her
will with magic. She answered him like a child, once she had reached
him, "Yes, Bruce." Tracy was doing a good job of playing with his
mind. Bruce actually felt like he was manipulating her.

"You wanna dance wit' me now?" he asked.

"If you want me to."

Bruce took her hand for a slow song. The DJ played the Art Of
Noise's "Moments in Love." Tracy's emotions did not seem to be into
it. Bruce assumed she was angry at him for making her wait.

"Are you mad at me or something?" he whispered.

"Why would I be mad at you?"

Bruce felt it was a weak question and tried to cover up. "When are
you about to leave?" he asked.

Tracy lied. "As soon as my girlfriends are ready."

"Well, me and Bucky can leave with y'all."

"Okay," Tracy happily agreed. Her plan was beginning to work
perfectly, because she had to get home soon. Her mother was still
acting bitchy about the midnight curfew.

Bruce told Bucky their plans and they all left. Bucky flirted with
Carmen on the way to Tracy's house, but Bruce continued to keep his
distance from her, to keep her guessing, of course. He wanted to act as
if he was really in control of things.

As they walked, Bucky noticed they were nearing his cousin's house.
He secretly let Bruce know, and Bruce decided to try his luck. He
figured he had nothing to lose. He stopped and called Tracy over to
him.

"Why don't you hang out with me, Tracy?" he asked, while holding
her hand. "We can all chill over Bucky's cousin's house. He lives right
up the street."

Tracy jerked away from him. "No, I gotta get home."

"Look, it's only one night. Sometimes you just have to say 'Fuck
it,' " he told her, stealing a line from Tom Cruise's *Risky Business*.

Tracy laughed at him, recognizing the line. "Boy, you've been
watching too many movies."

Bruce felt a strong impulse to go for it, like Victor and the other playboys would do. "Look, if you don't go with me tonight, then it's over. So don't ever speak to me again," he ranted.

Tracy backed away and continued to laugh. She figured his threat was harmless. She could twist Bruce around her little finger anytime she wanted to. *Who is he trying to be?* she asked herself.

"Aw'ight then," she told him, walking away to rejoin her friends.

Bucky shook his head and imitated Fred Sanford. "You, big, *dummy!*"

Bruce sighed and said, "Man, I'll never get no ass."

Bucky headed for his cousin's house. "Don't worry 'bout it, 'Brucie.' Try again tomorrow," he said, imitating Tracy. He laughed even harder as his cousin answered the doorbell to let them in out of the cold.

After Christmas, Tracy and Bruce saw each other at the USA Skating Rink in Northeast Philadelphia.

Bruce kept his distance while Tracy stared at him, driving him crazy. And eventually he was drawn to her like a fly to fruit, while still trying his hardest to resist temptation.

"Why you always starin' at me if you don't like me?" he huffed at her.

"I didn't say I didn't like you."

"Well, do you like me or what?"

Tracy rolled her eyes. "I'on know. You tell me."

"You know what? You're really gettin' on my *nerves!*"

"So?" she snapped at him.

"So why don't you tell me what you want from me?"

Tracy lied. "I don't want nothin' from *you.*"

"So why the hell you keep staring at me?"

Teenagers turned to see what was going on. Tracy was amused by Bruce's temper. She giggled and said, "You better calm down, boy."

Bruce responded, skating away, "Fuck it, I quit. I'm tired of talkin' to you."

Tracy shouted, "Come here!"

"FOR WHAT?!"

"Just come here," she repeated, heading over to a water fountain on her skates. Bruce skated over behind her. "Do you want my phone number?" she asked, digging inside of her new white Sixers jacket.

"Is it gon' mean anything?" Bruce asked her.

Tracy snapped, "What 'chew think?"

Bruce started to skate away.

"Yeah, boy! God!" Tracy yelled.

"Are you sure? 'Cause I ain't playin' no more games," he warned her.

"You'll find out when you call me."

Bruce smiled helplessly. He was in love with Tracy's style. And for the rest of that night, she was the only thing that he could think about.

Bruce went home and dreamed about Tracy coming over to his house to make love to him. He imagined himself rolling over and spreading her legs while she lay in his bed. He would then melt into her naked body as she squeezed him and moaned his name. And when they would finish, she would cuddle up to him and whisper, "I love you."

Bruce called Tracy up and was invited to visit her. He was so excited that he immediately began practicing what he would say and how he would act. He planned to toss on some of his Polo cologne and get a fresh haircut for his shiny waves. And as far as Raheema seeing him, he told himself, "So what? She ain't fuckin' anyway. I wasted my time with her, just like Bucky tried to tell me."

"Mom, this is Bruce," Tracy said, leading him into the kitchen.

Patti looked him over and said, "How are you? I've heard so much about you."

"See, I told you I was talkin' 'bout you," Tracy bragged, grinning at him. Bruce felt important, but what he didn't know was that Tracy had only talked about how he looked and how he dressed.

She led him back to the living room and sat with him on the couch. Jason then ran and jumped on him.

"What's your name?" he asked.

"Bruce."

They shook hands, with Bruce's swallowing Jason's.

"You like Tracy?" Jason asked.

Bruce beamed. "I'on know."

Tracy butted in. "You want something to drink?"

"Yeah," Bruce said.

Tracy got him lemonade, and Bruce gulped it down in one big swallow.

"Dag! You want some more?" she asked, surprised by it. *He must be thirsty or something,* she thought to herself.

"Naw," Bruce responded with a nervous smile. But after playing with Jason, he began to feel at home.

Tracy took the cup back to the kitchen.

Patti grinned at her. "Tracy, he's cute."

"I *know,* 'cause I don't deal wit' ugly guys," Tracy said, walking back out to the living room with a slight bounce. She sat back on the couch with Bruce.

Bruce moved closer to her. "You just wake up pretty, don't you?" he asked.

Tracy responded with a giggle, "No, you have to ask my mother about that."

Bruce's eyes focused on the 27-inch RCA that Jason had turned on. "That's a big-ass TV y'all got."

Tracy whispered, looking at her brother, "Watch your mouth, boy."

Jason was a human tape recorder.

"Oh, my fault," Bruce apologized.

"Dag, you ain't got no manners," Tracy responded, still getting on him about it. She looked at Bruce's clothing and smiled.

"What's so funny?" he quizzed.

"Where you get your sneakers from?"

"From Footlocker's."

"How you be gettin' all them glasses?"

Bruce lied, thinking that Tracy liked adventure. "We stole 'em."

Her eyes ballooned. "For real?"

Bruce frowned. "No, girl. I bought them."

"Well, excuuuse me, Mr. Money."

Bruce cracked a broad smile while Tracy thought about making her move.

"Bruce?"

"What?"

"Won't 'chew buy me some stuff?" Tracy leaned into him.

Jason smiled, watching for Bruce's reaction to his sister's begging. Tracy was always begging for something.

Bruce chuckled and said, "Aw'ight. Give me the money."

Tracy sucked her teeth and nudged him. "For real, Bruce. Please. I'm serious." Her head softly met his shoulder.

Bruce insisted, "When you give me the money, I'll do it."

Tracy was pissed. "Dag, you stingy, boy!" she huffed at him, straightening up from his shoulder. "I *should* make you leave," she pouted.

Bruce didn't care if he left at that point. He had had a good time, and he could tell that Tracy was enjoying his company.

"Oh, well, I'll roll then," he said, getting up to walk to the door.

"Sike, Bruce. I'm only playin' with you," she said, pulling him back down on the couch with her. "But you gon' take me to the movies?"

"For what?"

"Because, I wanna go."

Bruce grinned. "If I take *you,* I won't be able to talk to no other girls."

Tracy rolled her eyes and sighed at him. "You a trip."

Bruce leaned back into her couch and enjoyed the rest of his stay.

• • •

Tracy's plan to get Bruce's materials without giving him anything was going nowhere. Bruce continued to avoid all of her money questions. He liked teasing her. He knew what she was after, and he began to ask her for a proper trade-off. They wore each other out with their demands. Neither of them seemed to be getting anywhere. And soon they began to talk to other people, fading off from each other.

By early March, Bruce had a new girlfriend, and Tracy liked a green-eyed, light-skinned boy who had clout in her school. "Green-eyed Timmy" had been approaching her for weeks, but Tracy refused to be his plaything. Timmy already had a girlfriend. And Bruce was going through the same old charades, struggling with every girl that liked him. He had the same old problems: not being able to keep the girls interested, and never being able to score.

It was early April before Tracy saw Bruce looking deliciously tempting again. She was going out for a track team, and Bruce happened to show up for a girl who was going out for the team as well. Jantel was already a star on the team, but she was still not as close with Tracy as they had been before Carmen entered the picture.

Bruce looked shockingly handsome in the bright spring sun. His legs were strong and masculine in his shorts. Maybe that was what turned Tracy on. Or possibly it was the haircut; his thick wavy hair shone like it was waxed. Or maybe it was the gold rope chain that he wore around his neck with a $ sign hanging over his red Polo tennis shirt. Whatever it was that turned Tracy on, it hit her like a bag of bricks that day, and all she could think about was how much she wanted him.

"Ay Marcy, tell that boy right there that somebody said he looks good," Tracy said to a new friend. She pointed the short, thick-built sprinter to Bruce, who was standing at the fence that surrounded the track.

Marcy walked right over to him and said it.

"Who said that?" Bruce quizzed, knowing who it was already. Only Tracy was *that* bold.

Marcy confirmed it, "Some girl named Tracy did."

Bruce looked over at her, and Tracy smiled at him.

Bruce felt desperate. "Well, tell her that I love her," he said to Marcy.

Tracy asked Marcy, excitedly, "What did he say?"

"He said that he loves you."

A burst of joy flowed through Tracy's body. She had made up her mind. She decided that she would *do it* with him. *No boy ever said that he loves me,* she thought.

She called Bruce up to talk, and he desperately tried to get her over to his house, but she refused. She wanted to wait to take her birth-control pills. Bruce was angry, having no idea why she had told him "no" again.

He tried unsuccessfully to score with other girls, becoming more and more pressed for a sexual encounter. Maybe it was the warm weather that was making him so restless for lovemaking, but Bruce was ready to *do it* with anyone who would let him. He felt as though he was being punished by the forces of nature. *I can't get no ass to save my life!* he told himself.

By the end of another sexless week, Bruce was devastated. His new girlfriend would not agree to consort with him either. He wouldn't dare to rape a girl. His mother would kill him, *after* she threw him out, so it was nothing that he could do to speed up nature's process but wait for his time to come. *Every dog has his day,* he mused, *but if I don't get some sex soon, I feel like I'm about to turn into one.*

"So what happened, man?" Bucky asked.

Bruce had returned from his girlfriend's house. He answered, sitting on Bucky's steps with his head down, "She said her period was on."

Bucky laughed, straightening out his Adidas tennis outfit. "You went for that *nut* shit?"

Bruce threw up his hands. "Look, man, what was I supposed to do?"

"You should have let her know, right off the back, that you ain't no *nut,* cuz'."

Bruce shook his head and said, "Yeah, well, it's too late for that now. Maybe it just ain't meant for me to get no ass."

"Man, shet up. That's probably why they all think you a sucka' now."

"Well, what we gon' do tonight?" Bruce asked, changing the subject. There had to be at least a million better things worth talking about, as far he was concerned.

Bucky tucked in his shirt. He wasn't "good-looking," but to Bruce, Bucky had poise and style. "I don't know what 'chew doin', but I'm gon' get with this bitch later on," he said. Then again, Bucky simply did and said what he wanted, and girls seemed to respect him for it.

"Damn, well, I might as well go to see this girl myself," Bruce suggested.

"Yeah, you betta' do somethin'."

Bruce left immediately. The early April night was warm and peaceful. He walked to the girl's block, where he found her standing with her slightly bow-legged girlfriend. Bruce could not help watching her friend's bow-legs for the twenty or so minutes that he spent with them.

"So what's up, Nikki?"

"Nothin'. You just decided to come around here and see me, hunh?"

"Why you say it like that?"

"Were you bored or somethin', Bruce?"

"What, I gotta be bored to come see you?"

"I'm asking you."

Bruce looked at her girlfriend. "Damn!" he said, laughing. Nikki knew what he was talking about, but she tried to let it pass.

"Are you going to that party tonight?" she asked him.

"Naw. What party?"

"At the playground center."

"Nope. I want to be with you tonight," Bruce said, glancing at her girlfriend again.

Nikki had enough. She snapped, "This is Kari, since you act like you want to meet her."

Bruce was caught, and all he could do was smile about it. "Why you say that?" he responded, still grinning.

"You know what, Bruce? You can go back home, because you don't have any respect for me."

"Aw, now, why you gon' say that?"

Nikki ignored him. Bruce decided to leave. There was no way he could keep his mind on one girl, when he wasn't getting anything from any of them. *What the hell is the use?* he thought.

Bruce went home and sat inside of his living room. He laid back on the couch, exhausted from his thoughts of hopelessness. It was one of those Friday nights when all of his friends would get drunk. But Bruce didn't feel like being drunk; he felt like being inside of a girl. He closed his eyes, dreaming about it.

BRRRRIIIINNNG!

He answered the phone on the first ring. "Hello."

"Hi, it's Tracy."

"Hey, girl. What's going on?" he asked excitedly. He straightened up on the couch.

"Are you mad at me for not coming to your house?"

"Naw, I'm just happy that we're talking to each other again."

Tracy was still his number one.

"Come up here," she demanded.

Bruce was shocked. "When?" he asked.

"Now."

"For real?" He thought about the suddenness of it. "You're not playing with me, are you?" he asked her.

"No, I'm serious," she told him.

"Okay. I'll be up."

Bruce hung up the phone, ran to his room, threw on some cologne, grabbed a couple of rubbers from out his drawer and broke out the front door. He ran up Chelten Avenue and onto Wayne. He only stopped running when he had reached the corner of Diamond Lane. He then calmed himself and rang Tracy's bell.

Tracy walked onto her front steps looking beautiful. She wore a small, pink flower in her thick, dark brown hair.

Bruce asked, "How you doin'?"

"I'm okay. You got a car ride or something?" Tracy asked, wondering how he had gotten there so fast.

Bruce lied. "Yeah, my boy dropped me off at the corner."

"Oh," Tracy said, looking womanly.

Bruce looked over at Raheema's door and then at Tracy. "Well, can I come in?" he decided to ask. He thought it would be embarrassing to have Raheema come out and catch him.

Tracy told him with a smile, "Come on."

It was dark inside. A red lamp was the only thing on.

They sat on the couch, and Tracy kept her distance, staring down at her lap.

"What are you doin' that for?" Bruce quizzed.

"I don't know."

"Where your mom at?"

"She went out."

Bruce wanted to make a move immediately, but Tracy gave him no hints. If he wanted to *get it,* she would make him come after *it.*

Bruce started to harden, thinking about the possibilities. He moved closer to her and attempted to feel on her breasts. Tracy didn't stop him. She wanted him to do more, but Bruce stopped in fear that she *might* stop him.

"Can I get something to drink?" he asked, standing up momentarily. He didn't know what to do with himself.

Tracy got up to get him some lemonade, thinking of how inexperienced Bruce was acting. He drank it down as if he was ready to die from thirst again. Tracy took the cup back to the kitchen. Bruce then told himself that he wouldn't procrastinate, and that he would go for it. *Now!*

Tracy came back from the kitchen, and Bruce gently caressed and kissed her as she responded positively toward it. Bruce then leaned up and went for her pants zipper, but Tracy stopped him.

"Hold up, my mom might be coming," she lied, hearing a car pulling up outside. Patti wasn't due to be home until late. It was only nine forty-five, and Jason had been knocked out and in dreamland an hour earlier. Tracy had made sure to exhaust him earlier that day so she could have the nighttime all to herself.

Bruce got scared and leaped off of her.

Tracy walked to the door, holding in her laugh. She looked through the shades. "Nope. I was wrong."

Bruce held her up against the door and tried to kiss her again. Tracy turned her head from him to avoid it. Bruce kissed her neck instead.

"Stop, Bruce."

"So what we gon' do then?"

"All right, I'll *do it* with you. God!" she snapped at him.

"Are you sure?" Bruce asked, no longer believing anything that she said.

"Yeah, just let me go."

Bruce let her go, feeling victorious.

Tracy walked away from him and sat on the couch. "Why we gotta *do it?*" she whined.

Bruce sighed. He shook his head disappointedly. "I bet Victor ain't have to go through this shit!"

"Fuck him!" Tracy hollered in response. She walked over by the stairs.

Bruce said, "Look, I'm gettin' out of here, 'cause you ain't doin' nothin' but playin' with me." He grabbed his jacket and bolted for the door.

Tracy yelled, "Where you goin', Bruce?"

"I'm goin' the fuck home! Where you think I'm goin'?"

"NO!"

"Well, why you call me up here if you didn't wanna do nothin'?"

"Because, I wanted to talk to you."

"When I get home, I'll call you up then."

"I SAID, 'NO,' BOY!" Tracy hollered at him again.

"What we gon' do then, Tracy?"

Tracy looked away and sighed. She then walked over to the bottom of the stairs. "Get your stuff and come up to my bedroom," she told him.

Bruce struggled to keep his composure. He headed up the stairs, walking up first and feeling aroused. Tracy followed him sluggishly. Bruce got to her all-pink room in the dark. Tracy stood in the doorway behind him.

"Well, come on," Bruce turned and said.

Tracy shied away from him. "I'on wanna *do it* with *you,*" she whined, still playing games.

Bruce was about to go out of his mind, but he figured he was too close to lose. "Aw naw, that's it," he said, grabbing at her pants.

Tracy fought him. "Get off of me. I'll do it," she said, peeling his hands from her jeans.

Bruce frowned. "Come on, girl, stop playing with me," he said as if he was about to cry.

Tracy started to laugh. She loved Bruce's temper. "You get on my *nerves,* boy," she said, finally taking off her pants.

Bruce's heart beat wildly as he began to strip. Tracy became the first girl that he saw butt-naked in his life, except for the time when he walked in on his cousin taking an afternoon shower.

Bruce tried to lay Tracy's smooth honey-brown body on the bed, underneath his chestnut-brown frame.

Tracy stopped him. "No, Bruce."

"What 'chew mean, 'no'?" he asked, confused.

"I wanna *do it* on the floor."

Bruce cracked a colossal smile. He was in heaven. Everything Tracy said added to his excitement.

She stretched a blanket out on the floor, spread her legs and raised her knees up high, like she had done for Victor, more than a dozen times.

She whined, "Hurry up, Bruce. It's cold."

Bruce climbed overtop of her and tried to enter, but he could not find the right place.

"No, what are you trying to do?" Tracy asked.

"It's too dark in here. I can't see," Bruce said, making excuses. He tried again and failed, falling on top of her and breathing like he had done something.

Tracy asked, "What's wrong?"

Bruce laughed it off. "I don't believe this."

"What?"

"I ain't even hard no more."

Tracy sucked her teeth. "Well, get off of me then."

"Naw," Bruce responded. "But see, if you wasn't playin' with me, this wouldn't have happened," he said, making up more excuses for his inexperience. They lay there for a while, doing nothing. Bruce then tried to make himself erect by rubbing himself against her leg.

"Help me, Tracy," he whined.

Tracy was repulsed. "NO! I'm not touching *it.*"

Bruce sat up, playing with himself to become erect again. "Come on, help me," he begged Tracy.

Tracy grabbed at him and moved her hand back and forth. Bruce began to suck her breasts. Tracy then ran her fingers over his back, and he was *up* like a ladder.

"Put it in," he told her. Tracy did it with ease, making Bruce feel stupid that he could not do it. He leveled himself on top of her and started to move around in circles, not really knowing what he was doing. He didn't *feel* anything *special. Sex* was overrated.

Tracy felt nothing either. It wasn't like when Victor *did it* to her. Bruce did not have any of Victor's experience.

After a few minutes of feeling nothing, Tracy tried to push him off of her, but Bruce tightened his grip on her body. He continued to do what was meaningless, squirming around in circles and finally tired himself out.

Tracy shoved him away and sat up to think, *This boy ain't know what the hell he was doin'*. She figured she had given him a fair shot, and Bruce had grossly disappointed her.

"Put your clothes on," she demanded, slipping on her own.

Bruce refused. "Naw. I want to see what I got with your light on," he said, smiling and feeling proud of himself.

Tracy slid on a long, baby-blue nightshirt, refusing to show Bruce her naked body in the light. He then pulled his clothes back on in defeat.

Tracy walked to the top of her steps and froze. "Oh my God! Bruce, it's my mom!'' she said hysterically. Patti had come home earlier than expected. "Hurry up and hide in the closet." She forced Bruce in before he even had a chance to think. He fell in over all her shoes and under her clothing, which dangled over his head.

Tracy frantically straightened up the room and sprayed air freshener. Patti walked into the house and headed straight for Tracy's room, knowing that she wasn't asleep yet. It was a quarter of eleven on a Friday night.

Bruce was crunched and scared, listening in the closet.

"Well, how was it, mom?" Tracy asked. She really wanted to ask why she was back home so early, but she didn't want her mother to get suspicious.

"It was nice and all. Was Jason all right?" Patti didn't suspect anything.

"Yeah, he went to sleep like eight-thirty," Tracy told her.

Patti looked surprised. "He did?"

"Yup."

"Well, he must have been rippin' and runnin' all day, hunh?"

Bruce's long legs tightened in the closet, feeling severely cramped.

"Mom, I need some new jeans," Tracy was saying.

"I just bought you two pair."

Bruce was praying that her mother didn't walk over to check out her closet.

"Yeah, but I wanted some black ones, 'cause my other ones are too small now."

Tracy had enough clothes, which were beating Bruce up in the closet. *This girl is spoiled as shit,* he thought. *I pay for my own gear.*

Patti finally left for bed after what Bruce thought was eternity. Tracy then snuck downstairs to open the front door. Bruce was dying in the closet, balled up like a snail, when she made it back up to get him.

As she opened the closet door, Tracy whispered, "Come on."

Bruce struggled to his feet while Tracy hurried him down the stairs. Bruce then fell out on to her lawn, stretching out his legs on the grass.

"What are you doin'?" Tracy asked.

Bruce pouted, "Look, my legs are messed up. Aw'ight? Let me stuff you in a fuckin' closet."

Tracy giggled and said, "Get up, boy."

Bruce did, and headed on his way home.

The cars were shining, the streets were clean, the wind was blowing, the moon was glowing, the grass was shimmering, the sky was filled with stars and the poor were no longer hungry as Bruce jogged home. He was on cloud nine. He was *satisfied*. He had gotten *some*. And he couldn't wait to tell his friend Bucky.

cops-N-robbers

Tracy was wearing the black leather shoes and the Chanel perfume that she had gotten from Bruce as gifts. Bruce came religiously to sit around in her house and in her company, incensing her neighbor Raheema. Tracy was practically through with him after receiving more than four hundred dollars worth of accessories. But Bruce continued to buy her things, hoping that she would stay with him.

"Do you go with Bruce, Tracy?" Patti asked at breakfast.

Tracy drank down a cup of orange juice. "No, mom. We're just friends."

"Well, he's been buying you a lot of stuff lately."

Tracy grinned and said, "I know."

"You two don't like each other in a relationship way?"

"No, mom. God!"

Patti looked at Tracy with a smirk. "You know, *using* people is not the way to be."

"Ain't nobody *using* him."

"Okay, but what goes around comes around. Take it from your

mother, girl. I know this to be a fact." Patti warned, walking out of the kitchen.

Tracy thought about her mother's relationship with her father while heading to school. *I'm still young,* she told herself. *I'm just having fun right now. I'm not gon' to be dependent on guys all my life, but while I'm young, why not enjoy it?*

Tracy entered school that morning with a new project on her mind. Bruce had been conquered.

"Ay Joy, does Timmy still go with that light-skinned girl?"

"No, they broke up weeks ago," Joy said, frowning at Tracy's lack of knowledge on the recent gossip.

"You walk my way to class, right, Joy?"

"Yeah," Joy answered, standing a full head shorter than Tracy.

"Well, let's walk and talk then."

"So why you worried about Timmy all of a sudden? You thinkin' 'bout gettin' with him or somethin'?"

Tracy answered with a smile, "I don't know."

They dodged the other students as they walked through the hallway.

"Well, I wouldn't get involved with him if I was you, 'cause he's always in trouble for stealing and stuff."

"For real?"

Joy nodded. "Yup, girl. Guys be after him all the time. But I like that boy's *eyes* though. He got some pretty-ass eyes."

Wham! Timmy walked out from the boys' bathroom.

Joy's eyes popped, surprised to see him. "Speak of the devil," she said.

Timmy grinned with sparkling green eyes, strolling tall and slim with rusty brown hair. "What, you was talkin' 'bout me?"

"Yeah, I was just tellin' Tracy how much trouble you be gettin' into."

"Ay, don't believe her, Tracy, 'cause I wanted to make you my girl."

Tracy was shocked. Timmy was reading her mind. Things were happening too fast.

"Don't listen to him. He don't respect women," Joy warned, leaving Tracy alone with him.

"So where's your next class at?" Timmy asked Tracy.

Tracy smiled and said, "Around the hall."

"Can I talk to you now, Tracy? I'm free."

"If you want to," she answered, glancing at his greens.

Tracy had turned down Timmy's offerings before, but like he said, he was "free," and she was more than ready to move on from Bruce.

"So what's your number?" he asked, taking out a pen to write it on a scrap of paper. Timmy was confident she would oblige. And Tracy gave it to him with no hassles. She then asked him for his number before they parted ways to head to their classes.

Timmy, a sophomore, walked down the hall in the opposite direction. He stopped and looked to see if anyone was spying him. An accomplice had told him the combination to the locker in front of him. Timmy got it open and searched through it. He watched up and down the hallway as he took the Polo baseball cap along with a Sony Walkman radio, planning on selling them. Timmy had a second locker to hide his stolen merchandise in until the heat cooled down.

"Ay Tim, what's up, man?" asked a golden-brown-toned friend, sitting at the long cafeteria tables inside the lunch room.

"You know me, cuz', I'm just hangin' in there, makin' money and things," Timmy said, taking a seat to join him.

"See that girl right there?" Golden-brown asked, directing with his eyes.

"Yeah," Timmy said, following them.

"I'd love to be *her* boyfriend. *Forever,* cuz'!"

Timmy smiled slyly. "I been hit that, man. She a nice little somethin'."

"For real? You had her?"

"Her *and* her girlfriend."

Golden-brown shook his head, grinning with admiration. "Damn, cuz'! How you be gettin' 'em, Tim? Oh, that's right, you got them green eyes and shit."

Timmy laughed. "Everybody think I be gettin' bitches because of my eyes. All my cousins have light eyes, and they don't get *half* the ass that I get."

"So you're tryin' t' tell me that they don't notice?"

Timmy shook his rusty-brown-colored head. "Naw, I ain't sayin' that. You know the girls gon' notice. But just because I got green eyes, don't make me get the ass no quicker than the next nigga."

Golden-brown contested, "Yes the fuck it do. Let me get some hazel-ass eyes. I'd have many and plenny bitches."

They laughed as the bell rang for the next period.

"DAMN!" Mark Bates shouted after opening his locker.

"What's wrong, Mark?" the girl with him asked.

"Somebody got my shit!"

His curvy, light-brown companion wanted to laugh, but she held it in. She had slipped the combination to Timmy before first period.

"Well, what did they take?" she asked, faking concern.

"My hat and my Walkman." Mark thought for a moment. "You know what? That boah' Timmy is good for stuff like this."

His curvy-light-brown companion had to cover up. "That green-eyed pussy. Naw, I doubt if it was him."

Mark thought about it and went with his intuitions. "Yeah, he may be a pussy, but he *do* be stealin' shit. That ma-fucka think he slick, but I'ma whip his ass. Watch me."

Mark walked off and began looking up and down the school halls, stairways and bathrooms, searching for Timmy. He then stormed into one of Timmy's classes. He cared nothing about interrupting it. Timmy had his shit!

Mark stepped right up to the desk and asked the teacher if he could speak to Timmy out in the hallway.

Timmy looked up from his desk, knowing that it was time to *Hollywood,* or in other words, to play a perfect role of innocence.

"Well, what about?" the short brown teacher asked. She looked toward Timmy. Timmy frowned at her, expecting conviction.

"I had some things stolen from my locker, and I think he has somethin' to do with it."

"What?" Timmy shouted toward them both.

"Dude, I know you ain't gettin' loud wit' me," Mark said to him.

"Man, people better stop puttin' my name in shit," Timmy responded.

"Watch the language, Timothy," the short brown teacher said.

"Well, can I speak to him outside, in the hallway?" Mark Bates asked again.

"Be my guest," she agreed. She had never liked Timmy anyway.

"Man, I'on even know what he talkin' about," Timmy said, not budging. *Shid', I ain't slow,* he thought to himself.

"What's the problem in here?" the disciplinarian came in to ask. He just happened to be in the vicinity and heard the confusion.

"Well, this student feels that one of mine has something to do with stealing from his locker," the teacher answered. She was embarrassed that the disciplinarian had walked in.

He stood solid, light brown, and wearing a suit and tie. His voice boomed with authority. "Which one?"

"Timothy Adams," the teacher answered nervously. Timmy could accuse her of inappropriate activities. She had agreed to setting him up for a fight.

Suit-and-tie looked at Timmy sternly. "We can get this straightened out in my office."

Timmy gathered his things, expecting to Hollywood again in the main office. The teenagers walked behind the disciplinarian as he led them to his small office and closed the door. It was a usual event for Timmy. He felt at ease.

"Now what is the problem here?"

"Some things were stolen from my locker, and I think it was him," slim-brown Mark Bates started.

"Do you have any proof?" Suit-and-tie asked him.

"Naw, but I was gon' ask him about it to see what he had to say."

"And you really think he would have told you if he did it?"

"Naw, but he would have said somethin'."

Mark had no proof and no witnesses, so Timmy started to giggle, feeling that the accusations were ridiculous.

Suit-and-tie asked, "Is something funny, Mr. Adams?"

"Naw. But I mean, he gon' come out of the blue and say that I took somethin' from his locker."

"Oh, cuz', you 'bout to get punched in your mug," Mark retorted. He could see that Timmy was pulling a fast one on him. *Most thieves are good liars,* he told himself.

"Yeah, aw'ight," Timmy snapped back at him.

Suit-and-tie butted in. "Well, let's check his locker. And if it's not in there, then there's nothin' left I can do."

"Aw'ight," Mark said, getting up from the chair.

Time to Hollywood, Timmy thought. "Hold up, we gon' check my locker when I ain't did nothin'. That ain't even right. What if I just walked up in here and said somebody stole something from me? Are we gonna go check their locker, too?"

Suit-and-tie stood from his big brown desk. "Probably not, but you have a history of accusations, so we're definitely going to check *your* locker," he said, getting in the last word.

The bell rang as they arrived at Timmy's locker. "G-Town" students, including Tracy, watched out of curiosity.

"Well, it's not here," Suit-and-tie announced to Mark.

Mark wasn't satisfied. "Aw'ight then, but if I find out that he knows somethin', I'ma break 'im up after school. If he thinks *Peppy* beat 'em up, watch what I'll do to him," he said. Mark was putting on a show for the students who watched.

"Go on back to your classes, Mark. He doesn't have your things," Suit-and-tie said.

• • •

Tracy walked home, wanting to hold off from calling Timmy on the first night. She wrote his number in her phone book just as her doorbell rang.

"Who is it!" she hollered from her living-room couch.

"It's me!"

"Hold on," she responded, recognizing the voice.

"What's up, pretty?" Bruce asked from her top step, wearing a Hawaiian shirt and sunglasses.

"Hi, Bruce," Tracy said nonchalantly.

"Can I come in?"

"How many times do I have to tell you? NO!"

"Come on now, Tracy, after all we been through, you still won't bend the rules for me?"

Tracy had stopped letting Bruce in her house when no one was home. She shook her head and walked down her patio steps to the pavement. "Nope."

Bruce sat, watched and grinned. "You know, I feel good as hell when I'm with you," he told her, despite her apparent mistreatment of him.

"Why you come here every day?" she asked, giving Bruce a hint. Tracy didn't want him around anymore. *Dag, he must have needed some bad, because he won't stop bothering me,* she told herself.

"I just told you why: you make me feel like nothing else exists in the world."

Tracy roared with laughter. "You need to go get yourself checked out or something."

Bruce frowned. "Why I gotta get checked out for feeling that way about you?"

"You don't have any *other* girls?" she asked him, glancing at Raheema's house.

Bruce shook his head. "Naw, 'cause I don't want any other girls . . . I just want you."

"You crazy!" Tracy exclaimed.

Bruce got up to walk near her. Tracy ran around him on her lawn and back up her steps.

"Now why you gon' act stupid like that, Tracy?"

She eyed him crossly from her door. "Look, I gotta go pick up my brother," she said.

Bruce left her feeling disappointed with himself. He was being played again.

Tracy was bored after picking her brother up from day-care. She stared at her blue phone book while doing her algebra, thinking, *Timmy probably has a lot to talk about since he gets into so much.* She was still hesitant to call him on the first night, but she decided, *What the hell? He gave me his number to call him, so what's the difference?*

"Hello. Can I speak to Timmy?"

"Yo, it's me."

"Hi. It's Tracy."

"Oh, what's up, girl? You musta' been bored, hunh?"

"No, why you say that?" Tracy asked, embarrassed.

"'Cause, why did 'ju call me already?"

Tracy snapped, "Well, *I won't* call you, if you don't want me to. What 'chew give me your number for?"

"Oh, well, fuck you then, 'cause I ain't the one for sweatin' bitches anyway," he blurted out, hanging up in her ear. Joy had warned her from jump-street that Timmy had no respect.

"Ay, I'm sorry about cussing you out. I was in a hyped mood," Timmy apologized at Tracy's locker the next day at school.

"Yeah, aw'ight," Tracy responded, unfazed.

Timmy caressed her gently from behind. Tracy felt his body pressed on her backside. His hands held her waistline perfectly. But she didn't want him to know that she liked it.

Tracy pushed him away silently.

Timmy chuckled and said, "Oh, not in school, hunh?"

Tracy tried her damndest not to smile. *I don't believe he's just gonna walk up and be all nice now,* she mused.

"Well, you gon' call me tonight, ain't you, Tracy?" he asked her.

Tracy faced him, noticing his freshly cut, rusty-brown hair. "So you can tell me off again?" she asked.

"Naw, so I can tell you what time I'm gon' pick you up for the movies this weekend."

Tracy cracked a smile. Timmy had caught her off guard. He had nerve, but he was definitely exciting and unpredictable. He was a major change from Bruce.

"So, we goin' to the movies, hunh?" she asked.

"Yeah, on Friday night."

"What we gon' go see?"

Nightmare on Elm Street: Part Three, or four or five; one of them ma-fuckas. I forgot which one they up to now."

Tracy laughed. She could not help it. Timmy was funny, too. "Well, what time you plan on goin'?" she asked, losing her apprehension for him.

"Like seven o'clock, but I'll let you know though."

"So you gon' pay my way?" she asked with a child's grin.

Timmy grinned back. "Yeah, but don't get excited about it, 'cause I ain't no rich nigga. I work hard for my shit."

"I heard," Tracy mumbled under her breath as Timmy walked off.

Friday night came quickly. Tracy wore a navy blue silk outfit, draped with her gold. She met Timmy out on Chelten Avenue to catch the bus. Timmy was impressed by her knock-out style. He was proud enough to make her his girl.

They walked through the Cheltenham Mall, and many jealous teen-aged boys were staring. Green-eyed Timmy had another young star on his arm.

Timmy ordered and paid for everything. Tracy felt like a woman.

They took a seat in the theater, and Timmy promptly wrapped his arm around her. He grabbed her tightly when the scary parts came and gently during the love scenes. He made Tracy feel secure. He never left her side to get popcorn or anything. And she enjoyed his company.

After the movie, Timmy walked her to get ice cream while holding her hand, and Tracy wanted him to finish the job. He had proved himself worthy of her. He had class, and he made her feel good, so she wanted to repay him for it with good lovemaking. Yet Timmy had other thoughts in mind. He didn't have anywhere to take her at the time anyway.

They rode the buses back to Tracy's house, and he was anxious to leave her.

"You not even gon' kiss me good night?" she complained, standing at her door.

"No, but I do have something to say to you though."

"What?"

"From now on, you're my girl. Aw'ight?"

"Oh, you just gon' tell me, hunh?"

Timmy raised his brow. "What, you don't wanna be?"

Tracy responded quickly, "I ain't say that." She didn't want Timmy to blow up and tell her off again. He seemed to have a serious temper problem. And his temper was not childishly entertaining like Bruce's. Timmy's tantrums were of a more violent nature.

Timmy was devious, proud and bold, spending money like a windmill blows wind. Tracy was weak for adventure, a fiend for fashion and a money hawk.

He took her downtown to the Market Street Gallery and to Chestnut Street that Saturday afternoon, where he bought her huge, triangle-shaped gold earrings with *Tracy* etched in gold across the middle. He bought her leather pants with matching pocketbooks. He then charmed Patti into liking him with his greens when they had arrived back at Tracy's house. Tracy lied to her mother about where Timmy's finances came from, and together they were a match of teenagers headed for no good.

. . .

"Dag, girl, Timmy sure is spending a whole lot of money on you," Carmen said, sitting out on Tracy's front steps. She could not seem to take her eyes off of Tracy's new earrings.

"I know, but I'm scared to tell him to stop," Tracy commented.

Carmen frowned at her, confused. "Why would you tell him to stop?" she asked. *I wish he was my man,* she thought to herself. *I could use a bunch of new gear in my empty-ass closets!*

"He's buying *too* much stuff for me," Tracy told her, "like he *owns* me or something. That shit scares me."

"Where does he get the money from?"

Tracy grinned. "Stealin'."

Carmen had already heard; she just wanted to see if Tracy knew. "Yeah, that's what people told me," she said, smiling back at Tracy. "And if he's stealin' stuff, then that means that people are gonna be after him."

Tracy nodded. "Yeah, I know. That's why I make sure that everything he gives me is new."

"You better make sure," Carmen warned her.

They both watched as Tracy's neighbor, Raheema, approached her house, walking home late from school.

"Y'all still don't talk to each other?" Carmen asked.

Tracy shook her head, standing up to greet Raheema. Their displeasure with one another had gone far enough, and Bruce was no longer in the picture as far as Tracy was concerned.

"I'm about to make up with her, because we were only fighting over Bruce, and I don't talk to him no more," she answered.

Raheema did not appear to look in Tracy's direction as she headed up the walkway.

"Raheema, can I talk to you for a second?"

Raheema stopped and waited for Tracy without a word.

"Are you still mad at me about Bruce?"

"Why should I be?" Raheema knew that Tracy had been using

Bruce for free clothing and things. *But that was Bruce's dumb fault,* she figured.

"Well, because he had liked you."

Raheema was mute again. She did miss Bruce's company for a while. Nevertheless, life goes on.

"I was mad at first, Tracy, because you just had to have him, when there's a whole lot of other guys that you could have talked to. But I can't say that it's all your fault, because he did try to talk to you."

"Yeah, because I didn't tell you about the time when he asked to come in my house," Tracy alluded.

"Yup," Carmen added. "Y'all should never fight over a boy, because most boys will *do it* to anything that moves."

Raheema looked at Carmen and smirked. *You too,* she felt like saying. "Well, I'm no longer mad at you, Tracy," she said to her next-door neighbor instead.

Tracy opened her arms to hug her and Raheema obliged.

"Awww, now ain't that sweet," Carmen perked.

The girls shared a smile before Raheema excused herself and walked into the house.

"I'm goin' over Timmy's house tonight," Tracy suddenly announced. She felt joyful after making up with her neighbor.

"Oh, so y'all gon' do 'the nasty,' tonight. Hunh?" Carmen assumed.

Tracy smiled bashfully. "I'on know. He don't even touch me."

"Yeah, well, he gon' *touch you* tonight."

They giggled together before it was time for Tracy to leave for track practice. Patti began picking Jason up from day-care when Tracy went to practice. She didn't mind it much, as long as her daughter was doing something constructive.

Timmy waited until eight o'clock to pick Tracy up. They walked to his house, five blocks from hers, down dark and windy row-house streets. Once at his house, they went in and up to a stuffy dark room that Timmy tried, hopelessly, to straighten up. He then got a couple of strawberry coolers and poured them into two tall glasses. Tracy had never drunk before, but she was not planning on telling Timmy "no" at such a romantic point in their relationship. Timmy had been able to make all of his girlfriends feel as if they had known him for years when they barely knew him at all. He gave them all a perfect illusion of comfort.

"Don't drink it so fast," he told her, as Tracy rushed to finish her tall glass. She stood up and wobbled, before Timmy grabbed her.

"Look at you, girl. And that was only one cooler."

"I ain't never drank one before," she said, falling back.

Timmy laid her out on his bed and examined her for a moment. "That's because you drank it too fast," he told her. "You acted like you was drinkin' a damn soda."

Tracy giggled at him. "You know, you haven't kissed me since we been goin' together," she said, out of the blue, with her head stuck to the pillow.

Timmy leaned over and kissed her, weakly.

"Oh, you call 'lat a kiz?" she asked, slurring her speech.

Timmy laughed. "Girl, you drunk as hell."

"Well, you did 'dis to me, boy."

Timmy x-rayed her curvaceous body. Tracy was wearing a long yellow skirt with a white silk blouse, laced with gold. But something was missing.

"Where my earrings?" Timmy fumed.

Tracy slurred, with heavy drunk eyes, "In my criiib, Tim-e-e-e. Wh-i-i-i?"

"Why you ain't wear 'em?"

"Cuzzz, it wuz too loud ta' wear wit' 'dis."

Timmy gripped her tightly by the arm. "When I buy you somethin', I expect you to wear it."

"O-kay," Tracy said, jerking away from him.

Timmy looked at her, from head to toe, trying to decide what he wanted to do with her. "You wanna make love?" he asked.

"I'on have no choice. I know you want some. 'Dat's why you got me all drunk and shit. I ain't stupid, boy."

Timmy giggled. "Yeah, but you fucked up, I know 'dat."

He sat down beside her and ran his hands over her breasts. Tracy struggled to turn herself over, feeling good.

Timmy asked, "What 'chew doin'?"

"Button down my blouse," Tracy told him.

He did, along with unfastening her bra.

"Take off my skirt."

Timmy did that as well, as Tracy lifted up her legs. He then stood up, shut his door and began taking off his clothes. He pulled the covers back when he was fully undressed and climbed in with her as their naked bodies met under the sheets.

Tracy kissed up and down his chest, and Timmy responded with a long wet kiss on her lips. In no time at all, Tracy was stimulated. She pulled Timmy's body on top of hers and grabbed his private parts to do the honor herself. Timmy was shocked by her assertiveness, as he held her firmly by the waist.

Tracy squirmed, enjoying it. She ran her hands up and down Timmy's smooth spine as he breathed heavy in her ear while uttering undistinguishable expressions of bliss. Tracy's snug fit made the sex more desirable.

"Oh, girl!" Timmy squealed, increasing his speed and losing control of himself. His hands ran through Tracy's hair and all over the bed as he tried, desperately, to grab ahold of something. Tracy squeezed him even tighter as she felt his body becoming rigid and tense. Timmy's last attempt to calm himself was unsuccessful. He began to vibrantly kick his legs and beat his hands against the pillow, as he pushed his naked, perspiring body as close as it could get to hers. All the while, Tracy continued to caress him roughly.

Timmy had done it *right,* as he inhaled and exhaled deeply to regain his energy. His eyes rolled up toward the ceiling, and the cool breeze chilled them, blowing in from his open window.

"That was good as shit," he told her.

Tracy smiled and leaned over to kiss his pinkish lips.

• • •

"Ay Timmy, did you get it yet?" his golden-brown friend asked, sitting at the lunch tables again.

"Get what?"

"Your girl, cuz'."

"Oh, yeah, I got it Friday night. I thought you was talkin' about something else."

"Naw."

Timmy leaned over the lunch-room table to whisper in his ear. "Yo, man, she had the best ass I ever had in my life."

Golden-brown smiled. "She did?"

"Cuz', no bull-shit."

"She do look like she got some good shit though."

Timmy snapped, "Ay, man, what the fuck is wrong wit' 'chew? Don't talk about my girl like that. And don't be lookin' at her that hard either!"

"Damn, cuz'. My fault."

"Yeah, but don't let that shit happen again!"

Timmy left the lunch room pissed at everyone for his friend's slip of tongue. He howled at Tracy at her locker. "Where the fuck was you at last night?"

Tracy was puzzled. "I was at my next-door neighbor's house," she answered, surprised by his rashness.

"Doin' what?"

"Talking to my girlfriend. She lives there."

Timmy looked her in her eyes, as if he wanted to reprimand her. "If I find out you wasn't there, I'm gon' break your neck."

Tracy was confused and frightened. Unlike Bruce, she suspected that Timmy would do what he said. *What the hell is he pissed off about now?* she asked herself. Timmy seemed to be always on the verge of an explosion.

"Ay, what's up, Ra-Ra?" Bruce asked, on the way to Tracy's house.

"What are you speaking to me for? I thought you liked Tracy?" Raheema asked him sourly.

Bruce decided not to respond to her while taking a seat on Tracy's steps.

Raheema stared at his back, standing inside of her doorway. "She got a new boyfriend now anyway," she added vengefully.

Bruce faced her with his eyes flaring in shock. "How long she been goin' with him?"

"Ask her. It's none of my business to tell."

"Well, you told me that she had one."

"She would have *wanted* me to do that."

Bruce was puzzled. *How come she didn't tell me then?* he thought to himself. *Then again, maybe Raheema's lying to get back at me.* "I thought y'all was enemies," he quizzed.

"Not anymore. That was just *you* in our way!" Raheema shut her door on Bruce's crushed face, feeling avenged.

Bruce got up to leave, inflamed, with pulsating nerves. He spotted Tracy heading home from school, and he calmed himself as he waited for her on the sidewalk. Tracy wore a dark-blue, velour sweat suit with red trimming running up the sides and accentuating her curves. Bruce wanted desperately to be loved by her, but Tracy tried to ignore him and walk on by.

"Ay, you not gon' even say 'hi'?"

"Hi, Bruce," she answered blandly.

Bruce cheered up with the sound of her voice. "That's a nice sweat suit," he commented, following her.

"Thanks. My boyfriend bought it for me."

Bruce swallowed his rage. "Who is he?" he asked.

"Don't worry about it," Tracy flared.

Bruce thought about snatching her arm, but Tracy marched ahead too quickly for him to react.

Tracy continued to her house, thinking about her situation with Timmy. He was too compulsive. She opened her door and tossed herself on the couch. Victor appeared in her daydream. She never stopped wanting him. She felt like going to the playground just to see if he was there, playing ball or hanging out.

Tracy went to pick up her brother from the day-care center and saw Victor anyway. He stood out in the sun in a blue, terry-cloth, Fila sweat suit. A small gold V hung on a link chain around his neck, and his hair was freshly cut, as always. Yet, as usual, he was spending time with another girl.

Tracy met his eyes, still feeling controlled by him. Victor was still her first love, but he had not spoken to her for nearly a year.

Victor was there again, in Tracy's eyesight view, on her way home with her brother. And his companion had left him. Once he spotted Tracy walking back with Jason, he walked over to their side of the street and sat on the hood of a red Dodge Omni, holding an unlit cigarette. He played with it in his smooth black hands, flipping it over in circles between his fingers, waiting for her as she approached him. He then smiled at her and said, "I heard you go wit' punk-ass Timmy now."

"Yeah," Tracy answered, beaming helplessly.

Victor leaped off of the car and moved toward her. "Come here, Tracy."

"I can't," she responded. She wanted to talk to him, but could not allow her hormones to get her into trouble with Timmy, who was crazy with jealous rage.

"So it's like that now, hunh?" Victor asked her as she continued on her way.

Tracy turned back to face him. "No, I just can't."

"Are you sure?" Victor asked, giving her his winning smile. He simply wanted to see how much Tracy liked her new guy.

Tracy looked him over and shook her head. "I can't." She then turned and took a deep breath as she continued home with her brother, happy to have spoken to Victor again.

Victor stared at her back and muttered, "Damn. She's still loyal to a nigga. I like that. But I could still have her if I really wanted to. I can tell by how she looks at me."

•   •   •

"So Tracy, are you and Timmy going out this weekend?" Patti asked her daughter. They were watching *Dynasty* together in the living room.

Jason interjected, "No, 'cause she gotta watch me."

"Shet up, boy," Tracy told him. "I don't know what we gon' do, mom," she answered.

"Yeah, well that's a nice suit he bought you there. And I can never get over those gigantic earrings."

Tracy laughed as she played with the huge earring in her ear. Patti didn't seem to mind her having little boyfriends and going out on dates at fourteen. Why should she? She and her sisters had done it when they were young and growing up in North Philly. Patti didn't mind her daughter wearing expensive clothing and accessories either. After all, she had always wanted her daughter to look her best. She wanted to look fabulous when she was young, too. A lot of young girls wanted to be "flyy." It was the next best thing to being a movie star.

Tracy said, "He was gonna buy me a big nugget ring, too, but I acted like it was ugly, and he changed his mind."

"Well don't get too much into letting him buy you things, because you'll end up in the same boat that I'm in with your father. He thinks that just because he pays the bills here, he can do what he wants to do, but I got news for his ass."

Here she goes again, Tracy thought. *She compares everything to him now.*

"That's just how they are, honey," her mother added. "They just wanna do whatever pleases them."

And what about us? Tracy wanted to ask. *I know I want what I want, and you do too, mom.* But she decided to keep her thoughts to herself as they continued to watch *Dynasty*'s Carrington family.

"Mom, guess who was up here today," she asked.

"Bruce."

"How you know?"

"I seen him in the supermarket last night with his mother, and he told me to tell you he said 'hi.' "

"Well, how come you didn't tell me?"

"To tell you the truth, it slipped my mind. But what are you worried about it for anyway? You don't like the poor boy."

Tracy laughed. "I know, but I just like to know stuff like that."

"It's a shame, how you did that boy," Patti said, walking to the kitchen. "I should have married myself a nice little boy like him," she mumbled.

Tracy watched Blake arguing with Alexis. She smiled, thinking about Bruce's childish temper. That was the only exciting thing about him, except for his money. Yet Timmy bought her more expensive things.

"Yo, man, you know some dude named Timmy?" asked a lemon-skinned boy on Timmy's block of row-houses. He was eighteen, wearing a plain blue baseball cap.

"Naw, why?" a tall, dark brown neighbor asked.

"I mean, if you don't know him, what you worried about it for?"

"Yeah, I know him. So what's the problem?" another resident said from the patio. He walked down to the pavement and stared. He was thick built, and nineteen.

Lemon-skin said, "Well, I heard that this is his block, and I wanna speak to 'im about somethin'."

"About what?"

More neighbors gathered as Lemon-skin backed up and pulled out a gun. They all wanted to scatter but remained calm, scared of becoming a statistic in the *Daily News*.

"Y'all tell that pussy that I'm gon' kill his ass," the boy responded. He jammed his gun back inside of his jacket and dashed around the corner. A few of the neighbors ran into their houses to get their guns. They all ran around the corner after him, but the quick-footed boy was long gone.

Only two minutes after the incident, Timmy walked around the opposite corner with Tracy. All eyes were glued to them.

"Yo, man, come here for a minute," the thick-built neighbor said privately. He didn't want to alarm Tracy.

"What's up?" Timmy asked him.

"Some dude just came around here and pulled a gun out, looking for you."

"A light-skinned dude?"

"Yeah, why? You stole some shit from 'im?"

"Aw, man, that was Doug. He a *nut*. He probably didn't have bullets in the gun," Timmy responded with a chuckle.

Tracy waited for him at his door.

"Ay Tim, man, you better watch yourself, boy," Thick-built warned.

Timmy had just turned sixteen, and he was headed for jail or the morgue.

He entered his house with Tracy.

Tracy asked, "What was that about?"

"Oh, don't worry about that, girl. Everything is taken care of." Timmy hugged her and snatched her firmly by the backside. Tracy threw her arms around him. They kissed, and Timmy hastily led her to his room, where they undressed, going at it again.

Tracy walked to the avenue to get some morning cereal for Jason. Wayne Avenue was empty. Tracy looked around, feeling peculiar and decided to walk ahead to the supermarket. Summer had just begun; all the public schools had let out two days earlier. It was hot and sunny, and Tracy figured that there should have been a crowd of people out on the avenue.

Tracy came out from the store and noticed a lanky boy wearing a red hat with a C on it. She paid him no mind. The boy then glanced at her and turned his head quickly away. Tracy thought about it, wanting to take another look. She turned in his direction just as the boy ran past and grabbed the chains from around her neck, pulling a few of them off. It happened too fast for her to even let out a cry for help.

Tracy cursed him, feeling helpless. He had dropped the two smaller chains, but he had gotten away with the larger, more expensive ones, a Gucci link that Timmy had bought for her and the herringbone that she had saved to buy only a year ago.

• • •

"Mom, I just got my chains snatched," Tracy mumbled, walking into her mother's room with tears in her eyes.

Patti jumped up from her bed. "Oh no, girl. Look at these scratches on your neck." She took her daughter to the bathroom and poured some rubbing alcohol into her hands to apply to Tracy's neck.

"OOOWWW!" Tracy squealed, tensing from the sting.

"Did you see what he looked like?"

Tracy sucked in air to take in the pain. "Yeah, he had on this red Cincinnati baseball hat. He was about my height, and skinny." Tears streamed down her face.

"Which chains did he get? He didn't get all of them, did he?"

"No, but he got my herringbone and the Gucci link that Timmy bought for me," Tracy whined, showing her mother the smaller chains in her hand.

"Hmm," Patti grunted. "How much did that Gucci thing cost?"

"Like three hundred," Tracy admitted.

"Three hundred dollars?" Patti responded, expecting as much. "He didn't have any business buying you no three-hundred-dollar chain anyway," she commented protectively. She figured that any young man would act like a fool about losing something that he had bought for his girlfriend. But it wasn't Tracy's fault. "So you're gonna tell Timmy about this?" she asked, knowing that he would worry her about it.

"I wish I didn't have to, 'cause he gon' get all out of shape about it. Watch. I know he is."

"Well, maybe you should stay away from him for a while," Patti suggested.

Only hours later, Tracy ended up on the avenue explaining to Timmy a blow by blow of what happened.

Timmy grimaced. "So where was he standing at?"

"I told you, right here," Tracy said, pointing to the spot.

Timmy shook his head, frowning. He was nagging the hell out of her. "You gon' tell me that nobody was out here?"

Tracy sighed. "Jantel said that it was a fight that everybody went to see, down the hill."

"Get the fuck out of here, girl! What I look like? You tellin' me that the whole avenue went to see a fight?"

"Yeah, Timmy. DAG!"

He angrily grabbed Tracy by the neck and pushed her toward the corner.

"Won't you stop, Timmy?" she pleaded.

"What you gon' do if I don't?"

Tracy's voice cracked. "It's not my fault."

"Why was you down here wearing your chains in the first place? You probably just wanted to see some nigga."

Timmy dragged her off of the avenue by her arm.

"GET OFF OF ME!" Tracy screamed, as he pulled her along.

"Shet up, before I punch you in your fuckin' mouth!"

A silver Mercedes Benz pulled up to the curb. The door swung open, and Victor Hinson jumped out from the passenger side. "YO! What the fuck is your problem, man?" he yelled at Timmy.

Tracy was stunned.

"What?" Timmy responded hesitantly.

Victor approached him as if he was ready to fight. "You got a problem with her, man?" he asked.

Timmy backed away, still holding on to Tracy's arm. "This ain't got nothin' to do with you," he told him.

Victor clenched his hands together and said, "Cuz', I'm gon' tell you one time to let her fuckin' go. And after that, you gon' wish you never heard of me."

Timmy gave Victor an evil eye and let go of Tracy's arm. He then trotted down the street away from them, ready to kill. He had been embarrassed beyond belief. *She gon' pay for this shit!* he told himself. *Fuck that nigga, and his brother!*

"You want a ride home?" Victor asked Tracy.

She looked toward the car and shook her head as she began to walk away. Victor had only made her situation worse.

"Yo, you need to pick a new friend," he told her as he climbed back into the car. "That's the young-girl that I was telling you about, Todd," he said to his brother.

Todd shifted his Mercedes back into drive and said, "She got a lot of growing up to do."

Victor nodded. "Yeah, I know. But she gon' be aw'ight."

Todd looked at his younger brother and smirked. "Sounds like she got your nose open."

Victor smiled and shook his head. "Naw, never that. I'm just lookin' out for her, that's all."

Even though Tracy felt much admiration and respect for Victor's actions, she was still dedicated to Timmy, but he did not speak to her for three days. Each event made her feel strangely closer to him, yet further apart. She was learning him, his pain and his loneliness. She understood that violence and crime were Timmy's means of letting out his frustrations.

Tracy remained loyal and at his command at the ball games, the parties, the movies and every other place he took her to be showcased. Timmy no longer allowed her to hang out with girlfriends like Carmen, who had a reputation for being loose, nor with Raheema, whom he hated simply for acting snotty and spreading gossip about him. And as far as Victor was concerned, *He's too busy for me anyway,* Tracy thought. *I'm not gonna be one of his girls,* she told herself. She preferred to be with Timmy, despite his attitudes. At least he was consistent.

"Damn, cuz'! Who is that?" Timmy's tall, dark brown friend asked. Jay watched Raheema walk up to her house.

"Go ahead and find out, Jay," Timmy told him, knowing better.

"Hi," Jay said to Raheema. Jay was a basketball addict, morning, afternoon and night.

"Hi," Raheema responded, opening up her door to go in.

Jay asked, "Can I talk to you real quick?"

"That's all right."

Timmy giggled as Raheema went in and closed the door back. "See, man, I told you. That bitch a *nut*. Nobody gets along with her, cuz'."

Tracy came out and overheard him talking about her neighbor. "Stop talkin' about her then," she interjected.

"So you goin' to that concert tonight, hunh, Jay?" Timmy asked, changing the subject.

"Yeah, man. You should take her. It's gon' be Run DMC, Whodini, LL Cool J, The Fat Boys, them white Beastie Boys. Cuz', it's gon' be live!"

Timmy contested, "Naw, you never take your girl to no shit like that. It's always some muthafuckas acting crazy, tryin' to talk to her. And them niggas be a hundred thick from South Philly."

Tracy said with an attitude, "Oh, it's gon' be thousands of other girls there, and they just gon' pick me, hunh?"

"Ay, you gettin' a little bold, talkin' that shit, girl. You better shet the fuck up," Timmy responded to her.

Tracy went in the house and took a seat on the couch, disappointed. Timmy followed her, leaving his friend outside.

"Now you wasn't even thinking about that concert until he said somethin'," he commented.

Tracy crossed her legs, and pouted, "You the one who brought it up. You just wanted to tease me about it."

Timmy chuckled.

"Now why you laughin'?" Tracy asked, standing back up and in his face.

Timmy sat her back down. "Come on now, stop playin' wit' me, before I have to hurt you. Now you know me better than that, girl."

Tracy looked away. "That's all you know how to do is hurt me."

Timmy sat down beside her and kissed her ear. "Well, we gon' go out to eat tonight or somethin'. Okay?"

"I don't want to," Tracy told him with a long face.

"What 'chew wanna do then? 'Cause I'm not goin' to that concert. I'm tellin' you that shit right now."

"Let's go to the movies," Tracy suggested.

Timmy nodded his head. "Aw'ight. We can do that."

Going to the movies with Timmy became less exciting for Tracy. Their relationship was slowly falling apart. They always ended up in bed, no matter what they did. Timmy was "whipped." Tracy knew it. There was no longer any foreplay to stimulate her, and they were always in danger from someone chasing after Timmy. It was more than Tracy could handle. They could not go out in peace. Timmy was constantly watching his back.

I never felt scared all the time when I was with Victor, Tracy thought to herself. *But he never really took me anywhere.*

"I'm tired of this," she complained. She and Timmy ended up naked again, inside of a hotel bedroom that one of Timmy's older friends had gotten for him.

Timmy asked, while stretched out in the bed, "What are you talkin' about? Look, we went to the movies, right?"

"I'm talkin' about how we always do this routine stuff."

Timmy laughed. "I thought you said that I was full of surprises."

"Well, I was wrong. And the only surprise that you have is doing things without warning."

Timmy looked puzzled. "So, that's still a surprise."

Tracy yelled, putting on her clothes, "Well, it ain't shit new!"

Timmy gripped her arm. "Where're you goin'?"

Tracy snapped, "Oh, wow, I'm not even fifteen yet, and you think I'm your fuckin' wife."

Timmy thought about it. *Yeah, we are kind of young for this, but that's what makes it cool.* "Well, you act and look old enough," he told her, pulling her back in bed.

Tracy sighed. "Come on now, Timmy, this is boring. I wanna go home."

Timmy frowned at her. "So what 'chew sayin'?"

Tracy thought for a moment. "Did you treat your other girls like this?"

"What does it matter?"

"Because, I didn't think you was this possessive."

"Well, you're my girl, right?"

"But I still need room and freedom."

"What?" Timmy snapped. "Okay, you want *freedom*. Get the fuck out then!"

Timmy led her to the door and pushed her out.

Tracy pleaded, "See, why you gettin' mad like this."

"'Cause I feel like it!"

Tracy yelled through the door, "You a pussy anyway!"

Timmy rushed out in a fury, wearing his drawers. He chased Tracy down the hall, caught up to her and punched her in her mouth. He then banged her head on the wall and threw her to the carpeted floor.

"NOW! Call me a pussy again. BITCH!"

Tracy ran to the elevator and rode it down to the lobby level with a busted lip and a headache. She wept and sucked her lip as she walked to catch a bus back home. It was ten o'clock, and Timmy had humiliated her for the last time. She was tired of him.

Tracy got home and snuck into her bedroom, not wanting her mother to see her. She wiped the tears from her eyes and iced her lips.

It was the first time she had ever been beaten on. She felt that she had experienced everything that makes a woman, as if she was in a bad marriage. *I'm too young for this,* she told herself. *He don't own me.*

"How you get that bruise on your lip?" Raheema asked Tracy on the steps that next day.

Tracy stared out at the street. "Timmy did it."

"What did you do?"

"I told him I didn't want to be around him no more."

"And he just punched you in your lip?"

"He kicked me out and chased me first," Tracy answered. She didn't want to tell Raheema that they had been inside of a hotel room.

"So you're going to quit him now?"

"I don't know," Tracy mumbled. She wanted to hear what Timmy had to say first.

"Mmm," Raheema grunted. "I would quit him if I were you."

Raheema went inside the house and left Tracy alone with a busted lip and damaged pride in ninety-degree weather, while she watched her brother all day. Tracy figured she had been through enough emotionally to last for the rest of the summer.

Timmy and his friends prepared for a major theft inside of a department store. They drove to a suburban mall and waited inside until it was almost ready to close. With limited cameras and theft detectors, the only thing that concerned them were the aged security guards.

Timmy unfolded a trash bag and started throwing in jeans and shirts as his friends followed his lead. Once it was half full, Timmy dropped the bag and pushed it under a clothing rack. He watched all sides for walkers-by. He then kicked the bag closer to the door. It was an easy nighttime job. Timmy and his friends made it out undiscovered and tossed the stolen merchandise in the trunk.

Timmy grinned. "I told y'all it would be an easy-ass hit."

Mat, the chubby brown driver, shook his head. "Damn, man, I don't believe that security."

Basketball Jay said, "Yup, but we got to keep things low, 'cause we took so much that they might put a word out on the streets for a snitch."

Mat contested, "They can't touch us anyway. We're not in their district."

Timmy retorted, "Y'all can talk all that shit if y'all want, but I'm gettin' *paid.*"

• • •

Timmy had an increasing hunger for stealing since Tracy was no longer around him. He started romancing a new girl and had moved out of his mother's home. No one knew where he was staying.

He continued to steal, deviously, sticking up stores and everyday citizens around the city. His friends feared his destructive path. Timmy was developing into an all-out criminal at the tender age of sixteen.

"Y'all wanna stick up that spot up on Seventeenth Street?" Timmy asked his friends. He was visiting on his mother's Germantown block. "They be gettin' paid in that bitch, y'all. I just peeped that shit," he said.

Thick-built responded, "Naw, man, and you crazy to even be up here."

"Did the cops come to my house?"

"Fuckin' right they did. I mean, they huntin' for your ass, cuz'. You better start wearin' shades," Thick-built joked.

Timmy did not look as well groomed as he usually did. He had been drinking and doing drugs, and his rusty-brown hair was growing wild under a blood-red Phillies cap.

"Aw, man, as long as they don't know where I'm at, fuck the cops."

Thick-built said, "You crazy as shit, man. I don't see how you be doin' that dumb shit."

Timmy persisted. "Look, cuz', is you down or what?"

Basketball Jay stepped up. "Fuck it. I'm wit' it."

"Dig, cuz', I'm down," Chubby Mat agreed.

Timmy directed. "Bet. Let's go steal a lemon and roll."

Thick-built shook his head. "Y'all niggas is crazy to be listening to him. That muthafucka out his mind."

They went with Timmy anyway.

Timmy left it up to Mat, the car specialist, to hot-wire a car. They drove with the lights off until they were out of Dodge. Timmy then showed Mat where the place was. They got there in a hurry, filled with nervous energy. Timmy pulled out two small-caliber guns, giving one to Jay.

"Where you get these from?" Jay asked him apprehensively.

"Look, man, don't worry about it. Let's just do this," Timmy snapped at him.

They stopped the car. Timmy got out and told Mat to keep it running. It was a dark restaurant in West Oak Lane, off of Ogontz Avenue. Timmy knew where they kept the money.

Small crowds frequented the place, especially on Friday and Saturday nights when the bar had entertainment and an open dance floor. Timmy had watched the sexy waitresses taking money alongside the bar for safe storage on a previous visit, when he had asked to use the bathroom.

He and Jay walked in slowly, wearing shades and baseball hats. Timmy told Jay to watch the outside, as he approached the back room.

"Yeah, I was wondering if I could get change for a fifty?" he asked a honey-brown employee, who was heading toward the back. His adrenalin level was stable. Timmy was used to the action.

"Sure," Honey-brown answered, taking his fifty-dollar bill and walking into the back room.

Timmy ran in behind her and pulled out the gun and a small bag in his left hand. "Aw'ight, just throw all that shit in the bag!"

The manager was shocked. He did what Timmy demanded. Jay eased up against the door, making sure no other employees walked back.

Timmy reached over and smacked the short, fat manager in his curly head with the butt of his gun. He then eyed Honey-brown. "You try some dumb shit, bitch, and I'll kill your ass!"

Timmy dashed out of the back room with the bag. The other employees were puzzled. *What the hell is going on?* By the time they had gotten word that they were being robbed, the car was speeding up a side street.

The angry manager ran out with his own gun in hand and decided not to shoot. He ran back in and called his friend from the police force instead. Two cruisers happened to be in the vicinity. Ogontz Avenue was a busy strip.

Timmy was frantic. "Yo, let me out right here!" he yelled, only five blocks from the hit.

Chubby Mat whined, "Aw, man, you gon' get us stuck wit' the fuckin' ride!"

Timmy leaped out of the front seat and ran for the Broad Street subway. He took all of the money with him.

Jay and Mat turned paranoid.

Mat yelled, "See, I knew we shouldna' tried this shit!"

Jay roared, hopping in the front seat, "Fuck it, man, let's get the hell out of here!"

They turned a tight corner and crashed into a parked car.

Jay shouted, "SHIT! Get out and break, man!"

They sprinted in opposite directions. Philadelphia police cruisers whipped around at both ends only seconds later. The officers hustled in hot pursuit as Jay dashed up a street perpendicular from Mat and tried to jump over a fence. The fence snagged his leg, slamming Basketball Jay to the hard concrete. The officers caught up and pinned him down.

"MOTHER-FUCKA!" Jay spat, with tears in his eyes.

One officer smiled. "Your father can't help ya' now, son." They smashed Jay to the ground and put the handcuffs on.

BOOMP! BOOMP! BOOMP!

"Open up! It's the police!"

Patti marched to the door. "What the hell is going on?" she demanded, answering it.

"We would like to talk to your daughter concerning the whereabouts of a Mr. Timothy Adams."

Tracy walked out of the kitchen with big eyes.

"Do you know Timothy Adams, ma'am?" the officer asked her on sight.

Tracy's voice cracked. "Yes," she squealed nervously.

"Would you happen to know where he stays?"

"No," she responded, looking over his clean stern face and dark uniform.

The officer shook his head. "Now, nothing is going to happen to you. We just want to find out where he is."

Tracy wouldn't have told if she did know. But she didn't. "No, I don't know where he is. I haven't talked to him in weeks," she answered.

Stern-face said, "Well, if you hear from him, could you do us a favor and let us know? 'Cause from what I hear, it would be to his benefit if *we* caught him first."

Stern-face walked out while his partner radioed the station from the squad car.

Patti closed the door and watched until the police cleared out. She then turned and stared at her daughter, shaking her head. She went to the kitchen to think. Tracy followed her.

"Well, what's it about, Tracy?"

Tracy stiffened. "Stealin'," she admitted.

"Oh, so you knew what he was doin', hunh?"

Tracy pondered. "I couldn't stop him . . . I wonder where he's at though."

Patti frowned and said, "What? I don't believe you even said that. You remind me of your aunts, girl, datin' troublemakers and then wondering why they get all wrapped up in it. You stay away from those types! You hear me? That boy is no longer allowed in this house."

The word was out that Tracy was the former girlfriend of Timothy Adams. He was in deep trouble with the police and no one knew where he was. And although he had busted Tracy's lip and assaulted her, she *still* felt for him.

"How long you plan on staying here, Timmy?" his new girlfriend asked. She was twenty-three and had her own apartment in Southwest Philly.

"I'on know," he answered, stretched out on her bed, with only jeans and sneakers on.

"You're crazy as hell. You know that, right?" she asked, grinning at him. "You could have been a cute, green-eyed, light-skinned boy, growing up to go to college. I don't understand you. I mean, you lived in a nice neighborhood and all. You already had money."

The twenty-three-year-old figured that Germantown had its "good parts" and "bad parts," but it was still a nice area compared to where she lived, in a drug-and-crime-infested apartment complex. She took drugs herself. Timmy was giving her money to feed her habit while he stayed there.

"Ay, Gina, just shet the fuck up! Nobody asked you shit!" he fumed at her.

"Just explain to me where you're comin' from."

"Look, life ain't shit unless you live it."

"What does that mean?"

"That means I'm gon' do what the fuck I want! SHIT!"

"And then what?"

Timmy smiled. "I'on know . . . I guess you die."

Gina retorted, "See, all you criminal-minded niggas think the world is a joke, but you only get one chance to live, and you messed yours up."

Gina began to get ready to leave for work.

Timmy asked, "Gina, what the fuck are you doin' with your life? I mean, you strung out on drugs and shit."

Gina snapped, "I ain't headed for jail, I got my own place and a good job. Muthafucka!"

Timmy grinned and shook his head. Gina had a temper, too. He sat on the bed, thinking about what she had said after she left. She let him stay with her, thinking that she could help him out, while he gave her money for *her* habit.

Timmy shook his head and smirked. "Life is fuckin' crazy," he mumbled to himself. Like father, like son was his story. His father had died in a shoot-out years ago. Timmy was raised by his mother and stepfather. He had never respected either one. He had to compete for attention. His mother then had a thing for abusive men, after divorcing his stepfather. She never had another child, and Timmy was lonely and miserable. He used females and mischief to fill his void. And before his wild lifestyle would end, he wanted to be with Tracy again.

Timmy dialed her number. "Hello . . . Yeah, it's me," he answered.

Tracy got excited and asked, "Where you at?"

"That's not important. I'm sorry, and I wanna come see you."

Tracy smiled, willing to oblige. "Where do you want me to meet you?"

"I'm gon' come up to your house, late at night, like two o'clock in the mornin'."

"But the cops gon' be after you."

Timmy sighed. "I'm goin' to jail soon anyway. It don't matter no more."

Tracy was weak for him. She wanted to see him. "You want me to sneak you in the back door?" she asked.

"Yeah, you do that."

Tracy paused. "I love you," she said, hanging up.

Timmy began to think that if he had not been so demanding with her, he would have never followed such a path of destruction and robbery. Tracy kept him out of trouble when they were together, and her words of affection launched Timmy into emotional turmoil.

Timmy snuck out that night while Gina took a shower. He packed his gun and five hundred dollars to give to Tracy. He had gotten away with twelve hundred dollars on his last robbery. He figured Tracy could use the money better than he could. At least no one would be after her. He had about four hundred left for himself after giving Gina her share for letting him stay with her.

Not trusting the buses or the subway, he called a freelance taxi driver, or a "hack," to ride him up to Tracy's house. He stopped for snacks at a Korean corner store to stall for time. He paid the hack to wait with him. He then told the driver to let him out three blocks away from Tracy's house, so that he could watch for cops. He didn't want the driver to know all of his business either. Timmy wasn't *slow.*

He walked up the familiar streets toward Tracy's house, watching his back from all directions with his gun loaded and ready. He arrived at Tracy's driveway, feeling secure that no one had seen him, and knocked on her door. Tracy stood glimmering, naked as an angel, ready for them to make love.

Timmy did not say a word as he undressed. They then stared at each other and held hands in the darkness. Their kiss was soft, gentle and calming. Timmy's hands rubbed her body, and Tracy's hands rubbed his as they caressed, standing in the middle of her blue-carpeted basement. And they proceeded to lay together for the last time.

Tracy asked, "Where are you going?"

Timmy sighed. "I gotta get outta here." He jerked up his pants as he dressed in a hurry.

Tracy pleaded, "Stay till the morning, Timmy."

Timmy frowned at her. "Shit, girl, it's like four o'clock. It is the fuckin' morning."

"Well, where do you stay?"

He shook his head, refusing to tell her. "I told you that's not important," he answered, walking toward the door.

"I love you." Tracy told him again.

Timmy smiled. "Yeah, I know."

He walked off with a quick pace, slipping around corners and making sure there were no police cars positioned around her block. He ran down another driveway and around another corner, heading for the Broad Street subway station.

Once he had arrived, he waited nervously. A train pulled up after five minutes. Timmy rode the Broad Street line to Center City, feeling like he had escaped. He then transferred to the Market Street line. Fatigue pulled him into sleep while he rode. He awoke to find that he had missed his stop. He got up and crossed to the other side to head back. He was thankful that it was summertime. The sun would not rise until six, and it was already five-thirty.

Timmy wobbled on the streets, trying to stay awake until he could reach Gina's and fall asleep for the rest of day. He arrived at Gina's apartment building and pulled out the key that she had given him.

"FREEZE! YOU'RE UNDER ARREST!" a plainclothes detective hollered from behind him, with a raised gun.

Timmy was too tired to notice them ducked inside of a parked car across the street from the apartment complex. He was a wanted man, and the officers had waited for him to arrive, arresting him for the sake of hard-working citizens.

"Now drop the bag and turn around with your hands up high, son, or your life will end right here!"

Timmy dropped the bag and did as he was told.

drug Money

Crack cocaine was not on the popular scene in Tracy's neighborhood until the end of that summer of nineteen-eighty-six. A few boys sold marijuana and beer, but cocaine was new, highly addictive and in more demand. It was also the most profitable. It became an achievement for a girl to have a drug-dealing boyfriend. The status, the glamour and the money were beyond compare for teenagers.

Drug dealers in Philly drove Cadillac Eldorados, Ford Bronco jeeps, Mercedes Benzes and BMW's. They became the most talked about, instead of the athletes, the fighters and the pretty-boys. Drug dealing was the new *in* thing to do, with dealers making hundreds to thousands of dollars a day. No one knew who was the first to sell drugs in Tracy's part of the city. The word was out that drugs were moving into Germantown from North and South Philly, where crack cocaine had been popular since as early as nineteen-eighty-one.

. . .

Tracy remained in shock after the police arrested Timmy. She decided to leave boys alone for a while. She sat outside on her patio, watching flashy teens drive by in fancy cars with thumping sound systems.

Tracy could not help but be curious about them. All of the neighborhood gossip became focused around who's who in the drug world. Victor was one of the primary young sellers in the area, running things under his brother. Bruce's friend Bucky began conducting "business," as he liked to call it, for Victor's brother in his area. College basketball was not profitable for Todd "Hoops" Hinson, but the cocaine business was booming.

Tracy was attracted to a few of the dealers, regardless of her efforts to leave guys alone. On occasion, her growing curiosity had led her to the playground to learn more about them.

As Tracy looked up and down her block, she noticed Bruce, walking up toward her house. He wore a light-blue Izod tennis shirt with matching shorts. Tracy knew that he and Bucky had broken off. Bruce was not fond of drugs.

He walked right up to her steps and sat next to Tracy without a word.

"What, you just gon' sit here and not say anything?"

"So, what's been up, Tracy?" Bruce asked, as he looked into her hazels glittering in the sunlight. *Damn, she's beautiful!* he told himself. Obviously he was still not over her.

"Nothin'. What's up with you?"

"I'm 'bout to go to the Bahamas." Bruce hoped that she would ask more about it.

Tracy ignored it. "How come you don't hang out with your friend anymore?" she asked, wickedly. She already knew why; she just wanted to hear Bruce's full explanation.

"Because, Bucky got his own life now."

"Are you mad at him or something?" she pressed, wanting a more precise answer.

"Did I say I was mad at him?"

"Well, I thought you and Bucky were best friends."

"Oh, we still cool, we just don't hang out no more."

Tracy was guiding Bruce slowly but surely to where she wanted to go with their conversation: to talk about the drug trade.

"Why not?" she asked him.

"He got new buddies now."

"So what does that mean?"

"Look, I don't like his new friends, aw'ight," Bruce finally snapped at her. Although he was glad she was being cordial to him again, he was growing weary of her questions.

"Well, don't get mad at *me* for it."

"Stop asking me about it then."

Bruce was giving her the run-around instead of saying what she wanted him to say about drug dealing.

A blue Eldorado with white trimming whipped around the corner. Tracy noticed Victor driving, with Mark Bates in the passenger seat. Victor had recently turned eighteen, the same age as Bruce. Tracy would be turning a mere fifteen in September, but she *looked* eighteen.

Victor shouted, "Yo Bruce, come here, man!"

Tracy felt queasy about Victor and Bruce being out in front of her house together.

"You know where Bucky at, man?" Victor asked him.

"Naw, I don't be with him no more."

"Yeah, what's up wit' 'dat, man? You ain't down with this money or something, cuz'," Mark interjected.

Bruce never liked Mark. Mark Bates faked being cooler and tougher than what he really was, perpetrating like he was a real somebody. He was nothing to talk about to Bruce.

Bruce quizzed him, "How much money you gettin' out of it?"

"Oh, I'm makin' mine."

"Yeah, sure you are."

Victor knew that Bruce could easily beat Mark in a real confrontation. Bruce may have not been so good at enticing girls, but he was nobody's punk.

Victor said, "Bruce, if you wanna get put down just get wit' me, man. And tell Bucky I was lookin' for 'em." He then looked over at Tracy and smiled. "Oh yeah, tell my young-girl that I said, 'hi.' "

Bruce nodded as Victor's "El-dog" sped off, thumping Schoolly D's "Gucci Time."

Bruce walked back over to sit with Tracy.

"What did he say to you?" she asked him excitedly.

It was clear to Bruce that she still liked Victor, even though he seldom said anything to her.

"Nothin'," he lied jealously.

Tracy begged, "Come on. Tell me."

Bruce smiled. "What 'chew gon' do for me?"

Tracy looked at him and frowned. "Oh, well, never mind then. And if you're not gon' tell me, you can get off of my steps, too."

"Look at you actin' like a kid."

"Well, tell me then, and I'll do somethin' with you." Tracy smiled seductively.

Bruce laughed. "You a trip, 'cause I ain't tellin' you nothin'."

"Please, 'Brucie,' " Tracy begged, pulling on his arm. It was just like old times again. Tracy had not changed a bit.

"You want me bad, hunh?" Bruce asked her sarcastically.

Tracy released him, disgusted. "Boy, I don't want you. I'm goin' in the house."

Bruce knew he had gotten her goat. He strolled off with a big smile on his face.

"And don't come back here no more," Tracy yelled at his back.

Bruce continued to smile, and he took her ranting to mean the exact opposite.

"Tracy! Bruce is down here," Patti yelled up the steps that next evening.

Tracy ran down, excited about seeing him. But she kept her liking for him incognito. It was more fun that way.

"Didn't I tell you not to come here anymore?" she said to Bruce with a grin. She was wearing a red Le Coq Sportif sweat suit with an asymmetric hairdo, and the gigantic *Tracy* earrings that Timmy had bought her. She refused to listen to her mother about not wearing them anymore, especially since Timmy had purchased them with what she called "dirty money." Tracy argued, "Unless you just got new dollar bills from the bank, *all* money is dirty, mom."

Bruce sat on her couch and said, "I was around the courts, and I thought I might as well stop by."

"Was it a game around there?" Tracy asked him. She joined him on the couch, keeping a space in between them.

"Yeah, but it's over with now," he answered her. "And you know dude named Peppy?"

Tracy frowned. "Yeah, I know that punk."

Bruce smiled. "Dig, I don't like dude either, but he got busted up at the courts though."

"By who?" Tracy asked, hungry for gossip.

"Some drug-dealing dude named Cash. You know who I'm talkin' about?"

"Unt unh. I heard about him though. What he look like?"

"He a cool-looking dude, tall, brown and slender. He look a little like Rudy on the *Fat Albert Show,*" Bruce told her with a laugh.

Tracy shook her head. "No he don't," she responded. She thought about getting a chance to meet the boy. She then turned her attention back to Bruce.

Tracy asked him with a smile, "So Bruce, when you gon' buy me somethin' again?" She gestured passion with her hazels.

Bruce slapped his hand on her knee and whispered, "As soon as we make love again."

Tracy figured he was serious. "You ain't making love to me," she snapped, turning away from him. She wanted to see if Bruce would pursue her. He would be more exciting that way.

"Why not?" he asked, begging already.

"Because I said you can't," Tracy told him, annoyed by his weakness. Bruce was still *slow.*

"Well, the fuck if I'm gon' buy anything then," he snapped in a low tone. Patti was right in the kitchen. Bruce added, "You ain't givin' me no ass. So what I look like, Santa Claus or some shit to you?"

"Watch your mouth, boy," Tracy said, tickled brown. She chuckled at his radical response. Then she lied. "I don't want nothin' from you, Bruce. I just wanted to see if you were still stingy."

Bruce looked in between Tracy's legs. "Look how stingy you are."

Tracy grinned. "You nasty."

"Aw, girl, don't even try it. You know damn well you be givin' them panties up."

Tracy laughed aloud.

Bruce asked, "Can I get some water?"

"No, you can't have *nothin'* from me." She was hoping that Bruce would keep talking nasty to her. Tracy liked it.

Patti came out of the kitchen.

"Is Jason still in front of the house?"

Tracy responded, annoyed, "Yeah, mom."

Patti was in the way.

She walked to the front door to see for herself.

Bruce figured it was a perfect opportunity to get the upper hand on Tracy. "Oh, I can't get anything to drink, Tracy?" He was sure that Patti would hear him.

"Tracy, get up and get him somethin'."

Bruce giggled at his success.

Tracy said playfully, while bringing him a glass of lemonade, "I hate you."

"Yeah, I know you love me."

"I don't hardly love you, boy."

Bruce chuckled, gulping from the tall blue glass. "Well, I'm 'bout to roll," he said, finishing the lemonade. His mother had told him he had to start packing for their trip to the Bahamas.

Tracy asked, "Why you leavin'?"

Bruce lied. "I gotta go see my girlfriend."

"What girlfriend?"

"None of your business," he answered sharply, walking toward the door.

Tracy followed him out of her house, disappointed that he didn't stay longer. She was jealous, thinking that he was telling the truth.

"Don't leave, Bruce," she pleaded. She then whispered, "Fuck that girl." She looked back toward her brother, who was playing on the lawn with a neighbor, to make sure that they didn't hear her.

Bruce felt in charge. He wanted to keep Tracy begging. "Nope. I gotta go. Bye-bye. Seeya' later. *Buenos noches*. Don't forget to write." He laughed as he walked off down her block.

Tracy retorted, "Well, don't come back then."

Of course, she meant the opposite. Bruce was fun.

She looked and noticed a brand-new jeep at the opposite corner. She waited for Bruce to disappear before going to inspect it further.

"Where you goin', Tracy?" Jason asked, tagging along. His friend had been called inside.

"Nowhere, boy. Get back in front of the house," she told him. Jason remained at her side as Tracy looked the Bronco jeep over. It was two-toned, black on the top and gold across the bottom.

Jason squealed, "Deeeeep. This truck is *decent.*" He was four years old.

"Shet up, boy," Tracy told him, being evil.

"So you like my jeep, hunh, pretty?"

Tracy turned and spotted a tall, handsome, brown-skinned teenager wearing white leather shorts and a purple t-shirt. A wide gold chain was wrapped around his neck, and he wore no socks with his Timberland shoes.

Tracy said, "It is kind of nice." Feeling nervous, she seized Jason's hand.

Tall-and-handsome asked, "What's your name?"

"Tracy."

He leaned up against his jeep. "You live on this block, Tracy?"

"Yeah."

"My name is Jason," her brother said, reaching out to shake Tall-and-handsome's hand.

"Oh, you a cool little dude, hunh?" he responded. He picked Jason up, shocking Tracy with his friendliness. She stood there, waiting to be sweet-talked, as he put Jason back down and looked her over.

"So Tracy, I got an aunt that lives here, and whenever I'm up here to see her, I can stop by and shoot the breeze with you."

"Aw'ight. I live right there," Tracy told him, pointing to her house. "What's your name?" she finally asked him.

"Everybody calls me 'Cash.' My name was Ronald three years ago. But hell, you might as well call me Cash now, too."

Tracy asked, "Was you just fightin' some boy named Peppy at the playground?"

Cash nodded with a grin. "Yeah, I had to smack dude up a bit, you know. He was talkin' shit to me like he was hard or something."

Tracy liked his sense of authority and his nonchalant attitude. "I hate that boy," she told him.

"Yeah, well anyway, won't you give me your number so I can call you when I come back around to see my aunt?"

"Aw'ight," Tracy responded, refreshed by a new boy with a Bronco jeep. She wrote her number on a business card that Cash had pulled from his dashboard. He seemed to have everything in control. Tracy loved his organization. He gave her a beeper number and a three-digit code before he left, pumping Roxanne Shante from his booming system.

"Yo Cash, we gon' pick up that package later on?" asked a short, tanned-skinned friend.

"Naw, man. We ain't got the money together from the last one yet. And I ain't trying to owe no niggas nothin'."

Cash sat on his apartment couch, back in North Philly, counting ones, fives, tens and twenties.

"So you busted dude up today, hunh?" Short-tan asked.

"Oh yeah, Ed, 'cause dude thought I was a sucka'." Cash was still preoccupied with counting money.

"It be some babes up there, Cash?" Ed asked. He was watching *Black Caesar,* starring Fred Williamson, on the VCR.

Cash said, "Up in Germantown? Yeah, they got some good-lookin' chicks, cuz'. I met this young chumpee named Tracy up there t'day. She live on my aunt's block, on Diamond Lane. Mount Airy got some bad bitches too though. Straight up. Them rich hoes be lookin' gooder than a muthafucka."

"They got any connections, runnin' things up there?"

"Yeah, my man Victor Hinson and his brother got things rollin'. We went to school together in elementary. Victor's people's from North Philly."

Cash stood up to look out of the window. "Yo Ed, here come that girl, man. Get the shit."

Ed went outside and met her at the corner.

The ragged woman spied him nervously. "Give me a twenty, man."

He made the transaction and went back to the apartment.

Cash said, "That bitch come like every two days, cuz'."

"Yeah, I know."

Ed gave Cash the ruffled twenty-dollar bill.

"Man, she gotta get that monkey off her back," he responded, chuckling to himself. "Ay, man, I'm gon' call that young-girl up. Fuck it, you know."

Cash walked to the phone with the number in his hand and dialed it.

"Hello . . . Yeah, is Tracy there? Yo, what's up? It's Cash . . . Yeah, well you know what? That's for young-boah's, 'cause when I get a babe's number, I'm gon' use it when I want to . . . Yeah, well I was thinking 'bout coming up on Thursday, if you really wanted to ride around and all."

Ed interjected, while peeping out of the window, "Yo Cash, that bugged-out bitch is back again."

Cash spied out the window, four stories down. "Ay Tracy, I'm gon' call you back in a few." He hung up the phone and went back to the window. "Aw, man, I'm 'bout to punch this girl in her mouth."

They watched the young woman marching up the stairs toward their apartment complex. She was flyy, sporting gold and gear.

Cash sprinted outside, catching her before she made it inside of the building.

"I want my shit!" she screamed at him.

"Look, girl, I told you I ain't got it."

"Well, you know somethin' about it."

"Why you think I know, out of all people?"

"'Cause you down wit' Victor and them."

"What he got to do with it? You fuckin' him or some shit?"

"Look, all I know is that I was at that damn party up Haines Street, and my three hundred dollars are missin'. Now one of y'all know about the shit."

Her good looks were beginning to decline from being out in the streets too long. She was twenty-four years old, still dating young hustlers.

Cash said, "Well, you should'na had all that money on you anyway. You knew everybody was damn-near drunk in 'nere."

"I was holding it for my boyfriend."

"Who's your boyfriend?"

"Shawn Matthews."

Cash roared, "That dick-head is your boyfriend?" Another customer came up as he laughed. "YO, ED, come out and get this, man!"

Ed was watching from the window and came down to make a transaction with an older man. The gray-haired man wobbled in his stance. He then walked away shoving the twenty-dollar pack of cocaine inside of his pocket as if it would fly away from him.

The young woman who had been arguing with Cash stopped herself to think about things for a second. "It's a shame, what y'all do to these people," she commented.

"We ain't doin' nothin' but business. They takin' the drugs themselves. Nobody's forcin' 'em," Cash argued.

"Well look, I just wanna get my money back," she told him, getting back to the matter at hand.

Cash quizzed her, "Ain't that money your boyfriend had from drug-selling? Shawn sell drugs, too. He a *nut,* but he still sellin'."

"Look, I'on even know. Okay?"

Cash smiled and said, "Yeah, you know, you just don't wanna say it. So you can't say shit to me about gettin' paid, 'cause I'm gon' try to live it up as best I can."

Cash never did call Tracy back. He had "business" to take care of.

Tracy went school shopping with her family.

"So how much money you gon' milk for today?" her father asked.

"Well, you haven't been around for a while. You owe me *a lot,* now."

"I owe," Dave responded to her sternly. Tracy was referring to him as if he was one of her little boyfriends. "Your mother told me about that boyfriend you had, so I think I'm 'bout to start showing up around the house more often. You're getting way out of hand, to be living on the edge like that. You're not even fifteen yet."

Tracy grimaced. "I'm about to be fifteen though."

"Yup," Jason added, holding his mother's hand.

Patti still had few words for her estranged husband. He knew where she stood in the matter. She wanted his ass to stay home or stay away, but he could *not* do both.

Dave retorted, "Girl, jokes and games are over. Now you better start thinkin' before you get out here in them damn streets."

Tracy listened, but she didn't plan to adhere to anything. Where had *he* been? Who was *he* to give advice?

"In fact, I don't know why you need so many new clothes anyway. It seems to me that all this extra stuff is the main reason that you're out here running the streets," her father commented.

Tracy rolled her eyes. "Well, forget it then. I don't need any clothes."

Dave grabbed her arm. "So you think that since I'm not in the house with you and your mother that you can say anything you want to me now? Is that it?"

Tracy snapped, "Wait a minute, nobody *asked* you to leave. *You* wanted to leave us, so don't start acting like you wasn't welcomed home. Maybe if you *was* home more, I would have something else to do," she said, as she walked away from him.

Jason anxiously threw his hand to his mouth, expecting Tracy to get in trouble.

Dave looked to Patti, but she was not ready to sympathize with him. "If you really want to help her, then you know where your daughter lives," she told him.

Patti sat and listened all that night as Dave lectured Tracy about the "hot-ass girls" he knew when he was a teenager. Patti had been a "hot-ass" herself, she *and* her sisters. Nevertheless, despite Dave's efforts, all Tracy could think about was how her father had the audacity to tell her how to live when he had basically walked out on his family.

Dave was gone again, talked out, after only an hour of shopping and three hours of lecturing.

Patti sat on the living-room couch with her son after his father had walked out on them again. "You see that? Now I'm stuck to raise *you* and Tracy *all* by myself. And that sister of yours is just too fast for her own good."

"So where are we goin'?" Tracy asked Cash, hopping inside of his black and gold Bronco.

Cash was going on nineteen years old, older than any boy Tracy had dealt with. He pulled off without responding to her. The air-conditioner pumped into Tracy's face, and the bass from his stereo system made it feel like she was at a live concert. They whipped down the street doing forty miles per hour to an unknown destination as Tracy enjoyed the scenery. Cash then stopped at a gas station to fill up while Tracy leaned back in the passenger seat, thinking that she was dreaming. Yet it was real. She was not yet fifteen, cruising in a brand-new jeep with a young drug dealer.

Cash said, "Look, I gotta go pick up this package, and then I got some other stops to make."

Tracy nodded. She had been on several car rides before, but a jeep ride with him was the best.

They drove through neighborhoods in Philadelphia that Tracy had never been to before. Outside of Logan, where she had had dance classes, Tracy never had any reason to visit other areas. Germantown was her home.

They stopped in the middle of a block, in the heart of North Philly. Cash jumped out and was surrounded by five or six tough-looking friends.

"CASH MO-N-A-A-Y! What's up, man?"

They looked into the jeep at Tracy, reminding her of the type of rough-looking guys that her cousins dated in Logan. Cash then walked around the jeep to let her out.

"Come on," he demanded, opening the door.

Tracy climbed out, feeling terrified. Her father tried to tell her about living in the fast lanes. She looked around, realizing that Cash had every motive in the world to sell drugs. The streets were ripped up and aged, along with the cars and the houses. Down at the opposite corner, two girls were fist fighting and trying to nearly kill each other, but the neighbors seemed unconcerned. They were used to the chaos.

Cash was showing Tracy off, or "sportin' her." "Come here, I want you to meet my boy, Wayne," he said.

Wayne looked Tracy over: pretty face, honey-brown complexioned, hazel-eyed, tall, full of body, asymmetric hair and glittering with gold.

Wayne responded, "Damn, girl, you got any older sisters?" He was older than Cash. Tracy suspected that Cash was working for him. Wayne looked about twenty-four and was loosely dressed with Adidas gear. He had a neatly trimmed goatee and was walnut-brown like Mercedes.

Wayne looked important. Tracy could not help staring at his thick, gold nugget bracelet. Then again, her earrings were just as big, shining ostentatiously. And she could sense that the North Philly girls were jealously staring at her. She was taking one of their players.

"No, I don't have any sisters," she answered Wayne. "All I got is a little brother."

Cash butted in. "Yeah, her brother gon' be aw'ight, Wayne. Little dude ran up and spoke, shook my hand and everything. Oh, these my partners, L.C. and Trap," he told Tracy, introducing two others. They weren't as glamorous or as handsome as Wayne.

"Hi y'all doin'?" Tracy said politely.

"Not as fine as you, unfortunately," L.C. said, laughing boisterously. "You know, cuz'? Unfortunately," he repeated, still chuckling to himself. L.C. was short with a missing tooth, wearing an old Todd 1 sweat suit, which was out of fashion at the time.

Trap said, "Dig, 'cause I'm 'bout to run on up to Germantown and get quite *fortunate* myself, *I must say.*"

Tracy was pleased and tickled by their lighthearted *Saturday Night Live* attitudes. But she was smart enough to know that they were only friendly because Cash was their boy and she was his young-girl.

She followed Cash into his house to meet his young-looking mother and friendly sisters. His family was large. Tracy envied that. With three older brothers and four sisters, Cash would always have someone to talk to.

"So did you like my family and all?" he asked with a smile, as they traveled to the next stop in his jeep.

"Yeah. I wish I had a big family like that."

Cash chuckled and said, "I wish I had a crib like yours. Girl, I would have loved to grow up up your way."

"Why you say that?"

Cash grimaced as if it should have been obvious. "'Cause, it would have been a lot more peaceful, compared to the shit that I had to go through down North. And the thing that takes me out is how y'all got those fake-ass punks in y'all area, like that boah' Peppy, thinkin' he tough and shit. That's why I had to smack him around for a second."

Cash rolled down the windows to catch the night air. The sun was starting to set and the wind blew in, shaking Tracy's earrings.

"That feels gooood," she squealed.

Cash giggled at nothing.

"What's so funny?" she quizzed him.

"I was just thinking about how scared you looked when I told you

to get out the jeep," he alluded. "GET OUT OF THE STREET, YOU
LITTLE KNUCKLEHEAD!" Cash screamed out of the window to
a kid.

Tracy chuckled, watching the brown boy scatter to the sidewalk.

They arrived at their second destination, all the way down Southwest
Philly. There weren't as many people around as on Cash's block in
North. He told Tracy to stay inside the jeep, while he jumped out and
ran into a house.

"Yo, you got that set-up for me?" he asked an older black man.

"Yeah. HEY SAM, give him that package, man!"

Sam said, "What took you so long, young-boah'? We thought you
was gon' be here at six-thirty." He brought the package out with him
from the kitchen. It was a clear sandwich bag with small packages of
crack cocaine, all individually wrapped.

Cash said, "Yeah, well, I got this little young-girl out in the ride,
and she just met my mom and sisters, back the way."

"You got a little young-girl in the car, hunh?" Sam responded,
looking out of the window at Tracy, who was sitting inside of the jeep
impatiently. She didn't like the idea of waiting outside of a drug house.
"Damn, she a *fine* thing!" Sam said. He was at least thirty-two, and
too old to be concerned about the latest fashions. He had on a plain
pair of blue jeans and a red Nike T-shirt.

"How old you think she is?" Cash quizzed him with a smile.

"What, she's like seventeen, eighteen, right? 'Cause I'm assuming
she got to be younger than you. You ain't got no game for no old-head
pussy yet," Sam told him. He laughed and slung an arm around Cash's
shoulder.

"Yeah, aw'ight, cuz'," Cash responded, smirking. "But umm, naw.
That girl only fifteen years old, Sam. Matter of fact, she fourteen,
'cause her birthday's in two weeks."

"W-o-o-o-o, slow down! You better watch them babies," Sam told
him seriously. "I don't wanna see my man goin' ta' jail and shit, over
some ass that still smell like piss."

They roared laughing, like at a Richard Pryor concert.

Cash said, "Naw, Sam, it ain't even like 'dat. She know what time it is. You gotta bring 'em in the right way, 'cause them young-boahs' would just waste her potential. And I'm 'bout to blossom this young buck."

Cash walked out with the package in a brown paper bag and hid it under his seat. It was the first time that Tracy had been around any crack cocaine. She tried to hold her tongue about it, but it was no use.

"What if we get stopped by the police?" she asked, laughing to camouflage her concern. She was serious, and Cash knew it. He rode down another street and turned the corner to park. He then turned the key off and took a deep breath.

Cash looked Tracy in her hazels and threw down *his* game. "Now I know that you're spoiled and all, and that you grew up in a nice neighborhood, but this is the way I stay on top of life. I'm not tryin' to get you involved in any dumb stuff, either. All I do, myself, is buy it and have it distributed. This the only time that I even touch the stuff.

"Now I'ma let you know right now, I like you, but this is how I do things. Now if you can't deal with that, then fuck it. And after I drop you off tonight, just don't call me no more."

He turned the ignition back on and zoomed the jeep to the next stop, his distribution house. Tracy was not afraid of Cash like she was of Timmy; she just had some serious thinking to do about the drug trade. She was indirectly involved, but she knew that situations could turn hostile when the money didn't add up right. Yet she liked the suspense of it, and she loved riding around in his jeep, but it was getting late.

Cash sprinted inside of the distribution house to organize his workers and kept some product for his buddy Ed. By then, it was ten thirty-five on a Tuesday night. Cash realized that Tracy had to be home soon, and by the time they had finally made it back to her Germantown block, she had fallen asleep and it was after twelve.

Cash howled, "Ay, girl! Get up!"

"What?" Tracy answered, pushing him off of her. Her hazels were sealed shut.

Cash hopped out of his jeep and walked around to the passenger side to carry her out.

"Dag, what time is it?" she asked, stretching in his arms.

"Just go in the house, girl." He tossed Tracy down on the sidewalk. Her Reeboks hit the pavement with a plop, and she headed for her door.

Patti was asleep when Tracy crept into bed, but she knew that her daughter had been out later than usual. She figured she would catch her in the morning, or after she got in from work.

After cruising for six hours in Cash's jeep, Tracy had a good sleep that night, straight through to eleven o'clock that next morning.

Jason announced, "Mommy said you gon' *get it* when she gets home." He was smiling, leaning overtop of her head when she awoke.

"Shet up and leave me alone."

"Mommy told you to fix me some cereal when you get up."

"Well, I ain't up yet."

Jason leaped on her demandingly. Tracy tossed him from her bed, and he landed on his head.

BLOOM!

"OOOOWWW! I'm gon' tell mom on you, Tra-cy!"

"You shouldna' been playin' wit' me!" she screamed at him. She climbed up out of bed to see if her brother was okay. Jason then punched her in the stomach and ran. Tracy smiled and shook her head, tickled by his revenge.

BRRRIIIINNGG! . . . BRRRIIIINNGG!

Jason called from the hallway, "The telephone, you dummy."

"Hello," Tracy answered, wiping sleep from her eyes.

"Yo, it's Bruce. I haven't heard from you in a while."

Tracy didn't want to be rude and just hang up on him, but she was in no mood to be hassled that morning. "Look, Bruce, I'm 'bout to fix my brother something to eat, so I'll call you back," she told him.

Bruce took a while to respond, as if he was thinking about something else to say. "Yeah, aw'ight then," he finally responded to her.

"Come on, boy," Tracy said to her brother, leading him down the steps and into the kitchen.

• • •

She expected her mother to be angry at her, but Tracy was not *that* concerned about it. *I mean, what can she do to me? Put me on punishment,* she pondered.

Tracy and Raheema gossiped all that afternoon about the boys and girls from around their neighborhood, while Jason had his playtime out in the sun. Raheema had been talking about boys more after dealing with Bruce, but she still did not date any of them, so Tracy told her all of her news, hoping that her neighbor would learn something for when she felt comfortable enough to try another boyfriend.

When a quarter after five ticked around, Patti pulled around the corner and parked out in front of the house.

"Here she comes, Tracy," Raheema commented with a smile.

"I can see, girl," Tracy snapped at her nervously. She then got up and walked into the house to make sure that she was not embarrassed outside. She strutted into the kitchen and poured herself some water to calm her nerves, wondering what her mother had in store for her. By the time she had finished, Patti was right behind her.

"Where the hell was your grown-ass last night, Tracy?" Patti was taking off her rings.

Tracy said, "Mom, honest t' God, I fell asleep. I didn't know what time it was."

She watched her mother set her rings on the kitchen table, as if they were going to fist fight. Patti was still an inch or so taller than her daughter, and she was nearly twenty pounds heavier.

Patti grabbed Tracy by her hair, which was all piled up on top of her head. "Girl, I'm 'bout to whip your motherfuckin' *ASS!*" she yelled violently. They slammed up against the long kitchen cabinet, next to the refrigerator as Patti attacked her daughter, smacking her face and flooring her with fists and elbows.

Tracy hollered with tears rushing down her face, too petrified to try and get away, "I'M SORRY, MOM-MEE! I WON'T DO IT AGAIN! PL-E-E-EASE! OH GOD! HELP ME!"

"GOD AIN'T GON' HELP YOUR ASS, GIRL!" Patti roared. She

stopped herself, seeing how helpless her daughter was and took a couple of deep breaths.

Tracy slid to the floor, crying hysterically.

"Take your hot-ass upstairs to your room! And you best not come the hell out until it's wintertime!"

Tracy jumped up and sprinted past her mother and up to her room. She closed her door and jumped into her bed before Patti got a chance to mumble her last sentence.

Jason had walked inside wearing a smile, to see what was going on.

"This ain't nothing to laugh about, Jason, because if you start acting up, you're gonna get some of this too," his mother warned him.

Her son's smile quickly faded as Patti continued to rant while pacing her living room:

"If Tracy thinks that she's gonna do whatever she wants, and come home anytime that she wants to, while out here running around with these damn boys, then I'm gonna tear fire to her ass more often.

"I don't know who she *thinks* she is, but she ain't old enough to make her own rules and schedules in *this* house, and when she *thinks* that she is, then she's gonna be hittin' that damn door, 'cause I'm not losing my my mind chasing after her. I already have to go though this shit with your father."

Jason cringed from his mother's unexpected rage and snuck back outside.

Patti walked back to the kitchen and took a seat to slip her rings back on her fingers. "I simply *refuse* to be stepped on," she told herself.

Tracy didn't see Cash for three weeks. She was in no rush to get back out into the fast lanes. She stayed around her house and played with her brother, figuring that she needed a resting period.

Patti eased up and let her off of punishment once the new school year started. It was the first Friday night that Tracy was allowed to go out. Raheema, Carmen and Jantel weren't home when she called them. She then decided to sit out on her front steps in the cool, nighttime breeze, hoping that neighbors, or anyone, would decide to come out on her block. No one did.

Tracy could hear crickets chirping, it was so quiet. She looked at the stars to amuse herself, thinking about Cash's black and gold Bronco. If she could wish for something, it would be for him to pick her up. Then she laughed at her ridiculousness, remembering how ready her mother was to beat her senseless.

A voice seemed to fall out of the night air, "Hey, pretty."

Tracy snapped out of her daze. It was Bruce. "What's up?" she perked, happy to have his company. Bruce could not stay away from her.

"Nothin'. I was up here, so I figured I'd come talk to you for a while," he told her.

They fell silent for the first five minutes.

Tracy said, "I thought you came up here to talk to me."

Bruce chuckled. "You know I'm going into the Air Force, right?" He turned to look up at Tracy's asymmetric hairdo and those big *Tracy* gold earrings. She was fifteen years old, in high school. He was eighteen, heading into the United States Air Force, but Bruce couldn't help being attracted to her.

Tracy grunted, "Unt unh." She shook her head and looked even prettier to him. "Why you goin' there?"

"'Cause, college is for those education-type people. I'd rather be doing somethin' physical."

Tracy glanced up the street at a car that was driving by. She thought that it was Victor, but it wasn't.

Bruce said, "It's peaceful out here tonight, ain't it? I feel like we on a romantic date or something. Yup, Tracy, we can put a candle right in front of us. Then I would stare at your pretty eyes and all."

Tracy started to giggle. "How come you don't sell drugs instead of going to the Air Force?" she asked, just for the hell of it. Bruce had never commented about the drug trade since the last time she had asked.

"Oh, you into that too, hunh?" he commented glumly. "I see that as an easy way out for people that don't wanna work hard."

"Well, why should life have to be hard work?"

"'Cause that's the way that it is, Tracy."

"Who says so?"

"I don't fuckin' know, girl."

Tracy laughed at Bruce's temperament before she quizzed him. "How come you can't tell me why?"

"'Cause I don't know why. Shit! What a nigga know in this world? Tell me."

Tracy answered with sparkling hazels, "Well, if you don't know, then leave things alone and live." She played with her right earring and looked into Bruce's placid face. "See, the way I see it, Bruce, is that everybody knows these things about life and all, but no one lets them get in the way of living. And that's how it should be, 'cause no one wants to be constantly reminded that the world is dull and boring. Now I know I'm still young and all, but that's how I see things."

Bruce nodded. They sat and talked for hours about the times they had had in the year gone by. Tracy got Bruce to lighten up enough to talk about his life. He was delightful to be with when his mind was not on his letdowns and his shortcomings. They had good rapport.

Her sophomore year, every boy in the hallway was impressed with Tracy's flamboyance and her stunning outfits. She scared off the boys who lacked self-confidence, attracting only the players, and she liked it that way.

The first week of classes took forever. Tracy wore smashing outfits, Monday through Friday, catching all eyes, while the guys whispered, "Damn, she flyy."

One boy got up enough heart to ask, "Excuse me. Can I walk you home?"

Tracy turned and spotted a well-dressed, cool-looking, tanned-skinned boy, surrounded by hungry-looking friends.

"I'm getting a ride home today," she told him. She wore a black suede skirt with black fishnet stockings and a gold silk blouse; her usual gold was around her neck, wrists and fingers, and her earrings dangled from her ears. Tracy's full package glared like a teen model strutting down a concrete runway.

The boy responded, "Oh, don't tell me you got a car, too."

"No, but my boyfriend is picking me up in his jeep."

The cool boy cracked a charming smile.

"What's so funny?" Tracy asked him.

"Your boyfriend got a jeep, hunh?" He shook his head and added, "So everybody wants a drug dealer nowadays."

"How you know he a drug dealer?"

"'Cause he got a jeep. And ain't no young niggas ridin' around in no jeeps, unless they sellin' drugs."

"Who told you that?"

"Everybody knows that shit, girl. Where you been at?"

"Everybody *don't* know it. It's some blacks who don't need to sell drugs to buy a jeep. My boyfriend's father bought it for him," Tracy lied. At least her heart was in the right place.

"Yeah, right. Don't run that game on me, girl. Save that corny shit for the next *slow* nigga, 'cause I ain't him." The cool boy strolled to rejoin his admiring friends. He had set Tracy straight, and he knew it.

Tracy smirked and rushed to the spot where Cash said he would pick her up. He was running late. He then whipped around the corner blasting Rakim's song, "Eric B For President."

Tracy yelled through the heavy bass of the rap song, "What took you so long?"

Cash turned the volume down. "Oh, this nut dude tried to get over on Wayne, so we had to smack 'im up a bit."

Tracy leaped in and slung her book-bag to the floor. "You gotta fight a lot?" she asked, curiously.

"Naw, just when somebody tries some dumb stuff. But don't start gettin' all worried about that, 'cause I know how you start thinkin'. So we just gon' go to a movie and chill tonight."

"We gotta go to an early show though, 'cause I got school tomorrow," she told him. Tracy didn't want her mother going crazy again.

"Yeah, aw'ight. I'll pick you up before seven, and have you back before ten."

"All right," Tracy agreed.

Cash pulled up at the corner of her block just as Raheema was going inside of her house. She saw them kiss good-bye at the corner, and she decided to wait up for Tracy.

"I thought you said you weren't gonna go with him anymore?" she asked her hard-headed neighbor.

"Mind your business, Raheema," Tracy said in a sing-song fashion. She was too happy to argue.

"Well, you did say that."

"So what? I changed my mind."

"What if your mom finds out?" Raheema had heard about Tracy's ass-kicking through *her* mother. Patti told Beth, and Beth passed it down to Raheema as a warning. Tracy assumed that she knew, because of the big smile she displayed.

Tracy snapped, "Then I'm gon' kick your ass. You bitch!" she spat.

Aware that she had unintentionally hit a weak spot with Tracy, Raheema decided to slip inside. "I'm not a bitch. I'm just worried about you," she retorted. She slipped into the house before Tracy could get ahold of her.

"Well, worry about yourself!" Tracy hollered at her neighbor's door. She was pissed! Her feelings were hurt. "God, I hate that fuckin' girl!" she shouted. She marched inside of her house and said, "That bitch gon' mess around and dime on me. *Watch!* And if I get my ass kicked, then I'm gon' kick her ass."

Tracy had cooled out with boys and mischief for a little while, but as they say, *A hard head makes a soft behind.* Her mouth was getting worse as well.

"Girl always worried about somebody," she continued to rant, worried about what would happen if Raheema started running her mouth. She paced back and forth in her living room. "That's why her face is breakin' out. She need a new boyfriend. All she do is sit around the house and gossip. Little fuckin' nerd. She need to live her own damn life."

• • •

Times were hard and dull for Raheema. The two rebels of life, Mercedes and Tracy, seemed to be getting a lot more out of it.

Raheema thought back to her childhood years, and she was suddenly able to understand Mercedes' changes. Mercedes was a victim. It simply did not pay to do right in a world where so many enjoyed doing wrong.

Raheema did all of her homework on time, and continued to get straight A's in Cardinal Dougherty high school. She was bored and miserable, learning to gossip for enjoyment. She had lost her only boyfriend because of her mistrust and inexperience with the opposite sex, and to top off her misfortunes, a case of teenaged acne had slowly begun to invade her face.

What did obedience to her parents do for her? Raheema felt as if she was being robbed of her teenage experience. She felt as if she would have nothing to tell her children, except gossip about what everyone else was doing. Her self-esteem was as low as a worm's in the mud.

She went to the bathroom and looked at herself in the mirror. The image reflected her inside and her outside. Her acne pads sat inside the cabinet, with a strong smell of alcohol. It was a teenage thing. Everyone would get it. But Raheema only saw the miserable people with it. *Mercedes never had no stupid acne,* she thought. *And Tracy doesn't either.*

Books and homework no longer had their hold over her. In Raheema's state of depression, the bed seemed a lot more rewarding, and she was beginning to take naps for hours at a time, tormented by her "Plain Jane" lifestyle. She went to her room and got into bed.

Beth walked in and clicked on her daughter's light, concerned about her. It was eight-thirty. Raheema had not left her room. "Ra-Ra? Are you sick or somethin', honey?"

Raheema ignored her, playing possum. She didn't feel like talking about it, not to her mother. *She put me in this situation in the first place, by marrying my mean-ass father,* she thought. "No, mom. I just want to rest."

Beth placed her hand on Raheema's forehead to see if she was coming down with a fever. "Are you sure nothing's wrong with you?"

"I just wanna sleep, mom." Tears slid from Raheema's face and into her pillow, revealing her despair.

"Did something happen in school today?" her mother pressed her.

Raheema remained speechless.

"Well, did you fail a test or something? Honey, please, I'm here to help you."

Raheema felt that her situation was hopeless. She mumbled into her pillow, "You can't help me, mom."

"Well, what is the problem?"

Raheema sniffed and wiped her eyes. "I hate myself because I'm ugly. I haven't been happy since my sister left. I want to be with her. She's the only one that has a real life in this family," she cried, wiping her watery eyes and sniffing more rapidly.

Beth hugged her, attempting to sooth her pain. "Honey, this is just a passing phase. It'll go away," she said, referring more to the teenaged acne than the reference to Mercedes. *Lord knows I don't want to go through that again,* she thought. Keith still talked about "that damn Mercedes" this and "that damn Mercedes" that.

Raheema retorted, "I'm tired of hearing that. Tracy didn't start breaking out." She angrily pulled away. They had had teenaged acne discussions at least five times before.

Raheema put her hands over her face and mumbled, "I've done everything that dad tells me to do, and he doesn't even notice me. All he talks about is Mercedes. He always liked her more than me anyway. She didn't do anything he told her, and yet he still talks about when *she* was here. He never talks about me. And I hate him anyway. I hate him, mom."

She looked her mother in the face with spiteful eyes, as if she hated her too. Then she asked her, "Why you marry that man, mommy?"

There was nothing Beth could say to soothe her. *Why did I marry him?* she asked herself. "Baby, things will get better," she said.

Keith roared from down the stairs, "BETH! WHERE 'DAT DAMN GIRL AT? Tell her to get down here and wash these damn dishes!" He walked to the kitchen to get something to drink. He was just getting in from work. He took out a KOOL cigarette to calm his nerves from the hype of his laboring job.

Beth came down to meet him. "I'll do it. Raheema's not feeling too well."

Beth had bags around her eyes, appearing thin and frail, as if the exuberance and the energy of life had been sucked out from her body. She wore droopy, dull clothing, navy blues, charcoal grays and dark greens. She had married Keith because she thought it was the right thing to do. She was pregnant with his daughter, Mercedes, right out of high school, and even then he had forced his will on her.

Keith asked, "Well, what's wrong with her?" He gulped down a cold Miller and burped.

"She's having emotional problems."

"Emotional problems!" he exclaimed with a frown. "So she's about to start up with that dumb shit, too, hunh? I'm gon' straighten *this one* the hell out!" Keith put out his cigarette and headed for Raheema's room.

Beth asked, "Now what are you gonna do, Keith?" She hurried behind him, forcing herself not to allow him up the steps.

"What the hell is wrong with you?" he yelled at her. He shoved her and continued on his way up.

Beth pleaded, grabbing onto his waist, "Please, Keith, I beg you. It's not what you think it is."

Keith pushed her away to release her hold on him.

Beth refused. "You're torturing her!" she screamed at him. "That's her problem! Now if you have any love left in your heart, then let her rest in peace. PLEASE!"

Raheema jolted from her room and saw her parents struggling on the stairs. She ran back to her room and slammed the door, locking it shut. She then proceeded to trash her room, wishing she had the power to do the same to her father. All her life she dreamed of having *that* power. For five minutes Raheema screamed and hollered how much she hated him.

Keith finally got the message. He turned and walked into his room, locking *his* door. He paced inside of his room and lit up another cigarette, thinking about how his father had tortured him and his family when he was young. He didn't want to blame himself, yet he realized that was adding, blindly, to a terrible chain of mental cruelty.

Raheema made her mind up, in her despair, that she too would have sex, just to see how it felt. But everyone hated her snotty attitude. And she had acne. Those were problems. Tracy had previously joked that sex would clear her face up, and Raheema was willing to find out if the myth was true.

Makeup covered her blemishes, with lipstick adding the finishing touches. Raheema pumped herself up to have a positive attitude. The first couple of days in school she pulled it off. She held meaningful conversations with a few more people than what she usually had spoken to, and specifically with more boys. But no one tried to approach her about a date until her second week on the prowl.

"Hi, Ra-Ra. You real look nice today," a fellow student said inside of the hallway. He had bright eyes and rust-colored skin, and he was friendly.

Raheema smiled. "Oh, how you doin', Darin?"

Darin had known her since freshman year and had a crush on her. He was attractive, but not glamorous. Raheema did not count him as a likely prospect.

"Can I walk you to class?" he asked her.

Raheema slammed her hard-to-close locker. "If you want to," she answered carelessly.

"So what did you do all summer?"

"Nothing, really."

"Well, how is your mother?"

What is he asking about my mother for? Raheema thought. She felt guilty about it, but she was annoyed with Darin's small talk. He wouldn't have gotten a second of Mercedes' or Tracy's time. He was slow-witted, and his conversation was weak.

Raheema tried her best to remain cordial when she asked him, "Why are you asking about my mother?"

Darin answered, shakily, "Oh, I just figured I'd ask. You know?"

Raheema smiled and nodded to ease his embarrassment, but she didn't know. *He's never even met my mother,* she told herself.

They arrived at her class, and she was relieved when Darin turned to walk away. He felt good about it. He had enjoyed himself. He was grinning as if he had received an award at a banquet.

"I saw you, D. What did you say to her?" his brown and slender friend asked, walking up on him from behind.

Darin said, "Man, I was scared to ask her to the movies. But I tell you what, if I could get with her, I'd give her everything I have to give."

Raheema turned down several uninteresting offers that day while flirting in the halls. The girls talked about her, expecting her change to be for the worst. Her head was too high. She walked with a glow that she had never possessed. And they were jealous.

At the SEPTA bus stop, Raheema attracted more eyes than she did previously. The boys sensed that she was presently open for offers.

One boy asked, loud and clear, "What's your name, slim?" He was light-skinned with a scarred face, as if he was a fist-fighter. And he was not from Catholic school. He wore flashy public school gear.

Raheema asked, "Why you call me 'slim'?" She was attempting to establish her new sociability. The boy was not as well-groomed as Bruce or Darin, but Raheema thought he was more confident and cool. *So what if he's not a pretty-boy?* she told herself.

Scar-face sat down beside her and responded, "Does the shit matter?"

His friends chuckled. He had always been rash with his words.

The boy reminded Raheema of Bruce's friend Bucky. She had never gotten along well with him. Bucky had been able to read all of her inconsistencies.

Blood rushed to Raheema's face with anxiety. She began to feel inferior and not secure enough to deal with the boy. Her new self-confidence was weakening.

Scar-face asked, "So what's your name?"

He put his hand on Raheema's knee. She could imagine her father doing something of that sort to her mother, some twenty years ago.

"Raheema." She tried to hide her nervousness with a piece of gum.

"You got one for me too, right?"

Scar-face did not look all that bad with a smile on his face. Raheema gave him a stick.

"So where do you live?" he asked, popping the gum into his mouth.

"Diamond Lane."

"Yeah? Do you know some girl named Tracy?"

"Yeah, why?" she asked, still craving gossip.

"Oh, 'cause she think she the shit. I be wantin' to take her head off, the cat-eyed-lookin' bitch."

Raheema giggled, feeling more comfortable. "What's your name?" she asked him.

"Chuck." He looked at her silky long hair and touched it. "I like this. It'll be good to run my fingers through."

His friends looked at him and laughed again.

Raheema smiled it off, apprehensively. *I don't think I want to do anything with him,* she told herself. Yet Chuck had established more authority with her than the other boys who had tried her.

He asked for her number, but Raheema bashfully asked for his instead, so Chuck wrote it down for her.

She arrived home with a certain smugness about her day. She had accomplished something outside of schoolwork for the first time in a long time. It was even enjoyable to go boy-shopping. She began to feel some of the excitement that she was sure her older sister and her neighbor had felt.

Tracy had turned down Cash's offer to go to the movies. Raheema had "busted her groove," or in other words, gotten in the way of her plans Cash then promised to take her to the Gucci shop in Atlantic City, New Jersey. He said he was going to buy her some Gucci gear, since he had missed her birthday. He gave her all kinds of excuses for a couple of weeks before he finally took her on the shopping spree.

They left for Atlantic City early on a Saturday morning. Tracy lied to her mother and said that she would be attending Jantel's cross-country track meet. She knew she was pressing her luck, but she surely was not going to pass up a chance to go to Atlantic City.

When they arrived, Cash counted out three thousand dollars. Tracy pretended as if she was not looking, but Cash knew that she was. The only time she had seen that much money was in the movies.

"You gon' spend all that on me?" she asked with a loose tongue.

"Naw, my sisters wanted some stuff, too."

Tracy smiled and said, "I know. I was just jokin'." She felt embarrassed about her hasty comment.

Cash grinned at her and responded, "No you didn't. You really are greedy like that."

"No I'm not," she retorted.

They walked ahead toward the casinos. It was cloudy along the beach, and the first three casinos they had entered were wrong.

Tracy whined, "Dag, we gotta walk all way back there."

"Won't you stop complainin' so much?"

"I don't feel like walkin' all way back there." She dragged her feet like a child. She wore her white Sixers jacket, black Gloria Vanderbilt jeans and red Reeboks.

"Fuck it. We goin' back home," Cash teased.

"Sike, Cash, I'm only playin'. God."

Cash shook his head. "You somethin' else, girl. And you think I'm a sucka', but that's aw'ight." He looked at her and grinned, thinking about leaving her in "A-C." "You lucky I like you," he told her.

"Why?" she asked, confused.

"Oh, don't worry about it now."

"Don't worry about what?"

"Nothin', girl."

What is he talking about? Tracy thought to herself.

They reached the right casino and walked through crowds of gamblers before coming to the Gucci shop. Prices ranged from twenty-five dollars for key chains and umbrellas, on up to the thousands for everything else, including sweaters, jackets, shoes and outfits.

Tracy tried on the sneakers that she wanted. Cash bought them, a pocketbook and a key chain. He bought himself a four-hundred-and-fifty-two-dollar sweat suit, along with the items his sisters wanted.

Cash hung around the casinos while he waited for Tracy to use the bathroom. It was a perfect opportunity for him to get away long enough to order a hotel room. Tracy came out of the restrooms to find that Cash was gone. He came walking back with a smile on his face, and Tracy was curious about it. She thought he had snuck off to talk to some other girls who were there.

She asked possessively, "Where did you go?"

Cash lied to her. "Oh, I tried to get in the casino, and dude let me play a few games. But umm, Tracy, what we gon' do when we get back home?"

"I don't know."

"Well, let's put all these bags inside the jeep and walk around."

They walked around the casino grounds for another hour, laughing and talking about people. Every now and then, Cash would take a peek or two at Tracy's firm behind. He got her to jump on an elevator to ride up to the eighth floor. They got off to snoop around. Cash then stopped, taking out a key in front of room 812.

Tracy grinned. "Oh, so you got a room, hunh?"

"Yeah, I can't let us go home without celebratin'." He walked in with a serious face. And it was obvious to Tracy that he wanted something. "Come here and sit on my lap," he told her.

Tracy did, reluctantly. She didn't like the way that Cash had gone about it. *He should have just told me that he was going to get a room,* she thought to herself. *I don't know why he had to sneak around to do it.*

He looked at Tracy's lips before he kissed her.

Tracy pulled away, disappointed. She wasn't sure if she was up to doing anything with him. She just did not feel like it.

Cash asked her, "What 'chew stop for?"

Tracy sighed, without giving him an answer. She thought about lying to Cash and telling him that her time of the month was around. But she doubted if that would work. *I might as well just get this over with,* she told herself. She got up and went inside the bathroom to begin taking off her clothes. Cash was shocked! No young-girl had ever been so bold about it. Tracy figured it was the fastest way to get the sexual encounter over with, but Cash felt she was being exotic.

She walked over to the bed, butt-naked, with firm breasts, firm behind and a perfectly curved honey-brown body, and slipped underneath the covers.

Cash took out a three-pack of lubricated LifeStyles.

Tracy watched him. "I'm on the pill," she announced.

"So, them pills don't stop shit from burnin'."

"What?" she snapped defensively. "Oh, I ain't got nothin'."

Cash looked at her as if she was crazy. "Shid', I'on know you like that, girl. Even young-girls burnin' nowadays. I can't take no more chances with my shit, 'cause AIDS is killin' muthafuckas. And the shit that trips me out is that girls don't be knowin' when they're burnin'."

"You got burned before?"

"What 'chew think?"

There was a moment of silence.

Tracy said, "Well, I don't have anything, and if you feel like that, then we ain't gotta do nothin'."

Cash retorted, "Yup, and *we* ain't gotta go back home, either."

Tracy sighed. "Well, come on then," she said, throwing her head back against the pillow.

Cash looked at the pack of LifeStyles in his hand. "Aw'ight, fuck it," he said, throwing them on the dresser.

He climbed in bed and went for Tracy's breasts to stimulate himself. Tracy caressed him and guided him inside of her. Cash was shocked by her actions again. He moved in a fury as Tracy ran her fingers over his back, causing his early explosion. He breathed heavily as he re-leased himself, and it was over too fast for Tracy's comfort.

This boy fucks like a rabbit, she thought as she laid there, disgusted.

Cash was embarrassed. Tracy told him to be calm and try it again, as if she was the more experienced one. They laid there a few minutes. Cash then tried to make it last longer by ignoring how good Tracy felt to him. But it didn't work. He erupted a second time in just minutes.

"DAMN! You got some good shit!" he roared, amazed and embarrassed at the same time.

Tracy laughed and rolled out from under him. "I'm gonna take a shower," she told him. She giggled to herself while in the shower at how ridiculously quick he was. She ran the soap in between her legs, exciting herself, and dreaming of Victor Hinson. Victor would have made it last. He knew how to control his body and hers. And Tracy loved the way he whispered in her ear, confirming her pleasure every step of the way. He had never been repetitious or whipped like Timmy had been. He always tried something new. Victor made Tracy *feel* everything that lovemaking was supposed to feel like. All that was left for him to do was to tell her that he loved her.

Tracy dried herself to give Cash one more try at pleasing her. She playfully dove back into bed and squeezed his behind, attempting to arouse him again.

Just feeling her cool naked body next to his gave Cash a hard-on. They went at it for a third time. Tracy breathed heavy into his ear, rubbing his hips into hers. And finally, it had lasted long enough for her satisfaction. They laid there, exhausted and wrapped into each other's arms until they eventually fell asleep.

They awoke about seven o'clock that early evening. They redressed to have dinner and returned home before it got too late. They rode in the jeep quietly on the return trip. Cash still felt embarrassed, afraid to ask the "younger-girl" what she was thinking about. He assumed that she was thinking about them.

Tracy looked at him and smiled. "Ay Cash?"

"What?"

"How many girls have you had?"

"Don't worry about it."

Cash wanted to make up an excuse, but it was nothing that he could say without inflating Tracy's head about her sexuality. She had blown his mind, and most of the respect that she had had for him was lost.

Tracy hopped out of the jeep with her bags at the corner. "Well, I'll see you whenever," she said.

Cash responded blandly, "Yeah, aw'ight then." He drove off quickly.

Tracy snuck her bags into the house, stretched out on her bed and was bored with him. She thought about their experience at Atlantic City and cracked herself up. "I *gots* to tell Carmen about this," she mumbled to herself.

Raheema walked to her classes nervously on Monday morning. It was her big day with Chuck. He had convinced her to pay him a visit, and he was waiting for her after school.

Raheema walked quietly with him to the bus stop. While on the bus, Chuck threw his arm around her neck. She didn't want to break her promise to him, but she was really unsure about things. *You're not even my boyfriend,* she wanted to tell him. Nevertheless, she was headed with him to his house.

"So what do you wanna do?" Chuck asked with a grin as soon as they had arrived.

"I don't know," Raheema responded, looking away.

Chuck walked over and sat next to her on the couch.

Raheema jumped up and said, "Excuse me, but I have to go to the bathroom." She was lying, nervous as a cow in a meat factory. She sat in an empty chair when she returned.

"Why you sit over there?" Chuck asked.

"Oh, I just sat down. Why? Does it make a difference?"

Chuck shook his head at her evasiveness. "Come here and sit on my lap."

Raheema did.

Chuck then began to caress her breasts.

She hastily grabbed his hands. "Don't."

"What?" he responded to her, confused.

Raheema asked him innocently, "Why you gotta feel all on me?"

Chuck thought it was agreed upon that they would have sex. He pulled her down by her neck to kiss her, and Raheema could not stop him. They kissed longer than she expected as he caressed her breasts again. She moaned, feeling herself losing control. Chuck unfastened her bra through her shirt. Raheema then grabbed his head and bit into his high-cut hair.

Chuck pulled his head away from her teeth. "The fuck are you doin'?"

Raheema was embarrassed at her inexperience.

Chuck got up and yanked her hand. "Come on," he told her, leading her up the stairs and into his room. Raheema's heart was racing like the wind. She even wondered if Chuck could feel it through her hand. He took off his clothing, standing butt-naked and erect as soon as they entered his messy room. And he was quite muscular. He didn't have any scars on his athletically framed body.

Raheema turned to avoid staring at him. Chuck came closer to take her clothing off. Raheema stood terrified as she felt his hot, hard organ, bumping up against her while he took off her clothes. Chuck then tried to move her to the bed, but Raheema would not allow him.

"What's wrong?"

Feeling nauseous, she could no longer take it. She covered her naked, light-skinned body and told him, "I don't wanna do this."

"Well, what 'chew come over here for?"

Raheema sat on the bed, attempting to redress in a hurry.

Chuck howled, "Naw, fuck that shit! You ain't playin' wit' *my* dick!" He grabbed her, pushing her down on the bed and plying at her legs.

Raheema yelled, "No! Get off of me!"

"Why you come over here and play with me, girl?" Chuck asked, holding her arms down.

Raheema whined, "I'm not. Just get off of me." She made sure to keep her legs closed.

Chuck tried again to get them open.

Raheema screamed, "HELP! SOMEBODY!"

"Aw, you's a stupid bitch," he responded, nervously. He didn't want a rape charge on his hands.

Raheema rushed to collect her clothing from the floor. She dressed in a hurry and made a break for the front door.

Chuck roared, "Go ahead and leave, you retarded bitch. I never liked your stupid ass anyway!"

Raheema dashed out of his house and sprinted home in tears, determined not to tell anyone. "It's all my fault for going over there in the first place," she mumbled. She made sure she straightened up her face before she made it back to her house. She couldn't give her parents any clue about what had happened to her.

I won't try this mess again, she told herself, glad to have escaped.

Raheema went up to her room and sobbed helplessly into her pillow. She could never be like Mercedes or Tracy. It was too late to be like them. She felt too tense about sex, or relationships in general. Or maybe Chuck was the wrong person. She could feel new bumps already beginning to form under the makeup. She popped them, no longer caring about the scars they would leave. She washed the makeup off to see how unattractive her beautiful skin had become. Mercedes had not seen a bump on her skin. Life wasn't fair, but Raheema decided to hold on instead of joining the fast-paced streets. She had no other choice; she was not prepared to handle it.

"Ay Tracy, tell me when you through with your boyfriend, 'cause I wanna school you."

"Yeah, right."

"I'm for real, though."

"I know, but that don't mean that I'm gonna talk to you." Tracy walked to her class, wearing her Gucci sneakers and carrying her Gucci bag after dismissing another hopeful at school.

"Well, what do I have to do to attract you?" the boy asked, following her.

Tracy said, "Just be yourself. And if I'm not attracted to you now, I never will be."

Everyone in "G-Town" high school talked about Tracy. But none of them, except for Timmy, had been able to receive her favor. She had

dyed her hair honey-blonde on top with huge curls. It was long in the
back and pointed on the sides. Tracy was *the shit,* and no one could tell
her differently.

Cash continued to add something to her overabundant wardrobe each
week, like the long leather coat she had received after Thanksgiving.
He picked her up from school every day, watching her every move to
see if she would try to play him, or in other words, treat him with
disrespect. It was inevitable. Cash was giving her everything she
wanted, and he was starting to bore her.

"So what happened in school today?" he asked, driving her home
in cold December weather. Tracy wore her green leather bomber that
Patti had helped her buy.

Tracy answered, "The usual." She then looked away as if she had
no conversation for him.

Cash frowned at her. "What 'chew think, you're special now or
somethin'?"

Tracy smiled, realizing that she was getting under his skin with her
better-than-thou attitude. "No," she answered him.

Cash wasn't satisfied with just that. "I'on know about you, girl." He
kept his eyes on the road, listening to a Boogie Down Productions tape.

Tracy responded too boldly, "You got other girls anyway. You don't
need me."

Cash pulled over and stopped the jeep. He sat and stared out of
the window before speaking. "Now what are you tryin' to say?" he
asked her.

"I ain't sayin' nothin'."

"Naw, you actin' like you wanna call it quits."

"Did I say that?"

"Look, I'm gon' pick you up to talk about this later on, 'cause I got
some runs to make."

Tracy sat contentedly, deciding not to comment.

Cash let her off around the corner from her house. Tracy walked to
her steps and spotted Raheema, staring out of her window. They still
had not been speaking to each other. Tracy ignored her. She walked
into her house to clean up the kitchen like Patti had asked her. The

kitchen was extra messy after Patti had had a get-together party with friends. Pots, glasses and plates were everywhere. Tracy had not washed a dish load like that in years. She was not too pleased about it either.

"We need to get this damn dishwasher fixed!" she screamed. "Where's a good father when you need him?"

After she finished with the dishes and had returned home with Jason, who had started kindergarten, they sat on the living-room couch watching *The Transformers*. Tracy could not help thinking about a few dishes she had accidentally shattered in her hasty rage.

Jason said, "Tracy, help me get some cereal."

"No, Jason. Mom's about to come home and fix you some leftovers from last night."

"I don't want that," he told her on his way to the kitchen. "Come on, Tracy," he insisted, pulling at her arm for her to go with him.

He gave up on her and went to the kitchen to try and get the cereal by himself. Patti entered the door hearing a big crash. She ran to the kitchen behind her daughter and found Jason curled up into a ball on the floor, crying while holding his head, with spilled cereal surrounding him.

Patti asked, "What the hell is going on, Tracy?" Jason had a lump on the left side of his forehead. "Now what happened, boy? What were you trying to do?"

"I asked her to help me, and she ain't do it."

Patti looked at her daughter with evil dark eyes.

Tracy looked away.

"I asked you to watch him, girl, and I'm a little tired of your irresponsibility around this damn house. Look at this big knot on his head."

Tracy smiled helplessly at her brother's knotted forehead.

"You think this is a damn joke, don't you?" Patti asked. She smacked her daughter in the mouth as Tracy tried to back away.

"See, mom, all that wasn't even called for," she responded, grabbing her lip.

Patti challenged her, "When you wanna try me, you just let me know."

Tracy thought about her mother's challenge. She decided it was too risky.

Tracy sat in her room doing homework with a swollen lip.

Patti walked in with a bag of broken dishes that she had found hidden inside of the trash. "Tracy, umm, what the hell you trying to pull here?"

Tracy knew she was caught. There was no way out.

Patti said, "Girl, I'm about to rip your damn neck off." She reached across to smack her daughter again. Tracy was quick enough to duck. That only made Patti angrier. She rushed her daughter to the bed.

"I'm tired of you, Tracy. You're about ready to get on my last damn nerve. You think you're cute with this hair and this expensive shit you got on?" she asked, while strangling her daughter by the collar.

"No," Tracy whimpered. "Mom, you're choking me."

"Why should I let you up?"

"It was an accident."

"It ain't no accident that you think everything is a damn joke around here. And the *next* time something happens, I'm gon' be all over you."

Tracy was not as afraid of Patti as she was the first time.

Later that evening, through her front window Tracy noticed Cash pulling up in his jeep. She grabbed her coat to go with him.

Patti shouted, hearing the door slam, "TRA-CY!"

"Hurry up and get outta here!" Tracy told Cash.

Patti arrived at the door too late. She would be waiting for Tracy when she got back home, with a can of ass-whipping.

"Damn, what happened to your lip?" Cash asked, laughing.

Tracy looked in the vanity mirror. "My mom hit me."

Cash giggled. "I remember when my mom used to beat up my sisters," he told her.

"So where we goin'?" Tracy asked, ignoring him.

"Oh, we got one stop to make before we go to my crib." Tracy wanted to ask why they would be going to his "crib," because she was not planning on giving him *any*. But she decided to hold her tongue for a while. She was happy she had some money in her pocket though, just in case he didn't want to take her back home.

Once they had arrived at their destination, Tracy hopped out of the Bronco. "I'm comin' with you this time."

"For what?" Cash snapped. He didn't like the idea.

"Because, I'm not gon' be sitting out here in the cold, looking stupid."

"Well, I thought you didn't like these drug houses."

"I don't," she responded, following.

Cash knocked. Sam looked out of the window before letting them in. "Well looka' here. She's a beautiful thing, ain't she?"

Tracy felt disgusted that he was even close to her. She quickly moved away from him. Sam may have been an old pervert.

"I ain't gon' hurt 'cha," he responded to her. "What 'chew think I'm the 'Big Bad Wolf' or somethin'?"

Tracy sneered at him as she walked farther away, inside of the half-empty living room.

Cash asked, "So where's my stuff at, man?" He pulled out a roll of bills.

Sam said, "Oh, Lou got it. But he got a trick upstairs with him right now. Just wait a few minutes. He should be almost finish with that hoe by now." Sam smiled at Tracy and said, "Excuse me, young and beautiful, but if you're gonna be around the game, then you might as well know how it is."

Tracy sat on a couch. She thought about what low-life of a woman would fall to the point of giving up her body for cocaine. She played with her nails, taking peeks up at the steps. Cash and Sam continued to joke around, but Tracy was more interested in the "trick" they were referring to. She could hear the footsteps upstairs.

Cash roared, "AY LOU, HURRY UP, MAN! I ain't got all day!"

"SHET UP, YOUNG-BOAH'!" Lou shouted back down.

Tracy loosened up, still watching the steps. She could see and hear the woman coming down. She stopped to have last words at the top of the staircase. Her voice was deep and raspy, like an older woman's. Tracy could see her legs on the steps. They then met each other's stare, as Cash and Sam noticed the unspoken communication between them.

Tracy could not believe her eyes. She blinked at the nightmare. The young woman that she had known had lost at least fifteen pounds. She was frail and crooked in her stance. Her long hair looked damaged and oily, and her smooth walnut-brown skin had lost its shine. She walked from the stairs, wearing a dingy white leather jacket and turned her head from Tracy.

Tracy was embarrassed beyond words. She looked at the floor, and then at the walls and back at the floor again, avoiding further eye contact, while holding back her tears of empathy. Finally she cried, covering up her face to hide her watery eyes. Her expectations had been shattered. Tracy wanted to run home and slam her head into her pillow and wake from the nightmare. But it was not a dream. It was real.

"It's my God-damn life, Tracy. I don't have to answer to *nobody.*" She wiped her stuffed-up nose and staggered to the door, staring back at Tracy. But Tracy refused to look at her.

"Oh, you won't even look at me now, hunh? Well, life is hard, girl, and I fucked mine up, so get off my got'damn back." She began to cry herself as she walked out, ashamed to have been discovered by her young friend.

A tear dropped from Tracy's right eye and slid through her hands. She wished that she could keep her eyes closed forever. She realized her road had to change.

tHe reformatioN

Hard times

All of the lights were out at her home when Tracy had gotten back in. She opened the door and nearly tripped over four trash bags. She curiously looked inside of them and found much of her clothing. She then looked over to the living-room couch and noticed her mother stretched out as if she had fallen asleep while waiting for her. Too upset to think about the message her mother was sending, Tracy headed up the stairs to her room. Once she had made the journey up the steps, she crawled into her bed, which felt extra-soft after the shock she had been through. She ran her fingers over her face and through her honey-blonde-topped hair. If she had heeded her mother and stayed in the house, maybe she would have never experienced the nightmare.

Patti clicked on the light. "Get up, girl, 'cause you're getting *out* of *this* house!"

Tracy buried her face in the pillow. "Please, mom, I don't feel so good."

"Why, are you pregnant?"

"No, but I seen something that's making me sick."

Patti was still fuming, but she calmed down after seeing how distressed her daughter was. "You should have stayed in this damn house," she huffed, as she walked over and sat on Tracy's bed, tending to her. "So what happened?"

Tracy sat up and said, "Mercedes is messed up on drugs."

Patti shook her head and pondered. "Well, how do you know this?"

Tears rushed down Tracy's face. "I saw her. And she spoke to me."

"What did she say to you?"

"She said that it was her life and that she didn't care what I thought about it."

Patti muttered, "Mmm, mmm, mmm. What is this world coming to? Where were you at when you saw her?"

"I saw her on the street, and I went to go talk to her."

Patti frowned, knowing better. "You think I'm really stupid, don't you? I know that damn boy you been sneaking around with is probably mixed in with them damn drugs. And you probably seen her in one of those crack houses. Didn't you, Tracy?"

Tracy sat silently.

"See, girl, you think that your father and I don't know anything, and that *you* somehow got all of the answers. But I've been there myself, Tracy, and times don't change, they just *look* different.

"When I was growing up, it was the gang-war era, where you didn't date a guy unless he had a jacket. People were using heroin back then."

Patti got up to leave and said, "I hope that you learned something from this, because I don't know what else to say to you. This is *your* battle. I don't have the time nor the energy to be out here chasing you around in these streets. I have my *own* damn life to live, Tracy."

Patti walked to the door and added," Oh, by the way. I paged your father. He's going to be here any minute after work. I told him that I was ready to throw your ass out."

Tracy looked up at her mother from the pillow and remembered that her clothes were stuffed inside of trash bags and setting at the door.

"Do you think I should let you stay in this house, Tracy?" her mother asked. Patti figured that her hard-headed daughter may have learned a big enough lesson to stay.

"I'm sorry, mom," Tracy pleaded.

"Answer the damn question, girl," Patti snapped at her.

"Yes," Tracy answered meekly.

"Why?"

Tracy thought of a good answer and came up empty. "I don't have no place else to go," she mumbled.

"You *act* like you got somewhere else to go. Do you wanna move in with that boy you've been running around with?" Patti had a lot of assumptions about her daughter's whereabouts. All she needed was the proof.

"No," Tracy answered.

Patti nodded, pensively, deciding that she would let her stay. *She ain't ready for them damn streets anyway,* she told herself. *She's been spoiled all of her life. Philadelphia would eat her alive, just like it did Mercedes.* "You know that you're back on punishment, right?" Patti was telling her more than asking her.

Tracy nodded, conceding to it.

"And I want them earrings, *and* the chains," her mother added.

"Hunh?" Tracy uttered, confused.

"You heard me. Take them off and give them here." Patti walked back over to the bed and reached out her hand.

Tracy was still reluctant. "What are you gonna do with it?"

"Tracy, give me the damn jewelry! I'm gonna put it up, until I *feel* like giving it back to you."

Tracy took off her jewelry and handed it over.

Patti held the relatively weightless gold in the cup of her hands. "Mmm," she grunted. "Cheap. If you tried to pawn this stuff downtown, they'd barely give you fifty dollars for it." She then put the seized items away in her room and went back downstairs to wait for Dave.

Dave unlocked the front door with his key as soon as Patti had gotten comfortable on the couch. It was close to eleven o'clock.

"So what's this about?" he asked her, stumbling over the trash bags of clothing, just as Tracy had done earlier.

Hearing the front door creak open and close, Tracy snuck into the hallway bathroom, which was right by the stairway, to eavesdrop on her parent's conversation.

"I'm kicking Tracy out," Patti lied to him. She was ready for an argument. She wanted one. *I'm ready to kick his ass in here, too,* she thought to herself. She had done a lot of maturing in the nine years that they had been apart.

"For what?" Dave asked her.

"Because she's grown."

He walked over and joined his wife on the couch. "Let me speak to her."

"She's asleep."

"Well, let's go wake her up."

"For what?" Patti snapped at him.

"So I can see what's going on here."

Patti looked at him crossly. "I just fucking told you what's going on here. Tracy thinks that she's grown, so she's moving out."

Tracy stood inside of the bathroom door enjoying it, especially since she knew that she wasn't going anywhere. "Get him, mom," she whispered to herself. Dave had not been a good daddy.

"Patti, the girl is barely fifteen years old," he argued.

"And?"

"She's nowhere near grown."

"Well, since she's *not* grown, then maybe she needs a damn father around here!"

Dave fell silent. He wanted to come back home, he just didn't know how. He had gotten used to his freedom, and it had become destructively addictive. "So what are you saying, Patti?" he asked her, wanting her to cut to the chase. They had not discussed the topic in a while.

Patti took a deep breath. She had been thinking about this moment practically for all of the nine years of their unofficial separation. "Either you're going to stay here, or you're not. You can't have it both ways. Not anymore. So either we're gonna get a divorce, so you can marry this bitch, or whoever the hell you've been staying with, so I can move on with my life, or . . ."

She stopped herself, not wanting to believe that she actually still wanted him back. *We're not divorced yet,* she told herself.

Tracy had stopped breathing after hearing the word "divorce." "Oh my God!" she mumbled. "I can't believe she said that." She was listening for her father's response before she could continue breathing.

"I've never been staying with any woman. You know where I stay," Dave commented to his wife, avoiding her ultimatum.

"Well, I've never seen the place," Patti responded to him. "But that's beside the point, Dave. The point is: why are you there in the first place?"

Dave grimaced. "Look, Patti, what do you want me to do? I mean, we can't even have a conversation anymore."

"Is that my fault? Oh, go ahead, blame everything on me."

Dave was speechless. Patti was finally backing him up against a wall. "How do you think we can do this, Patti?" he asked her.

Patti was confused. "What the hell, Dave? Is there some kind of a process with you moving back in?" She had been saving up to move into her own place if he failed to agree. *Life goes on,* she told herself. And she was no longer willing to remain captive in his house.

Dave sighed. "It's not as easy as you think it is," he told her. He realized that Patti had matured, but with that maturity, she was also more demanding.

"You don't have much longer to think about it, Dave. You told me, or *us,* rather, that you were moving back in years ago, after I had had Jason. What happened to that?"

Dave wanted to run away again to think it over. He knew he did not want a divorce. The only *right* thing to do was to start over. He had been dating on and off like Patti had, yet no woman could take her place either. She was the mother of his kids, still his wife and still living inside of his house.

"All right, I'll think it over," he told her.

Patti got up and walked over to the steps, unsatisfied with his answer. "You can let yourself out. And by the way, I decided to let Tracy stay before you came."

"Well, you still haven't told me what she's done."

"You ask her."

Tracy eased into her room before her mother reached the top of the steps.

Dave sat for a while and thought things over. "Well, I guess this is it," he said to himself. He was as nervous about moving back in as he had been when he first told Patti "I do." But he had had his way long enough. The stability of his family depended on his presence.

That next day of school was like a funeral for Tracy. She did not want to be in school. There were too many things on her mind. She wore no glamorous outfits on her back that day. No earrings, and gold chains.

"Hey Tracy, you hear about Mark?" Jantel asked glumly.

"What Mark?" Tracy responded, absent-minded.

"You know, the one that hangs out with Victor and them."

"Oh, Mark Bates. Yeah, what about him?"

"He dead," Jantel told her.

Tracy stopped what she was doing at her locker. "How? What happened to him?"

"Some guys were after Victor for some money, and they shot Mark when they couldn't find him."

Tracy shook her head. "They always get the ones that really ain't into it, 'cause Mark never knew what he was doin'."

"I know, and he had started goin' to night school and all to better himself, too."

"He should have never dropped out," Tracy commented. They parted ways for class, and Tracy arrived late.

"Is there any reason why you're late, Ms. Ellison?"

"No, I just lost track of time."

"Well, make sure that you keep track of it while in detention today."

Tracy was appalled. "Oh, so I get a detention for being late *one* time?"

"Yes you do, and just for your outrage, you've earned yourself another one."

Mr. Roberts was a no-nonsense English instructor, and Tracy hated him.

Bald-headed fool. That's why he ain't got no wife, she snapped to herself. *Nobody wants his behind.*

The detention ended faster than Tracy thought it would. She headed home after school with a girlfriend. A fast-running crook snatched her girlfriend's earrings right off of her ears. Both girls screamed, but he was long gone before any help arrived. The pull had ripped the corner of one ear. Tracy's companion bled while crying hysterically.

A concerned citizen summoned a policeman, and Tracy explained to the officer what had happened. The girl was then escorted to Germantown Hospital, with Tracy comforting her until they had arrived. *Dag, I'm glad my mom took my earrings,* she thought.

Afterward, Tracy rode the bus back home, bewildered by all of the unfortunate occurrences. She dropped her book-bag inside of the house and rushed to pick up Jason. While on her way past the playground, she noticed Victor and his friends loading up into cars. She suspected that they were heading to get revenge for Mark.

Jason was the last child to be picked up, and on the way back home Tracy could have sworn that she saw Mercedes in a long brown coat and wearing a black baseball hat. She turned away, hoping it wasn't Mercedes who was walking toward them. Tracy still had not gotten over the shock of her desperate drug addiction.

"Tracy, let me talk with you. I feel a need to express myself," the figure in the long brown coat said from behind. She was wearing a pink sweat suit with brand-new Reebok tennis shoes.

"I don't want to talk to you out here," Tracy responded to her. She looked around to see who saw them.

"Well, I'll walk you home, so we can talk in your house like we used to."

Tracy asked, "Have you spoken to your mother?"

"No, I haven't, and don't plan to, either."

"Well, what if they see you?"

"It don't matter. I have nothin' to say to them," Mercedes said out of spite.

But won't you be ashamed of them seeing you like this? Tracy wished she had the courage to ask.

Mercedes sniffed and followed Tracy and her brother. She then took out a Newport.

Tracy sped up her pace to get inside quickly, nervous about Raheema spotting them.

Once they had made it inside, Mercedes sat on the couch. She began to shake and rub her hands together as if she were still cold and decided to keep her coat on.

Jason asked, "What's wrong with her?"

"Nothin', boy. Go on upstairs and watch TV in my room."

Jason peeked at Mercedes disgustedly before he ran upstairs.

Mercedes looked at Tracy harshly. "Yeah, I know what you're thinking, but it can happen to *you,* too. It can happen to *any* and *everybody.*"

Tracy felt Mercedes had a lot of explaining to do. It was a quarter to five. Patti was not expected home until five-thirty.

Mercedes shook her head. Her baggy eyes were bloodshot under the black hat's brim. "Look at me now. A year ago I thought I was the *toughest* thing walkin'. And I thought I could get out of taking drugs, but I had more and more problems, so I needed more shit."

She wiped her nose and continued. "Yup, Tracy, I had some good men that wanted to be with me, even marry me, but I turned them all down. I don't know why, and shit. I guess I thought I was too much for these motherfuckin' niggas out here." She looked at Tracy and shrugged. "It might be over with for me, but I figured I could turn you around. It's the least thing a sorry bitch like me can do now."

Tracy interjected, "Naw, it ain't gonna happen to me. And your life ain't over with yet. You're only twenty years old."

Mercedes stood up to get her point across. "LOOK, GIRL . . . it ain't that easy to say!"

Tracy backed down nervously, thinking that "junkies" were violent. She didn't want to alarm her.

Mercedes calmed down and continued. "Every time you turn one nigga down, you gon' go for another who's more ruthless than the last. And they just gon' dog you out and waste your damn time. It's not the right way to go, but you put yourself in that boat when you're young. And you're never fuckin' happy, because eventually you get bored with every one of them niggas. They don't really like you and you don't really like them. Y'all just buying time. He gives you some money and some clothes, while you're giving him the pussy. And that shit ain't changed in a hundred fucking years."

"Have you talked to your sister?" Tracy asked, holding back her tears. Mercedes sounded as if she had given up on life.

"No. I haven't seen her," she answered. "How is she though?"

"She got acne all up and down her face. She needs some attention," Tracy assumed.

Mercedes shook her head and sat back down. "See, all women got the same problem. I think we were better off in the caveman days when the men just took and fucked us . . . So what about that boyfriend of yours? The drug dealer?"

Tracy frowned. "Who, Cash? Oh, I'm gettin' out of that, because I'm tired of that drug shit."

Mercedes nodded. "That's good, because once you get in it too deep, it's hard to get back out. And all you'll do is go run to the next one. But shit, at least I ain't have no damn babies. That's all I needed to drive me crazy."

"But what about you? Are you gonna get help or something?" Tracy asked, concerned about her.

"Yeah, I'm going to this rehabilitation place tomorrow. And I guess I gotta be goin' now." She looked outside to see if her mother or Raheema might have been walking in. She then turned and faced Tracy. "Watch after my sister for me, all right? You're stronger than she is."

Tracy nodded. She shook in her stance as she closed the door. *That could never happen to me,* she told herself. *I don't even smoke.* But Tracy would watch after Raheema. She felt that *Raheema* needed guidance, not her, and just like old times, she decided to call next door and make up.

· · ·

Tracy answered her phone on the first ring, expecting it to be Cash.
Patti still allowed her to have phone calls; she just could not leave the
house.

"Where was you at today?" he demanded.

"I had a detention. And you don't have to ask me like that."

"A detention, for what?"

"You know what, Cash? I think you better call me back when you
calm down."

"Naw, fuck that! We gon' talk right now!" Cash was paranoid again
that Tracy was trying to play him. He suspected that she had evaded
him on purpose.

Tracy smirked. "Cash, you gots to chill with all that hollering."

Cash was annoyed. He figured he would try to scare her into submission. "Aw'ight young-girl. I'm gon' break you up when I see you.
Watch."

Tracy retorted, "No you're not."

Cash slammed the phone on her ear.

Tracy sat on her bed, worried about tomorrow and unable to focus
on her homework. She was too busy thinking about her situation. Cash
was from a rough neighborhood, and most likely, she figured that he
meant what he said.

"Did your father call you yet?" her mother stopped in to ask.

Tracy shook her head. "No."

"Mmm, hmm," Patti grunted. "All right then. Go on back to your
homework."

Tracy took longer than usual to put her clothing on that next morning.
Before and after school, she watched her back for her safety, looking
out for Cash. And after her second detention, Cash was nowhere in
sight, so Tracy rushed home with her key in hand.

A voice roared, "HAAH!"

"AAAHHH!" Tracy screamed, throwing her hands to her chest. She
then noticed that it was only Raheema. "Girl, what's wrong with you?"
she snapped.

Raheema laughed. "You're lucky, girl, because Cash was up here looking for you in his jeep."

"He was?"

Raheema followed Tracy into her house. "You should have seen this rabbit-fur coat that he had on," she commented. "It had like five different colors, and a hood."

Tracy sucked her teeth disdainfully. "Yeah, he can buy anything that he wants with his drug money."

Raheema watched Tracy take off the long black leather. "Didn't he buy that coat you're wearing?"

"He got me a lot of stuff, but ta' hell with him though," Tracy insisted. She walked into the kitchen.

Raheema followed her. "You're a trip, Tracy. You just go from one guy to the next, and you don't even care," she said, wishing that she could do the same. In a way, Raheema was beginning to admire Tracy's free spirit.

"You can't care, 'cause then they try to get *new* on you, and start acting all differently, like they got you in check or something."

Raheema sighed. "Why can't boys just like you and be with you for who you are?"

Tracy washed the dishes, glad that her mother was picking up Jason after a field trip his kindergarten class was having. She would not have to worry about seeing Cash for at least another day.

"Here you go talking that trash. You probably got boys who like you, but you don't like them," Tracy assumed. It was the same with most girls. *If you look even half decent, somebody is gonna like you,* she told herself. And in her opinion, light-skinned, long-haired and virtuous Raheema still had a lot going for her.

"Yeah, that's true," Raheema responded with a smile. "But when do you get the guy that you *really* want?"

"I guess when you get married. But some girls don't even get him then."

Raheema said, "Yeah, like my mother."

"Everybody ain't meant to play the same role in life, Raheema."

"You right, but my role is stupid."

"No it ain't, Ra-Ra. You might get that 'Mr. Right' before I do. And men love to marry virgins."

Raheema was caught off guard. Neither of them knew how to react after it had been said.

Tracy decided to laugh it off. "Why do people get all upset when you call them a virgin? That ain't nothin' negative."

"It's because of the way that people say it, like it's something to be ashamed of."

"Well, it don't make no difference, as long as the guy knows what *he's* doing."

"Why can't *he* be a virgin?" Raheema asked with a smile.

"Because, girl, you don't want no guy who don't know what he's doin'. And if he's still a virgin by the time he gets married, then most girls must didn't like him anyway."

Raheema suggested, "Maybe he was saving himself."

Tracy cracked up at that one. "Oh my God! You really *don't* know anything about guys, do you? Because I guarantee you, any man who's still a virgin by the time he's like twenty-one has a serious social problem."

Dave had finally gotten over his inhibitions about moving back in with Patti and his children, but he wasn't prepared to take the dive overnight. He took his sweet time about it. And with his work schedule as it was, he still did not seem to be home much. He and Patti had to get used to sharing the same bed and bathroom again, and it was no cake walk for either of them. They had both gotten used to having extra space.

I hope that this shit wasn't a mistake, Dave would routinely tell himself. It felt weird being away from home for so long and then suddenly coming back for good. For nine years, he could leave in and out whenever he wanted to, and that liberty was gone.

This shit seems more stressful than him not being here, Patti thought, apprehensive herself. She was not sure if she could cuddle or hold him at night without scaring him away. Dave coming back home was nothing like being newlyweds. They were more like a couple coming home after a marriage-counseling session, and every move between them was tentative.

Tracy was confused as well. *I wonder how things are gonna change with my father moving back home for good?* she pondered. She was not quite sure how to take it. What if Dave became restrictive about who she went out with, where she went, and how long she stayed. Yet Dave was not as pressed about it as she thought he would be. He knew that he had been absent, so he planned to walk his way through a new understanding with Tracy, and that understanding did not include stepping in and controlling her life. He simply wanted to guide her from a man's perspective.

For Jason, having both mom and dad home more often was heaven. He even wanted to stay up longer just to see the two of them in bed together. His reaction to the move in eased all of their doubts, making the new transition they were going through a hell of a lot more hopeful.

Tracy had moved on from Cash and began to date "respectable" guys, to impress upon her parents that she too had matured.

Keith Branch was a popular basketball player at Cheltenham High School, outside of Philadelphia. He was the talk of the school, tall, brown-skinned, well-dressed and well-spoken. He was exactly the type of young man that Tracy could introduce to her parents. Yet he had a problem with correcting her speech and making her feel illiterate. She could stand that, but his pretentious attitude was unacceptable. She had been around too many sociably astute guys to settle for a phony who pretended to be better-than. So Tracy dropped him in a heartbeat.

Her next friend, Charles Webster, was from Chestnut Hill, west of Germantown. Tracy had met him downtown inside of The Gallery while out boy-shopping with Raheema. He was half-white, or "mixed," and he had never met the white side of his family. His German-born mother had been shunned, so Charles only knew his black kin, from down south.

Charles had a yellowish-tan complexion and floppy light-brown curls. The only boy who could match him for sheer prettiness was Bob. In fact, Tracy only talked to Charles because of his looks. She never listened to anything he had to say. "Light-brown curls, with pretty, smooth skin" was all that she talked about. And she took him with her wherever she went, protecting him possessively, as if *he* was the girl.

After they talked on the phone for a couple of days, Charles began to meet Tracy at her house nearly every day after school, and they would sit around and innocently do homework. Soon though, his eager peers began to pressure him into asking her for their first sexual encounter. Tracy was only sporting him, and did not consider herself in the sexual market anymore. *Those days are over for me,* she told herself.

Less concerned about her own wardrobe, Tracy began buy and pick out things for Charles to wear. She felt that his gear was not flashy enough for her taste, and in no time at all Tracy had him wearing clothing that quickly boosted his young image. She even paid for his haircuts, getting his curls cut the way *she* wanted them to look.

Tracy had reversed the roles, but unfortunately Charles' new status attracted girls who *were* still in the sexual market. A Chestnut Hill girl, three years older than Charles and four years older than Tracy, made a strong move for him. Charles went over to her house to help lift a new television set into her bedroom when no one was home to help her. According to Charles, she then closed her door and locked him inside with her, where she proceeded to take off all of her clothes and supposedly lick him from head to toe before forcing him to have sex with her.

Tracy was furious after he told her. She didn't believe one word of it. She felt as if he could not control himself, and that he knew what the girl was up to when she had invited him over to her house. "And if he thinks that his story is gonna make me wanna give him some, he can forget about it," she had huffed to Jantel after telling her Charles' story. They had become good friends again, and Jantel was by then one of the most popular track stars in the city.

Tracy could not believe that Charles had played her after she had bought him clothing and taken him places with *her* money to *make* him who he was. Girls were only attracted to him sexually after Tracy had schooled him. He was nothing but a slow-wit suburban boy before she had met him, but after Tracy, Charles ran free like a teenaged stud, getting all of the girls.

"That's it, Ra-Ra. I hate all guys!" Tracy snapped after school.

"Why you say that?" Raheema wanted to know.

It was April. Raheema was turning sixteen in another month. Tracy's birthday was not until September.

"That pussy-ass Charles is actin' like he's all that now," Tracy hissed. She took a seat on her steps, with the April sun shining through the breeze. She winced, looking up at it.

"Well, you shouldn't have been pimping him, and buying him all that stuff," Raheema told her.

Tracy smiled at her neighbor's choice of words. "Pimping him?" she repeated. "Let me find out Raheema's trying to sound hip."

Raheema grinned. "Well, that's what you were doing, dressing him up and showing him off and stuff." Raheema secretly liked Charles herself, yet Tracy practically jumped down his throat to get his phone number when they had first met him at The Gallery.

"Yeah, well fuck him," Tracy fumed. "And see if I spend *my* money on another boy in *my* life."

Raheema chuckled. "I wish I could have went with him," she revealed. "I would have never let him leave."

Tracy looked at her neighbor's pimpled face and felt sorry for her. Raheema was living off of her life. "So you would have had sex with him?" she asked, still wondering if the myth was true that sex could clear up acne.

Raheema thought about it. "I don't know. But I mean, why not?" she piped.

Tracy shook her head at her, remembering her first experience with Victor and how she had turned into his plaything. "You don't wanna do that. Just hold out until you get married."

"You didn't," Raheema reminded her.

Tracy paused, thinking about what she had actually gotten out of having sex, and why she had been so quick to engage in it the first place. "I think I just got ahead of myself and got mixed up into boys for the wrong reason," she admitted. "I mean, I had no business at all being with a guy like Victor. He wasn't no good for me. And I can see that now. He was *way* out of my league. And after him, I just kept doing it."

"What about now?" Raheema asked, curiously.

"What, me and Victor?"

"Yeah? Do you think he's still out of your league?"

Good question, Tracy thought. "Umm, I don't know."

"Whatever happened to Keith?" Raheema asked, changing the subject. She had begun to enjoy talking to Tracy about boys since she was older and more interested in them. And Tracy had many stories to share.

"Fuck that boy. He thought he was better than somebody," she snapped.

Raheema frowned. "You do too."

Tracy grinned, feeling guilty. "Yeah, but I don't do it the way he did. I mean, I don't really think that I'm better than people. I just—"

"Yeah, whatever," Raheema said, cutting her off.

Tracy chuckled to herself. "Have you seen your sister lately?" she suddenly asked.

"No," Raheema answered quietly.

"She might just don't want to see y'all."

"Are you saying that my sister hates us that much?"

"No. Maybe she's too ashamed." Tracy was speaking more for herself than for Mercedes. She was ashamed. Mercedes had been her big-sister figure as well.

Raheema was speechless. She was utterly confused about what road to travel in her life. She definitely did not want to go through the things that Mercedes and Tracy had been through, but yet they still had lived fuller lives. Raheema continued to believe that she was being cheated.

Raheema asked out of the blue, "Tracy, when was the last time you had sex?"

Tracy was shocked. She laughed and asked, "Wow, where'd you get that question from?"

"I don't know. I guess because I never had sex."

"Well, Cash was, when he took me to Atlantic City, last September."

"Dag, I didn't ask you *who*. I asked you *when*."

Tracy laughed. "You probably was gonna ask me that next, any-way."

"But you only *did it* with him once, though?"

Tracy grinned. "Well, you can say that, if you're talking about on different dates."

"He didn't try you again?"

"Not really, 'cause he was embarrassed. He got other girls though. *I* just wanted his money. His jeep was nice, too."

Raheema quizzed, "What do you mean, 'he was embarrassed'?"

Tracy smiled and said, "Because, he didn't *last* too long." Then she chuckled and said, "Look, I gotta go get my brother. I'll be back."

Tracy left. She shook her head on the way, thinking of how much Raheema appeared to be missing out on. It was no surprise to see Victor again when she turned the corner. He was close enough to speak to her.

Tracy could sense him watching her as she walked. She then turned and caught him smiling at her, still giving her tingles up the spine. She was immediately angry at herself. *I don't believe that I still get nervous around him,* she told herself.

"Ay Tracy, can I walk with you?" he said to her.

Why not? she told herself. "I'on care."

Victor walked up beside her and grinned. "So I hear you been keepin' some big-time company."

"What 'chew mean by that?"

Victor always seemed to have information on her.

He took out a roll of twenty-dollar bills and said, "Cash Money."

Tracy sucked her teeth and responded, "Oh, he ain't nobody."

"You was even talking to my man, Bruce. And that young-boah' 'Charley' schoolin' all the girls after dealin' with you." Victor smiled and said, "I guess I must have trained you well, hunh Tracy?"

"No, I don't *think* so," she responded. *I don't believe he said that to me,* she thought. *He makes me sound like a whore.*

"Anyway, I hate that boy Charles," she told him. *I'm starting to hate your ass, too,* she mused.

Victor said, "You know, hate is confused love sometimes, for real. You probably said you hate me to somebody. I mean, we both know you still like me. Don't we, Tracy?"

Tracy was speechless. "Oh my God," she mumbled with a helpless grin. *I was just thinking that.* "Why were you asking about me and stuff?" she wanted to know. It was obvious to her since he knew what she had been up to.

Victor cracked a smile, displaying all of his charm. "I'm just keeping tabs on you, making sure you're all right."

"Why?"

Victor grimaced at her. "Would you rather I just forgot about you, like we never did nothin', and we never knew each other? Just like that," he said with a snap of his fingers.

Tracy thought about it, experiencing an unexpected moment of panic. *What if Victor never even knew me?*

Victor was smiling again, in love with his own wit. "You know what? You don't even have to answer that. I'll just see you around." He then turned and stepped off in the springtime breeze.

Tracy stared at the white sweatshirt that covered his back, still in a daze. Then grinned at herself. "I guess I'm not in his league," she told herself. Victor still had her hooked.

Another summer rolled around, and the years were passing by like days. Tracy's "sweet sixteen" would be at the summer's end, and she planned on moving up the social ladder. She had already been accepted into a new clique of older college girls that she had met at the Ayunde Cultural Festival downtown on South Street. Her popularity had escalated, but Tracy wanted to change her priorities as far as guys were concerned. She desired more intelligent relations. She was tired of dealing with guys who had nothing on their minds but sex and life out in the streets.

A college boy

"Tra-cy! Pick up the phone!" Patti yelled up the steps.

Tracy sprinted to her room from the bathroom. "Okay! I got it! . . . Hello."

"Yo, it's 'Brucie.' "

"Well, I haven't heard from you in a while."

"Yeah, I told you I'd be away. But what have you been up to?"

"Nothin'."

"Well, who's your new boyfriend?"

"I don't have one."

"Yes you do."

"Boy, how you gon' just come home and tell me that I got a boyfriend."

"Because, you can't function without one."

"Yes I can. I don't need y'all."

"Yeah, you need *us* more than you think."

"Well, if I do, I don't need *your* ass," Tracy snapped, getting annoyed.

"I know, because I'm not a celebrity."

Tracy sighed and said, "You know what Bruce? You need to get a life."

"What?"

"I said you need to move on from me."

Bruce thought about it. "What if I don't want to?"

"Well, I don't know what to tell you, but you can't keep calling me up and acting as if we still have something going, because we don't. I'm just trying to be straight with you. I mean, we can be friends and whatnot, but we're never gonna be anything more than that."

"That's all I wanted to be."

Tracy smirked. *Yeah, right,* she thought to herself.

Bruce said, "So that's how you feel about us, hunh?" He still had visions of being her only man.

"I'm just trying to be truthful with you."

Bruce was silent for a moment. "All right then, if that's the way it is . . ."

Tracy could only wish that there was some other way to ease his longing for her, but there wasn't. Bruce did not attract her in a long-term relationship way. There had only been small moments of pleasure between them, and nothing that would last.

"Look, Bruce, I'm about to go out," she told him. "I'm sorry, but you're gonna have to find yourself someone else."

Frustrated by love, Bruce hung up on her. He did not slam down the phone, but he simply did not know what else to say. The girl of his dreams had shattered them.

Tracy looked at the phone in her hand and exhaled. "God, that was tough," she moaned. *But it was no sense in leading him on about it,* she pondered. *The sooner I told him, the better.*

On the way with her mother to a Cheltenham store that sold boxes of party snacks and accessories, Tracy thought of Mercedes.

Not a word was spoken on their half-hour journey. Once they had arrived at the store, a young cashier was guilty of watching Tracy with

lustful eyes and undercounted their total. Tracy laughed when Patti
brought it to her attention, but it was not funny enough to disperse her
depressing thoughts about Mercedes.

She got back home and stretched out across her bed, reflecting on
her own life. A photo on her dresser of when she was ten reminded her
of the times when she had first begun her interest in boys. She smiled,
remembering the arguments she had had with her young girlfriends
inside of the schoolyard. *I wonder what they're up to now,* she pondered. Then she began to frown, remembering the misguided things
that Mercedes had told her. "Boy, was she wrong," she mumbled to
herself. "That stuff she told me ain't get me in nothing but trouble.
And look where it got her."

Tracy wished that she could return the favor and give Mercedes
some advice. Yet her advice would be of a much more constructive
nature. She did come to a realization, however, of the double standards
of gender through her experiences. Boys were much less inhibited.
They could sex over a hundred girls and be "the man." A girl would
be considered a whore if she did the same. And guys never had to
worry about monthly cycles slowing them down.

"It just ain't fair," Tracy told herself. She then giggled and said, "I
wish that some of them could experience a period."

Tracy's sweet-sixteen party was packed, but she did not invite her
college friends. She didn't want to remind them how young she
was.

Patti felt a lot safer about having Tracy's party with her husband
around. The rowdy boys who showed up at their front door immediately took notice of him. Dave had never looked like a pushover. He
had come up through the Philadelphia gang era, so a group of rowdy
youngsters did not ruffle his feathers at all.

Raheema had even enjoyed herself, while hanging out with Jantel.
They made good companions. Jantel was a lot more stable with her
virginity. "You just have to find something for yourself to do," she
advised.

"Like running track, hunh?" Raheema asked, with a cup of punch in her hand.

Jantel smiled. "Well, everybody can't run track, but find something that *you* like to do, and something that you're good at."

Like what? Raheema asked herself. She had participated in dance class, but she did not consider herself *good* at it. Dance had taken too much out of her. Neither she nor Tracy had taken another dance class. It was a one-time event, for sure.

All that Raheema could think about that gave her any kind of enjoyment was reading books and gossiping, which basically did the same thing for her; both took her away from thoughts about her own dull life. She figured if she could not do some of the wild and crazy things that other people did, she could at least read or converse about them. Raheema could write her own book on the things that Tracy had told her about her life. And it was far from over.

Tracy had a way of drawing engaging life stories in everything that she did, yet her junior year of school was boring from inception. Her elaborate style of dress slacked off, allowing the other girls at school to steal her show. What was the use of it? She had already been flyy. She was more interested in moving on.

Tracy began to think about her friend Carmen while she walked through the halls. Carmen was still living fast. She did not seem to care about reevaluating *her* life. She had started *doing it* earlier than nearly everyone. Carmen was the one girl that Tracy knew of personally who had had venereal diseases. Nevertheless, she kept right on *doing it.*

Tracy began to daydream as she sat in class, cringing at even the *thought* of having a socially transmitted disease. "What did you say, Tasha?" she commented, catching a whisper about her less-than-fashionable jeans. She had borrowed the bell-bottom style from her college friends, and bell-bottom jeans were not yet acceptable among high school circles in Philadelphia.

"I ain't say nothin' to you," Tasha lashed out at her.

"Girl, I heard you."

"How you know I was talkin' 'bout you?"

Tracy grimaced and said, "I'm the only one I see in here with bell-bottoms on."

The class then broke into wild laughter. Tracy had a lot of courage trying to establish her own dress code in high school. Conforming to what was hip and what was not was the basic rule among teens in any town.

"What is the problem?" the teacher interjected.

"No, she gon' accuse me of talkin' about her," Tasha said, speaking up first through a smile.

The teacher grinned at their youthful silliness. "Girls, cut out the pettiness and finish reading the two paragraphs, please."

Class ended shortly after the outburst. Tracy then went and joined Jantel inside the lunch room. They had the same lunch period.

Jantel announced, "I hate that little bitch!" She had gained a few pounds and looked good in her toned brown frame, like the track star that she had become. Jantel never wore anything glamourous, and she kept her hair short for sprinting purposes.

"Who are you talking about?" Tracy asked her.

"That freshman girl with the Gucci sweat suit."

Tracy smiled. "You're getting jealous, hunh?"

"No, but I mean, that girl think she's *it.*"

"So what? You got your own life to live. People know you all over the city. Especially after the Penn Relays. Y'all almost beat William Penn last year," Tracy alluded. She was proud of her good friend, and she was glad that they had squashed their differences.

"Yeah, we're gonna go up against them again this year. This is the fastest team we've had in a while," Jantel added with a smile.

Tracy nodded and said, "See that? That girl won't be running in the Penn Relays with thousands of people watching her. She's just having her fun."

Jantel thought it over and shrugged. "Yeah, I guess you're right."

The Gucci-girl flirted in the lunch line. She was pretty and dark brown-skinned, with a big butt. The guys were all up on her info. *Who is that?* they asked of themselves.

Tracy said, "We did the same thing our freshman year."

"Yeah, but I didn't have three-hundred-dollar sweat suits on either."

Tracy grinned. "Oh, that's why you don't like her?"

"No, not only that, but they be actin' like they own the school or somethin'."

"Come on now, that's kid stuff. We're getting too old for that," Tracy commented. She went to her next class after lunch break and daydreamed about being married with kids, and living in a nice house with a charming husband. Her urge for security was rising, especially after her father had come back home. With the lack of a boyfriend, she was becoming envious of her mother's happiness. Tracy wanted what Patti had, a handsome guy to be there for her.

"Okay, Tracy, I just want you to know that college is a different atmosphere from high school. Things move extremely fast here."

"I can handle myself, Lisa." Tracy folded her legs in the back of Lisa's blue Toyota.

"See y'all, she think she's grown, and she doesn't know anything about college life," Lisa responded to her two college friends. They were headed for City Line Avenue, on the west side of Philadelphia, to attend a Cheyney State University party.

"Unh hunh. I got a little sister like that who's pregnant now," said Joanne, sitting in the front passenger seat. She was dark and thick-bodied, wearing African Kente fabric wrapped around her head that matched the cloth bag that she carried. Lisa, on the other hand, was real light-skinned, or "damned-near white." She had her hair twisted in baby dreadlocks.

"Well, I'm on the pill," Tracy said proudly.

"Oh, well excuuuse me. Girlfriend is ready for the world," Joanne retorted sarcastically.

Lisa added, "Yup, and we better watch out for who tries to get her. Because you know those pressed freshmen boys are dying to get their hands on some fresh, high-school meat."

"Unt unh," Tracy grunted with a grin. "Ain't nobody gettin' *this* meat."

"Do your parent's know that you're on the pill?" the girlfriend sitting in the backseat with Tracy asked.

Tracy looked at her as if she was crazy. "Unt unh."

Kiwana was a shade darker than Tracy. She had long silky hair, looking like Mercedes used to look. Kiwana had been in music videos, and aspired to be an actress and a playwright. Tracy was impressed with her, and she secretly coveted her name. She repeated it to herself as if it was her own: *Kiwana Ellison. Kiwana Ellison.*

"Yeah, they have that confidentiality rule," Joanne informed her.

"Oh, yeah, that's right," Kiwana said with a nod.

Lisa said, "Well, birth control doesn't have anything to do with being a tramp or not. And we got a 'Ms. Goodfoot' in here, y'all. She thinks she knows all the right moves."

Lisa loved to talk. She hadn't stopped since they picked Tracy up. Everyone else was enjoying the ride.

When they pulled up at Cheyney State, the campus grounds were packed, and it was an interesting change of scenery for Tracy. The students possessed an air of importance. But a lot of them dressed like black hippies to Tracy. She chuckled at that. And she had already begun to copy their fashions.

After paying to enter the party, fraternity members were bouncing around, dancing and screaming, "WE ARE THE BROTHERS!" from such and such. Sorority sisters began meowing like cats. Others made hooting noises. Fraternity members wearing purple and gold then barked into the party in a single-file line and began removing their shirts and pants, displaying their underwear while they entertained the crowd with their ritual of a dance. The whole thing was a totally different world to Tracy.

So this is college, she thought with a smile. *They are bugging out in here.*

Tracy turned down her first dance offer. The second guy was more handsome, so she danced with him. She had been used to dealing with older guys, but none of her flings were with college types. Tracy was curious.

"So, are you a freshman?" Mr. Handsome asked her.

"Nope. I'm still in high school," Tracy answered, too proud to lie about it.

He gave her a second look and said, "Damn! You look old as hell to be in high school. You got a boyfriend?" he asked.

"No."

"Naw? A pretty girl like you?" He began to stare into Tracy's hazels, but his tone turned her off. Mr. Handsome was too damned simple-minded for her idea of a *cool* college guy. She thought of him as a nag.

"Look, I'm about to go get some water," she told him, stepping away.

"Well, I wanna talk to you when you come back," he said, as Tracy faded into the crowd.

Lisa asked, "So, did anyone try to talk to you yet?"

"Yeah, that tall dude right there," Tracy responded, looking through the crowds and spotting Mr. Handsome.

"Oh, that's Sax."

"*Sax?* His name is *Sax?*" Tracy asked quizzically.

"No, girl. We just call him that, because he swear he can play some jazz. But he do be jammin' though."

"Yup," Joanne added.

Kiwana said, "Yeah, don't worry about him. The boy has a serious ego problem."

"Ay, what's up, girl?" a handsome, muscular guy with a golden-brown complexion stepped up and asked Lisa. He then slammed his big arm around her shoulder.

"Hey, Carl. When did you get here?"

"I'm just walking in now."

Tracy liked him immediately. He seemed cool, as if he had every-thing under control, and the tank top that he wore displayed his attractive muscular arms.

"Well, how come y'all not doin' this party, Carl?" Kiwana asked him.

Carl said, "We had this other party last night out West Philly. That party was s-o-o-o live, 'Kia.' "

"My name is Kiwana, Carl. How many times do I have to tell you that?" she retorted.

Carl hugged her with his thick, golden-brown arms. "I know, girl-friend. But I like to call you 'Kia' because you're so cute and cuddly."

Tracy was envious again. She wanted Carl to wrap that beautiful body of his around hers.

Lisa said, "Oh, so y'all just said the hell with this party, hunh?"

Carl answered, "No, but the plans were made weeks ago, and we didn't know if we would be able to do this one or not." He then looked at Tracy tenderly.

She responded quickly and before he could turn away from her. "Hi you doin'?"

"Oh, this my *little* girlfriend, Tracy," Lisa interjected.

Carl's golden-brown skin shined in the flashing disco lights. He had a soothing personality. Tracy felt relaxed around him, as if they had known each other for years.

"Well, can I dance with the charmer?" he asked Lisa.

"Yeah, I'll dance with you," Tracy answered.

Carl was impressed by her assertiveness. They eased out onto the dance floor where he asked her, "So, are you still in high school?"

"Yup," she perked.

Carl smiled at her exuberant energy. "I figured you were, since Lisa called you her *'little'* girlfriend. But it doesn't really matter too much to me."

"Why not?" she asked.

"Because, the social age of a person is more important than just a number. I started school early, because my birthday is in January, so I'm not much older than you are," he told her.

"Are you an English major or something?" Tracy asked, listening to his proper diction. He seemed a lot more easygoing with his speech than her previous friend Keith did. Carl did not seem concerned with putting on airs.

"Well yeah, but I'm more than that actually," he answered.

"What do you mean?" Tracy quizzed.

"I'm majoring in communications, which entails more than just an English requirement. I also play football."

"Oh," Tracy said, smiling. The more they talked, the more she liked him. "Do you plan on getting married soon?" she asked, jumping ahead of herself. She figured that Patti had met *her* husband at a campus party, so why not her?

Carl said, "You know, a lot of guys would shy away from that question, but I feel as though I could, if the right girl came along and caught me off-guard."

Yes! Tracy thought. *He's marriable.* "Why she gotta catch you 'off-guard?' " she wanted to know.

"Because, to be truthful, I'm not looking straight down the aisles of a wedding, or at least not yet. I mean, I'm only a sophomore. And since I was skipped, I'm only eighteen years old. You're acting as if I'm twenty-five already."

"Yo, what's up, Carl?" a tall friend interrupted, shaking his hand. Carl was just a few inches taller than Tracy, but his friend appeared to be a basketball-slamming giant. He looked into her face and stepped back. "Damn, you always get the good ones! Hunh, young-boah'?"

Carl smiled and said, "No, she's just my friend."

"Well, I would love to have a friend like her," the giant said, laughing before he walked away.

It was upsetting to be so close to such a gorgeous person and be called "just a friend." Tracy did not like the sound of that.

"You have a girlfriend or something?" she asked.

"No."

"Well, how many girls are you talking to?"

"I'm talking to you, right now."

Tracy raised her brow, confused. "What do you mean by that?"

"I mean, I want to talk to you. Matter of fact, come here." Carl led Tracy by the hand. Her college girlfriends were all doing their own things by then.

Tracy followed Carl over to one of his friends, who was standing near the turntables. She was wondering what Carl was doing. She was apprehensive about saying anything though. She figured that she would simply trust him.

Carl yelled, "AY JOE, you got some paper back there?"

"Yeah, hold up," Joe said, looking in the corner of the stage set.

Once he received the paper and a pen, Carl wrote his phone number down. He didn't ask Tracy for hers.

Tracy asked with a smile, "Don't you want mine?"

Carl checked out her earrings. Patti had given them back to her. "Oh, I'll get it from you when you call me," he said, touching them. Tracy didn't like guys to touch her earrings. But what the hell? she *trusted him.* Carl said, "You know, you don't need these big clumsy things, Tracy. You're already attractive in my eyes. You don't need any artificial additives."

Tracy beamed and thought, *That was a good one. I like that. He has class.*

Tracy and her college girlfriends squeezed back into the Toyota at the night's end. Patti had met Tracy's new friends weeks ago, deciding it would be good for her daughter to hang out with college girls, and Dave had agreed. "It'll get Tracy's head screwed on right, and get her focused toward going to school," Patti told him. She also gave Tracy a warning, "You make sure you keep them panties on up there, unless you feel you're ready to raise your *own* household. You hear me?"

"Tracy, wake up, girl!" Kiwana said, shoving her inside of the car.

Lisa asked from the wheel, "Is she asleep?"

"Girl, she knocked out like a baby."

Joanne said, "It looked like her and Carl were strapped together all night."

Tracy grinned with her eyes still closed.

"Oh, she *heard* that?" Kiwana said, noticing her smile. "So you're talkin' to him now, or what?" she asked.

"Yeah, I guess so," Tracy told her.

Joanne smiled. "Hmm, she went up there and booked a guy on the first night. A good one at that."

"Yeah, well, Carl's kind of young anyway. But he is nice," Lisa added.

Kiwana only smiled at the idea. She had turned Carl down before, but it wasn't because she didn't like him. She simply had someone else in mind for her affections, someone older.

Tracy slept good that night, finally waking up in mid-afternoon. It was a chilly Saturday, but the sun shined through all of the windows, warming her face, and Jason was busy running around the house, up and down the steps, letting Tracy know it was a normal weekend. She then began to smile up at the ceiling, wondering how she and Carl would get along as a couple.

Patti flung her door open. "Get on up, Tracy. You think you gonna lay up in bed all day? You got work to do. And you can start by hanging up all these clothes and mess, all over this damn room."

Her mother walked back out, leaving the door open, and Tracy continued to lay there, uninspired.

Jason yelled, "Mommy, she not gettin' up!" He walked over to the bed and sat on Tracy's leg. He wore a bright red, green and blue Oshkosh outfit, and he had a new haircut.

Tracy responded, shaking him from her leg, "Get off of me, boy!"

Jason laughed, attempting to sit on her again.

"Stop playin', Jason," she warned.

"NO! Mommy told you to get up."

"See, you gon' make me hurt you," Tracy said, leaning up to grab him.

Jason jumped up and ran out of her room giggling.

Tracy decided to get up and take a shower before she did her house chores. Once she was halfway finished cleaning up the house, the doorbell rang.

"TRA-CY, it's Raheema!" Patti yelled up the steps to her.

Tracy ran down the steps and spotted a huge smile on her next-door neighbor's face. "What are you so happy about?"

"What, I can't just be in a good mood?"

"Well, are you?"

"Yeah, because my father is goin' away for a week on a job trip."

Tracy grinned. "My father comes back and now your father is leaving for a week," she commented.

Raheema smiled back at her. "I know, right?"

Tracy was suspicious. "A job trip for a week, hunh?" she asked, contemplating the idea. "Sounds like your father is having an affair somewhere, to me," she wildly assumed.

"Well, I don't care if he is. Shucks! As long as he's not in my face for a week, the more power to him."

"But what about your mother?"

Raheema shrugged and said, "She's tired of him too."

"And that's why you all happy t'day?"

"Yeah, because things are more peaceful when it's just me and my mother. We're like girlfriends when he's not around. I can talk to her," she said with a smile. "But you know, you can't tell your mother everything."

"Yeah, I know," Tracy said, returning the smile. "Our mothers didn't tell their mother's *everything* either."

Raheema responded, "Yeah, but I bet you're glad that your dad is back. He's cool."

Tracy nodded. "Yeah. At first I thought he was gonna come back and start telling me what to do all the time, but he's been all right."

Raheema took off her jacket as they had a seat on the couch. She then asked, "You know what, Tracy? I wonder what makes one man cool and another man evil."

Tracy hunched her shoulders. "I would say the environment that they grew up in."

"So you think my father grew up in a rough environment?"

"Oh, I mean family environment."

"Yeah, that's what I mean too."

"Oh. Well, yeah. I bet your grandfather was meeean."

Raheema laughed and said, "I know. He probably was. I've never even met the man."

Tracy looked at her, surprised. "You never met your grandfather?"

"Nope. And I don't want to either."

"Dag, that's messed up."

"Well, how often do you go to visit your *cousins,* Tracy?"

Tracy answered, chuckling, "Never."

Raheema laughed and said, "See. So you can't talk about me then?"

Jason ran in to have a seat next to them on the couch, while Patti busied herself in her room. Dave had gone in to work earlier; he expected to be getting off soon.

Raheema stretched her arms and looked over at Jason, who was eying an afternoon horror movie on TV. "Dag, he's getting cuter everyday," she said.

"Yup, and he got all the girls in his school giving him candy and stuff," Tracy responded, smiling at him.

"Shet up, Tra-cy," Jason retorted, hearing them talking about him.

"Tell Ra-Ra your girlfriend's name."

"No, because I don't like girls. They always want me to play with them."

Both girls laughed as Raheema got up and headed for the door. "Well, I'll see you later, because my mom and I are going shopping," she announced to Tracy.

"All right then," Tracy said, getting up to shut the door.

"You a dummy, Tracy!" Jason hollered, facing her.

"Why you say that, boy?"

"'Cause, you always tellin' girls about me."

Tracy smiled. "So? They all like you," she responded to him.

Jason huffed, "'Dat's why I hate 'chew, Tracy."

Tracy was stunned. She bent over to face him for a response. "You hate me for real?"

Jason crossed his arms and mumbled, "Mmm hmm."

"Aw, that's a shame, Jason." Tracy felt hurt. She stood up, thinking to herself how badly she treated him.

Jason then smiled and looked up to face her. "Sike. I don't hate you."

Tracy then sucked her teeth and picked him up to hug him. "Boy, you gon' break a lot of hearts like that," she said, carrying Jason into the kitchen as he laughed. "You want something to drink?" she asked, noticing for herself how cute he was.

Jason said, while bouncing, "Yeah, and some cookies, too."

Tracy called Carl, feeling totally at ease with it. She liked their conversations.

"Hello, can I speak to Carl?"

"Yes, speaking."

"It's Tracy."

"Hey gorgeous. Did you take those earrings off?"

Tracy smiled and said, "I don't wear them every day."

"Well, anyway, what are you doing this evening?"

"Nothing at all."

"Okay, well, since you've called me now, what's your phone number?" he asked her.

Tracy gave it to him. "So are you gonna try to go to the pros?" she asked, referring to football.

Carl leveled with her and said, "I doubt it. See, most athletes dream the impossible, but at the same time, it's good to be realistic."

Tracy contested, "Well, like they say, 'If you think you can, you can.' But if you think you can't, then you can't. Or at least that's how I feel about it."

"Yeah, well, that doesn't work too well when you have college politics involved. They can make you or break you up here. And players at black schools don't get nearly enough national exposure as they do at white schools."

"Why didn't you go to a white school then?"

"My parents wanted me to learn something about my people. Plus, I've been in white schools all of my life."

His response made Tracy think about race and college. "Yeah, my father told me how hard it was for him to graduate from college in the seventies. He said he nearly hated white people. But he said he had to learn how to get along with them eventually."

"I know. I've already gone through that phase. I had to beat a few white boys down in high school. Most of them were afraid of me though."

"Did you play high-school football?"

"Yup, for all four years."

"You got older brothers and sisters?"

"Nope."

"Am I asking you too many questions?"

"No, but I'll let you know," Carl said with a chuckle.

"So you get a lot of homework in college?"

"Yeah, but if you keep to a tight schedule, you can do it. You know what though, Tracy?"

"What?" she quizzed, excitedly.

"No, forget it," he said, toying with her curiosity.

"What? Tell me."

"No. It's not that important."

"Yes it is. Tell me. Please, Carl."

"Well, I just wanted to tell you that you have some very attractive eyes. They remind me of my grandmother's. And I used to sit on her lap as a kid and listen to her while she told me stories. That's all."

Tracy beamed. "Oh, you so sweet, Carl."

"Yeah, I just thought I'd tell you that," he responded confidently, believing that the story was romantic.

"Well, thank you," Tracy told him.

Carl smiled and said, "So Tracy, when are we gonna go out and get some ice cream?"

"How you know I like ice cream?"

"I didn't know. But *I* like ice cream though."

Things were rolling along *too* smoothly. Tracy needed to know that it was *real*. She challenged him and said, "You know what, Carl? I don't believe a word you say anymore. I bet you just like my girlfriends said guys in college are. And you're just trying to get some young ass."

"What!" Carl snapped at her. He then calmed himself and told her what he was about. "Girl, do you know that I could do more to you with words, without ever having to touch you. Just being with a gorgeous black woman makes *me* happy. But you don't know me yet, so why would you pass judgments on the things that I say to you? Let me tell you something, Tracy. You have a lot of potential, but you have to stop that kid stuff if you want to be with me. So you call me back when you're a little more mature."

"Why are you hanging up?" she asked. She was curious to see what else he had to say.

"Because I have some work to finish up," Carl told her. "But I don't want to end this conversation on a bad note, Tracy, so I just want you to know that I like you. Okay? I like you a lot."

Tracy smiled. "Okay." She thought about telling Carl that she liked him as well, but she decided not to. She would tell him at another time, and possibly she would show him that she liked him. His muscular body was too tempting for her to ignore. *And I'm not a virgin anymore, so what's the difference if you really like a guy?* she asked herself. Yet she had not made up her mind on the matter.

One college weekend had helped distort Tracy's already negative attitude about high school. High-school classes that week were more boring than the last, and Tracy was beginning to look past her Germantown High days.

"Ay, what's up, Tracy?" a mere high-school boy asked at her locker.

"Hi, John," Tracy greeted him.

"Umm, does Jantel have a boyfriend?" John asked. He seemed very timid about it, as if he was afraid to ask.

"No, but she needs one. *Bad*," Tracy told him with a grin.

"For real? Why do you say that?"

"Because, she's jealous of these freshman girls," Tracy informed him. She felt that she was too mature to be jealous of new meat.

John asked, walking alongside her, "Do you think that I can get with her?" He was well aware that Jantel was a city-wide track sensation.

Tracy readjusted her earring, which was tangled inside her hair. "It's worth a try. She's free," she told him.

"Well, tell her that I want to talk to her."

Tracy frowned at the idea. "Look, John, if you really want to talk to her like you say you do, then go tell her. And if she turns you down, just stay on her back until she gives in."

"You really think that'll work?"

"Well, if it don't, then at least you know that you didn't go to lunch on your opportunity."

"Dig, that's right. Thanks a lot, 'Tray,' " he responded, energized by his chat with her.

"What I tell you about callin' me that?" she snapped.

John shouted, bouncing down the hallway, "Come on now, 'Tray,' we too cool for that!"

Tracy smiled and walked into the lunch room expecting to tell Jantel who liked her. It was noisy as usual, and Jantel was nowhere in sight. Tracy then sat by herself, happy that she was able to give John good advice. She began to picture herself as a mentor. *I have been through enough to advise people,* she thought.

"So Tracy, how was school today?" Patti asked.

"The same as always," Tracy answered. She sat watching *Sanford & Son* with a long face.

Patti said, "You haven't been excitable these last couple of days as you usually are. Is something bothering you?"

"Yup, mom. Life is long and boring sometimes," Tracy answered, falling back into the couch with a long sigh. "Sometimes I just wish that I was older already."

"Well, don't let a couple of rotten days spoil your weeks, because it's always a better day coming," her mother perked.

That's easy for you to say. You got my dad back, Tracy thought. "What if dad didn't come back?" she asked with a nervous smile.

Patti stared at her. "Then we'd be living in Chestnut Hill somewhere," she revealed.

Tracy was shocked. "For real, mom? You would have moved us out?"

Patti didn't blink. "That's right. One monkey don't stop no show."

Tracy laughed. "Are you calling dad a monkey?"

Her mother smiled and said, "If the shoe fits . . . "

"But I like this house," Tracy told her.

"You think I don't? But it was time for your father to either do right, or do wrong somewhere the hell else," she fumed. "And I should have made up my mind about that years ago. But you know what they say, 'If I would have known then what I know now, I woulda', coulda', shoulda'.

"All of my little girlfriends told me that I could never keep your father anyway," Patti alluded. "They all thought that he would have chosen 'an educated college girl.' But he didn't."

"Is it really that hard to keep a guy that you really like?" Tracy decided to ask. She had yet to experience pressures over losing any of her boyfriends. Outside of her fling with Victor, *she* had been the elusive one. She refused to count Charles. *I let him go so he could do what he wanted to do,* she told herself. *Charles would have stayed with me if I told him to.*

Patti gave some deep thought to the question. "You know, everyone wishes that they could just fall in love with the right person and remain happy, but it just doesn't work that way. Things change, people change, and some of us just get plain bored and aggravated by the stress in relationships."

Patti tried to sum everything up, but she couldn't find the right words. "Oh, I don't know, girl. Everything is confusing in this world anyway. I'm just glad that your father and I have been able to work things out, for the time being."

Tracy grimaced. "Are y'all still having problems?"

Patti shrugged. "Well, you never know, Tracy. I mean, it's only been a few months now." She then returned to the kitchen to cook dinner.

Tracy thought that her mother liked to cook. Patti would cook a different meal nearly every night. Cooking had, in fact, become a hobby for Patti during the years of Dave's absence. She could practically run her own restaurant with all of the different recipes she had experimented with. She had even made platters for her friends and co-workers from many of their leftovers. "That Patti sure can cook, girl," they had all agreed.

Overwhelmed with boredom, Tracy went back to her room to stretch out, napping for three hours. She had low energy and was in need of a rest.

Once nighttime had fallen, she decided to sit out on the patio and watch the stars. It didn't matter that she had no male companion. The stars, the moon and nature seemed company enough. Tracy felt at peace with the night. It had soothed her anxiety. She smiled, sitting there on her steps and thinking about how relaxed she felt. The elements of the night seemed to tell her not to worry. Tracy then decided to call Carl and start things anew, like a new day, after the nighttime had passed by.

"Hello, is this Carl?" she asked, pulling the living-room phone outside with her.

"Yes," he answered.

"You didn't think I would call you back?"

"I was hoping that you would."

"Oh, so you couldn't call me, hunh?" she quizzed him.

"Well, I mean, you were the one who started up the argument."

Yeah, he's right, she reflected. Tracy then asked him slowly, as if teasing him, "You don't wanna talk to me anymore?"

"Why are you putting words in my mouth? I didn't tell you that."

"Well, do you?"

Carl smiled and said, "Nope. I just want to take you out to the movies."

"And what we gonna do after that?" Tracy quizzed him again.

"Say good-bye," Carl responded to her with a chuckle.

Tracy sighed as a slight wind blew through her thick dyed hair. "That's a shame. And I thought you said you liked me."

"I do, but you're too complicated, so we'll just remain friends from now on."

Tracy wanted to snap on him, but the peace of the night directed her to be calm. There would be another day.

"All right then. When do you wanna go?" she asked.

Carl was surprised by her mellowness. "Are you serious?"

Tracy answered, beaming, "Yup, I'm serious."

"Oh, well, we can go out this Friday, then."

Tracy agreed and hung up just as her father headed up the walkway, coming home from work.

"Nice night out, hunh?" he asked her pleasantly. He looked beat, and Tracy wasn't sure if it was work or the strain of coming back to the family and being a live-in father again.

"Are you all right, dad?" she asked, concerned about his happiness. She followed him back into the house with the phone in hand.

"Yeah, I'm just tired, as usual."

"Does the pharmacy take that much out of you?"

"No, not really. I just have to work a lot of crazy different shifts. But why do you ask?"

"Well, I guess I'm just not used to seeing you so tired, that's all."

Dave smiled and had a seat on the couch. "You remember when you were a little girl and you used to fall asleep right here on my chest?" he asked, pointing to the spot.

Tracy nodded. "Yeah, I remember."

He chuckled to himself, remembering the times. *Things aren't so bad here. This is a good family,* he told himself. "Where's your mother?" he asked his daughter.

"In her room."

"And your brother's asleep?"

"Yup."

He nodded his head. "Good. That little guy's been trying to stay up too late."

Tracy was tempted to ask her father a few questions on his perspective on love, marriage and relationships. Yet she was unsure if she wanted to draw attention to herself. She was still hesitant about his views on dating. *Naw, I'll save that discussion for later,* she thought to herself. *Maybe I'll ask Carl a few more questions first.*

Friday afternoon, Tracy decided to wear a Kente outfit that Patti had bought for her at the Black Family Reunion Day celebration. Tracy had always thought that it was cute, but she never thought she would actually wear it anytime soon, especially not to school. Nevertheless, she felt that it was safe to wear it on her date with Carl.

She got out her brown sandals and some wooden earrings, waiting for Carl to pick her up, her first date since Charles.

Carl arrived on time, rang the bell and introduced himself to Patti and Jason. He was very respectful to Patti, and she was proud to have a college boy dating her growing daughter. She couldn't wait for Dave to meet him. Tracy had finally decided to move in the right direction.

"Well, are you going in or what?" Carl asked after the date. They sat outside of her house in his dark green Chevy Nova.

Tracy refused to leave the car. "Yeah, but only if you promise me something first," she said, smiling from the passenger's seat.

"And what's that?"

"Promise me you'll do it, first."

"No, you're gonna tell me what it is, first."

Tracy frowned. "Dag, you must don't trust me at all. Do you?"

"It's not about trust, Tracy. I just don't make blind promises."

"I only wanted you to come over tomorrow to meet my father. Dag. You act like I was gonna ask you to kill yourself."

Carl smiled and said, "Oh, I'm sorry."

"What did you think I wanted you to do?" she quizzed.

"I don't know, pretty. You could've said anything."

Tracy grinned at him. "You a trip."

Carl grinned back at her and said, "Yes, I know this. So what time do you want me to come over?"

"I'll call you in the morning and let you know. Sometimes my father works late, and sometimes he doesn't."

"Is he a doctor?"

"Nope, but you were close. He's a pharmacist."

Carl raised his brow and nodded. "Good profession. All right then. Let me walk you to the door," he suggested, expecting Tracy to hop out of the car. She looked him in the eyes and turned away with a giggle instead. She was wondering if he had been thinking about her sexually like she had been thinking about him.

"What's so funny?" he asked.

When was the last time you had sex with a girl? she felt like asking him. "Nothin'," she told him instead.

"Well, I'll see you tomorrow because I have to get back to the dorms and get some serious Z's," Carl said, pressed about ending their date.

Tracy looked at his car clock. "At eleven o'clock, you're going to bed, on a *Friday night?*" she asked, doubtingly.

"Yup, because I have to get up early tomorrow morning."

"Why?"

"I'm on the football team. Remember? We have a game tomorrow."

"Oh," Tracy responded, feeling stupid about her suspicions. "I'm sorry," she apologized to him.

Carl responded with a chuckle, "You know, you're something else. *No,* it's not another girl."

Tracy thought to herself and said, "Carl?"

"What?"

"When was the last girlfriend you had?"

"In April."

"And what happened?"

"It was a long-distance relationship, and she decided that she had other things to do, and I had other things to do as well, so we parted. We're still friends though. But I'm with someone now," he commented.

Tracy was shocked, thinking that he was coming clean to her about his girlfriend. "And who is this?" she asked, about to be enraged.

"Umm, some girl named Tracy," Carl told her.

Tracy exhaled, smiled at him and slapped his arm.

"What's that for?" he asked with a smirk.

"Don't worry about it," she told him. She was embarrassed by her jealousy. "All right then, since you're ready to get rid of me."

Carl leaped out of the car, sprinted to the passenger side, opened the door and carried her out and up to her steps. He then lowered her to her feet with his hulking arms.

Tracy was speechless. Carl waved at her as he hopped back into his Nova. Tracy didn't enter until he was out of sight.

Patti asked, "So how was the movie?" She sat on the couch watching late-night videos and eating ice cream.

"It was all right."

"Well, what's up with you and Carl?"

"Aw, mom, you only asking about him because he's in college," she answered with a smile.

"So what? This is a big step up for you."

Tracy giggled at her mother's forwardness. "You a trip, mom."

"And what's that boy's name that's always around here fighting? You know, the real cute dark boy?" Patti asked.

Tracy frowned. "Ill, mom, you talkin' 'bout Victor."

"Yeah, well I seen that boy with three girls inside of a Burger King. And they paid for his food."

Tracy sucked her teeth. "Mom, girls always buying him stuff."

"Unh hunh, just like you did for poor Charles," Patti alluded.

Tracy snapped, "Poor Charles? That boy runnin' around here with every girl he can get his hands on now."

"Well, that's what you get for toying with him. I heard you tell your girlfriend that he was your *'little slave.'* "

Tracy squealed, embarrassed, "Uuuw, mom, what 'chew doin' listening to my phone conversations?"

"Aw, go on somewhere, girl. I was passing by your room and just happened to catch that."

"Yeah, I bet. And you probably caught other things I said, too."

"Mmm, hmm, I did," her mother told her with a nod. "Like when you told Carmen to slow down with being 'Ms. Hot-Panties.' "

Tracy was shocked and ashamed. She howled, "That's it, mom! I'm gonna make sure I watch where you are before I talk on the phone again." Giggling, Tracy ran up the steps to get away.

Patti followed her up the steps. She had been in much better spirits since her husband had returned home, bringing his good loving with him when he wasn't tired. And Patti had a few things that she wanted to square away with her daughter about *her* sex life. It was about that time for a mother and daughter talk.

"Tracy, are you having sex yet?" Patti walked into her daughter's room and asked.

Tracy gasped for air, with her eyes ballooning. "Oh my God, mom."

Patti grinned, imagining how embarrassed Tracy felt. But it was time for their sex talk whether Tracy liked it or not. "Well?" Patti asked her. "I should have done this with you a long time ago. I guess I was too preoccupied with worrying about your father."

"Well, we can wait a couple more years, 'cause I'm not ready yet," Tracy tried to tell her mother.

"I don't think so," Patti snapped. "Now answer the question, Tracy. Have you been doing something or not?"

Tracy forced herself to lie, and it was a lot easier since she hadn't had sex in almost a year. "No, mom."

Patti glared at her and ignored her answer. "Have you been protecting yourself."

I can't believe this, Tracy was thinking, frantically. "No, mom I haven't—"

"NO!" Patti repeated, cutting off her daughter's explanation.

"I haven't been doing anything," Tracy insisted nervously.

Patti continued to stare at her. "Mmm, hmm. I know you have. And I can't stop you, but I'm telling you now, a whole lot of responsibility comes with sex, and we get girls down at the abortion clinic all the time, talking about 'I don't know how I got pregnant.' "

Tracy could not help laughing at her mother's imitation of a teenager. Patti had reached the over-thirty mark.

"Oh, don't laugh, because it's not funny, Tracy," she told her daughter. "Now if you're gonna start dealing with college boys and what have you, then I definitely have to have this talk with you."

Tracy thought about asking her mother how she would feel if she lost her virginity to Carl, but she declined. *Naw, that would be crazy,* she told herself.

"Now you're telling me that you're not doing anything, right?" Patti asked her again.

"Yes," Tracy lied, ready to crack at any minute.

Patti nodded. "All right, so if you end up pregnant or running around here with some kind of a disease, then I guess it'll be a mistake, like a million other girls."

Tracy didn't answer, and as soon as her mother had left the room, she began to breathe freely again.

Patti stuck her head back inside the door and startled Tracy.

"Dag, mom!" her daughter exclaimed.

"I just wanted to let you know that as soon as you're ready to talk to me about sex, I'm here for you."

Tracy nodded, begging for her mother to stop pressing her about it. "Okay," she said, "I'll let you know."

Once her mother left her room again, Tracy thought, *God! Wait 'til I tell everybody about this!*

Tracy, Patti, and Jason sat and ate dinner with Carl that Saturday evening after waiting on Dave. He called late and said that he had to fill in and that he wouldn't be home anytime soon.

"Oh, well," Patti piped. "Better luck next time. But I'll make sure and tell him how respectful you are, Carl. Okay?" Patti promised.

"As long as you let him know she's in good hands," Carl responded with a confident smile. He was eager to meet Tracy's father.

Tracy was a bit disappointed, but there was nothing she could do about her father's work schedule.

"Ay, Tracy, I hear you goin' out with a college guy now," Carmen said, joining Tracy at lunchtime.

"What, are you cutting from class or somethin'?" Tracy asked. She and Carmen had different lunch periods.

"Yeah, but fuck classes. So what's up wit' you and this college boy?"

Jantel continued to eat her lunch, minding her own business. She was still not fond of Carmen.

"Oh, girl, you much late, 'cause we been goin' together for three weeks now," Tracy answered.

"Oh, so y'all had sex by now, hunh? Was it good, girl?"

Tracy shook her head, letting Carmen know. "No, our relationship is not based on that. We started off as friends, and now we respect each other more. We don't need to have sex."

Jantel, with her mouth full of turkey and cheese on wheat bread, looked at Tracy and smiled. She could not believe her ears after how eager Tracy had been to explore sex in junior high.

Carmen laughed at her. "Check you out. What, you think you moved up now, hunh?"

Tracy responded sharply, "Yup, and I ain't coming back down either."

Carmen wanted to say something about the wooden earrings Tracy was wearing. But she let it slide. Carmen didn't comment on Tracy's new hairstyle either. She was trying to wear her hair like Lisa's, in twisted, baby dreadlocks.

Carmen broke it down and said, "It don't make no difference that he's in college. He's still a guy. And through all of that dumb stuff, all he really want, right now, is some ass, like all the rest of 'em."

"Well, you wouldn't know, Carmen, because all the boys who meet you already know they're gonna get what they want. They don't even have to *like* you."

"Well, I got a boyfriend, too, now," Carmen responded smugly.

"So, he only gon' drop you after he *gets* some."

Carmen smiled slyly, as if she knew something that Tracy did not. "Well, just to let you know, *girlfriend,* I already gave him some, and he's been with me since then. And you know what, that was four months ago."

Carmen walked off with the proud stroll of a model.

Jantel turned to face Tracy and laughed. "That's a shame," she commented. "I think she's actually proud of that."

"She is," Tracy agreed. Yet she realized that her relationships had not lasted much longer than Carmen's had.

It was nearly Thanksgiving, and Carl had finally met Tracy's father. Tracy feared having sex with Carl after her conversation with Carmen. At the same time, she was curious to know if he would leave her once they did anything.

Heading back to Cheyney's campus after a Saturday afternoon movie, Tracy expected Carl to try her for the first time. But after only talking, while up in his neat room for an hour, Tracy began to worry about "the chick on the side" theory that Mercedes had hipped her to a while ago. "Sometimes, when a guy wants to save his main squeeze, he'll have a chick or two on the side that he'll mess with until he gets you. And sometimes they keep them chicks on the side just in case you start holding out on them. So always watch out for them guys that act like they got iron balls and shit, like they don't need none, because it's all a big game." Therefore, Tracy feared that Carl was seeing someone when she left. But no matter how close they got, Tracy avoided bringing up the subject of sex.

After the chat with Carmen, sex with Carl was a waiting game that had turned into a psychological nightmare. Tracy was beginning to despise Carmen for it. Carl always seemed to be in a hurry to get back to his dorm, and Tracy was starting to believe that he was running back to catch a girl at a specific time.

Tracy called to make sure that he was home that night. "Hello . . . It's me," she answered.

"Yeah, how did you like the movie? I forgot to ask you," he asked her.

"It was all right," Tracy said, wanting to get to the point of her call. "What are you doin'?"

"Homework."

"Oh, so I guess you want me to hang up now, hunh?" she assumed.

"I didn't tell you to," he said to her.

What the hell is he doing homework on a Saturday night for? she asked herself. "Well, won't I disturb you while you doin' your *homework?*" she ranted.

Carl raised his brow and stopped writing. Something was definitely wrong with how Tracy was acting. "Hold on now, Tracy, what is the problem here? You act as if someone told you a rumor about me or something."

"Ain't nobody tell me nothin'. And how did you get that idea? You feel guilty about something?"

"Aw, that's it!" he snapped. "You think I'm cheating on you already, and I'm tired of having to prove things to you all the time, so the hell with it!" he shouted, hanging up on Tracy's ear.

Tracy held the phone, deciding not to call him back. She called Lisa, finding out that Carl was generally faithful. It was a mistake, showing how insecure she was. Tracy was still a growing teenager.

"So Jantel is really doing well in track, hunh?" Patti asked. She watched Tracy as she put on her winter coat. Tracy then grabbed her bag of clothing and personals. It was Friday night and she was staying over Jantel's house and planning on getting up bright and early to attend another of Jantel's cross-country track meets.

"Yeah. Colleges are looking at her for scholarships already," Tracy informed her mother.

Patti was excited for her. "See that? Now don't you wish you had stuck it out in track? You could've had colleges coming to see you."

Tracy laughed at the idea. "I'm not fast, mom. If I was, then maybe I would have stuck it out. But Jantel is one of the fastest girls in the city."

"Well, cross-country isn't sprinting," Patti said, confused.

"I know, but she runs all year round."

Patti nodded. "Yeah, I guess that's good for conditioning."

No, she's just afraid of boys, so she runs track all the time to have an excuse to stay busy, Tracy thought to herself with a grin.

"Well, have fun," her mother told her as she headed out the door.

Jantel lived across Wayne Avenue, four blocks away. Tracy insisted that she could walk instead of being driven, and she arrived at Jantel's in less than a half-hour.

"Ay, girl," Jantel greeted her friend at her door after looking through the peephole. Tracy followed her in and then up to Jantel's room to plot. They closed the door to speak in private.

Jantel whispered, "So what if your mom calls here?"

"She's not gon' call here. My mom ain't even like that."

"Okay then, 'cause I hope she don't find out."

"Stop worryin' about it."

"What would she do to you?" Jantel asked with a smile.

"Kick my ass," Tracy said, giggling nervously.

"Well, when you leavin'?"

"Like nine o'clock. And then I'll be back over here before we leave for the track meet."

"Okay then, girl, but you have to be back over here by seven-thirty in the morning."

Tracy snapped, "You told me five times already, Jantel. I know already. God!"

"I'm just trying to make sure, because if you're not here at seven-thirty, you're getting left." Jantel then shook her head and grinned. "I still think you crazy though."

Tracy, with her bags in hand, had her college friends pick her up on Chelten Avenue, claiming that she would be ordering a cheese steak sandwich by the time they would arrive. "So I'll just eat it there and wait for y'all," she told them. It was all right with them. They got Tracy to order them cheese steaks as well. They then headed for another Cheyney State campus party that Carl's group happened to be doing. The football team had off that weekend.

Tracy pushed her way through the crowds as soon as they had arrived. Lisa, Joanne and Kiwana were privileged to get in for free since Carl and his friends were DJing, and that included free entrance for Tracy.

Carl didn't see her at first. Tracy then shouted onto the stage, making her way through the crowds, "CARL!"

Carl looked down at her from the stage platform, and then back out into the crowds. Tracy waited patiently, deciding to sit on a nearby chair. She knew that he would eventually come to her.

Twenty minutes went by, and Carl still had not spoken to her.

"Ay pretty, you here by yourself?" a short fellow wearing glasses asked. He looked as if his last name was Peabody.

"No, I'm here with my boyfriend," Tracy answered, looking away. She was dressed like a bunch of the New York students, wearing a colorful rayon shirt, extra large jeans, an oversized belt, brown suede boots and twisted hair. Lisa and Joanne were from New York, too.

"Well, where is he?" the short fellow asked her.

"On the stage."

He looked up at the DJ table. "Oh, which one? Carl?"

"Yeah, and why you say it like that?"

"Oh, no reason. I just didn't know you were talkin' to him, that's all." Mr. Peabody backed off.

"So what are you doing here?" Carl finally came and asked Tracy.

"Oh, I can't come to see you?" she responded to him.

"For what? I have another girlfriend in here now."

Disturbed, Tracy snapped, "Well if you got another girl that fast, then you must wasn't serious about me, and you musta' been talkin' to her all along, and you think I'm stupid but I'm not." She jumped up to leave, embarrassed and angry, and her plan to spend the night with him was shattered.

"Come here!" Carl demanded.

"For what?" Tracy stopped and asked.

"All right, forget it then."

Tracy thought about it, hoping that he was only teasing about having another girlfriend to make her jealous. She then walked around to go up onto the stage with him.

"What are you doing?" he asked.

Tracy shouted, "COME HERE, CARL!" making a scene in front of plenty of college students.

Who the hell is she? students were asking themselves. Tracy was not a familiar face to them.

Carl could not deny her after her outrage. He followed her off of the stage and said, "You know what, Tracy? You're really getting on my nerves. I'm starting to wish I'd never met you."

"Well, tell me what you had to say then," she asked with sparkling hazels from the multi-colored party lights.

Her highly attractive presence soothed Carl, and he was suddenly filled with an urgent desire to make love to her. "I was gonna tell you that I was lying," he said.

"You were?"

"Yeah," Carl assured her, reaching out to hold her arms. "Who did you come here with tonight?" he asked more pleasantly.

"Me, myself and my bag."

Carl looked down at her bag. "What's all in there?"

"Clothing and stuff."

"Where are you going?"

Tracy paused. "To spend the night with you."

The words got stuck and lost in Carl's throat. He nodded, agreeably, waiting excitedly for the party's end.

Three o'clock came, and it was time to wrap up the party. The bright gymnasium lights were clicked on, and Carl's group packed up their stuff and loaded it onto a truck. There was an after-party being held at one of the dorms, but Carl had other plans. He turned down the offer to accompany his friends and walked Tracy's sleepy head back to his room. Tracy had already told Lisa that she would be staying with Carl, so they didn't wait up for her.

Once they arrived at his dorm room, Tracy fell face first into Carl's neatly made bed. Carl sat down beside her and began to rub her back. He then lit incense, turned off the lights and lit a candle.

"Carl?" Tracy said, face still pressed into his pillow.

"What?" Carl asked quietly, leaning over into her ear.

"Can you take my clothes off?"

Carl could not believe his ears. He obliged.

"Oh, that feels so good, Carl," she moaned, as he rubbed her bare back down to her waistline after taking off her shirt and bra. He then tugged off her oversized jeans. When he finished with that, Tracy turned over to face him.

Carl said with a hard-on and a smile, "Damn, you're turning me on, girl!"

"Shet up and take your clothes off," Tracy retorted with a smirk.

Carl did. He then began to lick down Tracy's neck, around to her shoulders and down to her breasts. Tracy grabbed his head and squeezed him into them, aroused. Carl licked down to her stomach, and Tracy wondered how far he was going to go with it. She could *feel* him moving farther down with his tongue, and it was too good of a feeling to stop him.

The room disappeared. Uncontested sensations exploded throughout Tracy's unexplored body. She tried to move away to lessen the excitement, but Carl pursued as her eyes squeezed shut, tearing in ecstasy.

Tracy began to shake, grabbing the sheets to keep from screaming. Mouth wide open with her fingers massaging Carl's massive shoulders, she finally managed to relax. And when Carl had pulled away from her, every muscle in her body tingled and fell limp across his twin-sized bed. Tracy was left too exhausted to move.

Tracy could not take her mind off of her experience with Carl. She sat at her desk in school Monday, thinking about marriage and children.

She thought she was in love. Carl had done things with her that she never thought would happen. He had even outdone Victor.

Tracy began to write out his name, Carl Thompson, over and over again inside of her notebook, and he was on her mind every hour of the day. He was her newfound treasure.

"Ay Ra-Ra? Where you been?" Tracy asked, catching her neighbor walking in from school.

Raheema entered Tracy's house to chat. Tracy quickly shut the door and rubbed her hands together to warm them. It was blistering cold outside, Atlantic Coast winter weather.

"Damn it's cold out there!" Tracy exclaimed, looking at Raheema's thick yellow coat. Her acne had gotten worse. "So where you been at, girl?" Tracy repeated.

"I'm in a glee club at this church, and we've been working on songs to sing on Sundays," Raheema answered her.

Tracy frowned. "Glee club and church? Since when did you get involved in that?"

"My mother thought it was a good idea."

"Well, are you happy now?" Tracy thought that *she* was definitely happy with Carl Thompson.

Raheema answered, "No, but it's good to be involved in something." She laughed, fighting off depression.

Tracy could tell that her neighbor was feeling miserable. "Look on the bright side, at least you have a good head on your shoulders. You're heading for college soon," she comforted, smiling to cheer her up.

"Yeah, yeah, everybody's always saying that, but boys aren't attracted to the books. They're more attracted to good looks and fat asses."

"Look, girl, we're only sixteen. We got a whole lot of time," Tracy snapped at her. "Your damn face ain't gon' stay like that forever. And all boys aren't into *'fat asses.'* "

"Yeah, right," Raheema retorted with a grin. The acne scars distorted her smile.

Damn, she's catching a bad break, Tracy told herself. *I'm glad my face ain't breaking out like that.*

Raheema sighed and said, "Look, Tracy, you were always the one who went after things, and your mother and father allowed you a chance to grow and be strong. Plus, you're pretty, and you know how to talk to boys and stuff and that's the kind of girls that they like."

"Well, you'll be pretty again, Ra-Ra. This is just a phase you're going through."

Raheema ignored her and said, "My father been haunting me since birth. And I don't even know how to act with guys, Tracy."

Tracy continued to listen as her neighbor went on:

"See, that's why if I have a daughter, I'm gonna let her be herself and just give her guidelines to follow, instead of trying to rule her life."

Tracy asked, out of curiosity, "What if you have a son?"

Raheema shrugged. "I'll do the same thing with him."

"Would you want your son to turn out like Bruce? You didn't like him." Tracy figured that Bruce was good enough for Raheema. *You should have stayed with him,* she wanted to tell her. But of course, she couldn't say it after having her own relations with Bruce.

"I did so like him, but that's when I was still running away from my sister's lifestyle. I didn't treat Bruce well."

I didn't either, Tracy pondered. *Poor Bruce.* "Well, what do you think about Carmen?" she quizzed.

"Oh, now *she's* a whore. I wouldn't want my daughter to be *anything* like her."

"What kind of husband do you want to have?"

Raheema smiled. "One like your father."

Tracy smiled back and said, "Me too." *And I think I already found him,* she thought. She didn't want to make Raheema jealous, so she kept her excitement about Carl to herself.

growing up

"Well, Carl, what are we going to do tonight?" Tracy asked. She was stretched out on Carl's bed inside of his dorm room.

"First, I have to take you home, and then I have to study for this upcoming test," Carl told her from his desk. He closed his book and stood up to leave.

"How come you all strapped into your grades, all of a sudden?"

"Look, would you get off the bed and come on."

"Oh, you don't want me down here or somethin'?"

"I didn't tell you to come down here anyway. I mean, you're just getting to the point now where you're inviting yourself." Carl opened his door.

"Okay then, since you have to *study* so much." Tracy jumped up from his bed and snatched her bag from off the floor. Not a word was spoken on their City Line Avenue ride toward her Germantown home. It was February, a new semester of college for Carl and the second half of Tracy's junior year of high school. She hadn't been able to spend a good deal of time with him since Christmas. It wasn't her fault that he

was on academic probation. Or was it? Tracy had been occupying a lot
of his time, but so was football and DJing. Carl simply had his marbles
in too many different jars.

"All right, I'll call you when I get in," he said. He had double-
parked his small Nova out in front of Tracy's house.

"Oh, you not even gonna walk me to my door, hunh?" she huffed
at him.

Carl looked at her as if it pained him. "Yes, I'm sorry," he said,
getting out to open her side. Just as he did, Victor Hinson and four of
his rough-looking friends approached them from the corner.

"YO, TRACY! COME HERE!" he hollered, drunkenly. He was
staggering from side to side as he walked, obviously filled to the rim
with alcohol.

Tracy didn't know what to do. *Oh my God, he's doing this shit
again,* she reflected, remembering when Victor had intervened to save
her from Timmy. "What do you want?" she asked him, nervously.

"Fuck you mean, 'What I want?' I said to come here. NOW!"

Tracy, noticing his drunken condition, tried to laugh it off. "You had
a little too much to drink," she told him.

Carl walked behind her cautiously. He was aware that Victor's
friends would intervene if he was to try anything bold and courageous.
And they didn't look like the types to allow any *Action Jackson* stunts
to go down.

Victor said, "Oh, okay. You gon' get new on me now, since you got
this muscle-headed pussy with you, right?" He walked up on Tracy's
sidewalk with his friends laughing in the background.

Tracy held in her own laugh. Carl did have a massive-sized head.

Carl turned and looked Victor in the face, as if he wanted to hurt
him for embarrassing him.

"Yeah, what 'chew want? We got the whole fuckin' street," Victor
responded to Carl's glare. "I'll break your punk ass up!" he shouted,
heading out into the middle of the street.

Victor took off his jacket and sweatshirt as Tracy watched, astonished and tickled brown. Victor was still black and beautiful in his own
muscular frame. His gold link-chain and small V around his neck,

glittered from the night lights along with the gold-nugget bracelet on his right wrist. "Come on, punk," he insisted, challenging Carl. "Come the fuck on out here."

Carl was contemplating about his friends.

"Ay Vic, stop that shit, man," one of his friends said, still chuckling. "Come on, cuz'. Put your shirt back on, you gon' catch a damn cold out here."

"Naw. FUCK 'DAT!" Victor hollered, staggering.

His crew continued to laugh.

Victor then kicked Carl's car. BOOM! "Now what, pussy? I wouldn't let you kick my muthafuckin' car. I'd put my foot in ya' ass, if it was my car. But I guess this piece of shit you drivin' don't mean much."

Victor's friends pleaded, seriously, "Vic, man, you drunk. You gon' have neighbors comin' out here, man."

Carl gritted his teeth, not budging, but he was starting to get worried. And Tracy's father was not in from work yet. *If this guy kicks my car again, I'm gonna have to fight all of them,* Carl mused.

Victor put his Adidas sweatshirt and winter ski jacket back on with his black Sergio jeans and Timberland boots. He had a fresh haircut to boot. Victor was *the shit,* even when he was drunk.

"Yeah, aw'ight," he said, straightening out his clothes. "That's my young-girl you dealin' wit', boah'. You treat her wrong, and I'm gon' break you the fuck up. Aw'ight, boah'?" he asked Carl.

Carl stared as if he wanted to hurt Victor. They were both about the same height, but Carl was thirty pounds heavier. Nevertheless, Victor was older and much more intimidating.

"You hear me talkin' to you, cuz'?" he asked, as he walked closer to them.

Carl and Tracy had not moved from the sidewalk since Victor started putting on his scene.

"Ay Vic, leave him alone, man. Dude don't want shit," his friend said, ushering Victor down the street.

"Fuck off of me, man! I can walk. And I know that big-head pussy don't want shit." They headed down Tracy's block, with Victor leading his friends. He then yelled, "PUNK!"

"Who was that?" Carl asked Tracy as they left.

Tracy lied. "Oh, that's just some guy that wanted to talk to me a while ago." She was surprisingly excited about the event. *Victor was ready to fight for me,* she thought.

Carl said, "That boy has a big mouth. I hate guys like that." He headed to his car and said, "I'll call you when I get in."

"Jantel! Guess what?" Tracy quizzed, jumping on the telephone as soon as she got inside.

"Okay, what Carl do now?"

"Nothing. It was Victor," Tracy told her.

"Victor? What about 'im?"

"He was ready to fight Carl over me."

"Get out of here! Victor?"

"Yeah. And he said I was his young-girl."

"For real!" Jantel shouted, getting excited herself. She then calmed herself down, starting to think for the both of them. "Yeah, but Victor still a damn dog. That boy done had more girls than I had track meets."

Tracy laughed and said, "I know." But she still could not help thinking about him. She added, all in a hurry, "I wonder if he gon' stop by and see me tomorrow. I wonder what he wanted. He might of asked me to come over to see him."

Jantel butted in and said, "No, girl. I can see it now. You gon' end up being his little plaything again." She was surprised she said it. Jantel always thought that way about Tracy and Victor, but she had never said it. She was slightly afraid of Tracy.

"WHAT?" Tracy fumed.

"I ain't mean it like that, Tracy. I just meant that Victor's just a dog, and that's all that he be wantin'."

"No. You ain't mean it like that. You callin' me a whore."

"No I'm not, Tracy. For real."

"Yes the fuck you are!" Tracy responded acidly, hanging up on her friend. She sat there in her room in a state of turmoil. *She's right,* she told herself. *I am still fuckin' hooked on him.* She was disappointed with herself for still liking Victor. Carl had become a drag like all her other previous boyfriends. Only Victor remained exciting for her. Yet he was the ultimate dog.

What the hell is wrong with me? she asked herself. She decided to push the thought of Victor out of her mind. *I'm not gonna be nobody's whore,* she insisted.

Tracy began to watch more television in Carl's busy absence. She even started taping shows when she knew that she would miss them. And every effort to stop from watching them and find something more constructive to do, only made her anxious to find out what she had missed. Tracy was a television junkie.

The glamour on television became the only perfect world. Adventures of *Dynasty, Knots Landing, Falcon Crest* and other network shows and movies of non-black people occupied a good portion of Tracy's imagination. She began to long for her own riches, imagining herself hosting large, elegant parties where handsome bachelors drooled over her and catered to her every desire.

"TRACY! GET UP OUT OF THAT BED, GIRL! Do you know what time it is?" Patti shouted, waking Tracy from dreamland. It was Thursday morning, and a school day.

"Hunh?" Tracy responded sleepily, tossing the pillow over her head to drown out her mother's screaming.

Patti yanked the pillow from her and turned the light on. "Girl, I'm sick and tired of you getting these damn late slips and detentions. Now get up, I said! What is wrong with you?"

"Nothin', mom."

Patti wore her white work coat, with a new wrap hairdo, looking good and young. "Are you pregnant or something?" she asked her daughter. Tracy had been at a loss of energy for weeks.

"No, I'm not pregnant," Tracy answered her with a frown.

"Well, what's your problem? All you've been doing is lying around watching those damn shows, with this nappy-ass hair of yours!"

"It's natural," Tracy retorted with a grin.

Patti had not said anything to her about the twisted-up hairstyle since Tracy had started wearing it. She figured it was a stage that her daughter was going through. But it was getting close to springtime, and Patti felt that Tracy would not be able to straighten her hair out in time to apply for a summer job.

"Girl, that ain't no nature," she responded with a smirk. "If you want a natural, then grow an Afro."

Tracy smiled herself. "Unt unh, mom. I don't believe you said that. See, white people got us hating our hair," Tracy rebutted, finally sitting up.

Patti said, "A nature is not using chemicals and whatnot, but you can still comb it. 'Cause my little do looks good, girlfriend. You hear me?" Patti chuckled, looking inside of Tracy's dresser mirror. "I got you an appointment with Donna tomorrow," she informed Tracy as she left the room.

"What?" Tracy asked, standing up to get herself together for school.

"You heard me," her mother responded before heading down the steps.

Already running late, Tracy took extra-long to shower up and get dressed. By the time she had arrived at school, it was after nine o'clock.

The security guard stopped her at the front door. "Excuse me, young lady, but are you just coming into school?" asked the heavyset and hungry-looking guard. He had a bunch of unnecessary hair on his face, untrimmed.

"Yeah," Tracy snapped.

"Well, you're gonna have to go to the office."

"I know that. That's where I was going."

Tracy rolled her eyes.

The security guard grabbed her by the arm and said, "In that case, let me escort you."

Tracy violently yanked away from him. "GET OFF OF ME! I CAN WALK!"

"That's it, young lady, you're in more trouble now," he warned her.

"Yeah, whatever," Tracy responded, unmoved.

Staff members came out of their offices, hearing the argument that erupted. Tracy strutted into the disciplinarian's office herself, ignoring their stares. She knew what was coming. She sat in the empty room, waiting for her case to be heard. *Dirty, hairy, greasy man,* she fumed to herself.

"Okay, I see we have a lot of problems going on here," Suit-and-tie said to Tracy. He was well-groomed as usual.

Tracy was a junior, believing she was old enough to demand respect from anyone. "No we don't, 'cause he shouldn't have put his hands on me."

Suit-and-tie let Tracy know. "Look, young lady, don't come in here with an attitude problem with me, 'cause you'll find yourself home for a few days, on suspension. Now, first of all, you've been late nearly every day for the past two weeks, and you have the audacity to come in here with this two-cent attitude as though we did something to *you.*"

"And?" Tracy asked carelessly.

"Okay, that's it." Suit-and-tie pulled out a pink slip from his desk. "Now I was gonna let you off the hook with a couple more detentions and a last warning, but it seems to me that you don't want any warnings."

"I don't care, 'cause I need to be away from this place for a while anyway."

Suit-and-tie picked up the phone, pulling Tracy's file. "Is your mother at work?"

"I don't know," Tracy lied, rolling her eyes again.

"Yes, may I speak with Mrs. Ellison please? . . . Yes, this is Mr. Waters from Germantown High School. It seems your daughter, Tracy, has a problem. Now I was originally going to give her three days suspension for her attitude, but now I think she needs five, unless you can come and talk to me about her. Okay . . . Mmm hmm . . . All right then. Well, I'll send her home, and you can come in on Monday with her to talk with me," Mr. Waters said, hanging up. He then filled out the pink slip and handed Tracy a copy. "Now you go on home and think about things," he told her.

Tracy left school, but she wasn't planning on going home. She headed down to Cheyney's campus after catching a taxi on City Line Avenue to pay Carl a surprise visit. There was no sense in going home. Tracy decided it would be better to stay on campus until it was time to pick up her brother.

"What's up?" she asked with a grin as Carl opened his door.

"What have you done now?" he asked.

"I got suspended."

Carl sighed, sick of all of her drama. "What the hell is wrong with you, Tracy?"

"Who you talkin' to like that?"

"I told you I have to study for my midterms this week, and here you come, crashing in here talking about you got suspended, as if you don't give a damn."

"So let's take a break and go to the movies."

Carl sat back at his desk. "I don't have time, number one, and no money either."

Tracy could not hold it in any longer. "You know what, Carl? I'm tired of just sittin' the fuck around while you do your homework, and then you wanna *get some.* You don't take me nowhere, you don't buy me nothin'. AND I'M TIRED OF THIS SHIT!"

Carl stopped studying. "Tracy, what the hell are you talking about?" he asked her. "You've been doing your thing, watching them damn television shows and BET videos for the past couple of weeks. I think you must be confusing characters or something. This is me, Carl Thompson, from college. Remember me? Earth to Tracy."

"All that smart shit can walk," she snapped at him.

"Yeah, and that's exactly what I feel like telling you."

Tracy was shocked. "Oh, is that the way you feel about it?"

"Yes, that's how I feel, Tracy!"

Tracy left his room without another word and slammed his door, hoping that Carl would come out after her, but he didn't.

Tracy got a ride back to the city and caught a bus downtown. She wandered around on Chestnut Street and looked over a pair of jeans inside of a retail store.

"Hey, bright eyes, you want a job?" an olive-complexioned Italian man asked her.

"Who, me?" Tracy responded with a smirk.

The Italian man walked over to her wearing an opened silk shirt that displayed his hairy chest. He wore two gold chains, and his black, curly hair shined as he slung his right arm up on a clothing rack, getting comfortable. "Yeah, you," he said.

Tracy stared at his gold-nugget bracelet.

He looked at Tracy's hairstyle and held back his comments. He wanted to hire her first. Tracy was obviously attractive, despite her twisted hair.

He smiled and said, "See, this is my store. I'm in charge of who gets hired here. Now I got a girl leaving soon for a spring break or something. You could replace her for me."

"What about when she comes back?"

"We'll worry about that then. But if you're interested, give me call. I'll hold the spot for you, but you gotta let me know by next week."

"Okay," she said, following him to the counter, where he gave her a store business card.

"Pamela! Come here a second. Wouldja'? This here is Tracy. She'll be in to work with us in a week or so," he said to a tall, light-skinned black woman. He assumed that Tracy would take him up on his offer.

"Hi you doin'?" Pamela asked, shaking Tracy's hand, lightly. She had huge gold earrings herself, with a sketch of Manhattan, New York, set inside of their circular shape.

Tracy responded, "Hi," while observing her earrings and her clothing.

"Now, Pam will give you all the details when you come in to work for me next week," the Italian man interjected. His name was Joseph

Bamatti. Tracy liked his name. She thought it sounded like a designer suit in *GQ* magazine. She walked out of the store, looking into several outside mirrors as she strolled along Chestnut Street, proud of her pretty face and attention-getting eyes.

"Mom, I'll straighten up now. I promise. I just needed something to do," Tracy was saying, after twenty minutes of arguing with her mother about whether she could accept the job offer.

"What makes you so sure?"

"Because, I just needed something to do to stop being bored, that's all."

"Well, I'm still gonna have to go and talk to Mr. Waters to get you back in school."

"I know," Tracy said, glowingly. She was very excited about her first job offer.

Patti conceded. "All right, girl, but you act up again, and that's it. And I have to tell your father first, to see what he has to say about it."

Why you gotta ask him? Tracy almost slipped and asked. She still had to get used to the shared chain of authority, since her father had returned. "Oh," she responded, walking away from her mother solemnly.

Patti went down the stairs and left Tracy in her room to think.

Jason walked in and asked, "Tra-cy, where's Carl at?"

"Why?"

"'Cause, I wanna know." Jason was decked out in another attractive Oshkosh outfit.

Tracy answered, "I don't know, and I don't care. He's a dumb jock anyway, that's trying to be a nerd now." She laughed and added, "That stupid pussy. Oops," she responded, catching herself.

Jason smiled. He didn't seem to make a big deal out of it, but he knew Tracy had said a bad word.

"I'm sorry, little man. You're not gon' tell on me, are you?" she begged him.

"No," he told her with a smile.

Pleased with his answer, Tracy said, "All right. I'll get you some cookies then, for being cool."

"And some milk, too," he told her. He was about to turn six years old, and was growing taller and getting smarter by the minute.

Tracy responded with a grin, "Oh, you're getting greedy now."

Jason said, "You shouldna' said it then."

Tracy chuckled to herself and headed down the stairs to get her brother the promised milk and cookies. *Dag, that's a shame. I'm being blackmailed by my little brother,* she thought.

"Girl, I got some news for you," Jantel told Tracy over the phone that evening. She was attempting to make up with Tracy after her slip of the tongue the night before.

"What?" Tracy asked flatly. She wanted to make up with her friend, but she was still hurt by what Jantel had insinuated about her.

"Guess who's pregnant."

"Who?" Tracy asked.

"Carmen. And she four months at that."

"For real?"

"Yup, 'cause I had just found out today."

"See, I told that tramp about runnin' around with everybody," Tracy said excitedly.

Jantel fell silent. She didn't want to say the wrong thing again. "I think she did it on purpose though, 'cause I heard that this guy got money," Jantel finally said, thinking that her comment was safe.

"That don't mean shit. She ain't gon' get none. That girl is dumb," Tracy commented.

Jantel sat silent again. *I wonder how you feel about me, Tracy?* she thought about asking. Tracy had been good friends with Carmen, but she seemed two-faced when she talked bad about her, a friend one day and talking about her the next.

Tracy was beginning to see the picture. Who was *she* to throw stones? "Well, I shouldn't say that," she commented apologetically.

"Anyway, what else is new?" she asked, deciding to change the subject.

"Nothin'. What's up with you and Carl?" Jantel asked.

"Fuck that boy!" Tracy exclaimed, without another word about it. "Oh yeah, I got a job offer downtown on Chestnut Street today," she said.

"For real?" Jantel asked.

"Yup," Tracy told her, beginning to warm up to her again.

"I can't even get a job with track and all. My schedule is too busy," Jantel commented.

"Ain't outdoor season 'bout to start?"

"Yup, next month."

Dave poked his head into Tracy's room and gestured to her.

Tracy held the phone away from her mouth. "Yes?" she asked him.

"I wanna talk to you for a minute."

Oh my God! Here it comes, she thought to herself, nervously. "Jantel, I gotta call you back," she told her friend before hanging up.

Dave took a seat on her bed while Tracy sat in her desk chair, anticipating their first father-daughter confrontation since he had moved back in almost a year ago. She knew that the moment would come eventually. It was only a matter of time.

"You know you have one more year of high school before you graduate, right?" he asked her. His tone was calm and conversational.

Tracy nodded, speechlessly. She wondered where her father was heading with the conversation.

"Do you plan on going to college?"

Tracy thought about how much fun she had had on Cheyney's campus with Lisa, Joanne, Kiwana and Carl. "Yeah," she told him with another nod. "I wanna go to college."

Dave nodded back to her. "Well, everybody don't get to go to school. Did you know that?"

Tracy paused. "I haven't really thought about it like that," she admitted.

"Most teenagers don't, until the last minute. And then they end up not being able go to the college that they wanted to, because they were unprepared for it."

Dave let the idea sink into his daughter's head before he commented on it further.

"Now what college would you like to go to?" he asked her next.

"A black school." Tracy told him.

"A black school? Why?"

Tracy hunched her shoulders. "Why not? Because I want to be around black people, I guess," she told him.

Her father began to smile at her. "I'm glad that you'd like to go to a black school and all, but it should be more than because you want to be around black people. You can go to Community College downtown and do that. You have to have a goal in mind when you start thinking about your future. I just want you to think about that before you start acting up in school, because you'll end up putting yourself in a bad situation that you'll be struggling to get out of."

He got up to leave her room and added, "By the way, congratulations on your new job. Maybe now you won't be digging in my pockets so much."

Tracy smiled at her father before he returned to his room. She was pleased with his method of getting across to her. *My dad really is cool,* she told herself, continuing to smile. She was proud to have such a thoughtful father. *He ain't nothin' like Mr. Keith at all.*

Monday morning, Tracy and her mother held the conference with Mr. Waters in his office. Several teachers had filed complaints on Tracy's lack of focus in class, but her grades did not seem to suffer. She had maintained A's and B's. She agreed with everything though, just to get the hour-long conference over with. She was dying to catch Carmen in school. She had a few words for her.

"Ay girl, I heard something big about you," she said.

Carmen was cutting her classes inside of the lunch room again. "I know, I know, but life is life," she retorted, annoyed with the gossip.

Tracy was not in school when Carmen's pregnancy news hit the fan and blew around.

"See, I told you about running around."

"Tracy, you're no better than I am. You just didn't get pregnant yet."

"That's right, and I ain't gettin' pregnant no time soon, either. I'm going to college."

"Yeah, well I'm happy for you. Anyway, I lucked up this time, 'cause he wants to marry me," Carmen informed Tracy cheerfully. She had not given her boyfriend an answer yet; she was simply proud that she had been asked.

Tracy said, "Well obviously, somethin' is wrong with him. And you're only seventeen." She was trying to cover her surprise. She was jealous.

Carmen took a sip of her Sprite soda. "People used to get married young. And my grandmother was fifteen when she got married."

"Yeah, well that was then, and the cost of living is much higher now," Tracy refuted, still shocked by Carmen's announcement.

Carmen said with a grin, "Well, his father is an engineer, and he's studying to be one, too. Plus, his mom is a physical therapist, and he said they make a lot of money."

Tracy was doubtful. It all sounded too good to be true. "Aw girl, that boy can tell you any damn thing, 'cause you don't know."

"Yeah, but I *do* know that he's treating me nice. He got a car, he's going to college this year, and since I'm carrying his baby, I got something that's a part of him forever." She got up to leave. "So now, Ms. Too-Fine. Or at least you think you are," she added, chuckling as she left.

Tracy had no words. Her plans to bring Carmen down had failed. She was the one who had crumbled. Security was something she had never known. Her father had only recently come back to the family, and her relationship with Carl was practically over, like the rest of her short-term flings. *Well, I wish Carmen luck,* she told herself, *'cause I sure ain't had none. At least my father is back home though, and my mom is happy again. But what about me?*

Tracy played with her left earring, watching the younger freshman girls flirting with the older boys. It was evident to Tracy that none of them knew what *love* and *romance* were. They were all too immature, looking for adventure, thinking it was love and falsely believing that they were grown.

The school day ended quicker than Tracy expected. She felt the usual stares while walking home from school. But they were coming from younger guys, who hadn't known her. She had been on a college campus and to college parties with a college boyfriend. What could a *high school boy* offer her? They were getting on her last damn nerves with, "Hey, baby. Can I get to know you better?" "You look like a movie star, sweetheart. Can I be your manager and keep that body healthy, with a little bit of *work?*" And one guy even got nasty. "Can I lick you where it feels good? Please. You know you would like it." Tracy told him off. "You a nasty little muthafucker. Do you know that? What kind of a mother would raise you?" Then she thought that Carl was nasty for doing it. Nevertheless, Tracy's attractive appearance drew attention, whether she liked it or not.

She walked around the same corners of Wayne and Chelten Avenues, seeing the same faces. The same older guys hung out in the playground, running ball, since Tracy could remember. And in the middle of that long playground block, in a blue Mercedes Benz, sat Victor Hinson.

Tracy slowed her pace, watching him as he talked on his car phone, hoping that he would look her way. She could not help herself. Empty of an outlet for excitement, Tracy found herself praying for him to light up her life for just a minute, but Victor did not seem to notice her.

Tracy speeded up to her house, dashed up the steps to her room, closed her door and threw her face into her pillow like a baby having a tantrum.

BRRRIIIIINNGG!

"Hello," she answered the phone snappishly.

"What's up?"

Tracy sat up. "Who is this?" she asked, just to make sure.

"What, you don't recognize my voice on the phone?"

"Well, you haven't called me in like *years.*"

Victor adjusted the channel on his car phone. "Well, that was then. I see you gettin' older now."

"Yeah, I'm gonna be going away to college soon and educating myself," she bragged, hoping that it would interest him. Victor was never the unintelligent type. And his older brother had gone to college, so Tracy was confident that he valued it.

"Oh, yeah? So that means that I could come down there and visit you, and spend the night in your dorm room?"

Tracy's heart raced as fast as when she had first met him. "We'll see," she teased.

"Do you still go with that dude?" he asked her, referring to Carl.

"Not really," Tracy told him. Their split was not official, but Tracy was ready to move on from Carl.

"Well, you know I was drunk that night," Victor said, stopping short of apologizing. He was not quite ready to fully apologize to a young-girl.

Tracy smiled, accepting it as an apology anyway. She knew about the male ego, and Victor had one of the biggest. "You know, I heard somebody say before that your real feelings come out when you're drunk. And it seemed to me like you were jealous," she alluded.

Victor chuckled. "That's what it seemed like?"

"Yeah."

"Well, maybe, maybe not."

Tracy was filled from head to toe with bliss, but then Victor's phone line beeped. "Yo, I'ma call you back. All right? I was just thinkin' 'bout you," he told her immediately.

Tracy wanted to ask why he didn't say anything to her when she had walked past his car earlier, but since he was on the phone at the time, she suspected that he was probably busy. She hung up the phone and headed out of the door to go and pick up her brother, and was energized. Victor was gone from the playground, but she was satisfied with his call.

She called Raheema over as soon as she got back home with Jason to tell her the news. Maybe Raheema would have a different perspective on Victor than Jantel. However, Raheema came over with her own news to tell.

"Mercedes is coming over to talk to my father tonight," she said.

"For real?" Tracy asked, shocked. Raheema's news was more important than her news. "Do your parents know?"

Raheema looked at Tracy as if it was obvious. "Yeah, they know. My aunt told them. Mercedes had started stealing and stuff."

"Oh my God!" Tracy exclaimed. "So what she wanna talk to your father about?"

"She wants to move back in while she goes to this rehabilitation place."

"Is he gonna let her?"

Raheema shrugged. "I don't know. But I doubt it, knowing him."

Tracy paused, thinking the news over. "Well, how do you feel about it?"

"She's my sister and she needs help. I would say to help her. But it's not my decision."

Tracy shook her head and grunted, "Mmm, this deep. Well, you know you gotta tell me what happened."

"Yeah, I'll tell you tomorrow."

"Tomorrow? Girl, I wouldn't be able to sleep. You gotta tell me tonight," Tracy insisted.

"I'll have to see," Raheema told her, making no promises. She was still apprehensive about the family meeting herself. She wanted to give herself time to digest it all before she would tell anyone.

Beth was apprehensive about what her husband would say concerning Mercedes' plea to move back into their home. Keith had only grumbled to her when she mentioned it to him a few days ago. "She walked out on us and now she wants to come back, hunh?" he muttered. So Beth was not optimistic about their meeting at all. But she nervously told him that if he did not agree to at least talk to Mercedes, she would be on her way out with her other daughter.

Raheema, on the other hand, felt that he would allow Mercedes to come back. He had never actually allowed his first daughter to leave, as much as he had talked about her. It was as if her image was imprinted on his mind. Raheema was only unsure about how she would take it. Mercedes had been an attention-stealer ever since she had started living in the fast lane, and Raheema feared being blatantly ignored again.

Mercedes rung the doorbell close to eight o'clock that evening. Her mother answered the door, and they greeted each other with a hug. Mercedes then followed Beth over to join Raheema and her father at the dining-room table, completing the four-member family again.

Raheema stood up to hug her older sister herself before retaking her seat.

Mercedes looked clean but thin. She had made sure to look her best and to be on her best behavior. She had to swallow a lot of her pride before finally deciding to ask her parents for forgiveness. She felt that her survival depended upon the support that only a caring family could give her.

Keith stared at his daughter, unstirred by emotionalism. "Why should we let you come back?" he asked, ice-cold.

Both Raheema and Beth stared at him, ready to defend Mercedes. Mercedes, however, kept her composure. After asking many questions of herself, she had finally learned to understand her father. He was as stubborn as she was, searching for an outlet to ease his frustrations. Their entire family was introverted and guarded. They all needed outlets. Mercedes was only able to understand that about them after leaving home.

"I'm not your enemy, dad. I'm a victim like you are," she told him. "And I know that I brought this on myself, but you have to understand that, in a sense, you forced me into making some stupid decisions."

"I didn't force you to do a damn thing."

"And nobody forced you to be so uptight with us," she responded, on beat. "I mean, you gotta understand that everybody has to have something to be happy about in life. There has to be something that they love to do. And we didn't have that here."

"You could have participated in anything you wanted to," he told her. He looked over at Raheema and said, "Your sister was in a dance class. We all went out to see her perform. Where were you?"

Raheema wanted to speak up about how afraid she had been about keeping her grades up, and how she had given up her weekends to study. Dance class had been more pressure on her than enjoyment. The only enjoyment in it was her final performance, and she had never participated in dance again.

"And I bet you found a way to make that hard on her," Mercedes commented, hitting the nail on the head.

Raheema was pleased with Mercedes' thoughtfulness. Beth nodded her head, remembering the night her daughter had come home in tears, fearful of the pressure of keeping her studies together while attending dance classes.

"You do what you're supposed to do, and you can do whatever you want on the side," Keith said.

"But that's just the point. Life is more than doing what you're *supposed* to do. Life is about living it while you're here. I mean, sure, you would like for us to get good grades and to go to school and all, but that ain't what makes people wake up every morning. They wake up every morning because of the exciting things that may happen that day."

Keith was suspicious. He did not believe that Mercedes could carry out such a clear and concise argument by herself. "Who been puttin' this stuff in your head?" he asked her, realizing that her points were valid. He had been living for a paycheck for so long that he had forgotten how to really enjoy himself.

Mercedes sighed, realizing that selling her program to her father was going to be just as tough as she thought it would be. "We love each other, dad, but we think too much alike to admit it," she told him.

Beth looked at her daughter and smiled. She had known that fact for years. Mercedes and Keith were both bull-headed.

"Yeah, well, this is still my house, and if you're planning on moving back in here, then you know that I have the final say-so."

"Do you?" Mercedes asked him.

"What?" he responded, confused. "You damn right!" he fumed, ignorant of Beth's feelings about it.

"So if Raheema walks out of this house with straight A's, can you guarantee her a college education?"

"If she continues to get the grades that she's been getting, then yes I can."

"And after she's finished college, can you guarantee her a job?"

Keith paused, knowing that there was no guarantee. "If she gets good grades in college, then she'll get a good job."

Mercedes nodded. "Maybe. But you can't guarantee that."

"What are you trying to get at, girl?" he snapped, weary of playing Q & A with her.

"What I'm trying to say is that, no matter what you do to prepare yourself for the world, there is no guarantee. You can only do the best that you can do to survive, but ultimately it's gonna be your will, and not how smart you are or how disciplined you are, that gets you over.

It's a lot of people in the world who are just like you, dad. They come home mad at the world every night and end up taking it out out their loved ones because they don't know any better.

"And by the way, I'm not a girl," she told him. "I'm a young woman in need of some help. And I'm also your daughter." Mercedes could not help the tears that swelled up in her eyes. It wasn't part of her speech, it simply happened. She wiped her eyes with the back of her hands. Beth jumped up to get her some tissues while she comforted her.

"Thank you," Mercedes said with a sniff.

Keith sat silently. There was not a word at the table for a couple of minutes. Keith loved his daughter. He loved his family. And Mercedes was right.

Beth felt optimistic after hearing his silence. She knew her husband, and silence from him meant that Mercedes had made a good-enough case to stay. Raheema knew it, too. She was no longer concerned about her sister getting too much attention. She looked at Mercedes as an important ally.

"So what do you want us to do?" her father asked her.

"I'm going into this rehabilitation program, and I just wanted your support and somewhere to stay when I get out in a couple of months. I need for somebody to come up there and see me and tell me that everything is gonna be all right. The counselors told me that the best way for me to pull through it is if I have my family's support."

"And when are you getting out?"

"As soon as I feel I'm strong enough."

Keith nodded and looked at his wife. "We can do that, Beth."

Overjoyed, Beth stood up from the table and said, "Now, can I see you two hug? I've been dying to see that." She began to choke up and cry herself.

Mercedes stood from her chair and walked around the table, eager to feel her father's arms around her. Keith slowly rose from his chair and approached her. Mercedes reached out and tenderly embraced him. Keith, feeling his daughter's frail body in his arms, began to choke up himself.

"Come on over here, Raheema," Beth told her youngest. She grabbed Raheema's hand and pulled her into a three-way embrace with her father.

"Thank you, dad," Mercedes told him, tearing uncontrollably. "Thank you so much."

Tears came leaking out of Keith's eyes for the first time in over twenty years. "Damn, girl, now you done got me crying," he told her, unable to stop them.

Beth kissed his cheek and said, "It's good for you. We needed this. All of us."

And after all that they had been through, Raheema could not agree more.

deſtiNY

Early on a Saturday morning, Tracy headed for Chelten Avenue to catch the bus to the Broad Street subway. She was decked out in white Gloria Vanderbilt jeans and a turquoise silk shirt, carrying her black leather Coach bag. She was on her way downtown for her fourth week at work in Jeans & Shirts. It had rained the night before, so the pavement was still damp, and a chilly wind blew through her asymmetric hairdo. She had done away with the baby dreadlocks, reverting back to the honey-blond-tipped asymmetric look, donning her triangular-shaped *Tracy* earrings again with her neck laced with gold.

Victor Hinson cruised up behind her in his blue Mercedes Benz. He stopped alongside her, rolled down his passenger-side window and leaned over the seat. "Hey, pretty. You want a ride?" He looked handsome, almost coal black with moon-white teeth.

Tracy was not sure if she wanted to oblige. After Raheema's news about Mercedes going into a rehabilitation center, the awareness that Victor dealt in drugs made him no longer acceptable to her. Morally, Victor was no better than Cash. "I don't think so," she told him.

Victor speeded up the street and double-parked. He then popped on his hazard lights, jumped out of his car and walked over to the sidewalk to wait for her.

Tracy was apprehensive as she slowly approached him. *Oh my God, I don't have time for this,* she thought to herself. She had to be at work in less than an hour.

Victor, in a sky-blue and white terry-cloth sweat suit with white BK shoes and no socks, danced to the music that rocked from his car, as he waited for Tracy to get closer to him. His sweat-suit jacket was zipped down to his stomach, and his gold V dangled from his chain and glimmered against his black chest. He then stepped in front of Tracy and grabbed her hands, ever so gently.

"I just wanted to hold you again, but I guess that you're over me now," he said to her with a smile. He knew that she wasn't.

Tracy stood there with him, at a loss for words, and was motionless. *Am I over him?* she asked herself, feeling his touch for the first time in nearly three years.

"I can't even give you a ride to where you're going?" he asked her. "Where are you going this early anyway? You got a job or something?"

Tracy was still trying to gather her thoughts. *Am I over him?* she continued to ask herself. "I gotta get to work," she finally told him. "I have to be to work in like forty-five minutes, and I need to get to Broad and Olney to take the subway." She still had not released herself from his hold on her.

Victor pulled her to his car and said, "Come on, then."

Tracy didn't want to get in, but she found no desire to pull away from him. She had never been inside of a Mercedes Benz, and before she knew it, Victor had shut the door on her and run around to the driver's side. Tracy found herself quickly relaxed as she leaned back into the blue leather interior, admiring the Mercedes Benz dashboard and the car phone. And the sweet strawberry incense that dangled from his mirror was pleasing to her senses. *Damn, this car is decent!* she could not help but thinking.

Victor glanced over and smiled at how sexy and tempting Tracy continued to look to him. He had a confession to make to her. "You know what? I don't know what it is, but every time I see you, I keep getting these urges to say something to you. And it's like I can't help it.

"I mean, to be straight up about it, I've been with a whole lot of good-lookin' girls, but none of them held my interest like you do."

Tracy cracked a huge smile. "Because you like me," she suggested to him.

Victor chuckled to himself and asked, "Why would you think I liked you, out of all the girls that I've had?"

Tracy thought as quickly as she could and responded, "Because I didn't sweat you like they did."

Victor burst out laughing. "Come on now. What are you trying to say? Are you trying to say that I never had you waiting for me at the playground and whatnot?"

Tracy grinned, embarrassingly. "That's when I was younger."

"So what 'chew sayin'? I couldn't do that to you now?"

"Hell no," Tracy snapped at him.

"But do you still like me though?"

Tracy paused. "Have you ever loved a girl before?" she decided to ask him.

Victor thought about it. "Love? You mean, like, 'I love you' love?"

Tracy laughed. The idea sounded alien to Victor. "Yeah. Have you ever loved a girl?"

"Damn, that's a good question. I mean, I remember girls that I liked a lot, and I still talk to them and all, but I ain't never said that I loved them or no shit like that."

"Why it gotta be 'shit?' "

"Well, I don't mean 'shit,' like in unimportant, I mean, 'shit,' like in complication. You know what I mean?"

Tracy sucked her teeth and stared at him. "Do you love me?" she asked. She was surprised that she had asked him, but once it was done, she felt good about it. She was finally beginning to assert herself with Victor.

Victor looked straight into her hazels with his piercing blacks. "Do you think that I love you?"

"Sometimes. Yeah."

"Why?"

"Because. I mean, you've been looking out for me and stuff, like I'm your little sister or something."

Victor shrugged his shoulders. "I've done that with a lot of girls."

"Have you *done it* with them?"

He shook his head. "Naw, not really. But you were big for your age, so I had to have you."

Tracy cracked up as they approached Broad Street a little too quickly for her. "You sound like a pervert," she told him.

"Come on now, I ain't *that* much older than you. How am I gonna sound like a pervert?"

Tracy grinned at her ill reference of him. "I was just playing with you. Don't take it personal."

"Well, ain't this your stop?" he asked, pulling right up beside the subway entrance.

Tracy was enjoying her conversation with him too much to leave. *Fuck it! You only live once,* she told herself. "You wanna ride me downtown?" she asked him.

Victor smiled and shook his head. "Naw, I got something to do."

Tracy then remembered her hesitancy to ride in his car in the first place. He was a drug dealer.

"I wanna talk to you about that when we get a chance," she told him.

Victor ignored her. He knew what she was getting at. Several other girls had asked him how he felt about selling drugs to his people, and Victor gave the same response as all the other dealers, *Nobody's forcing them to take it.*

"Come on now, I'm running late," he told her.

"Not until you tell me that you love me," she decided, playfully. *I'll talk to him about that drug-selling stuff at another time,* she promised herself, realizing that he had brushed her off about it.

"Well, you gon' be late for work then," he warned.

Tracy climbed out of his car and said, "You're gonna tell me that you love me one of these days."

Victor had another laugh. "What 'chew think, you're training me now or something?"

Tracy smiled at him as she walked toward the subway. "I think you wanna be my man."

"Oh yeah? Well, why would I want to be your man after I already had you?" he asked with a smile.

"Because I'm flyy. And you know that," she responded with confidence. *I'm finally on equal footing with him,* she told herself excitedly.

Victor rolled up his window and drove off, still grinning. "That girl's getting too smart for her own good," he told himself. "I like that."

Tracy's new job proved to be an effortless hype of self-esteem. Young black men from all over Philadelphia came to the centrally located store and bought more than they expected. They all wanted to keep "Flyy-honey-brown" in sight, pressing her for dates and for her phone number, while trying to give her theirs.

Tracy turned all of their offers down. Even her Italian boss, Joseph Bamatti, made moves on her whenever he could get close enough to her without the other girls noticing, and that only irritated her. Tracy feared losing her job in an argument about it, but she refused to be harassed.

Tracy called Pam into the dressing room in the back, so "Little Joey" could not hear her comments about him.

Pam quizzed, "What's up, girl?" She was big-boned and taller than Tracy.

Tracy whispered, "Did Joey ever try to hit on you?"

Pam smirked. "Hell naw. My boyfriend would kill his little ass. But he's sayin' dumb shit to you though?" Pam was large enough to have a huge boyfriend. Tracy could see why *she* had nothing to worry about from *Little* Joey. "Look, if that muthafucka is bothering you, then tell 'im the fuck off. I do. That's why he respects *me.*"

Tracy looked at Pam's size again, thinking, *That ain't the only reason why Joey respects you.* "Well, did he try any other girls?" she asked.

"He probably did, but nobody told me shit about it. And that's probably why 'dem two Italian girls don't like you in here."

"You think so?"

"Hell yeah, girl. He was probably playin' favors for them. And you the next *trick* on his list," Pam said jokingly.

"No the fuck I ain't," Tracy snapped.

Pam said, "Well, look, I'll talk to you on the phone about it, 'cause we losin' commission."

"Stop lunchin' and start working, Tracy," one of the Italian girls remarked.

"Ay Maria, come here for a minute," Tracy called.

Maria had an outright attitude. Disgust was written all over her olive-colored face. "What?" she answered skeptically.

Tracy asked, "Why don't you like me?"

"Who said I don't like you?"

"I mean, by the way you act toward me, it's obvious."

"It's not that I don't *like* you, it's just that you spend too much time bull-shitting around and not enough time working."

"Well, Joey ain't complainin'," Tracy said purposefully. She wanted to see if that was the problem.

Tracy hit pay dirt. Maria snapped, "I mean, are you fucking Joey or something?"

"No, are *you* fuckin' 'im?"

Maria rolled her eyes and said, "I don't think that's any of *your* business."

Tracy felt like smacking the color out of her. But it wouldn't look good for her image, since it would be painted that they were fighting over her boss.

Joey interjected, yelling from the front counter, "HEY! WHAT THE HELL ARE YOU TWO DOIN'? Come on, get a move on! We got customers in here ready to spend hundreds of dollars. Look, this guy here wants to buy a sweat suit. I mean, are yous' workin' or not?"

• • •

"Ra-heem-ma, let me tell you, girl-friend. I was so ready to kick this Italian bitch's teeth in today," Tracy told her neighbor.

Raheema was enjoying the spring night air as Tracy walked up. "Why?" she asked, smiling. Tracy always had a story to tell.

Tracy shook her earring-wearing head. "This bitch think that I'm fuckin' my Italian boss named Joey, and she be havin' attitudes with me. And oh my God, I felt like kickin' that bitch's ass t'day. But then everybody might think that I was fighting her over him. And I don't like this other Italian bitch in that store either, but I wanted to kill that Maria bitch."

Tracy was right out in front of her house, cussing up a storm. Raheema sat there chuckling.

Tracy finally calmed down and took a seat on Raheema's steps. "Damn, I hate petty bitches!" she claimed. "So what's the news, ABC Channel 6?"

Raheema paused. She didn't have any *good* news for Tracy. She said solemnly, "Victor got locked up today."

Tracy responded hoarsely, "What?"

"They said that he resisted arrest, and they had a warrant for attempted assault and battery against him, up in Cheltenham. Jantel told me about it."

Tracy trembled and choked up. "I don't . . . Why . . . Dag!"

Raheema moved closer, feeling almost as bad as Tracy did. She squeezed Tracy's hand, trying to comfort her.

"After all this shit," Tracy muttered sorrowfully. "Why did they have to get him now? Those muthafuckas just had to wait until now. Didn't they?" She bit her lower lip, trying to hold back the tears. They started falling rapidly down her face.

Tracy snatched her hand away from Raheema and stood up. "The Cheltenham police are racist anyway. Fuck the cops!" she exclaimed. She began pacing down her block toward Wayne Avenue.

"Where are you going?" Raheema asked her fearfully. She was afraid that Tracy might try something stupid in her rage.

"No-fuckin'-where!" Tracy fumed. Raheema followed her as she pouted. "I don't *believe* this! And the police are never around to lock up criminals when you need 'em to. They just know how to take niggas away, that's all. Punk-ass cops!"

Raheema realized that Victor was in the wrong, and although he had been Tracy's first love, Raheema suspected that her neighbor/girlfriend knew it, too. It was just the wrong time for Tracy to admit it.

That next Sunday morning, Tracy had promised her college friends that she would go with them to an African Cultural Festival in Fairmount Park. She tried to back out, but Lisa and Kiwana would not let her. Lisa had room in her car to take Raheema, since Joanne was back in New York.

"You gotta get out and shake this thing off, girl. And you should've never stopped hanging out with us in the first place," Lisa was saying to Tracy. "I mean, just because you and Carl couldn't work things out doesn't mean that you had to cut us off."

Kiwana said, "I know. Girlfriend just up and disappeared on us."

Lisa and Kiwana both wore African Kente outfits. Raheema and Tracy wore matching Nike sweat suits, looking like twins.

"So I guess you know what your name means, right?" Kiwana asked Raheema.

"Unt unh," Raheema responded shyly, especially around Kiwana. Kiwana looked so healthy. Her skin was clear and as smooth as a baby's.

"It's a Muslim name, meaning kindhearted and good," she told Raheema.

Raheema nodded, embarrassed by her acne-prone skin, wishing she could have Kiwana's.

"I'm gonna get you some vitamins, and some aloe vera products to heal your blemishes. You have to stop eating oil-producing foods, too."

Raheema was all ears and no complaints, with advice coming from someone as beautiful as Kiwana.

Lisa interjected, "Yeah, remember? Joanne had acne real bad when we first got to school."

"Yup. And we got her on a vegetarian diet and eating the right foods, and it straightened her right out," Kiwana said. "But the key is not to damage your skin. Acne can be taken care of. It's the scars that do the real damage."

"Yeah, and you just gotta start feeling positive about *you* as a person," Lisa added. She could tell that Raheema was guarded.

Tracy said, "I didn't know that Joanne had acne."

"Yeah, when we were freshmen," Lisa answered, as if it was years ago. They were only sophomores.

Kiwana asked Raheema, "What's your sister's name?"

"Mercedes."

"God. Why did your parents name her that?"

Raheema smiled. "Because my father wanted one."

They all roared with laughter inside of the small car.

Kiwana shook her head. "That's a shame."

Lisa asked, "So who named you?"

Raheema answered, "My mom did. She said that she knew this Muslim girl in high school, and she told me that she had always liked her name." She was beginning to open up to them.

"Oh," Lisa said. "So your mom and her are still good friends?"

"No. They didn't hang out or anything. My mom just liked her name, and she said that she moved to Washington years ago."

"Washington, D.C.?" Kiwana asked.

"Yeah," Raheema answered.

They pulled up to Fairmount Park and found a parking spot. Black men wearing black suits and bow ties were yelling and waving newspapers. "FINAL CALL! GET YOUR FINAL CALL . . . FINAL CALL! GET YOUR FINAL CALL!"

They were sharply dressed, clean-looking and masculine. Tracy heard her college girlfriends talk about "The Nation of Islam" before, but she had never seen any up close. They looked strong and upright.

"Hi are you sisters doin' today?" one asked.

"We're doing fine," Lisa answered for all of them.

"All right, now. Y'all have a good time," he said. He continued

waving his papers as they passed. "FINAL CALL! GET YOUR
FINAL CALL!"

Tracy said, "They look like they can kick some ass."

"Yeah, but I'll take an Afrocentric man, myself," Lisa retorted.

"Here you go with that again," Kiwana responded to her. "We gotta
stop separating ourselves like that. I'll take any black man who has his
head screwed on straight, and who is willing to go to battle culturally,
religiously, economically, academically and spiritually. I'll take a Muslim brother any day."

Lisa contested, "Yeah, you talk that stuff, Kiwana, but all the guys
at school say that you think you're *all that,* with your nose all up in
the air."

"Well, if any of them start knowing how to act on our campus, then
just maybe they would find out that I'm trying to become a queen first,
by getting to know who I am and my strongest aspects. And then I'll
look for my king, who knows who he is and what his strongest aspects
are. And that may take years," Kiwana announced.

Tracy and Raheema were thinking that Kiwana was already "a
queen." Tracy figured that she had found her king, but he was behind
bars, awaiting trial.

Tracy had never seen so many bright and cheerful colors in her life.
African descendants definitely had a way with using attractive colors.
Bright oranges, blues, yellows, purples, greens and earth browns were
everywhere, as they sold their handmade Kente outfits, clothes, hats,
and shirts, along with carved art, paintings and ethnic foods. The girls
were having a good time, and Fairmount Park was packed, vibrating
with the sounds of celebration and the drum.

The sun was out with a vengeance that afternoon, heating things up.
The African Cultural Festival lasted until seven o'clock. They then
planned to go see the Spike Lee Joint, *School Daze,* but first Kiwana
wanted Tracy and Raheema to listen to a lecture being given by African, Caribbean and African-American poets.

An older black man with graying dreadlocks held the stage. He wore
a long, earth-tone cloth from his neck to his ankles. He looked to be

sixty or more, and had the strong and steady eyes of wisdom, as if he could see through walls. And he spoke with a Caribbean accent.

"Our wi-mon in Ameri-ca, on de Islands and on de mainlands of Afri-ca must a-gain be the tea-chas of our chil'ren. We cannot raise any proper nay-shun without our sistuhs knowing exactly who dey are and what dey should be do-eng. Dey must know how to feed themselves propa-lee to be able to give propa nurturing to our future generay-shuns.

"Our wi-mon of old, have been our Nandi, raising Shaka, our Candice, fighting de white barbarians in Ethiopia, our Nefertiti, Hat-shepsut, Cleopatra, Harriet Tub-mon here on de mainland, sistuh Rita Marley in de Islands, and our mother goddesses, O-shun and Isis.

"Our wi-mon must know dare past to be able to plan for our future. Any nay-shun with mothas who do not know dare past to teach dare chil'ren can not possibly rise. So I say to de wi-mon on dees day that you must know your desti-nee. You must know your divini-tee. And you must know, dat through you, all nay-shuns live, all nay-shuns die."

"Well, you got one more year, Tracy, and then you're on your own," Patti said, getting Jason ready for his last week of first grade. It was also Tracy's last week as a high school junior. "I see you went back to that old 'natural look' again," Patti added with a chuckle.

Tracy smiled and looked into her mirror. Her hair was twisted-up again. She had stopped working at Jeans & Shirts after the first two months. She was turning down a lot of money, but she was tired of being exploited for her looks. For her last day of school, she was wearing a collage t-shirt, sunglasses, blue-jean shorts and no socks with her tan Dockside shoes.

"What is that?" Patti asked, noticing the small wood carving of a naked black woman hanging from her daughter's neck on a black leather string.

Tracy eyed the naked black woman, bouncing against her chest and held it in her hand. "It's a fertility symbol, mom." She smiled, feeling bashful. Kiwana had given it to her a couple of days ago. "Raheema got one, too."

"Well, what's with all this African stuff, all of a sudden?" Patti asked. She was curious, noticing the books that Tracy was reading.

"I don't know. I'm getting it from Kiwana."

"Tracy goin' to Africa, mom?" Jason asked.

"I don't know. Are you going to Africa, Tracy?" Patti said sarcastically.

Tracy grinned. "One day."

They then headed downstairs to the kitchen.

"And what's with this health-nut stuff you been getting into? Is that from Kiwana too?"

Tracy laughed. "Mom, I don't believe you."

Patti didn't know much about things outside of Philadelphia. But she wasn't stupid.

"I'm sorry, mom. I love you," Tracy said, realizing her careless thoughts.

Patti looked at her as if she was crazy. "I love you too, honey, but you're starting to act a little loony on me now. I'm gonna have to take you to a mental health clinic soon," she joked.

Tracy asked her mother while pouring some orange juice, "Did they teach you much about African health methods and whatnot when you were in that nutrition program, mom?"

"No," Patti said curiously. Tracy may have been learning some things that she didn't know. "Well, go ahead, 'Ms. Africa.' Teach me something," she responded. Patti smiled and sat down. And she was serious.

"Don't you have to be at work soon, mom?" Tracy asked, backing down from her mother's challenge. She was embarrassed.

Patti joked, "Oh, naw, Ms. Africa, ma'am. I ain't gotta be t' workin' for 'da massa till tin 'dis here mornin'."

Tracy giggled. Then she got serious. "Well, I was reading this book that Kiwana gave me, and it said that women only bleed with periods because of their appetites, and that the chauvinistic environment in America is stopping women from developing their full feminine capabilities. And Kiwana said that white women are not really developing power with their feminist movement, they're just getting to be as aggressive and destructive as men are, like Margaret Thatcher in Britain."

"Go on, girl, teach me," Patti said excitedly. She was proud that Tracy was using her mind and exploring things.

Tracy asked, "You ever notice that African women look a lot fuller than us, mom?"

"Yeah, I've always been saying that. And they don't be fat either, just healthy-bodied. But I got a nice shape though," Patti said, standing up to check herself out.

"Yeah, well that's because we lack proper nutrients and vitamins in urban areas with all this fast-food stuff and canned foods. You notice how women down South and out in the country are shaped more like African women? That's because their food supply is healthier."

"Go 'head, girl," Patti cheered her on. "Well, I've been feeding you the right foods in here, and I *do* know the proper food groups," she responded.

"But mom, I don't know if them white doctors are teaching us the right stuff, 'cause they're still experimenting with different foods and all. Africans mastered what and what not to eat thousands of years ago. But see, black people think that white people know everything and that we don't. But we've had vegetarian and fruit diets before the white man even came out of his caves. And they didn't have any fertile land to learn from, until the turn of the century when they started attacking everybody."

"GO 'HEAD, GIRL! THAT'S MY DAUGHTER!" Patti shouted.

Jason ran into the kitchen to find out what was going on. "What she doin', mom?" he asked.

"Dag, mom," Tracy responded, surprised by her mother's excitement. "I mean, I got a lot more to learn, but I'm getting there," she proudly added.

"Well, we all have to get a move on," Patti said, squeezing Jason's head as she walked toward the door. "Jason, turn that TV off."

Tracy and Jason followed their mother out.

Tracy said, out the door, "Yeah, I'm gonna have to buy Jason some books to read, so he won't get wrapped up into little white-boy fantasies."

Although he didn't understand what his sister was talking about yet, Jason nodded and said, "Okay."

"I am so proud of you," Patti announced, driving them to school. "My little baby's gonna be one of those sistas who puts the white man in his place. She's gonna be like Angela Davis and Assata Shakur. Yup, my daughter gon' be another Sojourner Truth."

Patti did know something. But Kiwana called Tracy "Camara," one who teaches from experience.

Throughout the summer, Tracy and Raheema enjoyed each other's company. It was the most inactive summer Tracy had had in her life. Mr. Keith was finally giving himself and his family room to breathe, and Raheema seemed a lot more cheerful. Both girls struggled to hold on to the vegetarian diet Kiwana had strongly suggested, and Raheema's acne slacked off with its use.

The girls laughed about all of the arguments they had and all the boys that had been on their block, trying to talk to either one of them.

Their futures looked bright. They argued about what colleges they would go to and the types of black men who would chase after them. "Probably some perverted professors," Tracy joked. But finding "the perfect man" was a mystery to them both.

"Do you still think about Victor?" Raheema asked Tracy while they enjoyed the moonlight and the cool nighttime breeze. They were not serious about boys anymore, unless anyone would ask Tracy about Victor.

"Yeah," she admitted, hesitantly. "I've never met anybody like him. . . . Remember Mercedes used to talk to Kevin?" Tracy asked, viewing the house across the street from them, where Kevin used to live.

Raheema nodded. "Yeah. That was her first boyfriend."

Tracy paused. "You know, sometimes I wish I could have one of those voodoo dolls, and just make guys act right."

Raheema laughed. "Me, too. But then again, girls don't really like guys they can control."

Tracy gave her a hi-five. "Ain't it the truth."

Raheema then got quiet, too quiet for Tracy.

Tracy quizzed her, "What are you thinkin' about?"

Raheema rubbed her long ponytail. "I was just wondering how your little brother is gonna treat girls."

"Oh. Girl, he ain't thinkin' 'bout nothin' but that damn television. But I've been trying to get him to read books though."

"Why do you think you like Victor so much?" Raheema wanted to know.

"Well, to begin with, you know that he was my first, just like Kevin was probably Mercedes' first. And that shit just does something to you if you liked the boy at all. You'll find out soon enough," Tracy assured her with a grin. "But outside of that, I see Victor as a black butterfly. And you watch him fly and land, and then you sit and admire him for a while, knowing that he gon' fly back away before you can grab him. And now his ass is in jail, just when I was getting close to him again with my net."

Raheema smiled.

"What?" Tracy asked, veeringly.

"I think that poetry you been reading is rubbing off on you."

Tracy sat silently, in thought. "I wrote a poem about Victor," she revealed.

"Yeah? Well, let's here it," Raheema piped.

"How you know I know it by heart, Ra-Ra?"

"Because you know Victor by heart."

Tracy grinned, admittedly. "Okay," she said. "It's called, 'King Victorious.'" She closed her hazels as Raheema looked into her smooth, honey-brown face. The moonlight was shining on them both.

Tracy started with a mellow voice, "I once knew a young black man who stole my heart. And then he gave it back to me when I begged for him to keep it. I said, 'Thieves don't give back the goods.' But he said, 'This thief can take all the goods in the world with his black skin and his kingly ways.' And I said, 'But these goods of mine are more precious than the furthest North and the furthest South, and if you run from me East to West, you will only run in circles of misery.' And he said, 'Yes, but this king can jump to the moon, and to Jupiter and as far away as Pluto, searching for more conquest.' So what could I do, but to say that I would follow him to the edge of the universe? And then he took me by my hand and ran me through the darkest pits of hell. And I yelled, 'Oh, my black king! I will still follow you, no matter how much you torture me!' 'Well then,' he said, 'you are a fool of limited wisdom and no self-respect.' And I then corrected him, saying, 'No, I am love eternal, giving you life, so who are you to take mine away, just because I love you so?' And he said, 'You should have known then, that I would deceive you because I am a warrior, who is not to be seduced.' And I said, 'Yes, but even black warriors need a place to rest and to feel secure in the warmth that only *I* can give you.' 'I need no rest,' he said, 'and I can fight on until I am no more.' And then *I* said, 'And with my tears, I can bring you back again.' And then he fell to his knees and cried, 'Then *I* have been the arrogant fool, while *you* have been the wise one all along.' And I said back to him, 'Stand up, my king of black skin, black as your thoughts before I gave them life. For you shall discard me again with your blind arrogance. And I shall chase you again to the edge of our universe, bringing you to your knees, reminding you that through me you became alive, with my eternal love. So love *me* as you would love your mother, who *is* me, before I separated myself to make more black kings, stretching to the furthest corners of my earth.' And then he nestled up beside me like my son, and I loved him, like my husband."

Tracy sat with her eyes closed, letting the moon feed her.

Raheema exclaimed, "That was *so decent!* When did you write that?" she asked, as soon as Tracy had opened her eyes again.

"I wrote it while sitting out here in the dark one night."

"Girl, you're gonna be rich and famous one day, if you keep writing stuff like that."

Tracy smiled and revealed her source. "That's from reading that Egyptian stuff, girl. Men have been forcing the world to follow their ways of aggression for a long time. So now we have to remind them that we gave them life. But first we have to know that *we* are the substance of dark that the Bible talks about. And the world was begun like a baby in our wombs."

Raheema simply stared at her for a moment. "Dag, Tracy! You're getting deeper than Kiwana. I can't even understand you anymore."

Tracy smiled and said, "Yeah, but I still love Victor though. I just can't help it."

It was a week away from Tracy's seventeenth birthday, on a Saturday.

"Dave, I think that you and Tracy need to just go away somewhere and be together for her birthday. I won't mind, because you haven't had a real father-daughter chat with Tracy in a while, and she's been learning a lot lately," Patti said to her husband as she climbed into bed.

Dave nodded. He was in bed already. "Sounds good to me. We can go out to eat at whatever restaurant she wants to go to."

"Yeah. My baby been studying about Africa," Patti alluded.

"Oh, really? How much does she know?"

Patti smiled. "I'll let you decide for yourself."

"Oh yeah. Well, hell, I'm looking forward to this."

"So you're gonna spend the entire day with her?"

Dave frowned. *Here she goes nagging again,* he thought. "Patti, I said that I would. Okay? Yes, I will."

Patti smiled and cuddled up with him, glad to have him back.

Dave grinned himself, thinking, *Women. You can't live with them, and here I am anyway.*

When Saturday morning came around, Jason was the first to shout, "Happy birthday, Tra-cy!" He hit her on her arm, trying to count to seventeen. His little punches were hard, but Tracy was too pleased to complain.

Patti didn't bother to buy her daughter any clothes for her seventeenth. She gave Tracy fifteen hundred dollars toward her college tuition next fall instead. It was part of the money she had been saving up to move out if Dave had refused to come back. Patti knew that her first baby was going to college. Tracy was still trying to decide if she wanted to go to Howard University, where all of the handsome men were, or to Spelman, an all-girls school, where she could study without distractions. Lisa told her that Morehouse, an all-boys school, was right around the corner, "in case you get horny one night," she joked. Tracy was not anticipating any of that. She wanted to learn more about being a black woman first.

"So your mother told me that you been studying up on Africa." Dave sat with his daughter at dinner later that birthday night, at Friday's restaurant on Philadelphia's City Line Avenue. They had been all over the city, and Tracy was pleased to have his company at a dinner for two.

"Yeah, a little bit," she answered modestly.

Dave started munching down the salad appetizer as if he was hungry. He wore an off-white sports jacket and a rayon shirt with navy blue pants and black leather shoes, looking jazzy. He smelled good, too. Tracy was damn proud that he was her father, but not by the way he was eating his salad.

"Dag, dad. That food ain't goin' nowhere," she hinted with a smile.

Dave looked up from his plate, watching the twinkling honey-colored eyes she had inherited from him. Tracy grinned, wearing a purple skirt and blouse outfit she had bought with the money she earned from working at Jeans & Shirts.

Dave said, "You know, you're starting to look like my mother a little bit with your hair like that."

What a coincidence, Tracy thought. But she didn't want to talk about Africa, fertility and heritage with *him.* Tracy wanted to ask her father *straight up* about men.

"Dad? Why do y'all act the way y'all do?" she asked him bluntly.

Dave was too cool to be startled by it. "Because most of us don't know any better. My mother spoiled the hell out of me," he responded, wiping the French salad dressing from his lips. "Hell, I thought I was women's gift to the world. But see now, some other cats get hurt by a woman and then start actin' real shady with them. But I never had to worry about that."

Tracy was surprised that her father was so willing to be open-minded with her instead of saying, "God did it." He still looked twenty-something, although he was forty.

"So are you saying it's my grandmother's fault?" she asked.

"Well, I can't put all of the blame on her. Of course not. I had my little quirks and things."

"And what really happened between you and mom?"

"Now see, your mother had her problems, too. That's why we need some type of support mechanisms with these families. And since you're studying Africa, I guess you know that the African family was extended. And if the black man could afford it, he took on several wives."

Tracy was surprised her father was talking so much. She was afraid to eat. "So you needed more wives?" she asked him, attempting to be objective about it. Like most American women, Tracy felt polygamous marriages were totally unacceptable.

"Well, I guess it ain't no secret that a lot of women were attracted to me. And I used to go to work, looking and smelling all good when I first started working at the hospital that I worked at. And them women used to say, 'Excuse me, but are you married?' And then when I said I was, they start making up shit. 'Oh, 'cause I got a girlfriend that you would make a perfect match with. But oh well.' And I'm thinkin', 'Who the hell they think they foolin'?' And then some women were straight up bold about it, telling me to call them if I *ever* had any problems I might need *worked out.*"

Tracy laughed at his candor, imagining older women falling all over him, like the girls did with Victor. "I liked this guy that reminds me of you, dad."

"So what's up with him? Is he your boyfriend?" Dave asked, trying to sound young and hip.

Tracy smiled. "You a trip, dad."

"Yeah, but you still ain't gave me an answer yet," he pressed her.

"Well, he's like you, hard to keep."

Dave didn't want to address that statement. It sounded convicting. He moved right along. "So is this cat in college, or what?" he asked, dodging Tracy's intentions. She wanted him to explain his own butterfly ways, so maybe she could understand him *and* Victor.

"No," she said annoyingly, ready to talk about *him*.

Dave was fast at being evasive. "He's not in school, hunh? So is he heading for jail or already in there?" he joked.

Tracy was shocked. She didn't want her father to know that he was actually right. She wasn't sure how he would react if she told him the truth, that she was in love with a drug dealer who took her virginity when she was only thirteen.

"What, are you thinking that just because a guy's not in college that he gotta be into something no good?" she retorted defensively.

Dave smiled, confused. "I'm just jokin' with you, girl. I want the best man for you. I want a man who can at least give you what I gave you and your mother."

"But will he leave me and run away?"

There was a sharp silence across the table. Tracy had struck her father's serious bone. Dave looked into his daughter's face with a seriousness that she had never witnessed from him before. "The black man in America needs a system where he has to stand up and correct himself. Now that ain't gon' happen on its own; sometimes you gotta go through hell before you realize it. But there's a lot of good brothers out there who got things workin' the right way.

"Now of course, I'm far from perfect, but I *did* take care of business while I was away. I had to do a lot of soul searchin', and I didn't have no damn support.

"My father died when I was eight. My mother was an only child, and I was an only child. So where was my support?

"Your mother was wearing me out before I think I was ready to be married. I mean, your mother loved this marriage thing, but I felt trapped, like life itself was kicking my ass. And the whole relationship with your aunts got on my *fuckin'* nerves.

"Now I have to admit that I got greedy and I stayed away longer than what I had planned to, and I'm sorry for that, baby. That was real selfish of me, but I just needed some space and some time to think alone."

Tracy smiled, loving her father more, because he was admitting that he was human, subject to mistakes and vulnerable.

"We needed to have this talk a long time ago, dad," she told him.

Dave looked into her glassy hazels and realized that she had matured a great deal. "I love you, your mother and your brother to death, but it was hard as hell to do things all on my own. I had too much weight on my shoulders. Something had to give. So whatever you do, you make sure that your man has some type of outside support. 'Cause no matter how strong us black men *think* we are, there's gon' come a time when we need somebody to lean on. And I ain't have nobody."

When Tracy got home that night, at almost one o'clock in the morning, she was exhausted. She headed straight in to bed after kissing her father good-night.

There was a letter on her dresser with no name or return address. It had a seven-digit I.D. number in the upper-lefthand corner.

"Oh my God!" Tracy yelped excitedly, wondering who it was. The intrigue was enough to make her want to read it out under the moon-light.

She sprinted outside to her patio energetically, and breathed in deep as she opened it.

Dear Tracy,

I know I'm surprising you by writing you this, but I think we understand each other. Here I am twenty years old and sitting in a cell now for three years and shit, and I don't know what will become of me. But I do know that you have eyes to see what I feel for you. Out of all the girls that I had, Tracy, and I stopped counting after 100, you were the only one that I kept up on. I studied you. And from my conclusions, I know that you're the girl that I would like to marry. Now I want you to go to college and all, but when you do go, make sure you study the right information.

The white man has set us up for all this shit we been through. And all I was doing was running around dicking every girl that I could get, beating up niggas, robbing and stealing and I even shot at some people. I realized that I was trying to outdo my brother. He always overshadowed me with that basketball shit. And I didn't know who I was, and what my mission was in life. But you know white people have a lot of pitfalls set up that distract us from searching for the truth. They be having us playing them "Supernigga" roles. But yo, it's some brothers in here that have been putting me down with the Nation of Islam and Minister Louis Farrakhan. And I've been getting educated. We need to be able to tell the truth as it is and we can't allow our parents or anybody else to stop us. So the brothers have told me that I must discipline myself by doing the right thing and choosing a wife for stability. Shit, the guards are closing shit down. I don't have much time to tell you more things that I want to do. But I want you to marry me when I get out and be the mother of my children. Me and you can raise a correct family, Tracy. And you are strong enough to understand me. All I want is three children and a wife who is supportive. You have that kind of drive that I need from a woman. You have that certain confidence. And I want you if you want me. But you have to wait for me, love me and never let another man come between us. I'll be waiting for you.

P.S. I hope this letter gets to you in time for your birthday September 6. I remembered even though you probably think I didn't know. And oh yeah, send me a pretty picture of you. A big naked one.

RIGHTEOUS LOVE
Victor Hinson "the slave"
Qadeer Muhammad "the man"

2158796

There was a return prison address under his name.
Tracy giggled and laughed, reading it over and over, touched to

tears, and still not believing it. Her desire had been fulfilled, and Victor was proposing to her in a letter that she would keep forever.

She wiped away happy tears, as she trembled blissfully. "I'll be here for you, baby . . . I'll be here for you," she mumbled with a smile.

A rush of elation overwhelmed her as more tears helplessly flooded her eyes. Tracy wiped them hurriedly, dreaming of Victor, Qadeer, black, strong and righteous, as the moon shone and the wind blew, adding to her birthday joy.

epilogue

Hey Dad!

My first year of college is almost over, and I've gotten all A's and B's. So . . . can I get a car? Sike, dad. Unless you really wanna buy me one.

I guess you know that Mercedes moved back home now. Raheema said that she's doing good with her rehabilitation. I'm happy for her.

Raheema sent me a letter from Cornell University a week ago. I was real happy that she got that scholarship to go there. She deserves it. She was saying in her letter how we had been through all of our fights and stuff and how we still came out close like sisters. And she is my sister in the communal sense. We helped each other through so much over the years, you know?

And as far as that 1200 that she got on the SAT's, I mean, all she did was sit in the house and study. Naw, that's my girl. She even got a boyfriend out there that's a Sigma and politically conscious, so she says. He's probably a nerd. No, let me stop. Anyway, I wrote her back and stuff. I told her to tell me if she's still a virgin, she left that part out.

Me? Well, let's just say that I've never gotten pregnant and I never got no diseases. And no, I didn't do any drugs, either. But remember that time you said that my boyfriend, well he wasn't my boyfriend, but you know, the guy that I liked back then when I was still in high school. His name is Victor, and you were right, he was in jail.

But anyway, he was my first love. He's up for parole from Holmesburg prison in three months, and I've been writing letters back and forth to him for almost two years.

I can't lie, dad. I went up there to see him a couple of times. I had to, dad. Cause it was people that kept calling me naive and stuff, saying that he was gaming me up, and that he couldn't have just changed overnight. But when I saw him it just made me want to wait for him even more because of how trapped it seemed he was. I mean, you gotta know Victor. He was always in control of things. But now he talks about going to trade schools and stuff when he gets out. And he was always smart. Victor's brother went to college.

I want to believe in him, dad. And all these girls up here who say they my friends are always talking about how I need to get a life. But I don't see how they're doing any better with these confused guys they talk to. It takes time for everybody to become who they're gonna be. Like who would have thought that I'd be going to Hampton and majoring in English, of all things.

Anyway, it's mostly because of Victor that I'm majoring in English now, cause we kept writing to each other and stuff. And dad, he would describe the bars and shit—oh excuse me dad, but I'm a big girl now— so the shit that he be going through in jail and all. And I used to cry and pray for him to get out soon, like a break-out or something. But it's hard being a young black man today, or a black man period. I wouldn't really know though, cause I'm having a hard-ass time being a young black woman.

Anyway. I love you, dad, and here's a poem that I wrote for you and fatherhood. It's called, "Stop the Critics," cause it's always people saying how they think things should be.

> My daddy wasn't home 24–7,
> but I do know him.
> He was the handsome dark brown face
> that my mother went crazy for.

I know my daddy wasn't like Bill
on the Cosby Show.
But he was real flesh
with real struggles
and I love him so.

Some people often criticize
and say that my mother and I were robbed.
But now I'm happily in college
with my daddy's support
so all in all
I'd say he's done a great job.

And still people argue
that my logic seems shabby.
But since they know so much
I ask them,
"Have you ever been a daddy?"

My creative writing teacher loved that poem. Cause she says she could relate to how I feel about you. I mean, hey, I only got one dad. Right? And you have to make the best out of what you can.

But anyway. Victor will probably get out when I'm home for the summer. And you don't have to worry about me getting into trouble or nothing with him, because I've cooled out a lot. And a lot of guys wanted to talk to me down here. I've gone out a couple times, but nothing serious. I was always thinking about Victor. But hey, if me and him can't work it out, then hell, I'm still living. I mean, people act like I'm gone die for waiting for him. I'll survive. And I'll be successful at whatever I do. Nobody can say that I haven't gotten what I wanted. So I'll just keep reaching for the sky.

Love Tracy, with hugs and kisses.
P.S.—Send me some money, daddy. Pl-e-e-e-ease.

AckNOWLedgMeNtſ

I would like to send out a special thanks to all of the people who supported me in my publishing efforts and my eventual ascension to national sales: Amos Drummond, John White Jr., Kevin Johnson; *News Dimensions* Staff: Barry, Chris, Patrick, John, Joy, Jeannie, and Sharon Jenkins; *The Capital Spotlight* Staff: Bill, Betty, Steve, Mary, and Ike Kendrick (RIP), Daniel and Tony McNeill, Mr. Harold Bell, Malcolm Beech, Kenny Gilmore; *MARS Productions* Staff: Lisa Chanel, Kim C. Barrington, TaMara Holmes, Diane Simpkins, Dr. Frank Render, Mercedes Allen, Pamela Artis, Larry Bradshaw Jr., Maroa Gikuuri, Sherry Bryant, and Kevin Watson; also the University of Pittsburgh's UCEP Counselors of 1987; and Howard University's School of Communications instructors of 1991.

To my family members who have always loved and supported me: Mom and Step-Pop Renee and Melvin Alston and brothers Mel Jr. and Phil; Grandmom Geraldine and the McLaurin, Briggs, and Brown families; Grandmom Mercyle and the Tyree, Simmons, Adams, and Tolbert families; the Robinson, Powell, Carvelho, Stewart, Hayes, Frazier, Ballard, Werts, Hilton, and Thomas families, including Karintha and the Randall and Rideout families.

To all of the buyers who pushed my book: Sister Lecia Warner and the Warner family, Sister Betty Jean, Brother Khalifah, Brother Hakim, Johnson-El and Karen, Sister Njeri, Shalada Sankofa, Margaret Holmes, Sister Carol, Brother Dwight, Sister Basiyma Muhammad, Brother Arnim, Brother Simba and Yao, Anne Miles, Brother Everett, Hodari Ali, Hakeem Rushdan, Brother Deke, George Siberian, Frank and Darlene Barber, David Reeves Sr., Brent Wilson, Nia Damali, Bruce Bridges, Larry Robin, Brother Bey, Edward Thomas and family, Ricardo Cunningham, Fred Hargrove, Mary Tate, Nati Natika, Al and Joe at Trover, David at Vertigo, and the Reprint Book Shop staff.

And to all of the supporters, friends, and organizations that helped me along the way: Cathis Hall, the African-American Writers Guild, Bill Neely, the MCY family, the Buttamilk and Incognito families, Kwame Alexander, John Ashford (DJ AyCE), Jennifer Williams (Flavors of the month), Stephanie Renee, Anne Lynn Smith and Gallaudet University, Tracy Hopkins, Warren Sledge, Marc D. Loud, Kenneth Mackel, Gambree Amlak, David R. Hancock, Doris Caffee, Vern Catron, J. R. Fenwick, Roland Mack, Ronnie M. Friday, Arletha Plummer, Thalia Sledge, William E. Wells Sr., the White family, the Underground Railroad family, the Carter family, Denise Slaughter, the WOL Radio family, the Valentine family, Wanda Wilson and friends, Aleatha C. Frederick, BZB International, Big City Comics, Anita and Rhonda, Io Handy, Cydnee Randall, Kala Threat, Yolandra Hickson, Preston Jenkins, Ronke Akinbulumo, Allie Thompson, Tyrone Greene, The DEAL Organization, Leslie D. Williams, Lloyd Murphy, Joseph Price, Jimmie Grayson and the Majestic Eagles, Tanika White, Vada Manager, VSJ Enterprises, *The Community News* and *The Hilltop*, Malik Azeez, Michael 3X and Brother Terrence, Danny Mc Queen, Charles Ford, Neche Harris, Gayle Cloudin, James Caldwell, Ray Mahari, Brother Oba, Manie Barron, Doug Lazy, Dr. Ronald Walters, Dr. Molefi Kete Asante, the D.C. Service Corps, WPFW Radio, WAMU and WYCB, Kojo Nnamdi, Stacy Ward, Courtland Milloy ("For Black Men Only" family), Tom Williams, Tonya Pendleton, Jane Hawkins, Natasha Tarpley,

Gelencia Dennis, Roxanne Rauch, Tonya Williams, Toni D. Blackman, Keisha, Trina Williams, Yolanda Sampson, Nicole Kasey, Jeff Morely, David Waters, Patrice Butler, and the Hospital For Sick Children family: Steve, Gary, Elaine, Harold, and Nate.

Peace and love to all of the people who first supported me in my hometown of Philadelphia, and in Washington, D.C., Baltimore, Maryland, and Virginia. And last but not least, I would like to thank all of my buddies (it's too many of y'all to name) from Pitt and H.U., who sat around listening to me philosophizing and straight up "talkin' shiz" on all those college nights that got me started writing in the first place, and to Teri Williams for introducing me to my hardworking agent Denise Stinson who sold the book to my editor Dawn Daniels of Simon & Schuster, who made it happen for us.

"Momma, I did it! I did it! I told you I would! Just look at me now! Momma, I'm shinin'! Whooowee!"

Omar Rashad Tyree

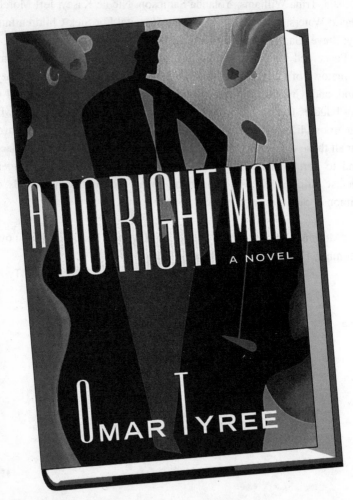